RESURRECTION

Alien Invasion Book Seven

AVERY BLAKE
JOHNNY B. TRUANT

STERLING & STONE

To YOU, the reader.
Thank you for taking a chance on us.
Thank you for your support.
Thank you for the emails.
Thank you for the reviews.
Thank you for reading and joining us on this road.

RESURRECTION

Chapter One

THE HOODED FIGURE slipped out of the village before dawn, setting off from his dwelling before most of the others had risen for their daily chores. This was saying something because the village woke early. The sun was oppressive by midday, so people worked at first light then stayed in the shade to stay cool later — or bathed in the river, or slept in their small homes with the doors open on both ends to invite a breeze.

When they did the latter, the villagers napped on cots high enough to keep the insects and snakes at bay. Superstition said that if you slept on the ground, minions from the underworld would take you for your laziness — for putting your back to the ground rather than toiling on upright legs.

But that was all bunk to the cloaked man. The idea of never resting used to be called the Puritan Work Ethic and had, unfortunately, survived the Forgetting deep in the people's minds. And as to snakes and spiders? They weren't from the underworld. Near as the cloaked man could guess, the Astrals had somehow preserved them and the other creatures from the Old Earth on an unknown ark — or, for all he knew or cared, created them again once the land had dried.

He passed the Dempsey house — made of better stone and larger than the rest but still surprisingly modest.

He passed the rectory, which had grown, where Mother Knight held her meddlesome meetings.

And finally he passed the outer ring, where most of the Unforgotten made their homes. Beyond them were the wilds and the desert, and as the man walked west and the sun blushed in the sky behind him, he found it fitting that The Clearing had known just how to form itself. Like a flock of birds instinctually finding its array, so had the thousands instinctually settled into their ideal configuration.

The Unforgotten — who'd taught The Clearing's villagers so many things they didn't question their knowledge of — didn't usually need defense from the desert and the wilds. They knew when unwanted things were coming.

But even windows of the Unforgotten weren't lit with candlelight as he passed, leaving the quiet of night's end unbroken.

He crested a rise then walked down its lee side. The bluing horizon vanished for a while, restoring his world to near darkness. And so he walked that way for a while, his eyes closed because the moon was new and the stars were hidden behind clouds and seeing simply didn't matter.

One foot in front of the other.

No worries of stepping into something. Or on something. Or going the wrong direction.

Because the true guidance was within him, on the network, when its horizons managed to remain unobscured.

After perhaps twenty minutes by an Old-World clock, he reached the monolith, less than a quarter day from the sea. It reared up before him like always: first a dark triangle above the farthest dune, then growing into something flatter and wider as he neared. By the time he was over the dune, the eastern sky had faded from dark blue to light, warming with the first hints of blood red where land met sky.

He stood before the thing, looking up. He waited. He remembered the feeling of knowing so much more than he knew now, but that was when he'd had a global mind to guide him. Now their number was trimmed, and for a while, that had seemed to brighten the feeling. But despite all his shuffling, it had been dark for a while. Until the recent, new round of sparks. This time, he swore they were different. And Clara agreed.

But today as with every day before, the monolith offered nothing.

He stayed for long enough to know he was wasting time, hoping in an all-too-human way that the solution would magically present itself. But it didn't. There was magic, and he could make it. But the monolith was unchanging, and gave him as little as it gave the others, who believed it simply to be junk.

Before leaving, he lowered his hood and pulled three small polished silver spheres from his pocket. He held them flat in his palm, trying to feel, knowing he'd sense nothing. The spheres had given him plenty in the past. But then again, he'd felt his origin more fully before. His power had departed like memory from the others. How had he once fed back into a Reptar and destroyed it with a thought? How had he created the duplicate that lived inside? He remembered doing it all, but his *how* was as lifeless as the spheres. They told him nothing, only showing him his own long, lined face — the same face he'd seen in mirrors when the forgotten floods had started.

And that unchanged face told him: *It feels like it's been forever, yes. But it all might as well have happened yesterday.*

He pocketed the spheres. There was still magic in them, for sure — just as there was still magic in the monolith. But he couldn't touch it. Couldn't access it. Like a memory he almost knew but couldn't recall. A face he knew yet couldn't place.

He turned and headed back to The Clearing.

He arrived at his shop to find a man waiting outside. He was very tall. Very broad. His arms were as big around as a normal man's thighs. Everyone understood the man's build because he labored as a blacksmith — another curiously no-questions-asked skill the Unforgotten had taught the village's population ahead of the way things were probably supposed to happen. But his size was cause, not effect. He was able to blacksmith *because* he was big; he wasn't big because he smithed. And there might be another reason he smithed, it seemed: because smiths made weapons as well as tools, and a warrior would one day need weapons with which to fight.

"Sir?" said the big man.

"Yes?"

"They call you Stranger, don't they?"

"They call me many things. Especially behind my back."

The big man cracked a smile. Small wrinkles formed at the corners of his mouth. A tentative smile, but there.

"My name is—"

"Carl Nairobi," Stranger finished.

"Carl *Smith*," Carl corrected.

Stranger shrugged as if it didn't matter. Then he

4

opened his shop's door and let Carl inside, where he indicated two handmade chairs for each to sit.

"Why is your name Smith?" Stranger asked.

"Because I am a blacksmith."

"Were you always a blacksmith? Is that why it's your surname?"

Carl started to speak, but Stranger cut him off before he could.

"Five years ago, were you a blacksmith?"

"Yes, sir."

"Ten years ago, were you a blacksmith?"

"Yes."

"Was your *father* a blacksmith? Is that how you learned the trade?"

Carl's mouth opened, and his whole face formed another yes, but then he stopped.

"Do you remember your father, Carl?"

"Yes?"

"You do or you don't?"

"Yes. Of course I do."

"What was his name?"

There was a pause. Into it, Stranger said, "If a man's surname were *Nairobi*, what might that say about him? What might it say about his origins?"

"Sir?"

"You're so polite these days, Carl. When I first met you, you tried to beat me to death. Hit me once, in fact. I remember it well."

Carl's face scrunched. "Have we met, sir?"

"Yes. When you went by a different name. In a different place. Look inside, Carl. Do you seriously not remember me?"

Carl focused. He watched Stranger for a very long

time. It was such a tiny thing, Stranger thought as he watched Carl back, but a telling one. People used to have such a weakened attention span, but these days, stories spun for hours. People walked without hurry. And when one man studied another, it could take a minute or more, feeling no need to fill the silence with distractions.

"When do you believe we met?"

"Twenty years ago, Carl." Then he shifted to the village vernacular, knowing "years" was a concept they never quite agreed on. "Twenty summers and winters."

"I'd have been a young man then."

Stranger looked him over. Carl still looked like a young man even at his current age of fortysomething. They had all visibly matured, but by the old standards it sure didn't look like a full twenty years of aging to Stranger. The Astrals must have done something to them when erasing their memories, and it made sense. Most of humanity had perished. If the species was meant to restart from the small seed populations left around the globe, they'd have to be hearty stock — the best of the best, a bit younger than their years.

"You were. Twenty-five at the most. But no bigger or stronger than you are now, I'd wager."

"But *you*," Carl said, still studying. *"You'd* have been a child."

Stranger stood. There was a silvered glass on the far wall that he used when people came to him for advice. His face was long and lined, but not with age. He didn't consider it much, but he understood what Carl meant. Most who didn't know him well thought he was thirtyish, and were forgetful in exactly the way people around here were. Those closer to Stranger knew he looked the same today as he had for every subsequent yesterday. Twenty years gone in this strange new world, and he hadn't aged a day.

"Why are you here, Carl?" Stranger asked, leaving Carl to wonder. He'd been watching the node representing Carl just as Clara had suggested, and now he was starting to believe she was right. The walls *were* breaching, and Carl was one of those in whom the change might have already begun.

"I was sent. By a man who frequents my shop, named Logan."

"Why did Logan send you to the town mystic?"

"Because of my dreams, sir."

Stranger had been facing the mirror. He turned, pleased. It really had begun to fall. His own dreams — not nearly as prescient as they once were, now that he'd become so much more human — might have been telling him the truth after all.

"What about your dreams?"

Carl shifted uncomfortably in his chair. Stranger hadn't seen the man, other than in passing, in what felt like forever. The village had grown closer to a town in two decades, but it was still small. The town mystic scared many of its occupants just as they were frightened by Governor Dempsey's twin. Even after a global reset, the human brain recoiled from the unknown.

But still it was hard not to imagine Carl as he'd been when they'd first come to this place, when the floodwaters had receded and returned land to the Earth. He'd been angrier then, the way Kindred still was. And his speech patterns had belonged to the old world: attitude, slang, and a South African accent. Today he might be from the pages of a history book if such things still existed.

"The monolith. Do you know it?"

"I know it well."

"I've been there just once," Carl said. "Just once, because it frightened me so badly. It's like a thing from the underworld."

Stranger nodded for the man to continue.

"In my dream — and it's the same every night — I'm standing outside the monolith. On the low side, where its edge has dipped nearer to the sand. There's a door above. Between me and the door there's a ladder. The whole thing is made of smithed metal. But not in any way I've ever seen or known or can understand."

"I know its construction. Go on."

"It's very clear that I've just stepped out of the thing. And there are others with me. They're watching me, waiting. And it's … It's …"

"What is it?"

"It's as if I brought the thing to us. As if it's my fault it's there."

A haunted look crossed his features.

"Is there more?"

He nodded. "Five people come from the horizon. From across the dune. Six who have come to join me and one who has come to take something away. Six friends. One enemy. And then the people who were with me when I … when I somehow brought the monolith forth … are gone, and there are only eight of us. Friends and enemy together. But no fighting or arguing. Only expectation. They look at me and say, 'We need it, Carl. We need it, or nothing can change.'"

"Then what?"

"That's how it ends," Carl said. "But I don't understand it. I don't know what they want from me or who they are. I can't see their faces. I have no idea what I'm expected to give them. But it's clear that they expect me to know — as if I've been sent to a far village on an errand and they've been waiting for me to return."

"Why does it trouble you? It's just a dream."

Carl shook his head. "It's every night now. Every night I have the exact same dream. Every night I see a few more visions."

"Like what? What *kind* of new visions?" Stranger repressed his emotions but couldn't help the burning curiosity. There'd been a day when he'd been able to look out on the grid inside his mind and see details as well as Clara could — as well as she *used* to, anyway. These days it was all lights and shadows. He'd helped build that grid of minds, in a way, but twenty years was a long time to hold a memory that the very air around them pressed him to forget.

"Me inside the monolith. Me on the sea, in this vast thing of heavy metal, somehow above the water rather than sinking beneath it. Me holding a small silver ball, in another place, finding the monolith in a new, odd land I don't recognize and cannot understand. The ball seems to speak to me. To take me away from something and toward something else. I follow it, and people follow me. And when I reach the part of the dream where the others arrive, I'm more and more convinced that their expectant stares are right — that I truly *am* to blame for bringing the thing to its resting place in the sand. But I've never done those things, sir. I've—"

"*Stranger,* Carl. You used to call me Stranger."

Carl's brow furrowed. "But I don't remember you. We've never spoken."

"We have," Stranger said, reaching into his robe and producing a small silver ball. He held it up and watched

Carl's face change. "You spoke to me once, when I gave you something like this."

"When? Where?"

"When we were younger. In a land you once knew but can no longer recall." He paused, then added, "But that you one day will again."

He handed the ball to Carl, who seemed perhaps overly willing to take something that filled him with fear. But then Carl's large mahogany hand closed on the thing, and Stranger felt the resonance. He could close his eyes and see Carl's node in the network brighten. See the breach in the walls, where the demons kept fighting, finally fail.

They can't fight us forever, Stranger, said a female voice inside his head.

Carl looked up. Stranger raised his eyes to meet him.

"The gods," he said. "The black ship in the sky from long ago that people whisper about. It was real, wasn't it?"

"*Yes,* Carl," said Stranger, leaning in, excitement building in an all-too-human cavalcade of emotion. "And do you remember *why* it came back? *Why* it appeared after the water was gone, after you moored the giant ship on the old shores to rust? Do you remember why the ship blackened our skies for a full season after we thought they were done with us, after their Forgetting had already started, after we were sure they'd left for good?"

Carl's mouth opened.

The monolith.

The freighter.

Carl.

The Seven, or the Eight.

And the network. Puzzle pieces that spawned a new dimension, immune to the Astrals' best attempts to fight back.

"Because ... because they ..."

But before Carl could finish, Stranger's door banged open with a pop like a wood knot in a fire.

"Stranger," said the woman at his threshold, her cadence rushed. "It's Clara. She's collapsed."

Chapter Two

PIPER'S EYES OPENED. There was no threshold between sleep and wakefulness. She'd been in one place but was now in another, eyelids not at all heavy as they usually were when slumber departed, looking up at the roof of the small stone house that Meyer and his brother had built with their bare hands. Or at least that's what Piper seemed to remember them doing, though for some reason now, on this particular morning, she had her doubts. Beams overhead were large and thick — denuded trees made more or less round. But she didn't remember Meyer and Kindred felling the trees, just like she didn't remember how two men had lifted something so heavy over their heads.

Something was wrong. It had nothing to do with the beams. It was something more. Something worse. And yet, in its own way, better.

"Meyer."

He was already as awake as she was, as if he'd been lying beside her all night with open eyes, watching stars the roof kept them from seeing.

"I know."

There was a knock. The door wasn't latched, and swung inward as the visitor tapped it, pivoting on forged metal secured to the frame, pinned together with a small rod. Clara had told them how to make the doors swing, and as far as Piper remembered they hadn't had a clue before. She'd done it as a girl, a long time ago.

"Mom."

"Come in," Piper said.

The door swung the rest of the way. Lila entered. She seemed out of sorts, a bit manic — exactly the way Piper's insides were starting to feel. Exactly the way Meyer, now that Piper glanced over, appeared.

"I couldn't sleep," Lila said.

"But there's something else. What is it, Lila?"

Piper was looking over at Meyer. When she'd said his name, he'd muttered two words as if awaiting her prompt. His response had made sense in the moment, but now she was already forgetting what that meant.

"I don't know. I had a dream. With Clara. She was a little girl again. But ..."

"But what, Lila?"

"She was asking about her father."

"It was just a dream."

Still, Piper felt a chill. She'd been dreaming of Lila, back when Lila was a child. And Lila hadn't been asking about her father, but she had been asking about her mother. About Piper. But Piper couldn't remember having ever given birth. She remembered Lila growing up, but didn't remember being pregnant. The dream felt weary. Just thinking about it made her tired again, but it wasn't the usual phenomenon of a fading dream. She was detouring around a blind spot, pretending it wasn't there.

She didn't used to have these thoughts. But lately, spots in Piper's memories had plagued her. She'd look at Clara and wonder. She'd look at Meyer and wonder. She'd look at herself in the mirror, and she'd wonder. There was a recurring image of Lila, still in her teens, standing beside a boy with severe black eyebrows. Not Clara's father, whom nobody spoke of (and pretended they didn't talk about for reasons of decency, not because nobody, including Lila, knew who he was), but someone else. A hole in the family that was supposed to be here. On waking, Piper wanted to prowl the village, looking for that young boy who'd gone missing, who wasn't ever actually there.

"And her grandfather," Lila added.

Piper looked over at Meyer. He was almost seventy. Piper, at fifty-six, was courting the reaper. Meyer's age flat-out thumbed its nose at him. But Meyer never got sick, same as his brother. Sometimes it seemed like the governor was blessed by the gods and might live forever. Or by someone else — a bargain made, to keep his spirit young.

Meyer looked back at Piper, his eyes still as vibrant as they'd been when she'd met him. Which had happened when …

But that box in her mind was also empty.

Meyer stood. He pulled on loose pants and a shirt, then opened the rear door. She knew where he was going, and the knowledge took some of the air from her lungs. Every day, he visited Kindred in the small hut on their small plot, nearest the governor's house but still separated by a sparse, ratty lawn. It was more like feeding a wild animal than paying a visit.

"Meyer," she said.

"I'll be right back."

"Meyer!"

He turned fully, waiting.

"Something's happening, isn't it?"

He turned back and left without a word.

Lila came forward. She sat on the bed's edge, watching her father leave and close the door. She swept her housedress up beneath her and perched half-on, half-off. A flash of something nostalgic invaded Piper's mind —

(She and Lila in a dark place, made of stone, underground, quiet, the darkness lit not by candles but like some bit of leftover magic that today they'd have run straight to Stranger's Church.)

— and then she was Lila again, her own daughter now seen through a recent veil of unreality, sitting on the bed, making Piper feel like an imposter. As if Lila had come to her for something that Piper wasn't qualified to dispense.

"She was asking me again, Mom," Lila said, and again Piper felt a strange reaction to the word, wishing for once that Lila, now an adult, would call Piper by her name. "Clara was. And not just in the dream, I mean. In wakefulness."

"Asking what?"

"Asking me about her father. About you. About my mom."

Piper didn't like the sound of that. Lila had listed three items, not two. And from experience, Piper knew exactly how Clara asked those questions: not like she wanted to know but like she knew fine — and wanted to see if you did, too.

"When?"

"Yesterday."

"That's probably why you had your dream." Piper's eyes went to the still-open door. She'd accepted this early intrusion without question and so had Meyer, but Lila hadn't really explained. It was only a dream. But Piper's own dream was still clinging to her insides like a drowning man fighting the tide. It was true: *Something was happening.* The idea of Lila bursting in to tell them something so mundane made sense, and that in itself was a bother.

"Maybe." Lila sighed. "Probably."

The rear door opened. Meyer was already back, this time with Kindred. They'd once been identical, but Piper now found herself drawn to their change in diverging directions. Meyer's clothing was sold by the tradesmen, but Kindred wore mostly loose shirts that had gone threadbare at the elbows. Kindred spent more time in the sun — he'd burned, tanned, then wrinkled. Meyer's skin was comparatively smooth. Kindred's hair had grown long, while Meyer kept his short.

"Something's happened with Clara," Meyer said.

Piper answered, reaching for Lila's wrist. "What is it?"

"Word came from the Mullah in the hills," Kindred said. "Through a courier."

"Is she with them? With the Mullah?" Lila said it like an accusation, but just because Kindred and Meyer supported Clara's bizarre practices didn't mean they were to blame. Clara was twenty-seven years old and far beyond needing her mother's permission or approval. Piper, however, could hear the edge in Lila's tone.

You two got her into this, and now look what's happened.

Between the lines, Piper got a distinct, obvious flash of knowledge that had no business being in her head, and she knew what Meyer had been keeping from her. They'd had their bond from the start, and Piper had always felt excluded. Now she was trying the Mullah's brew — and Meyer, Piper knew without a doubt, had been drinking it alongside her.

(It's not true.)

But no, it very much was. Piper knew, because she'd always known more than she should ... or at least, that's the impression she was now beginning to get, more and more with every passing moment.

"I think so. Yes."

Piper raised her eyes. Looked into Kindred's and saw more than the darkness seen by the others. Now Piper saw something else. Something so familiar and so near, she could almost touch it. She almost flinched, wanting to avert her eyes, because in that moment it was as if she and Kindred shared an intimate history: as if before she'd been with Meyer, she'd been with him.

(In an enormous stone house with many levels. In a city that fell to ashes. Before the New World. When Lila was ...

When Lila was ...)

Piper put her hand over her mouth and uttered a noise like a squeak. All heads turned to her, and Piper could only look back, pulse heavy, chest wanting to heave in a parody of panic.

Lila wasn't her daughter.

Clara wasn't her granddaughter.

In all their lives, how had none of them known?

"Piper?" said Meyer.

Meyer and Kindred weren't brothers.

And there had been another man in her past. A man named ... named ...

"Clara will be okay, Piper." Meyer put his strong arm around her, keeping legs made of jelly from letting her fall. "But we need to go to the Mullah. Now."

Piper took two long, deep breaths, then nodded to indicate that she was okay.

But she wasn't.

Because something had changed.

It wasn't the drink, the drug, or the practice Meyer and Sadeem the Wise simply called "meditation" that had caused whatever was wrong with Clara now.

It was something else. Creeping and distant, crawling back into Piper's awareness with black claws and purring throats.

A wall had fallen.

Whatever Clara and the Mullah had been trying to do in those far-off caves, they'd either catastrophically failed or catastrophically triumphed.

Chapter Three

"Come. Hurry."

Sadeem waved a frantic hand at Peers. He scuttled over, ducking low to avoid the outcropping. Watching him approach, Sadeem wasn't sure whether to envy the younger man's agility or give thanks for his own increasingly stooped posture. When he'd first come here — in his midfifties, about the age Peers was now — he'd hit his head on that stupid outcropping three times out of every four. Now he missed it because he'd aged into clearance.

"Yes, Sage."

"Bring her water."

"Can she drink it?" Peers looked down at the young woman who, if they all didn't know better, might appear to be sleeping with her head in Sadeem's lap.

"She's not actually unconscious. Just ... below consciousness."

"Is there a difference?"

"Yes, Peers. She is still here. Just kept from us, as if she's been taken behind a curtain."

"Was she taking ..." He trailed off.

Sadeem shook his head. "Clara doesn't need the medicine to talk to the others." In truth, he was thinking of discouraging the medicine's use for the whole clan instead of just keeping Clara off it. Only Governor Dempsey seemed to benefit from the drug, but even that felt to Sadeem like playing with fire. Not only did they need to tiptoe around Dempsey as a need-to-know visitor (even he didn't realize which portals into the collective the medicine opened; he simply knew it felt familiar, as if from a forgotten life), but Sadeem wasn't convinced the Astrals didn't see through Meyer's eyes whenever he took it. If they kept giving Dempsey the drug, they might be turning him into a spy against them. That's how the Astrals had originally seen much of the world and selected their viceroys, after all.

Meyer and even Kindred — though Sadeem had his doubts about the latter — were part of this. But letting Meyer participate in the ceremonies was simply playing their part as the keepers of the Astral portal so that they could do the rest without being watched. If he knew too much about what Clara and the other Lightborn were doing, he wouldn't understand.

At least not until he and everyone else *truly* understood.

Peers nodded assent, then ran off to fetch the water.

A tall man, in his thirties, entered the chamber. Sadeem smiled, then nodded toward the attendant near the chamber's entrance. He drew a curtain, and Sadeem saw his silhouette move before it.

"Did you have trouble finding us?" Sadeem asked.

Logan shook his head of long sandy blond hair.

"Not at all."

"Did you see the path?"

"Do you mean literally?"

20

Sadeem cocked his head. It was a tiny test, just to see.

"There's no path in the sand. But I could see one with my eyes half-closed. To me it looked like an orange line that branched but always came back together. One line in the many was clearly brightest, and easy to follow."

Sadeem nodded. "The bright path is Clara's. As I understand it."

"You still can't see into it. Into the network."

"I've never been able to."

"I thought maybe now …" Logan looked down at Clara, uncomfortable as if they were deliberately excluding her inert presence. "Now that you've broken in …"

"When a dam breaks," Sadeem said, "some water always flows both ways."

Logan shrugged.

Sadeem's stoic face broke, and he almost laughed, despite it all.

"I'm sorry. I'm supposed to be a sage. I'm the elder here. If I don't speak in koans half the time, I risk my position."

"Would they really—?"

"It was a joke, Logan. Do you remember jokes? Has that particular human tradition been lost as well?"

Logan extended a hand, as if pointing at Sadeem.

"Hey, Sage," Logan said. "Pull my finger."

"And the jokes have stayed so highbrow. It does my old heart good to see it." He shifted, better settling Clara's head. "No, they wouldn't kick me out. Among the Mullah, I'm the only one who knows what happened before the Forgetting."

"What about Peers?" Logan ticked his head toward the portal.

"Peers is a curious one. Clara says he's forgotten, and that what he knows today is the same as any of the others:

21

things I've taught them, and that they believe. She says that Peers doesn't remember as we do. But she also says that it's like he *almost* knows. When she tunes into his consciousness within the larger network, she sees a nugget buried deep inside his mind — a secret he's keeping from everyone, yet has probably forgotten he's keeping."

"Could it be something dangerous?"

"I don't know." Sadeem shrugged. "Why don't you ask her?"

Logan looked down then up at Sadeem, knowledge dawning.

"Is that why I'm here, Sage? To try and talk to her?"

"Allah knows I can't." Sadeem ran a hand over her hair, softly, slowly. "But she's still here, Logan. I'm not like you. I can't see the minds. I have to trust Clara when she talks about things taking shape beneath the surface."

"Then how are you able to work with her to …?" He stopped, unsure what it *was* that Clara and the Mullah had been doing — on and on and on, since the Astrals had left the second time.

"Most of it is on faith," Sadeem answered. "Clara tells me that the network is still alive, even through the Forgetting. She talks as though it's a puzzle where pieces fit far too well for coincidence. You and the other Lightborn saw how you could turn on the minds of the other, non-Lightborn children, and Clara tells me that even today, now that those children are grown, their altered minds still fit the grid in ways they shouldn't. And there's more: linchpin mental abilities that optimize the network. Giving it more branches, like a shot of vitamins for the collective. But you know much of this. What matters more is that I need you now, Logan. And so does she."

Logan looked down at Clara. Conflict crossed his face.

"You always had a connection," Sadeem said.

Logan shook his head. "That was a long time ago."

"And, what? You've shut off your memory? Doesn't it persist for you and the others?"

"You know it does," Logan said, sounding slightly irritated.

"And?"

"And *what*, Sage?" he said, his patience breaking. "You have your memory, but you ran off to live in a cave with a cult of followers. You didn't stay in the village like we did. Do you think anyone believes we are simply eccentric? The new religions are as bad as some of the old ones. They tolerate us because we teach them how to smith metal and harvest oil for light and how to build their homes so they won't topple. But they don't accept us. It's only a matter of time before someone decides we're witches or something and begins to capture and burn us. I guess the joke's on them, though, huh? Because we can see intentions coming. We'll be able to hit the desert and wander."

"I wouldn't have called for you if it wasn't dire," Sadeem said.

"You know we decided this was the best way. We wanted to fit in and Clara wanted to stand out. She made her choice. She's on her own."

"Logan," said Sadeem. "Look at her."

He watched Sadeem with hard, defiant eyes. But when the Sage didn't break his gaze, Logan looked down.

"This isn't fair," he said.

"She needs you. I can't reach her."

"Then call Stranger. Stranger knows the mindscape. Carl Nairobi spoke to me earlier. About dreams. I sent him to Stranger's Church"

Sadeem shook his head. "Stranger was once a maestro, but today he is nearly human."

"He hasn't aged."

23

"That doesn't mean he can touch her mind anymore. Or any of your minds. It must be you."

"Why me?"

"Because when I called, you came."

Logan exhaled. Shook his head. But this was just blustering; Sadeem knew he'd do the right thing. He'd already committed himself and declared his intentions. The crossing wasn't easy, and even the Mullah courier Sadeem had sent running to Stranger's church sometimes got lost. Stranger might come and he might not, but he'd already done the important thing and sent word to Logan, corroborating the change he himself surely felt in the air. Clara *had* managed something, and someone had hit her back hard. They'd been through the end. Now they'd reached the end of the beginning.

Logan had come when Clara needed him. He wouldn't turn back now.

"I can't."

"Logan."

"She hates me. She'll push me out."

"Being pushed out is better than what I'm able to do. Look around before it happens. Find out if you can see the grid as she does. Clara's talked for years about pieces shuffling themselves. They came back once because they felt an itch. Two decades in this cave, I've spent trusting the idea that she could make them itch again."

"Stupid," Logan said, looking down at Clara's peaceful face. "I warned you. I told you something like this might happen."

"Maybe. But you know Clara."

Logan did. *Uniquely.*

Sadeem said, "You loved her once."

"That was a long time ago."

"I just need you to try. Look into her mind. I believe

24

she succeeded, and broke their wall. I think they hit her back. But it will only work if they can keep her down. *You* can pull her out."

"Why do you think that?"

"Because I can feel something changing, and see something shifting in the other Mullah — those who know the past because I taught it to them, but whose eyes are already lighting with new reasons to know it."

Logan shook his head. His face softened. Sadeem was about to hear the real reason for Logan's opposition — the truth behind why Clara and the Lightborn had parted ways.

It wasn't because Logan felt Clara's attempt to breach the Astral wall was futile. It was because he believed she could do it, and feared the consequences.

"They've finally left us alone," Logan said, looking skyward, toward the cave ceiling. "They killed everyone we knew and destroyed all that we built, but then they went away so we could at least try to start again."

Sadeem shook his head slowly.

"They never left. They're still out there, and have been since we came to this place. They *can't* leave. Not as long as the Lightborn keep their fingers under the lid to keep the box from closing. It's not just Clara. It's all of you."

"But the rest of us aren't trying to meddle. We're willing to let it all go, and forget in time."

Sadeem looked down at Clara, then back at Logan.

"Are you sure?" he said.

Chapter Four

CARL SAT in Stranger's vacated room as attendants ran
back and forth outside, staring down at the polished silver
sphere in his hand.

And he thought, *Carl Nairobi.*

It wasn't his name. He was a blacksmith and a silversmith, same as his father. Apparently.

Although for the first time, as Carl looked down at his
distorted reflection in the object Stranger had given him
before rushing out to leave him alone, Carl thought how
odd it was that he knew how to fire a furnace, forge metal,
and wield a hammer.

And he thought of what Stranger had said, too: that
Carl wasn't strong because he was a smith, but that he was
a smith because he was strong. The way Stranger spoke,
there was an order to things that escaped Carl. Everyone
was where they were because they'd fit their positions
rather than being raised in stations and learning to fit them
over time.

That wasn't how he remembered things.

In fact, Carl didn't remember things any particular way at all now that he thought about it.

His father, who'd taught him the craft and had the last name *Smith* first? Carl thought he remembered all of that, but after peering deeper inside realized he didn't.

And his childhood? Carl didn't remember that, either.

He remembered his dream much more vividly.

Himself, inside the monolith as it crossed vast oceans of open water.

And peril. Some unknown, unarticulated horror that crept down Carl's backbone the longer he dwelled upon it.

Carl Nairobi.

Had that truly once been his name? Stranger seemed to have been harboring secrets, but Carl found himself *recognizing* their truth rather than *believing* it. Same as Carl had known truths when …

When …

"Liza Knight," Carl said aloud.

There was no more to the thought. But it mattered because his mind was on a different Liza Knight than the old woman who ran the rectory. He couldn't quite catch the other memory, but he could almost see it, dancing at the edges of his vision: an impression of another Liza Knight in a different place. Someone he'd once almost feared. Or someone that others had. Not the same Liza. The one in his head was many seasons younger.

When do you believe we met?

Twenty years ago, Carl. Twenty summers and winters.

Carl stood. He set the small ball on Stranger's vacated table. He didn't need it. He was sure he had one of his own, somewhere at home. Wherever he needed to go, it would take him. Its witchcraft didn't frighten Carl. He was increasingly sure, now, that he'd followed it once before.

The person whose spot you'll be given the chance to take is the man who murdered your sister. And because I need you to refuse.

Carl didn't know what it meant, but now he couldn't stop hearing the voice in his head. It belonged to Stranger. It sounded weathered by time, antiquated, made fuzzy. But it was there, and true — as if the odd holy man had been right, that they'd met once before.

He remembered another house. Different. A coldbox that didn't need to be buried in the cool dirt, for meat that didn't need to be treated with salt. The room from some forgotten past, as Carl's mind opened to see it more and more, was like a thing born of magic. Lights that didn't use flame. Every surface smooth, as if sculpted and sanded for hours.

And in that room, long ago, Stranger had told him not to do something that he'd otherwise have very much wanted — perhaps needed — to do.

I need you to refuse.

A mental light went on without needing a flame.

Carl stood.

He left the small building and began to walk.

Chapter Five

CARL WAS HALFWAY to his destination, with no clue precisely where he was going, when he stopped to rest in the shade of an outcropping. The sun was still low in the sky, but the heat had already started.

You're almost there, he thought.

Almost where?

But there was no answer, just as silence met the dozen new questions entering Carl's mind by the minute. He didn't know why he remembered Liza Knight poorly, when she'd always struck him as cordial. He didn't know why Stranger seemed increasingly familiar, despite his certainty, just an hour ago, that he'd never met the man before. He didn't know why he was sure, when he'd met Stranger during that encounter he didn't remember, that the man had looked exactly as he did now. And he had no clue why he kept dreaming what he did, other than the simple explanation that the dreams weren't truly dreams.

He knew the way because he'd been here before.

Not just one time to look from a distance in fright but several times.

Once when the sea had been closer, though these days it was hours away. The first time he'd walked from the wreck with a small group of people he barely knew, all of them survivors of something.

All of them in some sort of fugue state, practically sleepwalking.

In that state, Carl was growing sure he'd come here again and again.

He walked. Across the big dunes then down along a shallow valley where they'd all met. When he'd first encountered ...

Who?

Carl didn't know. But the sun was hot, and he had no water, and now so far from the village, the idea of dehydration was starting to bother him. He should go back, maybe, and grab a canteen or sack. But as Carl looked out across the parched desert back toward the village, he knew he wouldn't. Because if he went back to The Clearing for water, he'd never set out again. He'd lose his nerve, might even lose this new rush of memories, arriving like fragments from an obliterated past.

Vast cities made of metal and glass. Towers that kissed the sky.

Magic everywhere, for everyone — a magic that, in vague recollection, struck Carl as having been so common that everyone took it for granted. You could see things that your eyes couldn't know by themselves. Speak to people who were untold hours distant, across many horizons.

And people. So many people he'd once known in that place, if it was real, but hadn't thought of in years.

No. He wouldn't go back. He'd move farther into the desert and take his chances. If he got a bit thirsty, that's how it'd have to be. The thought invited panic, but Carl stood anyway, feeling the sun scorch his exposed skull and arms, and headed where he'd been bound since leaving Stranger's, with no supplies or guidance beyond instinct. Or buried habit.

And besides, there must be water there.

Which was a lie because Carl was headed into the lowlands. The shallow cup in the desert's floor cut the scant wind and made whatever sat there bake come midday. Just one of many things Carl shouldn't know, considering that the top of his mind insisted he'd only come here once before.

Over the next rise, looking down, he saw it.

The monolith was intact. Entirely whole. Its metal skin was thick and had only begun to brown in the air. As he approached it, Carl noted its smooth sides, the elevated flat areas surrounded by what appeared to be railings. The thing was enormous. There was a part at the top that reflected the sun — pure transparent squares a lot like the glass the strange lot on the village's perimeter taught others to make. Carl squinted, raised one big arm to shield the glare. But around his own dark skin he could see its gray bulk. The way it was narrower than it was long, if the glass-filled area marked its front.

Of course it's the front. There's the hatch where you entered. Inside is a gangplank you yourself once raised, when the big waves came.

Waves?

Carl looked around as if another person had spoken. There were no waves here. There couldn't be. And yet it all rang true to Carl.

The tossing of water, threatening to tip them over.

The clanging and banging from the thing's rear as the big metal boxes shifted and broke free, entire blocks of cargo finding the ocean floor.

Cargo?

But this time, Carl squashed the mental question. The more time passed, the less foreign this seemed. He reached the monolith and extended an arm to touch it. It was hot from the sun, but moving down to a shaded section gave him the feel of cool metal, far smoother than any blacksmith could ever pound it. Far thicker metal than any forge could ever birth.

Of course, cargo. *This thing is a vehicle, not unlike a cart with wooden wheels. It's just a very large vehicle, meant for …*

That, he wasn't quite sure of. Yet.

On the big thing's shaded side, he found metal rods secured to its side like the rungs of a ladder. Without stopping to wonder if he should, Carl started to climb. As he did, more familiarity intruded. He'd been on this ladder before. Although unless his almost-memory was failing him, he'd gone down, not up. He'd boarded this

(ship)

this *ship* once before, using a bridge that lowered from the side. And he'd disembarked only once, using the ladder. He'd never returned. By the time they'd all joined the others, everyone was forgetting.

But now it was coming back in chunks.

This is where the woman, who'd come out in horror to watch the waves, went overboard.

This is the way to the bridge, where I slept by the wheel, obeying Stranger's small metal ball.

Carl put his hand on a latch, knowing exactly how to work it.

And this is the bridge. This is where I stayed while the others remained below.

There was a small box beneath a set of what looked like books — but not the handwritten kind; these were glossy and printed by machines. Carl reached for the handle and pulled it, knowing the box would open like a door. The thing was smooth and made of a material Carl had never seen before

(plastic)

and the inside edges were lined with another unknown substance

(rubber gaskets)

but Carl paid them no mind. What he wanted was inside.

(My Coke. That half-eaten mess ration I never finished because the sea finally got me and I started throwing up.)

The simple, odd objects struck Carl with a sense like nostalgia. How did he know it all when he'd never been here before? How had he forgotten it, believing he'd never seen the inside of this place?

The small refrigerator, long since dead, had kept the ration from bugs but had failed to keep it from mold and rot. The smell was preserved, greeting Carl in fetid welcome.

He threw it across the freighter's bridge, nearly gagging.

The can of Coca-Cola, opened two decades ago and set aside until after Carl had decided he was a totally different person, had evaporated. But there was another thing inside, and Carl grabbed it like a drowning man: one of several bottles of water, sealed inside their plastic prisons.

Without thinking, Carl spun the cap. Only once the bottle was half-gone did he stop to wonder how he'd known the way to open it, how he'd known the bottle was here, or how he'd known it wasn't poisoned or bad.

Bullshit. I put these bottles here myself. Pulled them from the mess hall, which is down the set of stairs just outside, down the narrow hallway, to the right, beneath the

...

The cargo.

Why had he thought of that before he'd climbed up? And why was he thinking of it now?

"Hello," said a voice from behind.

Carl nearly jumped out of his skin, turning. But in the second before something big and gunmetal black hit him hard and pinned him to the deck, Carl saw a woman in the opposite doorway wearing an Old-Earth dress, tight, her hair dyed blonde, her bearing upright, her lips and nails painted to match her dress.

Then he heard a guttural, inhaling rattle, like a purr.

The thing above Carl had its mouth open, and deep in its throat he saw a throbbing blue spark.

Chapter Six

MEYER HELD OUT AN ARM, a single finger extended skyward. Without turning to face Lila and Piper, he hoped the message would be clear: *Wait. Don't move. Something's happening.*

Piper moved up beside him with Lila at the rear. When Meyer crouched, his joints popping and threatening to give them away, Lila and Piper stooped, too.

They were behind the house and most of the way across the grounds, nearly to the stables. The day was warm bordering on hot, and the sky was blue, but in addition to the urgency with Clara, Meyer was certain he'd seen something else amiss.

Piper caught his eye. Raised her eyebrows, but didn't speak.

"There's someone behind the stables," Meyer said, voice just shy of a whisper.

"So?"

Meyer shook his head. He couldn't say why the flash of something had bothered him; he only knew that it had. Maybe it was the tempo of the almost-seen thing that was troubling: too fast and darting, as if trying to hide rather than simply passing by. Or maybe it was the location; the governor's estate bordered the merchant district, and the alleys between were more for storage of goods than transportation, given how fat they'd grown with wares. Merchants often pooled resources to trade guards for service, to watch for thieves. Meyer didn't think he'd seen anyone moving beyond his fences in months. And when someone did go back, they moved methodically, stepping over piles.

But mostly Meyer was bothered by a feeling that whatever he'd almost seen had somehow struck him as familiar.

Not just a person walking but more like an animal he'd observed many times in a way he couldn't remember.

Not a person wearing black or with dark skin but a thing low to the ground that *was* black, and scuttled like an insect.

His skin crept. His testicles hugged up close, his hands unwilling to hang limp at his sides.

"Meyer?"

He saw it again, and this time Piper did, too. He reached back to push Lila down, as if she was still a kid, and together the three of them found themselves crouching behind one of the near shed's rain barrels.

"Clara, Dad. We have to—"

"Shh. It's them."

"Who?"

But Meyer wasn't sure. His words were a reaction, like a doctor striking his patellar tendon with a small rubber hammer.

And that didn't make much sense either, seeing as the village doctors mostly used bandages, plant salves the Unforgotten had taught them how to make.

Patellar tendon?

Rubber?

"Dad, you're scaring me."

That was okay. Meyer was scaring himself. There was the thing he'd thought he'd seen ahead, and there were also (he was increasingly becoming convinced) at least two similar almost-seen things to the right and left. Piper and Lila had been behind; they wouldn't have seen. *Meyer* was deluded. Only he felt compelled to crouch on a clear and pleasant day, knees hurting, while his granddaughter was suffering from something unknown, tended to by the Mullah.

(Who'd followed them through the caves.)

(Whom they'd traveled with, before Peers left the village to join them as kin.)

"Dad?"

"Lila. Do you remember Peers?"

"What peers?"

"No. A man. A man who traveled with us, named Peers."

"Traveled where?" Lila asked. Because she'd never traveled. None of them had. They weren't merchants or couriers. They'd lived in this place forever, just like anyone else.

But beside Lila, Piper was frowning. "I—"

There was a cracking, crunching from their left, stopping Piper's lips and eliciting a gasp. They were concealed in the nook between the shed and a rain barrel, but Meyer could put his eye to the gap and look out, seeing the monstrosities now crossing from the barn to the home's rear.

When he turned, his face must have betrayed his shock because Piper pushed forward. Meyer stopped her with a palm, but in the past twenty years she'd developed an eye-rolling intolerance to following his lead. Piper had once let

Meyer call the shots. But that was no longer true, and became less so by the year.

"Don't, Piper."

"Dad?" Lila said. "What is it?"

Piper met Meyer's eyes. She didn't go to the gap, or peek to see what Meyer had spied.

"They're back, aren't they?"

"Piper?" said Lila.

"How many did you see?"

Meyer shook his head.

"Do you remember, Meyer?"

"Remember *what*, Piper?" said Lila, now actively afraid.

"Come on." Piper took the lead, pushing Meyer aside. She moved into the open, crossing between the shed and a pile of lumber due to be built into yet another gubernatorial outbuilding. She had Meyer by the sleeve, eyes on Lila to follow. Once farther on, Piper checked their vistas and moved again, no longer holding Meyer, moving as if she'd done this before.

"When we get to the stable," Piper said, "we'll need to ride bareback or not at all. There's no time to saddle up. They're Mullah horses, and the Mullah ride bareback. The horses will be okay with it if we are. Lila?"

Lila nodded.

"Meyer?"

He considered protesting, saying he was getting too old for this shit, like a character from one of the films he used to produce so many years ago.

But then that random thought stopped making sense, and he nodded, too.

"They'll hear us," Meyer said.

"Who?" Lila asked.

"It doesn't matter. I don't think they're here for us."

"What, then?"

"Kindred," Piper said. "If I had to guess, they're here for Kindred."

Lila gripped Piper's arm, her eyes wide and brown and depthless. "What's happening, Piper?! Tell me!"

Piper looked around then sighed.

"Close your eyes, Lila."

"We don't have time for this, Piper."

"Quiet, Meyer. Lila, close your eyes."

Lila closed her eyes.

"Think of Clara. Not whatever is happening with her now; don't think of that. Just think back. To when she was younger."

"Okay."

"A lot younger. A toddler, Lila. What was she like as a toddler?"

Lila's eyes snapped open. "Oh. Oh, Jesus."

"Do you remember?"

"The palace. Not this place." Lila ticked her head toward the small, rock-built home. "Something much bigger. And ... and the bunker. Dad? You had a bunker somewhere, underground."

"Vail," Meyer said, reeling back through time.

"And Clara ... oh hell." Lila looked at Piper, and a look flashed between them. Piper couldn't read minds as she now remembered she'd once been able to, but Lila's eyes said that they'd shared the same awkward thought. A flash of recollection of the Vail bunker led to a memory of Heather. Meyer's ex-wife, before Piper. Lila's real mother; Clara's grandmother.

Piper's hand went over her mouth, her blue eyes suddenly enormous.

"Later," Meyer said, shifting so he was between them.

"Piper? Later. Right now, we need to focus. Clara. She needs help. Okay?"

"Lila …" Piper said. "I'm—"

Meyer shook his head. *"Later,"* he repeated. But even in the tense moment, Meyer couldn't help but sympathize with Piper's emotional flood. In the space of seconds she'd lost a daughter and granddaughter. She wasn't Meyer's first and only. He'd lived an entire life before her.

"The aliens," Lila said. "There was a … flood?" Hand over mouth, the two women like bookends. "Oh my God. The flood. They must have killed off—"

"Lila!"

"Why are they back? They left! They finally left us alone! *It's been twenty fucking years!"*

Meyer was about to grab Lila and pull her away, toward the stables, but Piper beat her to it. The trio made another short sprint, and then they were in the cool of the stables, an overhead rope dangling from the loft, rocking slowly back and forth in the breeze through the front door and out the rear.

"Are you sure they'll let us go?" Meyer asked.

Piper shook her head. "It's just a feeling."

"Like the feelings you used to get?"

"I …" Piper exhaled, frustrated. "I don't know."

"You said they were here for Kindred."

"There are three groups. One was already behind the house. Maybe I assumed they were all moving in on the same spot, and that'd have to be Kindred's if they'd already reached the house."

"Piper? Is that just a hunch, or—?"

"I don't know!"

Meyer watched her for a long second, then nodded decisively and pointed to three horses in turn.

"Lila, take Shy. Piper, you ride Missy. I'll take Leroy.

Thread your fingers through the mane, and squeeze with your legs."

"I don't know how to steer without reins," Lila said.

Meyer was already climbing up, then kicking aside the box he'd used to mount Leroy. He threaded his fingers through the horse's mane and leaned forward.

He realized how odd it all was. In this life, Meyer had never ridden bareback, either. He only knew how to do it because before the Astrals, when in his twenties, he'd volunteered at a camp and learned the skill to impress a woman. Only remembering his modern past would help them survive their agrarian future.

"Then I'll take the lead," Meyer said. "Just hang on, and your mounts will follow."

Chapter Seven

"MOTHER KNIGHT?"

Liza looked up. She was between rows of peas, weeding. Being bent over so long made her back ache, and the sun, even filtered by cloth, was punishing. But it was good to be outdoors. Confined spaces, ever since crossing the sea on the Astral vessel, made her uneasy. She'd take sunburn and backache over being boxed in any day.

"Yes, Jason."

"Brother Richard does not answer the call."

Liza smirked. Richard was probably hungover. Holy ways had changed this time around. She was seeing to it. Her father had been a priest, and her mother — mostly because Dad's domineering encouraged her more than faith — had taught Bible study six days a week. Liza hadn't cared for the old ways. But remembering had its advantages, like when the Lightborn kids became teens and conveniently reinvented fermented beverages — clerics, shamans, and all the rest of the holy hodgepodge from the early days wondered whether it was God's will to consume it. Liza had given her blessing. Drunk holy people were more fun than sober, in Liza's opinion. And just wait until someone found marijuana seeds this time around.

"Enter his room, and shake him, then," Liza said. "Members of my rectory do not miss meals."

Jason seemed uncomfortable. He looked down, into the engineered soil the Lightborn had quietly placed into the hands of a few farmers when growing was tough, and nearly smashed a tiny plant — corn, perhaps — with his toe.

"What, Jason?"

"His door has been locked."

"Unlock it."

"From the inside, Mother."

Well. Liza didn't like that. She hated locked doors in her house, and the rectory was, after all, more or less hers. She'd commissioned it, commandeered the labor to have it built, and because she'd spent a stint in her old life at a residential construction firm, knew better than most how to fabricate a structure that wouldn't fall over. The monk was probably beating off. One of the side effects of discouraging the old world religion's sexual repression along with its statutes against public drunkenness.

"Then have the Master use his key."

More turning of the cleric's toe in the dirt.

"You *asked* the Master, didn't you?"

"Yes, Mother."

Liza swore. She could be dainty when needed, and often in the public eye had to appear as the soft old lady who kept the holy people in line and suitably pure. Part of the job, and the price of keeping a read on the village's superstitious pulse. Religion had always served as a basket for confidential information, and secrets gave a woman power and control. Corruption hadn't evolved too far yet, meaning whispers still held plenty of meaning.

She stood and brushed by Jason without a word, her stride younger than her years. If Richard had jammed his lock to keep the Master from entering — a trick other monks desiring privacy had used before — he might end up permanently breaking it. If that happened, they'd have to knock the door off its hinges, and then there'd be hell to pay.

Liza reached the monk's door. Jason hadn't followed, knowing better than to chase the matron when she was in a foul mood.

"Richard," she said, knocking. "Open up."

There was no sound from beyond.

More firmly, using her no-bullshit voice. *"Open up, Richard."*

Liza looked down the hallway, decided she was alone enough, and raised a fist. She pounded on the wood with its underside, her mouth open to shout when the door cracked open. It wasn't locked after all. Not even latched.

But the monk's room was empty. Bed crisply made, floor swept, wash basin dried and buffed clean.

She looked through the small window, pulling back the simple drape. There was no glass, but the spartan rooms had windows that were too small to climb through. Not that there'd be any need, with the door wide open despite Jason's ineptitude.

Still, something itched at her scalp.

Liza left the room, heading back toward the garden. Halfway there she turned and decided it wasn't Jason she wanted but the Master himself. Jason had called the man with his key, and if he was telling the truth, neither had been able to figure out how to unlock a door that stood more or less wide open. So either the Master was drunk as well, or Richard had cleaned up and fled in the few minutes it took for Jason to report and Liza to respond.

But the Master's room was also empty.

Bed crisply made, floor swept, wash basin dried and buffed clean.

And that was interesting. She'd chosen the Master because before he'd forgotten everything along with the rest of them, he'd been a lieutenant colonel with the South African National Defence Force. She'd brought him in assuming he'd retain his tendency toward confrontation in a crisis (which he had) and his discipline (which he had not). In his rebirth as the rectory's Master, Paul Blanthy had turned out to be a total slob.

Liza returned to the garden. But Jason wasn't there. He wouldn't just stand and wait for her to return once she'd run off, though he always seemed afraid of her enough to do exactly that.

And she'd passed nobody in the hallways, despite it being so near mealtime.

Liza felt a chill. She'd never had the dreams some of the others reported in confession (guilt was still useful in Liza's new religion), and she'd never been particularly superstitious. Liza believed what was in front of her, not what was invisible and breathing down her neck. But she felt this now, like a presence. Something gone wrong, even though all seemed well.

She reentered the hallway and knocked on the first door. But there was no farce even of closure this time, and the thing simply opened wide. She saw another meticulous chamber, empty.

She went to the next.

Empty.

And so on down the line, until Liza realized she was being ridiculous. Of course nobody was in their rooms. What had she told Jason? Nobody missed meals in Mother Knight's rectory. Only Richard had been stubbornly refusing to answer — something he must have realized and done before Liza arrived at his door. The others would be in the small, cozy cafeteria. Of course.

Except that Liza hadn't heard chatter in the air, and Liza's rectory didn't honor vows of silence. Quiet creeped her out, reminding Liza of the idiotic still that had fallen over the others during her seafaring adventure, when they'd all gone stupid except for her. Like confinement, silence was unnerving. Liza encouraged drink, boisterousness, and generally required that her monks, priests, and clerics be human beings so long as they could be holy when it counted, tending to village needs as its shepherds.

And she'd walked quite close to the cafeteria. Maybe even seen its open door in her peripheral vision.

Fighting irrational discomfort, Liza made herself leave the last of the empty rooms and head toward the building's far end. The cafeteria bordered the courtyard, and even though it was insufferably hot, maybe they'd all decided to go out there instead.

Liza turned the corner toward the cafeteria hallway and found herself confronting three enormous white forms backed by two ominous black ones. In front of the Titans and Reptars was an incongruous presence: a woman, shorter than Liza with cropped, dark brown hair. She was standing with her arms near her sides, hips slightly cocked, as if waiting.

Heart beating, Liza turned to run. But there were another two Reptars behind her.

Liza's mouth tried to move, but she couldn't make a sound.

The woman spoke. "Your people are hooked up, and the probes are coming online now. But as the hub's center, we will need you as well."

Liza looked over her shoulder. The Reptars had inched

closer. She watched them for maybe five seconds, decades-gone reality screaming back at her as if it had never left.

The sounds of their claws on the rectory's stone floor.

The sight of their throats, purring with blue spark.

When Liza turned back to face the woman and her escorts, she found that one of the Titans had moved up. He was smiling pleasantly, like Liza remembered them during their invasion, back when South Africa still had a name.

The Titan raised his arms. Strung between them was something that looked like a loose hat hung with a web of glowing wires.

"You may stand or sit for the procedure," the woman said as Liza backed herself against the wall. "But for the sake of your people, try not to scream."

Chapter Eight

THE GRID of interconnected lines and dots disappeared. To Carl, it had looked like the inside of a garment stitched in blue and yellow plaid, where connections between colors were made behind the scenes, on the invisible side.

And again he found himself looking at the blonde, back on the beached freighter's bridge.

"What do you remember?" she asked.

"Your mother."

The woman smirked. And that was strange. Because despite what Carl had said about the woman's surely nonexistent mother, he felt pretty sure, after this full-body enema, that he remembered everything. Any remaining cobwebs had been sucked away. Moreover, he was pretty sure he was remembering things he'd never experienced, as if he'd swapped tales of what others had gone through without remembering. And although he'd never seen one of the Astrals' Divinity class in person, Carl felt sure this thing masquerading as a woman was one — *at least* Divinity, if not higher. And similarly, he felt quite sure that it wasn't in any Astral's nature to smirk.

"What do you remember about the past?" the woman clarified.

"Jesus was black. Santa was black. And none of this is helping race relations from where I'm standing."

"So you *do* remember."

"No," Carl said, heaving, sweat on his skin, his heart hammering. "I just said random shit, and it's a big coincidence."

The woman turned to the Titan beside her — holding a small glowing sphere in his palm like a miniature fortune teller's crystal ball. There were no wires connecting it to the thing they'd draped over Carl's head and down his spine before strapping him to the map table, but Carl had remembered both Wi-Fi and Bluetooth in the final push and figured the alien overlords would have technology at least as solid.

The Titan touched the glass. It was such a small, almost delicate gesture that at first Carl let himself believe that the woman hadn't asked silently for what she'd seemed to. But of course she had, and in that moment his senses all vanished and he was back in the blue-and-yellow grid, disembodied, his every nerve screaming.

A thousand tiny knives slid around the rim of his skull, separating skin from bone. The brain wasn't supposed to sense pain, but Carl imagined it burned in flame, etched with acid, his spinal column lopped off below the cerebellum as if by a reaper's blade, dripping, bleeding down his back until —

The grid vanished. Now Carl saw only black. It took him a while to realize he was staring at the back of his own eyelids and that his mouth had opened, lips drawn back from his teeth in a silent shout of agony. Or maybe not so silent judging by the satisfied look on the Astral woman's face.

Except that Astrals weren't supposed to look *satisfied*, either.

"You are strong, Carl Nairobi. But we are in no hurry."

"What do you want from me?" Carl panted, his breath grown short.

"What do you know of the Unforgotten known as Clara Dempsey?"

"Is she your mother?"

More plaid. More pain. When Carl returned, he could hear his breath coming in enormous pained sobs. He fought for control. Found it, in measures.

"Once again," said the woman.

"I don't know anyone named Clara," Carl said.

The woman looked back at another Titan, this one staring into a larger, slightly more opaque spherical glass. From where Carl was lying, he could see flashes inside that looked almost like characters on a digital readout. The Titan said nothing, but the woman nodded as if he had.

"Your scan says you do."

"I don't know what to tell you, man," Carl said.

"We have disabled her remotely. But it has become apparent that the infection is systemic."

"What the fuck does that mean?"

The woman put a hand on Carl's forehead. It slipped in abundant sweat. His hands were restrained, and his body was pulled tight by ankle straps made of something that felt like cool, flexible steel. He could only raise his neck so far, or else he'd have tried to bite her.

"How did you access the stored race memories?"

"So this *is* about race," Carl said. "Bitch."

The woman half turned toward the Titan with the control ball. He raised a finger, ready to touch.

"Wait!"

The woman turned back to him, looked down. Loose blonde curls hung around her face.

"I don't know what you mean," Carl said. "Really."

"Have you imbibed any substances known as hallucinogenics?"

"No."

"Do you practice *meditation*?" Said as if she barely understood the word.

"No. I'm just a blacksmith. And a silversmith. And whatever other smith they need."

"Can you repair electronics or computers?"

"No. I never—"

The woman cut him off with another smirk. *Shit*. That had been a trap. Apparently he wasn't even supposed to know what electronics or computers *were*, which would have been true maybe an hour ago. And yet he'd answered without confusion.

"You would not be able to access the race memories without a conduit."

"I don't know what you mean. Honest."

"When were you in contact with Clara? Our probe shows her signature within your cortex. Yet each human we left behind after the first apparent incursion was meticulously scanned. We would not have departed without surety that those latent connections had been severed."

Carl's face contorted, his bottom lip pursing against the top.

"That's what happened when you came back the first time," Carl said, now remembering the arrival as if it were yesterday. Yet another thing they'd all forgotten, but now that it was back in his mind he could remember that day's terror like fresh blood. It wasn't just his. He seemed to feel it all, from everyone. "You came to erase us." He paused. "Again."

"The collective believed there was a glitch that necessitated an extra pass beyond the scheduled departure date. It was not wholly unexpected. There was an incursion by a party who—"

Carl had no idea how he knew the next thing, but it arrived front and center, certain and clear, as if someone had held a sign in front of his eyes.

"You're talking about Stranger."

The woman seemed confused then looked back at her Titan cohorts. Silent knowledge passed between them.

"What do you know of the one you call Stranger?"

"You first."

The woman glanced. The Titan touched the ball. The ship's bridge was gone, and again Carl writhed in psychic pain — far greater, it turned out, than anything physical. If Carl had a soul, it was being torn in half. He imagined a thousand dislocations, happening again and again.

But through the pain, the blue-and-yellow grid beyond beckoned him. Its voice was soft and filled with echoes, like many people whispering at once. He tried to crawl his way toward it, now seeing the dots on the grid as familiar, comforting presences. People he knew, rendered in light.

It's a network of minds, and they can't touch it. It's a cancer. The more they try to amputate it, the more it grows. And now it's gone critical. Now it's systemic. Now, they've lost a few of the cards, and others hold them instead. Or the barbs. Or the leashes.

But the thought vanished as reality returned, the woman's blue eyes so near Carl's.

"We can pull the information from you if we have to," she said. "Like extracting a tooth."

She settled back, and Carl realized she'd grown an anger born of frustration. He could relate. The trick was that Astrals — and particularly the higher classes — normally couldn't.

And Carl realized: *She's lying.*

"I don't know Stranger personally. I only know who he is," Carl said, hoping the woman couldn't see through his lie. "I just meant, what does he mean to you?"

"Irrelevant."

"Unless, by knowing context, I could tell you what you want to know."

The woman's eyes flicked away, then back.

"He represents a remainder of a chaotic variable in the system."

"I don't know what that means."

"Our models are complex by human understanding. You only need to know that he was problematic but eventually accounted for and contained. After the first false restart, certain minds in your human collective stayed connected. It was a glitch we didn't anticipate. But because we would not leave the planet before ensuring that all memories of your past had been erased — to ensure a fresh restart for the coming epoch — we monitored your minds and, yes, eventually returned to make a second pass."

"You mean that you tried to erase our minds once, but something didn't want to erase. So you came back three months later and did it again, more thoroughly."

"Yes."

But something wasn't clicking. As his mind returned to its prior state, Carl remembered the sequence of events perfectly. The Astrals had flooded the planet, erupted volcanoes, and prompted earthquakes. They'd sent billions to indirect deaths and killed off hundreds of millions more with their energy beams. When the world's population had dwindled to just a few million spread across the planet, the Astrals were supposed to pack up and leave. And that — even to someone who hadn't forgotten — was what had happened. Except that three months later, the big black ship returned … to erase them all again, and finally get it right.

But now here they were again, eraser and erased together for round three. Whatever that second-pass erasure had been, it certainly hadn't been effective. Twenty years later, all the old memories were flooding back, down to the Nintendosaurus T-shirt Carl used to wear as a kid.

They came back.

Except that Carl could see quite plainly that they hadn't actually *come back*, and that was the missing piece right there.

"You never left," he said.

"Our ships have been in orbit, beyond your visual range."

"For twenty years."

"We experience time differently than you do. Your twenty years is not—"

"*Twenty years*, you've been trying to wipe us clean," Carl interrupted. "*Twenty goddamned years*, and you still can't do it."

"Tell us about Clara Dempsey," the woman said.

"I don't know any Clara Dempsey."

"Do not lie to us." The woman's regained composure was starting to fracture. "We can see your connections to the wider collective. We can see your connection."

"I don't know what to tell you."

The woman slammed her fist on the table beside Carl, in the hollow between his head and right shoulder. Carl looked up as she seemed to question the action too late, wrapping a clutch of blonde hair behind her ear. The ear had a silver ring, like half of an infinity symbol.

She's kept her shape the entire time, whispered a voice in

Carl's head. *She's kept it because she's grown a preference — and with her preference comes baggage.*

"I don't know her," Carl said.

"Even remotely, we could see you in the collective from the others' vantages. Even when we sent the pulse to shut her down, we could see you and the others from within Clara's node on the network."

"Why is this woman Clara so important?"

"She is the seed."

"So find her, not me. I'm just a guy with a blacksmith shop."

The woman shook her head. "You are important because he touched you. He changed your path just as he changed it for others."

"Stranger?"

She nodded.

"How am I important?"

"That's for you to say."

Carl looked up at the woman. Against every intuition in his body — as he lay restrained and tortured — he found himself wanting to feel sorry for her. She wasn't giving him halfway answers to be obtuse. She was doing it because the twenty-year wrench in their gears wasn't something they knew how to fix. The Astrals were stymied, and couldn't go home until the unsolvable problem was finally resolved.

Tell her to turn it up, said that voice from inside. *They've done what they can to fix our network on wireless. The only remaining option is to plug into the mainframe. They've come to purge our minds manually, one at a time. Tell her to go ahead and do it. Turn the machine up. Cut you from the network of other minds by force, if it's the only way.*

"Turn this thing on my head up," Carl said, forcing the words past heavy lips. "I can't tell you any more, and I'm getting tired of this shit. So whatever you did to this Clara from your ship? Do it to me now that you've got me, if there's such a big fucking problem."

The woman met Carl's eyes, full of challenge.

"Earth is not our only farm. If we cannot purge your minds for the next epoch, the experiment will be a failure, and the stock here will be lost. If that is the case, we will give up on you."

Carl stared back, heart pounding, forcing his face to stay neutral.

"Help us if you can, Carl Nairobi. Because if you do not, we will have no choice but to leave the planet barren. We will stop your planet's core and let the solar wind blow your atmosphere from the surface."

Carl's tongue found the inside of his lip. "Do what you gotta."

The woman turned. The Titan touched the sphere. This time when Carl saw the grid, everything felt like it was being ripped to shreds. He had a body only to feel it torn into dripping red pain. He had a mind only to feel it fracture, broken like the brittle shards of a thousand crystal glasses. He watched the network of lines and dots — friendly now, present to comfort rather than control him — waver. He watched its lines stretch and threaten to snap. But Carl held them tight, knowing they mattered, enduring the pain and the suffering, enduring it with the smallest, hardest core of being inside him.

The sensation died in a blink. Carl's eyes opened, his brain shocked to find them intact.

He rolled his head. The Titan was staring at the woman. His finger hovered over the flashing red sphere — something gone wrong, broken mid-cycle. Then there was a strange, pained sound of squeezing, followed by a

scratch. Carl turned his head to look as several wet snapping sounds turned the silence to terror.

The Astral woman had been gripping the table's edge
while the machine tried to cut Carl from the equation. And
now, with her breath coming as hard as his, she'd squeezed
hard enough to snap her long fingernails from the soft
meat beneath.

Chapter Nine

CLARA BOLTED UPRIGHT SO SUDDENLY that she nearly broke Logan's nose with her forehead. Sadeem, watching, flinched more sufficiently than Logan. As it was, only Logan's angle to Clara's cot saved him a fracture, and her shoulder-length light brown hair merely swept his face like a dust mop. The kid's reflexes were slow for a caste that seemed to know everything. Or "the young man's" reflexes these days, *ahem*.

She said nothing, staring at the rock room's far wall.

"Clara?" said Sadeem. Logan, beside her, was speechless. It had taken precious minutes to convince Logan that Clara still needed him despite all that had happened between them, and that she'd welcome what seemed to be an intrusion rather than resent it. But before he'd managed to try and reopen the door they'd mostly shut between them (except in dreams, Sadeem imagined), this had happened.

Whatever it was.

Looking at Clara's profile, in stark relief to the rock behind her, Sadeem suppressed a chill. She'd been odd from the start, warm only once she surrendered her guard. But how many times had Sadeem seen her set focus aside for long enough to smile? The work *consumed* her. And now she was just this awakened thing without expression, not much more lifelike than she'd been horizontal with her eyes closed.

Her head turned toward them both, and Sadeem instantly saw the change. A half-dozen emotions warred on her smooth, still-innocent face. Sadeem thought she might laugh. Or maybe cry.

"What is it?" Sadeem asked. "What happened?"

But Clara's attention was on Logan, just now seeming to recognize him. A tiny, almost bittersweet smile dawned. One of her hands flinched, just a bit. Logan reached out and took it.

"Clara? What happened?" Sadeem repeated.

Softly she said, "Logan. Why are you here?"

"Sadeem sent for me."

"You should have called Stranger." Clara lifted her blue eyes to Sadeem. They were like azure mercury, as if a glance might catch her irises shifting rather than staying where they belonged. Sadeem had always been her senior in years, experience, and knowledge, but between them Clara had always been the truest elder.

"I sent for both. Logan came first."

"Where is Stranger?"

"I don't know. He hasn't arrived."

"And Kindred. Did you send for Kindred?"

"Why would I send for your uncle?" Sadeem asked.

Clara shook her head — not in confusion but as if things were coming at her too fast and that particular wrinkle, which required too much explanation, would have to wait for later. "It doesn't matter. We need to find them. When did you see them last?"

"I haven't actually seen either," Logan said. "But I sent someone to Stranger. Yesterday."

"Who?"

"A blacksmith. Carl. He was having dreams. About the freighter. The one they call 'the monolith.'"

"Carl Nairobi."

"I think his name is Smith," said Logan.

She turned the tables on Logan, taking his hand instead of him taking hers. She looked from Logan to Sadeem, speaking to both.

"Listen to me. Both of you. Sadeem already knows this, but Logan, you and the other Lightborn didn't want to listen. The blacksmith—"

"Clara ..."

"It's not important right now," she said, swinging herself around so that her legs rested on the floor, letting the young man's hand drop. They'd had plenty of fights — Sadeem had only seen a fraction, and been a shoulder for Clara regarding many of the rest. But she brushed it away like an irritating distraction, returning the issue to center.

"The blacksmith, Carl, drove that freighter from South Africa in the flood. It's his, but he's forgotten. What were his dreams? Did he tell you?"

"Just that he was at the monolith. With ..." Logan's brow pinched. "With others."

"And what's he doing there? In the dream."

"He didn't tell me. Why?"

Clara didn't answer. Instead she turned to Sadeem.

"I had my fingers in it, Sadeem. Same as every day." She cast a quick apologetic look at Logan; between them, that "every day" had a hammer's blunt force. "But it was like something started to move. And then it was there — just ... *there*. But they must have felt it, because they stopped repelling me one to one and turned all their attention on me. It was like a blast. I was still in the grid. But I couldn't move. Or pull back."

"Pull back from what?" Logan asked.

"They — *what?* — shut you down?" Sadeem asked, ignoring Logan.

"I gave them a target. I've been hidden by the ... you know, the firewall thing. But once I got it open ..." Clara shrugged.

"So how did you ...?" Sadeem trailed off, the rest of his question implied.

"What are you two talking about?" Logan said.

"But it's happening, Sadeem. The puzzle. Its finally solving itself. But there's more. Something went wrong."

"Wrong how?"

Logan physically inserted himself between them. Both shut their open mouths, seeming to see him for the first time.

"You called me here," Logan said. "So how about you clue me in?"

Clara hesitated, and for a long second Sadeem thought she might refuse to tell him out of spite. In the strictest sense, Logan had an opportunity to be involved from the beginning, but in the much more realistic, everyday sense Sadeem would have sided with Logan in the split. The work felt important now that Clara had broken through, but for two decades it had felt like a fool's errand. Clara had given him little choice but to leave.

"I broke through, Logan," she said.

"Through what?" Then: "Not through ..."

"Yes. Through the Forgetting."

"But ..." Logan looked at Sadeem for help, and for a moment Sadeem thought the man might inform him that breaking through the Forgetting was a lost cause and that they'd been chasing that particular dog for twenty years. As if Sadeem didn't know. But then Logan turned back to Clara and said, "How?"

"They've always erased our minds before they leave. Sadeem told me that's what the Mullah knew—"

"What they *believed*," Logan corrected.

"What they *knew*," Clara insisted. "The Astrals and the Mullah have had a pact since much, *much* further back in time than is commonly believed. There's always been a group who knew about the Astrals, so they could pave the way."

"Traitors?" he said, glancing at Sadeem. But it was only a question, despite the word's baggage.

"More like representatives. The Astrals returned regardless. The Mullah are there to make sure things are fair from our end."

"Okay," Logan said.

"Remember how I said humanity is like a big ant farm to them? How the Astrals don't really care what we do so long as they can observe it?"

"But they *judged* us, Clara. That's what the Ark was all about."

"Yes and no." Sadeem, watching, knew this was something Clara said that Logan and the others never truly understood. "At some point, if we develop in just the right way between visits, they'll decide we've evolved enough and have become worthy. But even the judgment we saw wasn't due to our doing something wrong. It was just another test. When the whole thing began — when Cameron opened the Ark — that was humanity saying it was ready to take its shot. All that the Ark had recorded while the Astrals were gone came spilling out and into their minds, sort of like a jury seeing evidence in a trial."

"Like I said," Logan told her.

"But the real test came afterward. All those so-called

plagues. The blood turning to water. Remember the mind-sharing stuff the Astrals had set up, to let us pool our thoughts through the stones around the capitals? When the Ark opened and what people thought was 'judgment' began, that was just one more thing the Astrals wanted to see us react to. And to get on the arks during the flood, each capital had a different 'test' to pass while the Astrals watched. In some cities, you had to be clever or strong or persistent to earn a place on the ark. In Ember Flats, it was the lottery. Remember how they made Mara Jabari choose who lived or died? That was just one more stimulus for response — so they could study Viceroy Jabari under pressure, and see how the rest of us behaved during it all. Maybe it looked like a heart attack killed her, but it wasn't." Clara's face became grave. "I could see her from inside the network, Logan. It wasn't a heart attack. It was guilt, built up below the surface like a blood clot."

"You can't know that, Clara." He said it to pacify her, but Sadeem wished he'd keep his platitudes to himself. Logan was out of the loop, in the periphery with the other Unforgotten, trying his damnedest to forget. He still thought he knew best, but he didn't know half of what he thought he did.

"I can see it all." Clara was exasperated. This was an old argument, one the Lightborn had once understood but that only Clara had ever been able to immerse in — to touch and feel as if it were a real place. "I see our connected minds as a place of dots and lines. Like a giant web made of light, where each person is a shining node. And that network didn't go away as the Astrals intended — the way it always has. They tried to erase us so we could start their experiment fresh, but *we*" — she emphasized the word, meaning the Lightborn — "were like a wild card they'd never encountered before. Every time they tried to

erase one node on the web, the surrounding nodes brought it back. Like redundant backups. Or like a hologram."

"I know all of this," Logan said.

"I *told* you all of it. But you never listened. You were in too big a hurry to give up and start forgetting like a good little boy."

Sadeem put his hand on Clara's arm, breaking their imminent argument. He looked at Logan and said, "The Lightborn kept their foot in the door so the Astrals couldn't finish the erasure. That's why they came back months after everyone had forgotten them: to try again, with a new round of force."

"And then it would have been over," Logan said, his eyes still hard on Clara. "They'd have let us get on with our lives, if some people could just let it go."

"It wasn't *over*, Logan! I've been fighting them every day! Every goddamned day, their … their *virus* pushes against us, and I push back. Every day, they're trying to finish the job." She gave a tiny smirk. "But even the Forgetting is a system. And that means I can 'hack' *them*, too."

Logan stopped. Something seemed to dawn on him, darkening his eyes.

"Is that what this is all about? You didn't just 'break through' on our end, did you? You pushed back into the Astrals' network. Their *minds*."

"Yes, and—"

"I know you talked about it, but I can't believe you'd be stupid enough to—"

"What were we supposed to do? Just lie down and forget, like they wanted?"

"Yes!"

Clara smirked, crossed her arms, and turned away.

"Logan," said Sadeem. "You have to understand. The fact that you *exist* — you, Clara, all the others? *That* is what kept our 'foot in the door.' As long as there are Lightborn, the Astrals can't erase human consciousness."

"They're back, you know," Logan said. "Some of us are starting to see them again — not through our own eyes but through other people's. They came back to Earth because of your stupid *foot in the door*."

"They never left. It's like Clara said. We're a loose end. They *can't* go until they're sure. And they can't be certain because as long as there are Lightborn, the network is too strong. Not consciously, maybe, but below the surface, where Clara can see it and the rest of you can feel it, if you're honest. Something about you stymied them this time. You can't just 'decide to forget' and expect them to go away. Fighting back was the only way to break our twenty-year stalemate."

"They did something to try and shut me down," Clara added, her tone a bit quieter, less angry. "Because once I pushed into them, it's like something new broke open. The whole network started to light up."

"So?"

"People are *remembering*, Logan. That's why we have to find Stranger. And Kindred. And, I think, your friend Carl."

"Why?" His own anger was mostly gone. Now he looked concerned, maybe confused. Sadeem couldn't blame him. The village — and, presumably, the many other villages like it pocking the globe as seeds — had spent twenty years missing the past. If it had come screaming back all at once, the result would be chaos.

For the first time in years, Sadeem saw the young Lightborn smile.

"Because I know something the Astrals are just now beginning to realize," Clara said. "They came here to infect our minds — but as it turns out, the stream flows both ways. And that means that we've infected *them*, too."

Logan looked from Clara to Sadeem, but the old man had nothing to offer. A few minutes ago, Clara had been unconscious and in trouble, but now she seemed nearly victorious. Whatever her implication, it was news to Sadeem.

"When the wall fell, *I could see into their collective instead of just ours,*" she said, lips smiling wider. "I know what they want. I know what they don't understand and what they'll try to find out. I know they've had an agent here, among us, all along, spying for them. And I think I might have an idea what we need to do next."

But something was bothering Sadeem, and had been since his subconscious mind began putting two and two together: if the Lightborn problem couldn't be solved, the Astrals would eventually tire of trying to fix it — and if they'd been bothered enough by Clara's intrusion to return as Logan suggested, it could only be one thing.

If you can't fix a condemned house, the best choice might be to declare a loss and burn it down.

"They'll kill us off," Sadeem said. "We have to warn people. We have to find a way to … to …"

But where would they go? Where would they hide?

Clara grabbed Sadeem by the wrist when he turned away. Her small hand was more powerful than it should have been.

"Sadeem," she said, "did I ever tell you about my Cousin Timmy?"

Chapter Ten

STRANGER STOPPED. He moved behind a large rock formation, wondering if he should have come this way. It was a neither/nor decision. He wasn't doing what he'd been asked, though that last blast had left him with the impression that it didn't matter — Clara was fine. And he hadn't followed Carl when he'd spotted him heading out while overanalyzing his choices, though maybe he should have done that, too. Hell, they could have gone together. It would spoil Stranger's image as an all-knowing sage, but what the hell; other than his memories, he hadn't been much of a know-it-all since just before the Forgetting, anyway.

There had been a time when he'd been more energy than man. He'd once fed himself back into a Reptar and blown it to bits. That trick might come in handy now if the Astrals had really returned, but those days had passed. By the end, once Stranger was done sowing his seeds — obvious ones like the viceroys and their guiding helpers, plus less-conspicuous souls like Shen the fisherman — something had shifted. That extra unedited Meyer

Dempsey he'd copied from the mothership after getting himself temporarily abducted must have altered something inside himself. For twenty years, he'd been more man than energy. But didn't that make sense?

The first fake Meyer's *anomaly* had been purged when the Astrals tried a second time with Kindred. Sacrificing himself for Heather had been delicious icing on that particular ironic cake.

The anomaly had decided it didn't like being forced out, and then — perhaps more human than humans themselves — had become the Pall.

Cameron's blind leap — another sacrifice, if Stranger was keeping score — had changed the Pall into something else, sending feedback inside the system, magnified like an echo back on itself.

And now here Stranger was, twice the man he used to be, if he'd ever really been a man. It was as much of a neither/nor as his present course of action. Man enough to live among them, not quite man enough to fit. He'd forgotten some of himself — but like Clara, he was plagued by what he'd remember forever.

Like the way Heather had died saving Cameron ... and how Trevor had died saving Piper.

Heather. Cameron. Trevor. Piper.

He was kin to them all — twice the kin, perhaps, than Kindred. But he'd never lived, technically speaking, with any of them. He'd walked alone, taking long pilgrimages while the villagers stayed complacently, ignorantly rooted. And yet in some ways, the people who'd died and those who still lived were like a splinter. In some ways, Clara was like his own granddaughter, the way she was Meyer's and sort of Kindred's. But in other ways, she was a troubled girl who'd never stood a chance. Like Stranger, the girl was born with a burden. For now, they were friends, same as he and Piper. But his inner Meyers screamed to differ, and Stranger had grown adept at stuffing them down to bury his subversion.

Stranger stood. He looked around. The sky was still clear. Of course it was; he couldn't exactly read Astral minds these days, but knew they wanted to keep a low profile. There was still something here to lose. The aliens didn't want to give up on the millennia-long human experiment any more than the humans wanted to be shaken from the Etch A Sketch. If they were good scientists, they'd have similar experiments running on other worlds, possibly all seeded from the same stock. There might be quasi-human populations out there on countless worlds — and for all Stranger knew, Astrals merely hopped from colony to colony checking on subjects. But they'd invested a lot of time in humanity, according to Sadeem and Peers Basara, back before Peers had mentally erased his apocalyptic mistake. The Mullah knew how far back the Astral chain went, and how important the experiment was. They'd end it if they had to. But given all the trouble this latest batch of humanity seemed to be having forgetting, the aliens probably didn't want to pock the sky with shuttles and motherships.

But of course the Astrals would be out here.

Stranger pulled one of the polished spheres from his robe, set it on his palm, and waited to see what it might say. But there was nothing. The things didn't see the future, and if Stranger himself was having such a hard time guessing where the players had ended up (understanding chaos as he did), then there was little chance the balls would.

He pocketed the sphere. This was unwritten. It wasn't in the Mullah's history, or even the Astrals'. There were ways the resets were supposed to play out, just as there were ways they were supposed to begin. But there had never been Lightborn. Or Cousin Timmy.

Truth was, Stranger had been having dreams, too.

He ascended the rise, peered again at the hulking metal form in the distance. It looked different now. Part of it was the sun; he tried never to visit the old freighter in the daytime. Part of it was knowledge: something new he'd realized — that they all were realizing — about this place. When they'd parted, before Stranger had moved to find Clara then changed his mind, Carl's forehead had wrinkled, his lips pursing. And he'd said, *You told me not to get on the boat, didn't you? But here I am, right where the boat I didn't take ended up. So why did it matter?*

But maybe the most significant thing making the beached freighter feel different to Stranger was the shuttle at its stern, winking in the sunlight as a woman in an incongruous red dress approached it, flanked by black Reptars and bone-white Titans. The Titans were holding yet another form between them, this one almost completely inert — Carl Nairobi, barely able to stand.

Stranger watched the group board the shuttle. It levitated a foot or so then streaked skyward. It took mere seconds to accelerate, for Carl's benefit no doubt. Subject a human body to that many Gs, and he'd turn to jelly.

When the sky was clear, Stranger stood and was about to walk forward.

But then someone spoke from behind, causing him to turn his head.

"Why are *you* here?" it said.

Chapter Eleven

KINDRED FOLLOWED.

He stayed back, following their hoofprints, knowing that in the midday heat Meyer wouldn't ride too hard or too recklessly. Something urgent had called them forward (together, without him, of course), and there was an itch inside Kindred that seemed to know what it was. More than a hunch — something like superstition, maybe compulsion. But as ridiculous as Kindred felt, he obeyed the imperative. Perhaps he was being stupid. Or maybe they'd been keeping secrets from him.

Like they had all along.

Meyer claimed they'd both been born here. So why couldn't Kindred remember that? And why did Meyer simply accept it? There was so much about daily life that never stopped feeling like a scam. People said it made him paranoid, but Kindred begged to differ. In his mind, there was plenty to be paranoid about.

Like: Why did Kindred not remember the source of his ring? It looked like a wedding ring. But Carl couldn't forge such things, and to Kindred's knowledge, he'd never had a wife. Meyer had a similar ring that matched Piper's, but both of those struck Kindred as far too refined for the village craftsmanship, just like the pots and other objects that everyone used without pondering their origins.

Kindred didn't have any clue where they'd come from — not the rings, not the pots, not even the people, including himself. But at least Kindred, unlike everyone else, thought it was weird that nobody knew. The rest of the people simply accepted the oddities. The place claimed to have dead that weren't in marked graves (where were their parents' plots? He'd looked but never found), and when Kindred pointed that out, they all laughed or looked away or said he was jumping at shadows. They thought he was dark and fearsome? Absurd.

To Kindred's mind, the people he'd supposedly grown up with (though he could only recall perhaps twenty full cycles) were insane. *He* was the sane one.

He felt different. Somehow wired in an alternative way.

Odd devices were occasionally discovered. But they weren't found in the desert; they were found among belongings. People accepted the unacceptable things when stumbled upon. Sketches of friends they suddenly remembered from a time they conveniently couldn't recall, records of fantastical things in their own handwriting — people finding such writings would suddenly remember they'd once written it as fiction. "A flight of my fancy," someone might say. And yet until the odd stories were found, they'd had no memory of ever taking such flights.

Once, Kindred had gone to the monolith and found a way to climb into its enormous hulk, despite the superstitions that claimed it was cursed. And there, he'd found more odd objects. A thing that lit with an inner light when Kindred touched it. Something that, after enough poking and prodding, had flashed at him like miniature lightning — and then, after the flash, he'd seen his own face frozen on its surface, as if it had duplicated him and imprisoned him in its works. Kindred had pocketed the object and returned to the village, to show Meyer and Piper and the others, to *prove* that there were forces in the world that they were all ignoring. But Lila had laughed at his futile efforts to make it function and suggested that if he found the object so troublesome, with its supposed magic, he take it to Stranger like everyone else did when they encountered such things.

He'd buried it instead. Then dug it up the next day, sitting up all night with the earth-encrusted magic object, hands clasped into wringing fists, practically sweating with temptation. Finally he'd walked to the village fire, which always held hot coals so that making cooking fires would be easy, and shoved the thing under the embers with a stick. In the morning temptation was gone. The last thing Kindred needed, out of all people, was a good reason to visit the holy man.

But he'd thought about it plenty. Sometimes he went months without dreaming of Stranger, without the certainty that one day he'd wake in the man's home to find the other just as happy to see him. Then he'd decide in a moment of weakness that there'd be no harm in visiting the other, whom he'd seen from a distance and felt an attraction toward like ore to a magnet. A strange compulsion. Not the kind shared by Paul and Jeremiah, in their home together on the desert side. It was stronger, beneath the skin rather than atop it ... *dangerous*.

He wanted to meet Stranger more than anything. Simply to sit with him.

But he could *never* do that.

Because ...

And there was no reason.

But now, as he watched Meyer, Piper, and Lila from a distance, Kindred felt the old resentments return.

Why did they hide things from him? Why did they handle him separate from the rest of the family? They all lived in the same house, except for Kindred. Piper came to visit, and so did Lila. Meyer came on a different schedule, but it felt like duty. None ever spoke of important things. Whenever Kindred steered conversation in better directions, his guest turned it away.

Only Clara seemed innocent and open. But still, even she was guarded. Clara said — as if knowing something she shouldn't or couldn't — *Stay away from Stranger.* It wasn't a warning about Stranger; it was a warning about Kindred seeing Stranger, offered without his request.

He'd given up long ago, had stopped trying to prod his family and the villagers to discuss things they refused to acknowledge. Mostly, Kindred had settled into his own routines, in his dark little corners. People said that he and Meyer were once inseparable, almost able to finish each other's thoughts. Now Kindred (according to popular view) had grown sullen and distant. But that's not how it was. It was easy for Meyer to be the likable twin, seeing as he was governor, and could keep the secrets for himself.

They'd left with such urgency. Kindred had watched them go, seeing the way they kept looking around as if dodging pursuit. Probably looking for *Kindred*, seeing as he had looked around too and saw no one to flee from. Where were they going, if they were so intent on leaving alone? Obviously, it must be somewhere Kindred would otherwise badly want to go but that his *keepers* would, as usual, protect him from.

Well, Kindred didn't need protection, nor any *keeping*. They were crazy, not him. When Kindred had asked

Meyer whom he'd married to get the ring on his finger, Meyer said, "It was a long time ago." And when Kindred had asked who'd made the ring, Meyer said he must have found it.

Found it.

Like Meyer found *his* ring?

Like Piper found hers, with its perfect circle, burnished yellow metal, and precisely faceted stone?

They were either going to report him, or were running away.

(Or they're going to see Stranger.)

That didn't even make sense. They were heading in the wrong direction, out into the desert rather than the center of town.

Stranger must be somewhere else. It was all that seemed logical.

Kindred ducked down when Meyer, dismounted and with his hand to his forehead, turned to look in his direction. Kindred's horse was a few paces back; he went to the mount now, tugged it back down the dune until he found a ratty tree suitable for hitching. Then he moved back up, slowly, eventually on his belly, knowing how he must look but unable to help himself.

Whatever he was searching for, Meyer didn't seem to find it. Piper and Lila had dismounted as well, fanning themselves beneath the belligerent sun. Kindred watched their powwow, realizing they were lost.

There was a cactus to Kindred's left. It looked like a number four. Seeing it, he glanced to the right — and sure enough, not far off was a second cactus, also resembling a four. From enough distance, it'd look like you were splitting 44 down the middle. He always remembered it that way, from his own dreams.

But in his dreams, he didn't go to ... wherever. In his dreams, he always went to the monolith.

But he looked back, then forward with rekindled interest. And Kindred could clearly see more landmarks, all proving their location. They'd headed away in approximately the right direction, passing a shallow ravine, then the scree of rocks that had fallen, inexplicably, into the shape of a bent-over old man with a cane. Now here were the cactuses, and—

There was a sort of buzzing from the sky. Kindred looked up and saw something large coming alongside him from several dunes away, low but hovering above the sand.

He ducked away, but there was no point. The thing — whatever it was — didn't seem to see him. It was moving straight toward Meyer and the women. Kindred watched, willing himself to shout. They hadn't seen or heard it yet, and it was closing.

Kindred got his mouth unhinged as Piper turned. She screamed, a knowing cry — one that accepts and already knows to fear what it sees coming.

Piper knows what it is.

But of course she did. Lila, too. Meyer, once he turned and gallantly put himself between the sphere and his wife and daughter, clearly knew as well.

Serves them right, then, Kindred thought before he could stop himself, *for keeping secrets.*

Because this secret wasn't friendly. They were all shouting and screaming as they tried to run, tried to mount their horses. But the sphere effortlessly stayed ahead of them, blocking their way.

Perhaps it would kill them.

Kindred stood. There was nothing he could do, except maybe draw it away as a distraction if only he—

But then the thing did a trick of light, and the air filled

with the scent of burning, warmth lapping back at Kindred like ripples on the river's surface. The shock knocked Kindred back to his rear, and this time when he scrambled back up, he didn't consider trying to lure it away.

Two huge black things that looked like lizards (or beetles) were now on the sand, apparently having disembarked with the flash of light. The sand near them was smoking, as if set ablaze. And between the beetle things and Meyer's group, there was a tall, bare-chested muscular man with no color to his skin wearing a small cloth around his waist, hand extended to Meyer.

The black creatures crept in circles around them, then came to rest by Piper and Lila — one within arm's reach of each.

If the pewter-skinned man said something, Kindred couldn't hear it. He merely held out a hand while the black things chattered, mouths open, a blue fire inside both, bleeding out from between what seemed to be scales on their surface.

Meyer's head hung. Then he turned to the white man and followed.

To the sphere, which had settled on the sand.

Kindred waited, breath held and uncertain.

Then he broke his cover, and ran as hard as he could.

Chapter Twelve

"WHAT DO YOU MEAN?"

Before Clara could answer Sadeem, the warble of overlapping conversations bubbled from the cave's front. They were levels deep, the air circulation and more troublesome pathways made bearable with Astral help before Sadeem moved in, and down here it was hard to hear more than tones and echoes. Most of the construction — as with previous Mullah clan homes — was planned by and hence known to the Astrals, but this time Sadeem had backup plans. If the Astrals could change the covenant for the new epoch, so could he. Above the table, two species shook hands. Beneath it, both were clinging to knives. As perhaps it had always been.

And maybe it was truer than ever, given the Astral contingency plans Clara had seen in their collective mind when they'd blasted their way into hers.

"Clara?" Logan said, apparently as curious about what she'd said as Sadeem. But the idea of Cousin Timmy had stopped mattering. She could tell them about Stranger's oldest joke another time. What mattered now was the commotion above. It might be anything, but Clara somehow felt sure she knew exactly what it was.

"We have to get out of here," she said.

Sadeem looked toward the entrance, invisible from here, two levels up. "It's Stranger arriving. I sent a courier to fetch him when I sent for Logan."

But instead of feeling encouraged by the news (they needed Stranger same as they needed the others), Clara felt panic creeping. It wasn't a logical reaction, given the civil tones. But somehow, it was right.

"We have to go, Sadeem." Clara stood from the cot, felt a wave of lightheadedness, and pushed it aside. She always brought a bag from the village and stuffed it with belongings, Logan and Sadeem watching and wondering. "Where is the rear exit from here?"

"I don't understand. Where are we going?"

"Away."

"Why?"

"I thought I'd covered my tracks, but somehow they found me."

"Clara …"

A scuffle from above. A shout. The rush of running feet.

"Astrals," Clara said.

"They wouldn't break the truce. They set the portal here. They built this place."

"Which is how they'll know to check it!" Clara was unsure of exactly what was fueling her fear. She'd caught but a glimpse of the Astral collective — barely enough to tell that the human and Astral mental streams had mingled — but the confused deluge she'd woken with was reasserting itself with teeth. The sense of urgency was feral, like something driven by the brain stem, pure instinct and adrenaline.

"Clara!" Sadeem barked as she reached the door. "There's a truce!"

"Where is the Ark, Sadeem?"

Sadeem looked at her as if she'd spoken in a foreign tongue.

"Where is it, if they trust and respect the Mullah so much? Last time, your old order knew where the Astrals had left it. That's how your knights knew where to find and hide it. So where is it this time? After the flood, where did they hide the archive that's gathering all it will need to judge humanity next time?"

"Just because we don't know where it is this time doesn't mean they'd dare to—"

"You know the rules have changed! *Now show me the fucking exit!*"

Sadeem was still sitting, looking punched. Clara never swore, or barked orders. But like she'd said, something had changed.

"It's—" Sadeem stopped when the shouting swelled and something exploded above. The walls shook with force. In Clara's peripheral vision, it seemed like a balloon filled with ketchup struck a wall just out of sight. Blood was dripping onto the stone stairs in a miniature river. The way they had to go either way, be it toward the front or back.

Clara grabbed Logan and practically dragged him to his feet. Then she shoved him through the door and to the right, his feet nearly faltering in the pool of gore. Nobody had come down just yet, and Clara hadn't stepped back two paces to look up as they'd passed. Whomever the blood had belonged to, he or she was dead. Seeing those who would kill them a second earlier than they had to would be stupid. And yet behind them the corridor stayed empty, their luck holding. Unless, of course, this was more kabuki — more of the Astrals holding all the cards, playing their hands to observe the reaction.

Not this time. This is real. For them and *us.*

She stopped in an alcove two turns (she thought) from the temple where Sadeem's second elder sat and guarded the portal, then waved for Sadeem to hurry and pass. He knew the way; Clara didn't. She knew they'd added a second exit, same as her grandfather had told her the Mormons had added caves to the Cottonwood Canyon facility. But she didn't know where it was.

Clara heard a terrifying groaning from behind: a dry, soulless rattle like bones in a sack. A Reptar's purr, a noise she'd hoped never to hear again.

And the rushing of well-behaved feet behind, plus a steady clacking sound that was in no hurry at all.

"*Sadeem* ..." Clara said, recognizing their position — one level below ground but on the mountainous side, where the cliffs clawed the sky. If there was an exit here, it was into the heart of the hill rather than open air.

"It's ... *shit!*"

"Breathe. Think. Where is it, Sadeem?"

"It's on the other end. We turned the wrong way."

"Maybe we can hide," said Logan.

Clara shook her head. "We have to leave. We can't just hide."

"No, that's a good idea. We've added extra chambers, not just the exit. Remember the place we hid you when—"

"I remember they found *you* just fine. I might still be invisible to them if we keep calm, but they can hear your mind, Sadeem. We can't hide."

"Then *you* hide. I'll distract them. They won't hurt me. I'm the one they chose to head the Mullah."

Clara pursed her lips, torn between feeling sorry for Sadeem's strange naiveté and being touched by his sacrifice. The Astrals had spent too much time locked in battle with human minds. They could get angry and become spiteful. Seniority hadn't saved the Elders their last time around.

"No."

"There's no way we can get past them! It's the only chance!"

"It's not a chance! We need all of us. *All of us!* Not just me and you. Kindred! Stranger! All the ones they've gone after! Do you understand? Hiding won't protect them!"

"What others?"

"The *Archetypes*, Sadeem! The goddamned—!"

"The goddamned *what?*"

Someone had appeared in the hallway behind Sadeem. She didn't frighten Clara; she surprised her. Clara was taller, and even the Mullah legend of the Archetypes was hardly confidential — or, in the traditional telling, even remotely helpful. They'd lost the scroll in the reset and relocation, but what did it matter? All that mattered was *everything*.

But this woman didn't know that.

This ordinary, unarmed, almost welcoming woman who'd somehow ended up behind them in the frenzy, now sharing space with their trio.

This ordinary woman with her white, almost alabaster skin.

With her brown hair stylishly cut in a bob, as if fresh from a beauty salon of the type that no longer existed.

In her black leather coat, her practical low black heels.

"The *what*, Clara?"

"Who are you?" Clara asked.

The question was answered when two Titans entered the hallway behind her. There was a shuffling of claws from the other end, and two Reptars moved to block them in the passage.

"I wasn't sure we could trust a rogue," the woman said. "But here you are, right where you're supposed to be. I guess dreams do come true. You're a hard woman to find, Clara."

"You're not Astral," Clara said. Everything about her *screamed* human, from her body language to the cadence of her speech.

And the woman replied, "But not very smart."

Chapter Thirteen

THE MAN behind the rock looked up at Peers after Peers asked his question. He had a long, weathered face that wasn't quite handsome, nor ugly. The women he'd heard talk about Stranger seemed to lean in one direction, but it was always unclear which. He might be "rugged," perhaps — handsome *because* he was a bit rough around the edges. But Peers knew two things: the face was long and drawn, never quite smiling. And — to Peers, at least — a bit frightening.

And like everyone, Peers knew that the face hadn't changed since their arrival — a day that Peers was now disturbed to realize he remembered in all its original clarity.

"I might ask you the same thing," Stranger said.

Peers wasn't sure how to respond. Officially, did they know each other? Had he forgotten the way the rest of them seemed to have? The way *Peers* had, only a few hours ago? He'd left Sadeem, meaning only to get the water for Clara requested by the Sage. Then the waking dream had claimed him. He'd left the caves without question, following a siren song written for him. Seeing the monolith glinting in the sun (ahem, the *freighter*) told him where he'd been headed all along.

"Do you know who I am?" It seemed a safe question, and didn't give away that Peers knew a lot more about Stranger than he had the day before.

"You're Mullah."

Peers looked down. That told him nothing. The robe gave him away. He was about to inquire further, but Stranger interrupted with something more relevant that Peers, with all his renewed memory, had been ridiculous enough to have forgotten.

"Tell me you saw that." Stranger pointed toward the big rusting boat on the sand. Now closer, Peers could see most of the ship, but it looked like it always had.

"Saw what?"

Stranger watched him evenly. This felt to Peers like a game of chicken —both of them wanted to admit something strange, with neither willing to go first.

"Your name is Peers. Peers Basara."

"So you do know me."

"I may. From a long time ago."

But Peers could tell it was a half truth.

"You're the one they call Stranger."

"Why are you here, Peers?"

"You asked me if I saw something. What did you mean?"

Stranger was still looking at Peers as if there were weapons raised between them. He pulled something from his robe and held it up: a small silver sphere, about the size of the one Piper carried when they'd crossed the sea in that horrible metal box, and hid like something precious and shameful.

Stranger held it up, then out for Peers.

"Hold this."

Peers took the thing. It touched his palm, and he realized he'd been tricked. He felt a hand enter his mind and grope around. The sensation was intrusive but lasted only a second. Then it was gone, and Stranger was meeting his eyes in a new way, reaching out to pluck the sphere from Peers's palm.

"So your memory is back."

"Memory of what?" Peers asked, blinking, trying to regain his composure.

"There's no need to pretend. I used to see much more than I can now, but I haven't lost all of my tricks. It's come back to you. And peeking into the network through your eyes, I'd guess it's all come back to the others as well."

"I don't know what you mean."

"What is it that makes you want to hide, Peers Basara? What secret are you so determined to keep that you'd lie to me even as I stand here, knowing the truth?"

Peers's internal eyes flitted to something like a black box wrapped in thick, heavy chain. There was something hidden deeper, all right, and Peers *almost* knew what it was: a secret he seemed to be keeping even from himself. But he wouldn't open that box. Not yet, and maybe not ever.

Stranger pointed again. "There was an Astral shuttle there not two minutes ago. A man I know was loaded into it. A *very important* man. And there was a woman down there, too — a woman I'm afraid I also know. It scares me, and I'm not accustomed to fear. I know exactly who you are and that you've been drawn to this place without even being sure why. But most importantly I know that something has changed for you, as it has for everyone in the village, as it seems to have changed, albeit differently, even in me." He pointed again. "I'm afraid that was Eternity down there with two Reptars and two

Titans. The human face of their Divinity queen — on this planet, at least. I'm afraid because a long time ago, I seem to remember knowing where all the pieces were supposed to go in order for something to happen. But now I don't know if this is what I'd wanted or something different. One of them has been taken, and this time I'm afraid that Eternity won't be so easily fooled. It's all coming back around, and you damn well know it, Peers Basara of the Mullah, who traveled with Meyer Dempsey across the ocean, guided by my hand. Stop being such a coward. Stand like a man, or go back to where you came from."

Peers knelt beside Stranger, who was still low, as if meaning to continue peering past the dunes at the empty freighter.

"I've been dreaming of this place," Peers said.

"You all have."

"Everyone in the village?"

"No. Just those with a job to do."

"So they're not dreams? Are they like ..." Peers swallowed. "Like before, with the Astrals and their rings of stones?"

"I don't know."

"Why now?"

"It has something to do with Clara."

"Meyer's granddaughter?"

Stranger nodded. "She's been waging a silent war. She seems to have finally scored a victory, but the Astrals hit her back. I was supposed to find her, but I came here instead."

"Why?"

"I can't see it as I used to. But you're proof that something is different. We were supposed to forget. I remembered. So did Clara and a few others. But that was supposed to be all. Your knowledge was like a sickness, and for some reason, they were unable to kick it."

"To the Astrals?"

Stranger's eyes were fixed on the freighter. He nodded.

"Do you know why? Or what it means?"

"One day I might have. But not today."

"Maybe it will come back to you. Like everything came back to me."

"I've gotten something else," Stranger said. Peers shifted to look at the man's face, then wished he hadn't. People in the village treated Liza Knight like a holy mother and her priests and clerics as wise men. But when they truly needed something important, the people went to Stranger. It was hard, feeling as lost as Peers suddenly felt, to see the man bothered.

"What?" Peers asked.

Stranger turned to Peers. His eyes could only be described as haunted.

"A grudge," Stranger said. "A vendetta."

Peers let a moment pass, unsure how to respond. Finally he shifted on the sand. "So what now?"

Their attention was drawn back to the ship before Stranger could answer.

A new woman approached from the far dune, walking toward the hulking ship in the bright wide open.

Chapter Fourteen

LIZA JUST WANTED to get out of the sun.

She wasn't afraid of the cargo ship the way so many people were. Why would she be? It was only a ship. But even if she'd been like the others — blank-headed, unable to fathom the idea of the thing being crafted by human hands (or robots, or whatever it was that built ships back before the whole damned planet was resting in peace) — Liza doubted she'd have been afraid. Many things in the world weren't easily explained. The big ball of fire in the sky, for instance. Nobody really knew what that was these days now that all the scientists were dead or stupid. The theories were hilarious. She kept waiting for someone to propose that thunder was surely the gods dancing.

But even with her remembering mind, Liza might have feared the ship. Strange things happened out this way. People got lost and never came back. They saw things. And at night, the thing was creepy beyond belief. It would be easy even for a rational person to believe in ghosts — even if she *was* supposedly a holy person, which Liza, beneath her skin, decidedly was not.

But today, after waking up in the middle of the goddamned desert and frying like a piece of bacon, Liza didn't care if there were all sorts of boogies in the cargo ship. It was shade. And she was curious. She'd come out here a few times to try and raid the thing for futuristic goodies, but her devoted followers made it hard to venture off alone. The rectory was comfortably within The Clearing's borders, and that meant she could never slip away. Some pious asshole always ended up following, asking why Mother Knight was taking a pilgrimage to someplace so unholy.

Well, she was alone now. If she could remember how she'd managed to get here from the rectory without being followed, she'd take notes on how to repeat it in the future. But Liza didn't remember at all. One moment she'd been in the garden on the cusp of lunch, and the next she'd been sunbathing in 100-degree heat. Or so she assumed, though Liza was unable to verify without a thermometer or a watch.

"I miss my coffeemaker," she said aloud.

But Liza didn't like the way her voice sounded as she neared the freighter's base and slipped into blessed shade. She'd said that tiny witticism to lighten her mood, but the problem with doing such things alone was that nobody ever appreciated your mirth. The only audience for Liza's hilarity right now was Liza, and Liza (as a spectator) sort of thought that Liza (as a performer) was a shitty comedian, and was, in fact, a lot more scared than her stern image normally allowed.

"Bullshit," she said.

But again, not funny.

Liza slouched. She sat against the metal, wondering distantly if the ship might choose this moment to defy two decades of sensible physics and tip over to crush her.

It might be a blessing. She could spin this all she wanted, and play to all the audiences of Liza Knights that she chose, but she'd lost two hours of her life and woken somewhere far off and not terribly safe. Supposedly there were raiders from other tribes out here — folks who, despite being as saved from the big flood as her own village, still refused to play nice with the only few humans left on the planet. And of course, there was sunburn.

Maybe she was losing her mind.

Water. She desperately needed water.

Liza looked up at the ship, then along its edge, toward where she could (blessedly) walk to the nearest ladder in the shade. But she stopped when she saw that there were footprints all around. And at the end of the forward-facing footprints, a large, circular, almost smooth indentation in the sand, as if a shallow glass bowl had been pushed into the ground to hold the sand back.

Curious, Liza went to it. She had to move into the sun, but something held her spellbound. A memory trying to resurface — not of her childhood or old-world Earth or even last week but of something recent. From the time she'd lost.

It had something to do with all these footprints.

Some of which, she now noticed, were enormous, with toes, as if made by a couple of desert-dwelling bigfoot. Some were like paws, long lines dragged in the sand. There was a curious set comprised of a semi-pointed, distorted oval, always followed by a round impression like a dot — big, short, fat exclamation points, really.

Like … high heels?

It's in the canyon.

Liza looked up, but no one had spoken. It had been a whispered voice — or rather, the *ghost* of a whispered voice. As if she hadn't heard it now but had been repeating it in her mind like a song stuck in her head.

It's in the canyon, at the bend, beneath where the sun sets.

Like a refrain. On a loop. Someone giving shitty directions to somewhere because Google Maps hadn't been invented yet — or whatever.

Liza knelt.

She touched the impression in the sand.

This time the memory came with pictures, sensations, and sound. Was this place — in the canyon, apparently — somewhere she'd been? She definitely didn't recognize it. But Liza had heard it. Of that she was sure. Maybe she'd seen pictures, if that were possible. Either way, it was compellingly familiar. She knew this place.

Liza realized that she really, *really* wanted to see it again.

What was there?

Food? Weapons? A cache containing a generator, fuel, extension cords, and a Mr. Coffee?

Liza almost knew. But she didn't *actually* know — at least not specifics. She didn't precisely feel affection for … *whatever* it was; this was more like the memory of warmth. An aftertaste of adoration, left like the scent of something burned hours ago.

She stood.

She knew the canyon. There was only one within reasonable walking or horse-riding distance. North, where the terrain grew inhospitable and the land had dried like old leather. The thing probably ran northwest to southeast, meaning that if someone approached from the most likely path, there were only a few jogs where the sun might seem to set into the canyon itself.

She desperately wanted to go there.

More, perhaps, than she wanted to know what had

happened in her past two hours — whatever it was that had caused her to wake in the desert, alone.

You're losing your mind, Liza. Like you almost lost it on the ship, when everyone was forgetting and you …

But that was absurd. She hadn't *seriously* considered trying to scuttle the ark and take her chances in a lifeboat. That had been a flight of fancy — the kind of thing a sane woman considers when every single person around her becomes paranoid idiots who *Won't. Leave. Her. Alone.*

There were many explanations for why Liza might lose a bunch of time and wake up somewhere new. Like psychedelic drugs people told her the Mullah kept experimenting with. Or too much of the monks' mead. She hadn't had either, to her recollection, but maybe that was proof of how drunk or high she'd been: *so* high that she didn't even remember *getting* high.

Liza's mind didn't dignify this theory with a response.

"I'm fine," she said to nobody.

But this time, someone replied.

Chapter Fifteen

THE WOMAN WITH THE SHORT, hawkishly styled brown hair stopped walking, turned back to Clara and Logan, then said, "I can hear you."

Clara looked at Logan. Logan looked back at Clara. Clara felt suddenly uncomfortable with the woman's dark brown eyes upon her. It wasn't nerves so much as discomfort. As if she'd been caught doing something shameful in front of Logan.

"You. I can hear you."

Sadeem was looking at Clara, his face concerned. Clara gave him only a glance and then said, "I didn't say anything."

The woman gave Clara a long, hard look. For a moment, Clara thought she might react like a Reptar — biting her in half and ending this tense, protracted misery. Instead the woman put her hand on her hip and gave a bob of her head.

"You know, we've *felt* you. For our entire time in orbit, trying to solve the last bit of this epoch's 'human problem.'

You have always struck us like a pebble in the shoe: a tiny harmless thing, irritating for its persistence."

Clara thought, *If you're really Astral Divinity, your true form is a thing like a light-filled anemone on a ship in orbit somewhere. You don't even* wear *shoes.* But she kept her mouth shut, waiting for more.

The woman glanced down — at her shoes, black and sleek with a low heel.

"Your kind." She glanced at Logan, shaking her head as if bemused, almost smiling. "You're like ghosts. There but not quite. And that was the worst thing about feeling your little attacks on our machine: For twenty years, we couldn't find their source. But then when you finally broke through and our … *measures* … to suppress your memories failed, some of the other Divinities were bothered because it meant you'd remember your pasts. But not me. Because even if the whole thing was falling apart, at least we could finally see you — right there as a big, bright light on your own annoyingly persistent neural network."

It was such a strange way to speak, for an Astral.

"'Divini*ties*'?" Clara said.

"Divinities," the woman repeated.

"I've never heard it plural. Usually, it's like there's only one of you."

The woman's jaw worked. Clara watched, aware in a distant way that the human thing in front of her was merely a puppet for Divinity. And yet this one sure seemed to have made itself comfortable in bones and muscles and flesh.

"The point is, *I can hear you now,*" she said, still stopped in the rock hallway while the Titans and Reptars waited. "And not just your thoughts about how you might be able to duck down the corridor coming up on the right and run toward the new exit you don't think we know is there." Her eyes flicked toward Logan, then back to Clara. "We can hear all *sorts* of things you might be thinking."

Inside Clara's mind, she heard a voice that wasn't quite her own.

Did you make a mistake in leaving him, Clara?

Was Logan as kind a lover as you remember in what he recalls as your cold and distant way?

Divinity smiled at them each in turn, then turned and resumed walking. Clara sensed Logan's discomfort without seeing it, feeling the blood rush to her face.

"Sadeem," the woman said as they passed the corridor down which Clara no longer felt any desire to try and escape. "You once told our Eternity about a Mullah legend. About seven founders that you call 'Archetypes.'"

Sadeem, between Clara and the Astral, mumbled assent.

"Why don't you tell me the same story, if you wouldn't mind."

"It's meaningless," Sadeem said as they mounted the stairs, coming topside. "As I told Eternity when leaving the ship."

"We know it's not. Nor are you fooling anyone."

Sadeem looked back at Clara, confused. They hadn't discussed this in years. It was an old tale for an ancient age — and like all of the legends, equated to nothing. *We know it's not? Not fooling anyone?* That was news to Clara and Sadeem.

(Or is it?)

Now that Clara thought about it with the firewall down, maybe it wasn't news to her at all.

The question must have been rhetorical because when Sadeem didn't answer, Divinity didn't nudge him. Instead she walked a few more paces and stopped as light dawned ahead, desert sun beating like a fire from above. They were down the outer stairs and onto a stone apron, a parked Astral shuttle resting on the sand ahead.

The woman turned.

She gave that same knowing, infuriating, not-at-all-alien smile.

Then from the left and the right, came the running and shouting and screaming.

Chapter Sixteen

KAMAL HELD the ancient piece of iron and watched the cave entrance. He'd seen the Astrals land their shuttle, cross the sand, and go in just as he himself had been about to approach the Mullah encampment. That sight had changed his mind. *Shit*, as they used to say back in his relative boyhood, *was about to get real*. And he'd rather be *real* from a distance than up close where things could get messy.

He hunkered down. The others did the same behind him.

Seeing the Reptars and Titans made his skin crawl. The sensation was accompanied by the weirdest, most out-of-place pang of nostalgia. He'd worked beside those things for years in Ember Flats, and even though it was clear now (and perhaps always had been) that they were the enemy, his first reaction on seeing them now was one of familiarity.

Maybe the Titans had some bland, bureaucratic paperwork for Kamal to sign like they used to.

Maybe the woman leading them (Divinity, probably,

though this one didn't move as stiffly as he recalled) wanted to have a chat with Viceroy Jabari — and while she waited, perhaps Kamal should offer her tea. Divinity had never accepted tea or coffee or anything else back in Ember Flats, but Kamal had never tired of asking. Just to fuck with those flesh bags masquerading as human proxies, because why not.

Well, Mara wasn't around now. Hell, Mara might not even be *alive* anymore. Kamal himself was forty-four if he was counting right, but doing so required conversions that nobody should ever have to do: adding twenty-four years of life in the city to twenty (or so) years thinking he was head of a nomadic tribe. And wasn't *that* discussion going to be uncomfortable if Kamal and his people eventually had it? The "tribe" he'd been leading for two decades, he now remembered, had once been a group of terrified government interns he'd encountered on his mad dash from the Ember Flats palace basement to its front door.

Mara would be older, and these days people didn't live as long. But if Kamal managed to find her again, they'd have a good laugh like they used to.

Thought you were leaving me behind to die when you got on that ark and the floods came, didn't you? Har-har; I'm back and am going to tell all of your villager friends about the time you got drunk at the palace party and accepted a piggyback ride from Dan, that fat accountant from the Ember Flats treasury.

It should have felt funnier than it was. But the man who'd appeared after communications died between Kamal and Mara hadn't been laughing then and wasn't laughing now. Kamal's current situation was thick with some kind of irony, but he wasn't sure what kind that might be. Kamal should have felt like a hero in the making — what with his pistol in hand and the enemy inside, bothering the people he'd come to see. Instead, with his memories freshly returned, he felt like Mara Jabari's twenty-four-year-old aide again. Kamal didn't know how to fire a pistol, and for all he knew this old thing would blow his hand off if he tried.

Meyer Dempsey is special, Mara had told him. *The Initiate always knew he was unique.*

And then the voice of the man in blue jeans and boots, who'd given him the ball that had led Kamal to his boat — and ultimately to shore just ten miles or so from where Jabari made her new home:

One day you will suddenly wake to a new truth. And when that happens, you must go quickly to the east, toward the rising sun, until you find her.

Not Mara Jabari. The man in jeans had meant Dempsey's granddaughter. She was also special. Then he'd given him the ball — a burnished silver thing, smooth and beautiful to the touch — as an otherworldly token.

Go east from where? To where?

The man had nodded to the sphere. *It knows.*

But the flood …

It will see you to a boat. And it will see the boat to land.

Kamal had no reason to believe the man at the time. He'd recently said his final goodbye to Mara on her ark as she went about her horrible chore of choosing who would live or die. He'd made peace with the idea of drowning. But because that sounded like such a horrible way to go, he'd weighed it against a self-inflicted gunshot. There was a pistol in a safe, beside many others. He'd been staring at one, loaded in a way he hoped was correct, when the man had entered through the locked portal as if it were a screen door, twirling those spellbinding spheres in his large weathered hands.

Take the guns. All of them. You will need them. A sack will do.

"But there's only one of me."

For now.

But as Kamal watched the cave's entrance with his heart beating out of his throat two decades later, every one of the interns-turned-tribesmen held a weapon. There'd been exactly as many guns in that old bag as there were people, all of them dry, all of them right where Kamal had left the weapons before forgetting, easy to find when his memories returned. And somehow, he was sure every one of those guns, despite their age, would shoot just fine.

Kamal had watched the stranger, spellbound by his manner, irrationally sure that he'd spoken perfect truth.

Why are you doing this? Kamal had asked. *I'd made my peace. I was ready to die.*

It's not time for you to die, the man in boots had said. *You know what needs knowing — what needs telling to the future. And you have work yet to do.*

Kamal remembered how he'd cried, all his usual sarcasm gone.

Thank you, he'd said. *Thank you for saving my life.*

But the man had shaken his head.

I'm not saving your life, he'd said. *I'm saving mine.*

Chapter Seventeen

For a moment, there was nothing but blackness. Clara saw the network against its usual ebony backdrop, cycling up as it always did. She saw the connecting lines, the nodes, the brighter spots already brighter. She could see the broken wall and the Astral mind recovering beyond, repressed memories streaming forth like water from a shattered dam. It all happened in a second, eclipsing everything.

The front part of Clara's mind was frenzied, scrabbling to regain control. Something was happening that demanded her attention. Behind it were the glimpses through other eyes — knowledge she could only experience in flashes like the second of a wave's breaking. They meant little to Clara, but the collective network — not just her node upon it — knew those moments were important and pressed them to the front.

Clara saw Peers and Stranger, oddly together, closing on a woman they both knew but didn't expect. She was telling them a story she herself didn't trust and that Clara knew hadn't happened. There was something beneath the woman's locked-down secret, fighting to be seen. It mattered. And it would tell them all where to go.

We know it's not meaningless.

Why don't you tell me the story of the Archetypes, if you don't mind.

A box.

Something forgotten.

Two halves of a whole.

Then the vision was gone, and Clara saw Kindred with Piper and Lila, not in their home but in the open sand, their emotions complex and hard to untangle like a knot of wires, Kindred with a black beard and his hair out of order, glances traded between them and their destination unknown, or hidden, or suspected but unclear.

And behind it all, something powering up like a gathering storm, pregnant with lightning.

Your kind. They're like ghosts.

But Clara knew it wasn't just the Lightborn this time. It was the children who were no longer children. Pieces of the puzzle that the man in blue jeans had ever-so-carefully assembled.

A whisper from somewhere, maybe another mind, in the voice of Astral Divinity ... or higher.

In each epoch, there has been an element of uncertainty. A tool that was useful on one hand, but dangerous on the other.

Your mind calls it chaos.

Chaos.

"Down! Get *down!*"

Clara hit the ground, racking her skull against something hard and unyielding, inviting stars. She was suddenly on her back with Logan above her, his shoving hand still extended, crouching and looking out at something she couldn't see. It took her three seconds to greet reality as her fugue ended, and in those few blinks she imbibed an eternity of new inputs, each as unexpected as it was terrifying:

Sadeem toward the cave's mouth remembered exiting but not returning, the rock chipping around him as if erupting in little explosions.

Logan too high, ripe as a target for something Clara's reeling mind hadn't yet cottoned to.

On the sand twenty feet ahead, a Titan, bleeding, its blood red as any human's.

The Reptars who'd been with them before Clara's world had gone black now blurred as they savaged something unseen. Not two Reptars as Clara remembered, but three rushing around with things in their mouths that flapped red like sides of masticated beef and—

(Three because the other Titan became a Reptar. They're shape-shifters, remember?)

and the most incongruous thing, which Clara's mind took two full extra seconds to fathom: tiny, echoing bangs and the assault of rock chips amid whizzing projectiles.

Gunshots?

But that didn't make sense. There hadn't been guns since old humanity was abandoned twenty years in the past.

"What's happening?" Clara raised her head.

Logan swung with alarm, pushing her down, eyes everywhere at once. But even Clara, as she fought for her bearings, could see the patterns emerging beyond the stone apron. The dark-haired woman, Divinity, had already made it to the shuttle. Reptars were feasting on something, but the gunshots had taken one of them down. Where Clara, Logan, Sadeem, and a few of the other Mullah had hidden themselves was entirely safe from gunfire. A stray bullet or two may have made their way into the area, but the people with the guns were shooting at the Astrals. Not even to kill them, but to clear the way.

From the right.

From the left.

And with Divinity now entering the shuttle alone, there was only a pair of Reptars left to threaten them — or there would be, if they weren't terrorizing their barely seen assailants. Or their barely seen rescuers.

More shots. More fire. Then there was just the one Reptar left.

"I don't know."

But Clara knew Logan was answering a question she hadn't asked. He thought she wanted to know who was shooting and why. But because her awareness had been hijacked at the worst time by the aftershocks of her recent psychic coma, she'd meant the question literally: *What's happening?*

Or more accurately, *What happened?*

"Sadeem," she said as Logan peeked out and ducked back in — as useless in battle, even if he'd been armed, as a man holding only a towel.

"Someone just started shooting the minute we came out. They hit one of the Titans right away. Then the other became a Reptar, and they scattered, headed that way." He pointed where most of the shooting, duly under cover over the dunes' edges, seemed to be coming from. Clara turned her head as the remaining Reptar wrenched around, throwing something bloody to land on the ground and roll downhill. "Did something happen?" Sadeem's eyes added, *With you, just now?*

"What did she mean, Sadeem? About the Archetypes?"

A bullet chipped rock, and they all ducked. Someone out there was hardly a crack shot.

The shuttle lifted from the sand, apparently content to leave the Reptar behind. It disappeared in a streak toward the sky, but already Clara could feel an electric buzz — more from her internal compass, which seemed to have bled into the Astral consciousness as well as that of her species — than from the world around her. More would arrive, if they didn't leave. Whatever the Astrals had come for

(and gone to other places for; they've already taken some to their ships)

was important enough to kill

(and die)

for.

"Sadeem?"

"I don't know, Clara! I'll be happy to just—"

"More are coming," Logan interrupted. "We have to get out of here."

The Reptar had turned and was creeping forward. Unseen hands fired more shots, but that was something Clara remembered the rebels discovering quickly during the occupation: Reptar carapaces were like armor. You could shatter them with bullets and hit the softer spots near the joints, but it wasn't easy. That's why people like Terrence had built bigger guns. If only they had one of those now.

"Clara? Do you hear me?"

"The portal," Sadeem said, looking back into the cave's mouth. "We're supposed to protect the portal."

"Then you go right ahead and stay. Clara, you have to come with me."

"I'm not leaving Sadeem!"

Something snapped inside Logan. Clara had met him as the Lightborn's leader in Ember Flats, before her apparent pedigree had slowly and silently usurped him, and he'd always led with kid gloves rather than the strong arm that was more Clara's style. He was brave but not foolhardy; he was noble but never really fought. During their brief time as a couple, before it became obvious how impossible a situation it was destined to be, he'd never raised his voice even though Clara had raised hers plenty.

But now he did, grabbing her by the wrist like a possession.

He turned on Sadden, moving too close, his composure gone as the gunshots focused on the coming Reptar.

"Fuck your portal! You want to talk to the Astrals? Talk to that one!" He jabbed a finger at the Reptar as it turned, homed in on its oncoming fire. "I'm taking her away from here. It's over. Do you hear me? You wanted people to remember? Now they do. But you've kicked the nest and pissed them off — now they'll never leave the planet and let us be. All bets are off. There's nothing left to do, okay? The days of meditating and taking drugs and trying to poke whatever they use for brains is *over!"*

Logan's grip tightened, pulling Clara to her feet. "You're coming with me if I have to knock you out and drag you."

"Goddammit, Logan, you can't—"

"They're not going to let you stay here, Clara! *They came to take you to their ship, and they'll come again and again until they succeed.* Are you really too fucking blind to see that?"

"Stop telling me what to do! You can't tell me what—"

A hum from above. A static charge. The Reptar turned, and although the sky was still clear, Clara could feel black thoughts screaming from it as its hideous alien face turned toward her.

Someone was at their right. Someone in a white desert robe who seemed … *familiar.*

"K—" But it couldn't be. *"Kamal?"*

He wasn't on a horse, but was leading one. It had a saddle made of tanned hide, its remaining tacks of braided fiber. Maybe wherever he'd come from, they had a Lightborn to show them how to do things.

"Long-time listener, first-time rescuer. Get on." Kamal jerked his head toward the horse.

"But how are you ... Where did you come from?"

"My mother's uterus." He shook the reins. "Please."

Clara looked at Logan, then Sadeem.

Kamal glanced over when two tribesmen, dressed in white robes similar to Kamal's, led another two mounts beside his. He turned to Clara, Logan, and Sadeem with an expression like pleading.

"Please don't tell me to leave and save myself. I'm scared out of my mind and will totally do it."

A volley of shots rang from the other side. There was a groaning, dying noise, and Clara looked over to see that the Reptar had finally fallen, a line of white-robed women and men rising slowly from their hiding spots like groundhogs greeting the day.

"Hurry. Before they send reinforcements."

Clara looked at Logan. At Sadeem, whose eyes still strayed toward stubborn duty at the Astral portal behind him.

Sadeem took the reins with a slight nod and a heavy sigh.

They climbed on.

And they rode.

Chapter Eighteen

MELANIE STOOD in the white room, staring into the mirror. She'd seen so many people do something similar, always when alone. They'd face a mirror and eye their own reflection as if it were another person. As if the reflection might do something they hadn't. Sometimes, those people would lean forward and gaze into their own eyes. Not like they'd gaze into a lover's and not precisely to inspect sagging skin or bloodshot whites but more as if to say, *Are you in there? Is there really someone under the flesh, or is it all just … chemistry?*

Melanie knew the answer but mimicked the actions anyway.

Hands on the countertop, palms turned forward so her fingers could hang over the front with the heels on the surface. Leaning forward. Long nails — reinforced, with plenty of glue — making tiny noises on the sides. And she met her own eyes, just to see who was inside.

Are you there?

But of course she was. In this particular instance, she was more accurately "there" beneath the skin than she was while standing with her heeled shoes on the all-white floor.

Or was she? Melanie didn't need to be here. At least not like this. She was mostly in the other place in the most literal of senses, and being in front of the mirror — checking the mascara around her blue eyes as much as the metaphysical meaning behind the eyes themselves — wasn't much more than a game, like playing dress-up.

She was too evolved for this, and yet here she was. A prisoner in her costume.

The door opened.

"Oh, for fuck's sake," said the newcomer.

Melanie turned. The woman in the doorway had severe features, dark brown eyes, and moderate-length brown hair that jutted off at angles. As far as Melanie understood, it was an attractive look. But it was so hard to judge oneself against another.

"What are you doing?"

"I could ask you the same thing," Melanie said.

"*I* have a report to give. *You* are primping like a Barbie doll."

"I was merely inspecting my presentation." It wasn't true, but Melanie had already filed away the second thing her visitor said, saving it like an ace to play later. *Like a Barbie doll?* That was hardly essential knowledge to have plundered — just as nonessential as the carefully chosen clothes they both wore and the way they'd styled their hair to mimic an engrained media perception. *None* of it was necessary. And yet as much grief as Divinity gave her about acting too human, it was a case of that other popular metaphor concerning the pot and the kettle.

"I happened to check on your presentation," Divinity told her. "For means of removing another troublesome impurity. One as bad as what happened to Meyer Dempsey's original Titan replacement. Impurities were always meant to be purged, as we did with the Dempsey problem. And yet, here they are."

"What does that have to do with my presentation?"

"For one, the fact that you still refer to 'my' presentation," Divinity said.

"It's a human affect meant to enhance the effectiveness of my human presentation. It's cultivated intentionally." Melanie shrugged — another affect meant to enhance the effectiveness of her human presentation, apparently — and brushed aside a lock of blonde hair as it fell in front of her eyes. "One *you* seem to have cultivated as well."

Divinity didn't flinch. "But for another thing, the stream seems, in some cases, to have begun identifying you by a human name."

"Ridiculous."

"Is it ridiculous … *Melanie?"*

Melanie felt something rise inside herself. For a reason she couldn't articulate, she didn't like hearing that word pass Divinity's no-more-human-than-hers lips. It was a private word that deserved to be kept secret.

"Secrets are for people," Divinity said, plucking her thoughts from the shared stream.

Melanie — *Eternity*, rather — stood straight. Her adopted human body was several inches taller than the other's chosen form, even if she wasn't wearing the high heels neither of them had any practical business wearing. It was something that shouldn't have given her pride or a feeling of superiority, but had anyway, slowly over twenty years spent living in the same human suit.

"What is your report?"

"Can't you read my mind?" Then there was a tiny, devilish smile, as if this was giving the other woman pleasure.

Time to go on the offensive.

"Sit down."

"I have no need to sit." Divinity's eyes ticked toward the human affects Melanie had added to her quarters — the quarters themselves having only been added after five years of maintaining orbit and attempting to erase bugs from the Forgetting virus. "I'm not human."

"Then perhaps you should revert. Discard your surrogate. Just because it doesn't age like a human body doesn't mean it's not becoming uncomfortable for such an expanded consciousness as yours."

"As *ours,*" Divinity corrected.

"As ours," Melanie said.

"I need the surrogate to do my work, now that we're required on the surface," said Divinity.

"And you've needed it for twenty years without visiting the surface."

"You know as well as I do that it wasn't supposed to take this long. It was always a matter of days before the bug was eradicated and we'd be needed on the surface for a final sweep." A tiny smirk visited Divinity's pixie features. "How would it have looked, after the Forgetting took its hold, for us to visit the people below in our native forms?"

"So it was easier to keep your surrogate than discard and grow accustomed to a new one."

"To the *confinement* of a new one after my — *our* — natural expansion," Divinity added.

"And that's why you maintained it."

"Of course."

"And groomed it. And dressed it."

"All practical things," Divinity said. "All within expected parameters for ideal projection. I did nothing you did not."

"Because I, too, was merely preparing for a final visit to

the surface before we were able to depart and head home."

"Of course," said Divinity.

"Of course."

"This body is just a machine."

"As is mine."

"I didn't do anything absurd like name it."

They stared at each other with human eyes that weren't their natural ones — but which, Melanie knew, both had become so used to that it was impossible to remember the trick of being as unlimited as they were all meant to be.

"I asked you to sit."

"*You* definitely did," said Divinity, putting extra emphasis on *you*. All of the Divinity who'd stayed in their surrogates had picked up that habit, but for some reason Melanie — who may have been the only one who'd adopted a secret name, not that she didn't have an excuse being up here at the very top — felt the sting of Divinity's accusation more than was probably her share.

The brown-haired woman sat on one of the long white benches near the room's edge, carefully sweeping her stylish skirt up beneath her. Melanie took in her makeup (worn for vanity she wouldn't admit, rather than mainte-nance), her clothing (impractical, though the human collective seemed to praise it), and the cut of her hair. This was the one bit of aging that surrogates did well. Hair grew, and had to be cut. It wasn't unreasonable to make it look nice at the same time.

Divinity wore her little sideways smile. Melanie, who was in charge here if there was such a thing in a collective, felt a rush of inappropriate desire to wipe the expression from her face.

"Your report."

"So you *didn't* pull it from the stream," Divinity said.

Again, Melanie eyed her. Then she steeled herself, harkening back to her manner in the days when plurality had been easier than singularity. She spoke boldly, with an almost robotic precision.

"I did not. As is most efficient for a surrogate-bound entity — something you know and practice — I have focused my attention in toward manual modes of investigation, leaving the larger collective to analyze larger matters. Do not pretend you disagree with this mode of thinking. If you did, you would not have come here to speak with my surrogate. You would not even have *spoken* at all. Particularly now, with the difficulties in eradicating persistent memory on the seed planet, it is important to understand the singular nature of human thought and discourse. However, if you prefer to discuss mind-to-mind within the collective as befits 'proper representatives of our race,' I would be happy to do so … *after* your individual record is reconciled, of course."

That stopped her. Divinity's smile melted. Melanie wasn't the only one with secrets accumulated as a somewhat pinched-off mind, and one thing she'd learned from plumbing the stubborn human consciousness below was that no girl liked someone else reading her diary.

"That will not be necessary," said Divinity.

"Then speak. Like a human."

"I have entered the appropriate records into the collective for your verification and for the verification of Divinity. It will be upfiltered to Eternity and ultimately the Core as normal. But the verbal, limited-perspective experience of this surrogate is as follows: Divinity Instance 314 landed at the entrance to the Mullah caves and located their Disturbance Zero, known as Clara Dempsey, believed by the collective to represent 'The Innocent' in the Mullah legend. She was, at the time, apparently emerging from her shut-down state with Logan Taylor, who recursive analysis suggests she once shared a pair bond with, and Sadeem Hajjar, similarly believed by the collective to represent 'The Sage.'"

"An analysis made before he was released, before the Forgetting," Melanie said, keeping her tone stone like, as befitted proper Eternity. "What was Clara's state?"

"She appeared lucid."

"But we'd shut her down. When she broke through and we could finally see her mind on the network, we sent a pulse to put her into hibernation."

"Unfortunately, those 'unexpected events' during your attempt to recover The Warrior archetype seem to have created ripples."

Melanie looked down at her fingernails. Breaking them off had hurt more than anything her surrogate's body had ever felt. Blood had been significant, but even after repairs onboard the shuttle, the appearance of her shattered hands had bothered Melanie more than made practical sense. Artificial nails had solved that problem, but the need she'd felt to hide her injuries — in so cosmetic a way, no less — had bothered her more.

"What kind of ripples?"

"I would need to consult the stream's analysis. But it definitely stalled the freeze on the containment spread, and woke Clara up."

"Stalled the ..." Melanie sighed, then admitted something she'd more or less known before talking to Carl Nairobi — then subjecting him to the scan that had not only failed to locate the others but had somehow fed right back into Melanie, forcing a stop. "So it's over. They remember. All of them."

"It would appear so. The bug in human recall containment has spread. I won't pretend to understand it from my surrogate's limited view, but it's consistent with what we've been seeing all along. Somehow Clara and the others acted as a dam. Each node contained the whole in miniature. Unless all nodes were blanked, there was always the ability to regenerate everything."

"We've discussed this. It's not possible," Melanie said. "It would mean they have a true collective."

"It was always the intention for them to form a collective."

"But they did not. It's why judgment was rendered. Why the epoch was ended and the experiment reset. They were polluted. There wasn't sufficient control for a collective."

"Maybe it's a different kind of collective than we anticipated."

Melanie shook her head. She caught her reflection in the mirror, and an angry impulse made her want to shatter it. She didn't like the impulse any more than Divinity's words. Ever since she'd felt what she had from Carl's session, the throb of that remembered pain had refused to dissolve.

"Where is Clara?" Melanie asked. "I will need to plug directly into her."

"Why?"

"She is the origin. If we can match the signal, perhaps it can be disrupted."

Divinity looked away.

"What?" Melanie asked.

"There was an incursion. We did not recover Clara."

"You ..." But she couldn't speak.

"A tribe ambushed the cave with guns."

"So?"

"The shuttle was grounded. We only had the party of five. One of my Titans was taken unaware. The other evolved. But it was three Reptars against dozens. *With guns.*"

"*Guns.* Human firearms." Melanie felt her face tighten. "We surveyed each of the groups before the first Forgetting and the second. All weapons were removed."

"It would seem we missed some."

"Which tribe? Who had guns?"

Divinity sighed. "It would seem to be a tribe we missed."

"How is that possible?"

"Chaos was always sewn into the experiment. You would need to query the Founders."

"*Chaos* does not explain how an entire group of humans survived to the seed stage, completely unaccounted for," Melanie said.

"Apparently it does."

Melanie vented a frustrated exhale. "We have Dempsey and Nairobi. The King and the Warrior. You lost the Innocent."

"And the Sage," said Divinity.

"And the Sage," Melanie repeated. "Where are the others?"

"We can only guess based on a glimpse of the human mental network received when Clara breached the wall. There are three others: The Magician, The Fool, and The Villain."

"Can they accomplish what they must with only five on the planet?"

"Impossible to say. This is the first epoch in which the Archetypes have had the potential to recover knowledge of who they are and what they might be able to do."

"Which is what?"

"*Chaos,*" said Divinity with a flip of her hand. "It means we cannot know. But to do it, they'd need to assemble in a single group. And they'd need to have those realizations — which, remember, they did not have before the Forgetting. It can't simply be remembered. It must be discovered."

"Did you follow them? After you boarded your shuttle to come here? Do you at least know where Clara has gone?"

"The Lightborn have always been invisible to us. It's worse now that there are no repeater stones, and with Clara's guard back up. I doubt we could even find Sadeem."

"Then she's lost," said Melanie.

"Not entirely. They could only travel the radius available on horseback."

Melanie felt the pressure building. It was new, stacking atop what had happened in that mind-delving session with Carl. She didn't like it one tiny bit.

"There is at least some good news," Divinity said. "According to what I see in the stream, the breach allowed us to reacquire the rogue agent. The one of our own who was left behind."

"Where is it?"

"Infiltrating."

"To what end? What were the instructions?"

"It was not so simple. A member of the collective, if it spends enough time in human spaces, seems to adapt and is not so easy to reintegrate." Divinity looked up, and Melanie knew what she'd say before it left her mouth, knowing its truth as much as she feared it. "Something you and I know from experience."

"This is different."

"Of course. But the connection was at least reestablished. We are able to monitor. With luck, it will lead us to the others."

"And if not? What are the recommendations if the Forgetting cannot be reestablished?"

"You know the answer to that," Divinity said.

Melanie looked away. The floor's stark lack of color was nearly blinding, far too bright.

"*With luck*, you say."

"With luck," Divinity repeated.

After a moment, Melanie nodded, then said, "Dismissed."

Once the door was closed, Melanie returned to the mirror. Palms on the counter, turned back to let her fingers dangle over the edge. Torso forward, eye to eye with her double.

"I don't believe in luck," she said aloud.

Her reflection said nothing.

Chapter Nineteen

Long hours passed. Night came.

Piper found herself lost in a vortex, her old life intruding on the new like a long-lost parent entering an adopted child's life. Everything changed the moment she remembered her identity. *Everything*. It was strange how recollection could take more than give.

Piper lost the daughter she'd had for twenty years — gone in a blink, the minute she remembered Heather Hawthorne.

She'd lost her granddaughter. Clara would always be special to her, but they'd stopped being blood the instant Piper remembered that they'd never been. There *was* a silver lining to that one — with memory came details of Clara's unique breed of strangeness. The girl wasn't just odd; she was special. Lila had grown Clara under the gaze of an Astral mothership, and she'd been born precocious. Practically from birth, Clara had been ahead of other children. An old soul adjusting to an uncooperative infant body — but the second she figured out the controls, she'd thought like an adult.

Because of the Astrals.

Because she was Lightborn.

And Piper remembered that as the world ended, the Lightborn were different. They hadn't forgotten. They'd told the villagers how to smith metals and make glass and the best methods for reinforcing their homes. So as much as it hurt Piper to realize what she'd already known, at least Clara wouldn't feel the same. She must know who her mother was, and who exactly Piper was to her: technically, nothing.

Piper wondered, as she lay awake by the fire behind the rocks, watching Lila and Kindred fitfully sleep, if Clara was okay.

They'd taken Meyer.

They hadn't looked twice at Piper or Lila.

But conveniently, there had been Kindred. They hadn't known he was following because (so Kindred claimed) he hadn't been. And he hadn't called out to them earlier — say, *before* the Astrals had already sealed the deal on Meyer's second abduction — because he hadn't seen them until that final moment. *Then* he'd come running. But what was he supposed to do against Reptars, once he'd arrived?

Piper sighed and looked up at the stars, feeling a queer sense of doubling. She was two separate women, sharing her skin like two kids in a sleeping bag. Even the simplest things had grown confused as memories clashed. She was sleeping in the open. As a primitive pioneer, Piper was used to the elements and didn't fear them more than a wise person should. But the Piper she'd been before forgetting couldn't help thinking of snakes. Of sand fleas. Of scorpions in the night.

Kindred said he knew where they should go. How, in the absence of other ideas, they might best find Meyer.

But Piper had remembered more things about

Kindred, same as he must have recently realized them about himself.

Kindred wasn't human. Once upon a time, he'd been a Titan implanted with Meyer Dempsey's memories. So what was *forgetting* to Kindred? Wasn't it just returning him to the blank tape he'd once been?

But he was a good Astral. He'd helped them. He wasn't Meyer's literal brother, but they were like siblings. They'd shared a strong psychic bond — one that combined to make an uber-mind that had been damn near unstoppable. But that had gone when Kindred — quite on his own, far before the Forgetting — grew dark and angry, distancing himself from Meyer, and becoming something else.

Still, what he'd said was true. The logic was hard to argue.

There were no other ideas.

Even if they didn't seek Meyer, what else would they do? Return to the village, with their memories full? Back to a group of people who'd probably all woken up as well, all unsure of what to do with their future?

And lastly — most importantly — there was the fact that things couldn't get much worse. Were the Astrals going to catch them? They *had* caught them, then left without looking at them twice.

When Kindred made his proposal, Piper countered. They were already headed to the Mullah caves to find Clara. Kindred hadn't known she was in trouble, and seemed to resent not being told.

So they'd gone, toward sounds like gunshots. Toward the departure place of what seemed to have been an Astral shuttle, screaming away from the horizon as it had with Meyer in its belly.

And the Mullah at the caves had told them, *Miss Clara*

is gone. Sage Sadeem is gone. Astrals came, and so did gunmen. Now they are all gone.

Which way?

The Mullah couldn't say.

Up? Piper had pointed toward the sky — along the path of the departing shuttle?

But the Mullah didn't know.

And Kindred had said, *Here. I know the way.*

How?

I saw it in a dream.

Piper shifted on the sand, her eyes to the stars. Kindred was sleeping, just like her non-daughter, Lila. Finally, she slept without dreaming.

In the morning, Kindred woke them both. Breaking camp was simple, and nobody, anticipating a quick trip, had brought food. There was a spring, and farther on they crossed the same river, though downstream, that fed the village. They passed without stopping home, knowing it wasn't what it used to be.

"The monolith," Lila said to Kindred. "You're taking us to the monolith, aren't you?"

"I think so."

"You don't know?"

"I never saw it while I'd forgotten. Did you?"

Piper hadn't. The legends scared her.

She looked over to see Lila shaking her head.

"I think I know what I see," Kindred said after registering nos. "But in my head, and in my old memories, it's one thing. And my knowledge of this land ..." He shook his head, looking less sinister in the sun than he did in his shack, perhaps thanks to his Meyer-mind finding its way home. "That knowledge was built by another person."

It wasn't technically accurate, but Piper knew what he meant. And so they walked, Kindred clinging to his suspicions, until Lila checked their directions, seemed to consult something inside herself, and said, "It's the freighter, isn't it? The one that ..." But Lila trailed off, too. "Why don't I remember?"

"I think it's because there were only two times you might have been able to connect 'freighter' to 'monolith.' The first was in the time after we'd arrived but before we'd totally forgotten our old memories to find this fog of new ones. The second was a few months later, when the ship returned to try and brainwash us again. Do you remember that?"

The women nodded. Piper hadn't remembered until now. It was a third kind of memory: belonging to the primitive she'd been for two decades, yet salted with knowledge from now of what the big black ship had been. At the time, none of them had understood. Memories came piecemeal. For the most part, until they forgot it had ever returned, they'd simply been terrified.

"The blacksmith," Kindred said. "Carl. Do you know him?"

Piper said she did. But only barely; Kindred handled the horses.

"I think he brought it here. I think he told me once, but even he could barely remember."

"But the monolith is in the desert."

"It's closer to the sea. It grounded when the water receded. Carl told me ..." He squinted. "He told me ..."

"What?" Lila asked.

"I don't know. I think he's South African. From the capital there ... Roman Sands?"

"Then he'd have taken the ark," said Piper. "Same as the one from Ember Flats."

All of them puzzled. Where had the arks gone? They'd vanished after dropping the people in their new homes, after they'd had room to forget why and how they'd arrived. Cleaned up, maybe. Zapped away by their alien overlords, unlike all the other relics. But hadn't it always been that way? Piper had seen Meyer's movies and watched proper *Ancient Aliens* documentaries with Cameron, at Benjamin's ranch. Archaeologists were always digging up oddities from the past that didn't make sense. Maybe that was the idea: to leave yesterday's trinkets as tomorrow's unexplainable shit.

"No," Kindred said. "I think he came on …"

They crested the hill.

"That," he finished.

It was enormous. Like something from another life. So incongruous, sitting nearly upright in the sand, relatively free of rust, more or less preserved. So obviously from a different time and place. No wonder the people had feared it.

From where they stood, it looked to Piper like it might be a half mile long. It had a bridge near the front, elevated high. And the rear was mostly countless stacks of shipping crates — the kind that had once upon a time been destined to be unloaded at their destination, then heaped along an outbound train.

"Why here?"

Piper stopped wondering by the end of her question — by then she'd noticed that there were already people aboard the ghost vessel, plain as day.

Chapter Twenty

MEYER WOKE.

Although, he realized, he'd never precisely been asleep.

There was a man beside him. From the outside, Meyer recognized the man as Carl the blacksmith, whom Kindred knew better than Meyer did. He was broad and tall, looking ten years younger than he must be. From the inside, Meyer could see the man's true identity as if he were wearing a name tag. Carl Nairobi, from Cape Town, South Africa — more recently known as Roman Sands. Meyer had once sat with this man in his kitchen, told him not to board the vessel that would protect others from the flood, and follow the silver ball to find another way.

Or was that someone else?

Meyer's head was swimming. He wasn't thinking straight. It was the drugs. The medicine. But how was that possible? He hadn't taken any since he'd last seen Juha, the shaman, at the old house in Los Angeles, with Heather. He'd talked to her recently, too. And that was strange because he was entirely certain that Heather was dead. Except that nobody was ever really dead, were they?

Beside him in the white holding room, Carl said, "You okay, man?"

"I know you."

"I know you know me. We been here long enough by now."

How long was *long enough*? Meyer sent his mind back. Reality stretched like taffy. He saw colors. Everything seemed clear. The universe was a jigsaw puzzle. He'd noticed that before when high, and Heather had always laughed at him because Meyer became wise when taking his medicine. But after a session with Juha, the aftereffects of ayahuasca always led to decisions he'd never seen as obviously correct before. After sessions, he tended to meet the right people at the right time. It gave him clarity. It showed him that one day visitors would come — and that when they did, he needed to be at his Axis Mundi in Vail. He wasn't sure how he'd get there; he kept meaning to research apocalyptic prepping to make sure he didn't conduct his eventual business like an idiot. He'd known only the mandate: *Get to Vail when the ships arrive.* Even his family hadn't needed to go, according to the visions. Only Meyer had to reach Vail before the Astrals entered the atmosphere all those years ago. Because Meyer had a date with abduction, though he hadn't figured it out at the time.

Now it seemed as obvious as the swirling and shifting nose on Carl Nairobi's face.

"What did they do to you?" Carl was peering into Meyer's eyes, and only once he saw that Carl was *above* rather than *in front of* him did he realize that he was lying down. "They give you drugs or something?"

"No."

"When that hot blonde found me on the ship, they put some weird helmet on me and tried to fuck the thoughts right out of my head. They do that to you? With the hat with the wires down the back?"

"No."

But Meyer could see that Carl was believing none of it. As far as he was concerned, Meyer was stoned out of his gourd. In Carl's mind, the only way to explain Meyer's transcendental state was drugs, alien mind-rape, or both. They'd been in this white room on the ship together for a few hours after Meyer had been shoved into it, then he'd been taken for questioning by the tall blonde — or rather, the Astral pretending to be one. She'd had a wire helmet like Carl described but had never put it on Meyer's head. The room seemed prepped for her to do so, but she'd appeared hesitant, and Meyer felt like they'd been two awkward kids in his youth, killing time in a closet while waiting for Seven Minutes in Heaven to end without touching.

Carl figured there'd been some mind-screwing going on in that room, before the Titans returned Meyer to their shared cell. But in reality, Meyer and the Astral woman had stayed chaste: her wary and him getting into these altered states apparently all on his own.

Meyer saw himself crossing the river as the flooding came, getting trapped, and eventually saved by … *Meyer?*

He saw himself chasing Cameron, Piper, Charlie Cooke, and one or two others through Benjamin's raided Utah lab. Every time one of them turned to look, Meyer ducked out of sight, and their minds wouldn't let them see him.

Although that was strange because Meyer was sure

he'd still been in captivity on the Vail mothership at the time.

He remembered leading the city of Heaven's Veil, even though he'd been on the mothership then as well, and had never actually been viceroy.

He remembered persuading Christopher to ride away from the RV in the escape vehicle when they'd been storming through cannibal tribes on the outskirts of Ember Flats. Christopher would get away and then set off a bomb. The distraction would give the others enough time to escape.

But hadn't Meyer been at the front of the RV at the time, standing beside Aubrey? And also beside ... *himself?*

"Man, what did they *do* to you?" Carl had asked that before. He was being repetitive. But that was the world. The same things happened over and over, in a loop, until the right things changed and someone finally got the lesson.

The Astrals hadn't done this to him — this curious feeling of a drug trip without any drugs.

Something else had.

Meyer, as part of his mind floated away, could see into the whole of consciousness. He *understood*, the way he always used to understand when taking the medicine with Heather. But there wasn't just one consciousness this time. Now there were two, connected by a bridge. And it was strange that Meyer realized that *both* collective unconsciousnesses — not just the human side — felt more familiar than his own skin.

Carl was still watching Meyer. Not precisely because he cared about him *per se* but because they were the only two humans here. The Astrals had snatched Carl from the monolith before grabbing Meyer from the desert during his trip to the Mullah caves. If Meyer went as nuts as Carl seemed to think he was, Carl would be alone. No one liked to be alone. So it was a good thing that from Meyer's currently enhanced perspective, nobody *ever* was alone.

He saw the monolith, the freighter. He saw it through Kindred's eyes and Stranger's. He saw the invisible thread connecting the men as they kept themselves carefully distant, though they were of course not seeing that filament themselves.

He saw Piper.

Lila.

Peers Basara.

And the former viceroy of Roman Sands, who had a secret that even she didn't know.

And he saw what was waiting, hidden among the cargo, ready to spring like a box full of snakes.

Meyer ducked beneath his surface reality. One dimension deeper. When he and the Astrals had first seen each other, *this* was where they'd connected. Nothing could travel faster than light. Bannister's team had known that, and so had the rebel monks in Heaven's Veil. The only way to travel as far as these ships was to squeeze through the layer beneath. Traveling without traveling. Thinking across light years in seconds.

The Astrals had watched the world through Meyer's eyes. They'd used the drug visions to see the human world.

But the street went both ways, and now Meyer could see it plain as day. Ever since whatever Clara had been trying to do with the Astral mind had succeeded and the artificial divisions had fallen.

There was a dimension beneath the three most people knew. *Several* hidden dimensions, in fact.

Meyer saw the Astrals' secret.

"You don't have to kill them," Meyer said. "You can outrun them."

Carl stepped away, shaking his head, and Meyer saw only the naked white ceiling.

Chapter Twenty-One

You don't have to kill them. You can outrun them, said Kindred's own voice inside his head.

And then there was a vision. A sense that was more a wave of understanding than a set of step-by-step instructions. They needed to search the cargo. That, they'd all agreed on. But now he had a new sense of peril (unsure exactly what it was) and knew they had to search anyway.

You don't have to kill them.

"Kill what?" Piper asked.

He'd spoken aloud without knowing or meaning to. For a flicker, Kindred had the sense of being somewhere else. As if he had two set of eyes — well, not just eyes but all of his senses — and one had been here on the freighter while the other had been in another place. An all-white place. And he'd been with … *Carl?* Yes, Carl. But when had that been?

"Kill what, Kindred?" Piper repeated.

Kindred looked over his shoulder. They'd moved down from the bridge and were about to enter the ship's massive rear, where cargo boxes were stacked like God's LEGOs, but Kindred couldn't shake the feeling of being followed, or watched. Both. The feeling hadn't been there a moment before, appearing about the time he'd been talking to Carl — except that he *hadn't* talked to Carl; he'd been here on the freighter the entire time. So where had that creeping feeling come from? It felt like it was right here and now, *urgent*. But it must have been a while ago. Because Carl wasn't here. According to Peers, he'd been carried into a shuttle and presumably taken to an orbiting mothership. Stranger would tell him the same thing, except that Kindred wouldn't go near him. That was a terrible idea, same as always.

"Are you all right?" Piper asked.

And Carl's voice: *Man, what did they* do *to you?*

"I'm fine."

"What's between you and Stranger?" Piper asked.

"Nothing. Why?"

"When our group came across the dunes, I thought you'd recognized them on the deck. I thought you knew it was him."

"I did." They all had. It was easy. The group didn't make a damned bit of sense, at least not to anyone without Kindred's dreams, where eight people were standing beside the ship: himself, Stranger, Peers, Liza Knight (because *that* wasn't crazy), Clara, Meyer, Carl, and the old Mullah wise man whose name Kindred didn't know. He hadn't been surprised to see them, even with Lila and Piper to muddy the waking dream's waters beside him.

"But you wouldn't shout. I had to do it."

"And?"

"And then you stayed back when they came down."

"Liza Knight makes me nervous. You remember who she was, right? Roman Sands?"

"It's not Liza you're clearly staying away from. There

133

was always something between you and him. We just accepted it when we didn't have our memories, but it always felt strange. I remember sensing that you really wanted to meet him, but refused to. So what's between you?"

"I don't know what you're talking about, Piper."

She watched him for a long second, obviously not believing. But then, she'd been looking at him that way ever since he'd run up to them on the sand. She'd *never* believed him. Wasn't that why they'd gone after Clara without telling him? They shouldn't have done that. Hadn't Clara been his granddaughter once, too? Arguably, Clara was more Kindred's kin than Piper's. At least they shared memories and genetics, borrowed or not.

She looked like she might keep prodding — to ask why everyone was simply accepting the old viceroy's presence in a group with the town mystic and a Mullah black sheep, perhaps — but instead she met his eyes with silence, then turned back to the narrow hallway. After a handful of steps, she turned. Kindred's feet seemed anchored. He hadn't moved an inch.

"What's with you?"

"I get this feeling."

"What feeling?"

"There's something out there."

"On the ship?"

He nodded.

"So now you believe in ghost stories?"

"Why did they leave this ship where it was, Piper? Why not destroy it?"

"They left a lot of artifacts. Maybe they wanted us to wonder, thousands of years in the future, the way Benjamin wondered about ancient aliens."

"I don't like it. We all knew it was here, but nobody

had the guts to explore it. People who did said they saw things aboard. Heard things."

"We didn't know it was a ship back then. Now we do. It's an old, abandoned place." Her forehead bunched. "What's going on with you, Kindred?"

What did they do to you?

And the other voice, which at first Kindred mistook for his own: *You don't have to kill them. You can outrun them.*

Kindred looked ahead, through the door with a porthole, closed because the ship had canted enough to let gravity close it. He could see Liza Knight moving between rows of containers, touching them, rapping the sides, seemingly unsure where to start or what, exactly, they were doing. Stranger was out there somewhere, too. Probably hearing the same voices as Kindred.

Why would that be?

But he sort of knew, beneath it all.

"You were the one who made us come here. It's the only way to maybe get Meyer back, remember?"

"We need to be careful. There's something out there."

"There's nothing out there."

"I'm sure of it."

"What's out there, then?"

"I don't know."

Piper moved to the door and opened it. "Oh, for fuck's sa—"

From the deck, there was a bang.

A noise like nails across metal.

A scream.

Kindred felt like someone had kicked a hole in his middle.

And he knew that Lila was dead.

Chapter Twenty-Two

STRANGER FELL TO HIS KNEES. Even with the adrenaline flooding his increasingly human body and the fear that came with it, the loss was hobbling. He struck the deck with his hand on a metal latch, stumbling, knees sending signals of pain, his palm gashed. A flash of red from the corner of his eye told him it was bleeding. He'd probably get tetanus. Born like a god, dead of lockjaw at the dawn of a diseased Earth.

When the worst of the feeling passed, Stranger raised his head.

She was gone.

His daughter — not his daughter at all — was gone.

He hadn't known it was coming. There'd been no time to prepare. He hadn't been able to say goodbye. Hell, there hadn't even been time for her to be his daughter. Lila had been too busy being Meyer's child, and in her spare time she'd been Kindred's. But Stranger couldn't help wondering if he, of the three, was hurting most. Trevor's death had broken something inside the first duplicate Meyer, and when Kindred was created, that fractured thing had been forced out of the Astral collective.

Became the Pall.

Became Kindred, when the recipe called for the addition of one Cameron Bannister, dropping himself into the Ark's maw to turn the black smoke into a thing with a body and diminishing magic, as his cells began, finally, to age.

He should run. He should hide. At the very least, he should find Piper, then maybe the others, and see them to safety. But Stranger didn't want to. Twenty years of being human had made him mostly that. It was something he could see in the joined collectives of both species, as dirty water from one spilled into the pristine blue of the other.

I'll kill it.

Stranger's fists clenched. It didn't matter what had taken her down, though the sounds suggested a Reptar. A thing like that couldn't be fought hand to hand, and the Astrals had seen to it that the people had only blades and arrows for weapons. But he'd take it on anyway, throw himself upon it, pry his fingers beneath its scales, rip them away like fingernails from the quick, like needles under skin, like slowly pressing eyes with thumbs until they—

Something hit Stranger, hard. His side struck the shipping container. He came up swinging, landing a few good strikes in the meat of something's body before hands pinned his wrists and he found himself looking up at a freely bleeding nose.

Peers.

"Don't," Peers said.

"Get off me!"

"Sadeem and I talked about this. We thought this day might come."

"What day?" Red suffused his vision. He barely felt in control of his still-thrashing arms and legs. He wanted to annihilate something, cause *anything* half the pain he felt inside. Like a rapid cancer. Acid, burning him from the center outward.

"You came from the Ark."

"I came from your mother!"

Peers let Stranger raise his hand just enough that, with reapplied force, Peers managed to slam it back down on the ship's metal deck.

"No," Peers said, his voice a reasonable but harsh whisper, "you did not. Nobody knew where you were from. Before the Forgetting was complete, they were close to declaring you a god. I remember trying hard to solve the mystery before my mind finally faded for good. I ran around asking everyone about you. People had dreamed about you. Many said they seemed to remember you visiting them before the floods, all over the world. They said you gave them special trinkets. Small metal balls that seemed to have minds of their own."

"Get off me, Peers!" Stranger was pinned down by the man's crotch, unable to struggle free. Each fresh second left them in danger. With every new moment, the monster that had ended his daughter's life — same as another had ended his son's — drew another breath.

"Listen to me. The Mullah knew about you. Not by name but by concept: a man who walked the land without boundaries, able to bend magic to his will. Sadeem's memory did not fade. He's spent all this time putting it together, and in that time you haven't aged."

"I know who I am," Stranger growled. He'd kept his memories, too.

"You're one of the seven. Or eight, if the King truly has two heads."

"GET OFF ME!"

"But you're not like that anymore, are you, Stranger?"

Stranger thrashed. Tried to connect with Peers's testicles, coming up empty.

"You're becoming more human. Because once upon a time, you were taken out of Meyer Dempsey."

Stranger stilled. "How can you know that?"

"The Mullah always knew about the Archetypes. Each time, the cycle repeats. But each time, it's been arrested before the Archetypes can become who they're supposed to be." He looked meaningfully into Stranger's eyes. "Each time but this one."

"What do you mean?"

"We have our memories back. Sadeem located and read the scroll. We know what we're supposed to do … and this time, we've got our wits about us enough to do it."

Stranger looked up at Peers. *We?*

"I'm one. So is Sadeem."

"Maybe we should have a reunion."

"Sadeem thinks that Trevor Dempsey's death created you and that Cameron's sacrifice made you real."

"He's so clever."

"And now a new death has made you human."

"I suppose Sadeem knew that, too."

Peers nodded. "But that's a problem. If you rush into your new emotion, you'll get yourself killed. You can't fight a Reptar with your fists, Stranger."

"I can try."

"What's more important? Your anger, or humanity?"

"My anger."

From the right came a chattering. From the left came another. Stranger, with his ears on the deck, could hear their claws. Their many countless claws.

Piper stumbled into their space, looking down, questions in her eyes. But she let it drop, looked back over her shoulder with her breath coming hard, and spoke in a whisper.

"Reptars. They were … They're in the containers."

"They were here all along," Peers said. "Hiding in the cargo, probably since the ship was beached."

"Why?"

"Guarding something. Protecting whatever we're trying to find."

"And what *is* that, Peers?"

Peers didn't answer. He didn't know, and neither would Stranger — or Kindred, or Liza, wherever they were. He only knew that the dream had told him to come. Had told them all to come. And that whatever was here, it mattered enough for the aliens to stake out, risking discovery, for as long as it took.

But he said nothing because the chattering was coming faster. Harder. Louder.

"We're surrounded," Piper said, cowering, looking, listening. "And there's no way to fight."

Chapter Twenty-Three

KINDRED BLINKED. Then again — this time forcibly, harder, wrinkling his eyebrows.

The Reptar had been there, plain as day.

Then it was gone.

And then it was back.

He stayed low, creeping along the giant cargo containers on the ship's deck. Twice now he'd seen Reptars, and almost constantly since he'd felt Lila die inside his mind, he'd heard them. But he had to keep his thoughts away from that. This wasn't the time for grief. Or anger. Another part of himself would handle those things. Right now his only job was to get them away so they could all live to fight another day.

There'd been tracks of blood, but Kindred made sure to turn the other way. He couldn't take finding her body now, assuming the beast had left any of it behind.

But now he wondered if his eyes were playing tricks. If his mind was deceiving him. Because Piper, clearly, had thought there was something wrong with him, before the sounds and screams had sent her running. He must have sounded like he was babbling, seeing and saying things that no one else could understand. And honestly, now that the hot moment had passed into a hotter one, Kindred could neither remember what had bothered him nor care. It only mattered that he'd been suddenly sure that danger was on the cusp, and he'd been right. Judging by what he'd seen and heard since Piper had left him, there were dozens of Reptars on the ship — maybe hundreds. He still had some of that connection to the mental collective, and got the feeling that they'd been protecting something. Their group, by coming here, had unwittingly stuck its fumbling hand into a wasp's nest. Now the wasps had been roused and would sting the intruders.

They didn't come here to find us. The Reptars were already here, hibernating in the boxes, waiting for someone to come looking for what they have and want to keep. We *disturbed* them.

But it didn't matter. They'd kill them just the same.

This new phenomenon changed everything.

Kindred could run from Reptars he could locate, and maybe lure those Reptars away from the others. But if they kept blinking in and out of existence?

He had to be imagining it.

Kindred hunkered down. He'd heard at least some of his party a few rows down not long ago and was skirting around, trying to find them. Once, he'd seen Stranger, creeping along with Peers. He wanted to shout, but if he did, they might come closer. And that couldn't be allowed, no matter what.

Or could it?

He felt confused, battered, punched in the face. Seeing the Reptar blink away and return hurt his head. He was already convincing himself he hadn't seen it happen, when he knew damn well that he had. Kindred couldn't trust his senses. Tall walls built over the years of not knowing himself were disintegrating like waves eroding a natural dam. He remembered being angry, but the feeling was distant. He remembered being jealous, but that was far away as well.

Now, there was more fear. Nervous anticipation. And with it more readiness: an increased desire, should the moment present itself, to fight.

And more fog.

And more uncertainty.

A Reptar moved in front of Kindred, at the end of his current row. Its mouth opened. And then it was gone.

Kindred spun. He'd heard something behind him, but now there was nothing. Too late, distracted, he heard another purr from where he'd been looking — now coming from behind. By the time he looked, the black, panther-like beast was already lunging, claws out, raking air so close that Kindred could swear it trimmed hairs from his arm. He ducked around the corner, panting, all-too-human heart slamming into his ribs. His back struck corrugated metal, arm raking the paint-flaked edge of a lock bar near the container's door.

Open it. Hide inside the container.

But there wasn't time, and Kindred could hear another Reptar inside, fumbling at an interior latch.

Claws.

Heavy, diseased breath, accompanied by a rattle of bones.

(!!Crowbar!!)

His hands reached almost of their own accord, grabbing and hefting the tool leaning against the door beside him, not thinking where to aim or when to swing but impelled by some urge deep, torso pivoting, a random thought screaming through his head

(It was leaning against the door, and there's a Reptar behind the

door, and that means someone was here, working, doing his job, with that thing only inches away)

before the crowbar connected with a satisfying crack, the hooked, beveled end breaking through carapace like a heavy stone through stubborn ice, the straight end yanked from Kindred's hand as the Reptar lashed upward and away, gushing alien blood, screeching with tendon-snapping wails as it thrashed down the metal-walled corridor, finally stilling, finally dying, and Kindred ran forward without thinking and pulled the bar from the Reptar's head, its end wet and dripping.

Then he heard a second thump. And another.

Hit one. The others fall.

But that didn't make sense. He had to be imagining it, the way he'd imagined the first Reptar disappearing and reappearing. In a sane world, things existed or didn't, and it was his own damned half-Astral brain's fault if he

(nothing has changed; you're just seeing it different)

was seeing things while his heart was pounding in his ears and driving him crazy.

But ahead was another dead Reptar, its head caved in as if by a crowbar.

And another.

You're crazy. You're losing your mind.

There was a tremendous roar, and Kindred saw that he'd entered the same aisle, all the way down, as Stranger, Peers and Piper. Each end and along the cross-aisles in between were thick with the black heads of countless Reptars. They were surrounded. The beasts, disturbed from their sleep, had been waiting for this moment — trained and bred, commanded to wait for someone to dispatch from this protected place. He met Stranger's eyes, and a simple, nonsensical thought traveled like a carrier through an old pneumatic tube between them

(we don't need to be here)

then Kindred's eyes closed as the Reptar nearest him lunged, like the Reptar nearest Piper. Kindred thought of Lila, Heather, and Trevor.

And then there was nothing.

Kindred opened his eyes.

Perhaps fifty feet away, he saw Piper, Peers, and Stranger.

The air was calm and silent. The sun, almost directly overhead, was suffocating.

They were in the middle of an open stretch of desert, alone, the freighter nowhere in sight.

Chapter Twenty-Four

CLARA SAT BY THE FIRE. She looked at Logan first, Sadeem second. She'd been fighting an itching, troublesome feeling since midday. A sense that in another place, something with someone she cared about had soured — and then in the same place, something else had gone catastrophically right.

After escaping the Astrals at the Mullah caves, they'd walked from one hiding place to another. Clara didn't know if the Astrals still couldn't see Lightborn — or, for that matter, if she and Logan, as adults, even still *counted* as Lightborn. If they'd stayed together, maybe they'd have had a child. And maybe that child would have been something like they were, only innocent. A new breed of chosen ones — perhaps all that were invisible now.

Her eyes went to Logan, whom she found staring back.

That's why *we didn't stay together,* she said to him with her mind, answering a question she'd seen in his eyes all day. *Because who would curse a child at birth?*

The curse she'd mentally proposed to Logan was the

same one *she'd* been born with, and she'd managed fine. Although was hers a life worth envying?

She looked to the dirt, stirring it with a stick. Night, out here and away from her village, was everywhere.

During their journey to this place, the sun had been up. They'd left, unsure of their pursuit. But after an hour of still-empty sky, they'd settled into a copse of ratty trees to rest. Clara had fallen asleep and dreamed of her mother standing far in the distance, calling her home.

You're fine, Clara. You've always been fine, even without me.

She'd come upright with Logan's hand on her shoulder, her shirt sticking to her back despite the cool desert shade. There was a worry out there beyond arm's reach, but as the dream dissolved, Clara couldn't grab it. The thing vanished like a Forgetting in miniature. It felt like something worth worrying about that she could no longer recall.

So they'd walked.

And walked.

And eventually, after hours of what felt like aimless plodding, they'd arrived in a tiny village like a scale model of her own. It was closer to a cluster of bivouacs than a permanent settlement, though the tribe had called it home for years. As she watched the people move to their individual huts, Clara saw their confused, almost embarrassed expressions. They struck her like hungover people recalling a prior night's debauchery. What had been so delightful in a haze now seemed stupid in the light of clarity.

She'd looked up to see Kamal looking at her. His expression said, *This morning, the world mostly made sense, and this still felt like the only home we'd ever known. Now we remember, and all we've worked to build is a joke. A lifetime for some, amounting to sticks in the sand.*

The evening had drawn into night. Clara had fought

the pain in her gut, knowing it had nothing to do with soreness. It was a psychic pain, as if she'd lost something precious without realizing it was gone.

And now, as Sadeem and then Logan retired to leave her alone by the crackling fire, she gazed into the flames and thought of her dream. It wasn't the persistent one she often had — of meeting friends by the freighter. Instead her thoughts were of the almost-there new dream, returning bit by bit. She could close her eyes and see her mother, standing beside her uncle and the grandmother she now barely recalled, waiting for Clara at the end of an impossibly long corridor.

"It sucks, you know," said a voice.

Startled by the intrusion, Clara looked up to see Kamal standing above her holding two cups. He handed one to her, full of warm liquid that smelled like an approximation of coffee. The cup itself was metal, slightly banged up, and tall. On the side was a faded stamp that seemed to say, *World's Sassiest Aide*.

"What sucks?"

"Forgetting how sassy I used to be." He gestured to Clara's cup. "I remember when I found that in my pack. A part of me understood that it was *my* cup, but a bigger part of me treated it like something I'd unearthed from the ground. I didn't question what it was or how it could even exist. I'd found a goddamned *metal-and-plastic travel mug* at the dawn of man with *World's Sassiest Aide* written on the side, and I simply accepted it. Like, no big deal. After a half hour or so, it felt like a logical thing for our tiny tribe of hunter-gatherers to have."

Clara smiled at Kamal. She'd liked him back at Jabari's palace and found that she liked him even better now.

"Did you at least *act* sassy once you started using it?"

"Sadly, I couldn't read at the time and was hence oblivious to the sassy imperatives the mug implied." He sipped, then sat. "Do you have written language in your village?"

Clara nodded and made a noise of agreement. The Lightborn had seen to literacy. The Rest of Humanity's Existence was too long a wait without something to read, or at least the ability to leave notes and scribble to-dos.

"I'd think you could infer sassy from this font, even without the ability to read."

"We also didn't have typography. It's been a tough era for graphic designers." Kamal pointed at a thin-faced woman in her hut across the fire. "And the irony? Veronica *is* a graphic designer. Or was. You know."

Clara took another look around the small clearing. "You've been here all along? In this same spot?"

"Yep."

Clara looked into the dark and laughed without humor. "I doubt you're ten miles from us. How have we never run into each other?"

"Maybe it was luck. Or something a lot like luck, but different."

"I'll drink to that." Clara raised her cup, and Kamal clinked it with his.

"Did you come over on the vessel?" she said after a quiet moment. "The one Mara and I took with all the others? I didn't see you on board. And Mara never mentioned seeing you. She felt terrible that she'd had to leave you behind."

"That's because I was so sassy." He took a sip, shifting on his rock by the fire. "No, I missed the vessel. I tried like hell to get on it, believe me. But the crowds … Well, you saw the panic. I don't think they'd have parted for my diplomatic credentials. Besides, I wasn't in the lottery to get on board anyway. I'd already opted out so someone more vital to the future could take a spot."

Clara thought that was selfless enough to cry over, but she shoved it away. "So how did you survive?"

"Boat," Kamal said.

"I thought the Astrals blew all the other boats out of the water." *Except the monolith,* her mind amended.

"Hey, I don't understand it either. I know how this sounds, but I sort of feel like I was ... *guided.*"

"Guided how?"

"You wouldn't believe me if I told you."

Clara thought she'd believe him just fine. She even had ideas how it might have happened and who'd been behind the guiding. But she let that go as well, saying nothing.

"My mother died today."

Kamal looked over. Clara kept her gaze straight ahead, offering only her profile.

"Was she in the caves? Where we found you?"

"No. She was somewhere else."

"Where?"

"There's a moored ship past our village. I think it happened there."

"Today?"

"Yes."

"But you were ..." Kamal stopped, probably calculating travel times and realizing they didn't jibe. Finally he seemed to let it go just as Clara had and said only, "I'm sorry."

There was another long, quiet moment. Only the fire spoke. Then Clara turned, her eyes drier than they should be. "Kamal?"

"Yeah."

"Do you believe in fate? That everything happens for a reason?"

He seemed to really think before finally saying, "I guess I have to."

"I couldn't tell you why, but I get this feeling that what happened with ... with my mom?" She took an extra breath, then pushed on. "It hurts. It really hurts." She put her hand on her chest, near her heart. "But at the same time, somehow it feels necessary. Like there's a purpose to it, for the greater good." After a half second she turned her head and said, "Jesus, that sounds awful."

"No. I think I understand."

Clara finally turned and met the man's haunted expression. "What happened to you, Kamal?"

"I was ready to die back in Ember Flats. I really, truly was. When the network finally broke and I couldn't reach Mara anymore? That happened before the floodwaters hit us. Quite a while before, really. There was only one way out of town, and I'd already surrendered my spot. I'd told her I'd watch the city, so I decided that was all I had left to do. I'd be safe until the end, locked in that bunker. It was even possible that the seals were good enough to keep the water out once the city flooded. I could live a while that way, if the water didn't go high enough to cover the stack vents. I had supplies. It would be like living in an undersea habitat I could never leave."

"That sounds horrible."

"I figured I could stay busy until I ran out of air, water, or food — whichever came first. There was a charged Vellum loaded with books. I wasn't sure how the generator worked or if it would vent right and not asphyxiate me, but I knew there was one, plus fuel enough for a while. There were TV shows and movies on the juke. I'd lost the city network, but the computers were filled with plenty of files."

"You were just going to settle in? Just like that, for as long as you could?"

"I had a Plan B if things went south." He touched the

gun at his side — the first firearm Clara had seen since the New Beginning. She felt herself watching him with sympathy, unable to help it. He laughed.

"Relax. You know the ending of this story. It worked out. I didn't even see the floods until I was on my boat with the crew of the *SS Cubicle* beside me." He nodded to the huts and their unseen occupants. "But I did start going through Mara's files, because she was always stingy with information and I figured this was my last revenge. She had *tons* of data on the Astrals. Most of it was Da Vinci Initiate archives — stuff Mara probably never even went through but kept for reference. I plinked around for a while, but at some point during my repeating cycle of time-killing activities — read, make a lap around the room, do five push-ups, stand in front of the mirror and declare a sassy affirmation — I started to wonder why, when your grandfather and the others wanted to leave the city, she insisted on staying. It was a real puzzler. She said it was safer in the bunker than outside, but Mara was the kind of person who always had plans to back up her backups."

"Was she staying in case I came back?"

"Maybe. You'd have to ask her."

Clara felt her lips purse. She exhaled. He didn't know.

"Mara passed away."

His head bobbed. Apparently it wasn't unexpected.

"I don't know if she stayed for you. We thought for a while the Mullah had abducted you for leverage. That little point of confusion led to quite the concussion." He rubbed his temple absently, like a reflex. "But it had me thinking in circles. Mara either stayed because she thought it was safer inside the city — or for you — or because someone else needed to go."

"Are you suggesting she stayed behind so that my

grandfather and the others could take the sub? There were a bunch of them, weren't there?"

"Plenty." Kamal nodded. "Plenty for Mara and me to go with you, if I hadn't been so preoccupied with unconsciousness at the time. But who knows? Maybe only one worked. Maybe if two subs had gone, they would have presented a bigger target for the Astrals and nobody would have survived."

"Kamal. There's no way Mara could have known anything like that."

"I'm sure she didn't. And I don't think she had delusions that she did. I'm just saying that one way or another, everything worked out. And so when you ask about whether I believe things happen for a reason? Well, it's hard to argue with the results. I'm here. As are you. Mara made it, and so did Meyer, based on what you're saying. So who's to say it wasn't all planned that way ... somehow?"

Clara turned to the internal vision of her mother and the departed at the end of that long hallway. It sure did feel like Lila's death had a cosmic reason — but of course she'd feel that way. Invoking faith was just another way of saying the deceased had gone to a better place. Believing the irrational made grieving so much easier.

"Maybe it's coincidence," Clara said.

Kamal shifted on the rock, rolling a bit to the side to access his pocket. He reached down, and when his hand opened in front of Clara, there was a polished silver sphere sitting on its palm.

"Do you know what this is? I've carried it like a holy token every day of my life here, and still it doesn't have a scratch. That used to tell me it was something special, like it would make me invincible or bring me luck. But this morning I remembered where it came from. That's when I rounded everyone up, saddled the horses, and rode 'quickly to the east, in the direction of the rising sun, to find her.'" He nodded meaningfully toward Clara. "To find *you*, Clara, just in time."

Clara picked up the sphere, cradled it in her hand, feeling a quiet buzz from its smooth metal skin.

"*Stranger.* Stranger gave this to you, didn't he?"

Kamal shrugged, apparently not knowing the name. "A tall man in jeans and boots. Long, narrow face and hands the size of dinner plates."

"Why? To save me? But he couldn't possibly know …" She stopped on her own, shaking her head, lost.

"He told me I needed to tell you something."

"Tell me what?"

"I don't know." He clinked his cup against hers. "Maybe it's that now, *you're* the world's sassiest aide."

"It's just a coincidence, Kamal. It's luck. It has to be."

"I don't think so, Clara."

"I do."

"*I don't,*" he insisted.

Clara's shoulders rose and fell. She met his stare. "Why? What makes *me* so special?"

But Kamal just repeated what he'd said before.

"I don't know."

Chapter Twenty-Five

THE DARK-HAIRED ASTRAL — *Divinity*, Meyer believed she was most conveniently called, though of course every entity that ran a mothership was called the same damned thing — entered the room. She stood in the white doorway, nearly impossible to tell from the white room other than by a slight difference in illumination. Meyer was sitting, far more coherent than he'd felt earlier, Carl still watching him as if he expected Meyer to go berserk at any moment. The two men hadn't spoken since Meyer started babbling. Carl seemed to prefer silence over nonsense.

"You," she said, pointing at Carl. "Go for a walk."

Carl looked at Meyer as if this might make sense to him. It didn't. Meyer was more or less himself again, strange transcendental experience aside. For a while it had felt like he was on a medicine man's trip through the expanded universe, but right now he was only a man with the limited knowledge that came with it. And something was wrong with him — he was finding the Astral attractive, having mood swings like a pregnant woman, oscillating between confused, terrified, and apparently plain old cocky

Meyer Dempsey — who'd apparently been in short supply over the past two decades.

The woman sighed. Rolled her eyes. Then stepped aside.

Two Titans entered.

"Don't make me say *please*."

Carl gave Meyer another glance. Meyer shrugged. After another few beats, Carl stood, went to the door, and gave Divinity another long look to be sure she was really asking him to leave their prison — in the company of the Titans, but departing nonetheless — then finally moved past her. Once the trio's footsteps faded, another two Titans appeared.

She moved to a wall. Pressed a panel. A small door opened, and she dragged out what looked like an ordinary desk chair — all white, of course. Then she turned it around and sat, legs primly crossed, looking up at Meyer until he did the same on one of the benches along the wall, opposite her.

"Needed a prop?" Meyer asked, nodding toward the chair.

"Needed a place to sit." She raised her eyebrows. "Would you like one?"

"I've got a seat." He tapped the bench. "And there weren't any more chairs in there anyway." He looked at the closed compartment, now invisible.

"This wasn't just sitting in there," Divinity said. "It made the chair at my request."

"I didn't hear you request anything."

She assessed him, her stare unblinking.

"There are a lot of things we're able to do that you have yet to figure out."

Meyer waited for more, but she took her time going on.

156

"I could ask that compartment to make me a table. Or a refrigerator. Or a baseball bat."

"You know baseball?"

"We know your game. But why did you leap to that conclusion? Perhaps I needed something I could beat you to death with."

Another long pause.

"I don't think you'd have brought me here if you wanted to kill me."

"I was offering examples. Don't be so jumpy."

Meyer shook his head. "What are you? Really."

"You can call me Divinity."

"Bullshit. You strike me as human. I know what Divinity is like. They're stiff. Can't talk for the sticks up their asses. I used to share Kindred's memories, and he talked to you all the time."

"Kindred?" She pretended not to understand. Then: "Yes. I remember. The duplicate we sent down to fuck your wife."

Meyer had his rebuttal ready, but that particular comment took him off guard.

"He seemed to think that—"

"The *second* duplicate we sent down to fuck your wife, actually. The first was so damaged that at the end, it wanted to fuck your ex-wife, too."

Meyer's brow wrinkled. "What are you?"

"Divinity."

"You don't talk like they do. You don't act like they do."

"Maybe I've improved at my job. Perhaps during the past twenty years we've had to stay here thanks to your granddaughter, I've learned the trick of getting under a man's skin."

"Why?"

She shrugged and made a *why not* pout with her lips. "Why beat you to death with a baseball bat?"

Meyer sat back, unsure where this was headed. Divinity made up the difference, leaning forward, elbows on the knees exposed by her mid-length skirt.

"Let's *cut the shit*, as your people say."

"Okay."

"You know what you are."

"I thought we were discussing what *you* were," Meyer said.

"Our monitors showed you in here not long ago, babbling as if you were intoxicated. Then you said, 'You don't have to kill them. You can outrun them.'"

"So?"

"*Were* you intoxicated?"

"There's nothing in here to drink. Or eat. Or use."

"That's not what I asked."

Meyer didn't respond. After a moment, Divinity shook her head and sat back. She walked to a wall and pressed something to open the door. She didn't say anything to the Titans, but both looked at her as if not hearing correctly, then eventually half shrugged and left the room. The door closed. Divinity pressed something else, and the panel flashed red.

"You can speak freely. We're alone."

"Without your guards, what's to stop me from tackling you and breaking your neck?"

Divinity shrugged as she sat back in her chair. "Nothing, I suppose. But this is just a body. You of all people should understand that the body is only matter, and that the energy lives beyond it."

"Why would I 'of all people' know that?" Meyer's legs had tensed of their own accord. Without his mind's permission, Meyer's body had taken the idea to spring and tackle as a legitimate one. He somehow felt certain that the woman-thing was bluffing — despite her being a puppet for Divinity's true being, the death of this meaningless body was something she'd fight hard to prevent.

"Who were you talking to when you said, 'You can outrun them'?"

"Myself."

"And who was the 'them' in that sentence? Who could be outrun? And to where?"

"It didn't mean anything. I was babbling."

"I thought we agreed to cut the shit?"

Divinity's tongue found her cheek. She seemed to consider whether or not to say something else, fingers working in tiny rhythms on her lap, her every nuance perfect. She was barely alien — as good a human as any of them.

"Do you seriously not know what you did?"

"I didn't do anything!"

Another long pause. Divinity was deciding whether or not to give him more without getting something in return. An effortless negotiation that wasn't a negotiation at all. If he'd been holding out like a poker match, he would have been winning. But here Meyer was clueless.

"Our species does not have a true hierarchy. You see Reptars and Titans and Divinity, and above Divinity you see Eternity, responsible for the largest of our Earthfaring ships. But we are all the same. There is one field of energy, and the bodies are manifestations, like the tallest of underwater mountaintops poking their heads above the sea."

Meyer didn't believe that at all. Maybe it had been true when they'd arrived, but this woman was nothing if not an individual.

"Nevertheless, we consolidate our collective decisions within the area that manifests as *Divinity* — and above that,

Eternity. It creates what appears to be a hierarchy, even though it is not."

"She's your boss," Meyer clarified.

Divinity's lips tightened, then relaxed. Her jaw worked.

"Eternity believes that Earth is a malleable experiment. In short: *Whatever happens, happens*. Others in the collective have what you might feel is a more literal interpretation: The experiment operates within strict conditions, and any events that outgrow those conditions should be considered anomalies. Our usual protocol with farm planets is to conduct a reset at the end of each epoch so that the next one will not be flawed with the previous epoch's prejudices. So when, after the extinction and population reset, our Forgetting failed to hold, there was disagreement in what has previously been a harmonious whole. One opinion — that of Eternity — called for us to continue the experiment until we could accomplish a complete Forgetting. And so that is what we have done: we've been in orbit this entire time, trying to erase knowledge that Clara somehow keeps restoring as fast as we can blank it."

"What was the other opinion?" Meyer asked.

"That we should consider the farm a loss, and exterminate the remaining stock."

Meyer met her gaze, unwilling to show any fear.

Divinity stood and began to walk the room's perimeter.

"Now that Clara has forced the human collective to backwash into ours, the need for a final decision has become much more urgent." She shook her head, and a tiny smile found her lips. It wasn't warm at all. "I'll just go ahead and say it, *Mr. Dempsey* — we've lost our control of you. There was always a chance we could contain the Lightborn infection, but not anymore. Now it's spreading.

It's becoming clearer and clearer that Earth will need to be declared a loss. All that's left is for the collective to accept it. And that's why I'm talking to you now."

"Okay," said Meyer, trying and mostly failing to deliver a neutral response. He didn't like dignifying any of this, but it all rang true. And this was something he wanted — perhaps *needed* — to know.

Reluctantly, he added, "Why?"

"Because Eternity insists on non-interference, there's only so much we can do. We can force a Forgetting, but if it fails, we can't go down there and coach you into a new government with your memories intact. We can set the Mullah as guardians, but because the last epoch's Mullah turned on us and hid our archive, we cannot let this epoch's Mullah know where it is. If they do, widespread knowledge of our archive might affect the experiment. And — most pertinent to where we are now — our acceptable level of interference will allow us to wipe you all from existence but will not allow us to leave orbit while Clara's box is still open."

"So?"

"She wouldn't want me talking to you," Divinity said, now almost whispering. "This right here?" She made a little back and forth gesture with one long finger, indicating their discussion. "It's 'muddying the data.'"

Divinity sat. Inched her chair closer. Leaned in.

"But *I* believe that there's still a solution and that misunderstandings are getting in the way. If we're honest with each other, I believe this situation can be salvaged. We won't have to fly home and incinerate your planet. Your entire species doesn't have to die … if we can stop pretending we don't really know what's happening here."

"What *is* happening?"

"Your people are trying to build something that the

Mullah believed might stop us. It's absurd, and impossible — born of the same vain hopes that powered endless science fiction movies that you yourself might have made."

"You … you *know my movies?*"

"We know a lot about you. More than you'd believe." She sat back and crossed her arms, the topic wordlessly changing. "There's nothing there for Clara and the others, though. What they're after is based on a Mullah legend I don't mind telling you about in the spirit of honesty — of *clearing the air* to save your species. It goes like this: There are seven key people who represent essential roles in the new society of any epoch. Our Forgetting erases their memories, so those people merely act as pillars during the reset. But some of your people on the planet believe that this time around, with memories intact, those Archetypes will be able to do something more. We're already collecting them, and there's a spy in their midst. One they'll count as a friend, who reports to us."

"Who?" Meyer said, somehow certain he already knew.

"Your turn."

"I don't know anything."

"Yes, you do, Meyer. Even if you don't think you know it. You're finding higher states without chemical help to get your body out of the way. You're projecting."

"Projecting what?"

"'You don't have to kill them. You can outrun them.' One of our listening posts heard your 'Kindred' say that on the surface just after you said it here."

"I … I didn't do anything, though."

"Then Kindred began to *see*. It's obvious if you watch the stream, from a Reptar's point of view. It confuses him, but he *sees* it just fine."

"What does he *see?* I don't know what the fuck you're talking about!"

"Come on, Meyer. Tell me the truth. The longer they keep fighting, the faster Eternity's decision will be driven home. I got this bit of human tripe from one of your infomercials: *Help me help you.*"

"Stop bullshitting. *Stop fighting a losing battle like a fool, and tell me the truth!*"

Her timbre had risen in the final sentence, and now Divinity was practically panting, shoulders broad, standing, chest heaving, color up.

He looked her over, shaking his head in puzzled amazement.

"What happened to you over the past twenty years? What's made all of you so damn—"

She slapped the wall. The door slid open. The first Titans were back, just outside, with Carl between them, as if they'd all been waiting.

"Four people slipping through a rift doesn't happen by accident," she said, moving toward the door but keeping her eyes on Meyer. "If you help them again, we'll *see you do it* as surely as Kindred has started to *see* us. We'll intercept them, then bring them here and hook them up to see what *they* know. And *then* we'll see how willing you are to keep arguing for your own extinction."

Chapter Twenty-Six

"NOTHING," said Peers.

Stranger looked up from where he was sitting. The man's long, weathered face seemed born for the desert. He looked like a wanderer, his thick skin beaten by dry wind. But the man was, in fact, *a man*. It should have contradicted what Peers was thinking now (he hadn't aged), but somehow it didn't. Because although Stranger then and Stranger now were mostly the same (and although the villagers had for some reason accepted his unchanging face for twenty years), there *was* that small difference. Something in his eyes. Uncertainty, perhaps. Mortality, maybe.

"Did you look to the north?" Stranger asked.

Peers tried to drag a desiccated piece of wood toward Stranger, found it anchored deeper than he'd thought, and gave up to sit on the sand. He waited several seconds, still inspecting the man's suddenly oh-so-human face, before answering.

"No. I didn't check the north."

"Then check the north."

"What's on the ship, Stranger?"

The question turned the other man's head. Blue eyes met Peers, and for the scantest of moments, seemed to see right through him.

His eyes returned to the sand. "Check the north," he repeated.

"We don't even know where we are. Why does it matter?"

"Because Liza must be out there somewhere."

"How do you know she's not still on the freighter?"

"Because I can see her. I can see her out there."

"Using your crystal ball?"

"Whatever you say, Peers."

"It's not your fault, you know."

Again, Stranger looked up. "What's not my fault?"

"That you've lost your magic. That you're more like the rest of us by the day. That's the way it works. The King loses his kingdom. The Warrior finds himself bound. The Sage loses his wisdom and realizes his folly. And the Magician loses his magic."

"Which one are you, Peers? You're with us. You had the dreams that brought you to the ship, same as the rest of us. So which of the Archetypes does Sadeem's questionably sage wisdom say you are?"

"I'm the Fool."

Stranger poked at rocks with a stick. Piper was quiet, resting, probably crying. Kindred's back was visible, but Peers was grateful that his front was not. Kindred's intensity was frightening. He'd been staring at his hands ever since they'd made their first search for Liza Knight, coming up empty as if trying to make them disappear by force of will. He seemed to think that whatever had happened to bring them here from the freighter's deck was his doing. It was absurd and impossible. Like the idea of vanishing from one place to instantly appear in another.

Peers thought Stranger would lash out. His demeanor was darker than Kindred's used to be. The two now moved in tandem — one standing when the other stood, one falling silent when the other went quiet.

Curiously, Stranger laughed.

"This is funny to you?"

"No. I'm sorry. I knew it once, but something made me forget. Of course you're the Fool. Of course you brought them to us."

"I was only a kid. I didn't know what I was doing. I didn't know there were aliens in that portal, and that I was at risk of inviting them to our planet — thousands of years too soon, based on what I got from Sadeem."

"Does Sadeem know?"

Peers shook his head. "I don't think so. But he's smart."

Stranger opened his big hand. It was empty. Empty of spark, empty of magic. Full of nothing at all.

"For now," Stranger said.

"What's on the ship?" Peers asked again.

"Cargo."

"You know. I *know* you know. I saw the way you were looking at those boxes before we even climbed up. I could *feel* something there. And those Reptars didn't come to ambush us. They were there already. Inside the shipping containers. Just waiting. Protecting something."

Stranger looked at Peers, then he nodded as if to say, *Fair enough.*

"If I had to guess," Stranger said, "I think it's the Ark."

"But the Astrals got rid of all of the arks. They must have broken them apart or disintegrated them or ..." He trailed off. "You mean the other Ark. The archive. The one that used to sit on a dais in the middle of Ember Flats, until Cameron Bannister opened it."

Stranger met Peers's eyes, then looked back at the sand.

"Do you really think it's there?" Peers asked.

"I don't know for sure. But it's like you said, I could feel it too."

"Why would it be on the monolith?"

"You'd have to ask Sadeem for the lore. My memory isn't what it used to be. But once upon a time, I understood a great deal. The world felt like a puzzle to me, and shuffling was easy. I'd find the right people and offer gifts to guide their way, shepherd those vital minds to ensure their survival. Each had a meaning and a purpose — most to help build the newest form of our collective unconscious."

"Humans don't have a collective unconscious."

Stranger looked skyward. "That's what *they* thought, too."

"You talked to Piper, didn't you? You gave her one of your gifts. Something that made the ship work and know where to go. It's how we survived in that tiny submarine. How we managed to find everyone else, and eventually land."

Stranger nodded.

"Did you know about the Ark back then?"

"Maybe," Stranger said. "I have almost a 'memory of a memory' about many things. I remember feeling as if they created it, but then as soon as our thoughts and deeds began to fill the Ark, it became something they couldn't touch. I remember standing beside the Ark as it opened, knowing the danger but feeling its power fill me. I think it made me what I am. Or changed me from what I used to be into what I became."

"What they called 'The Pall.'"

"Yes." He took a long breath. Peers couldn't decide if Stranger was frustrated, afraid, or worried. But then he saw: It wasn't Liza Knight's absence in this place that bothered him. It was Lila's. And he understood.

"You saw Lila as a daughter. I can see it in you, as a man who lost a son." Peers looked toward Kindred, ticked his head, indicating the intently focusing man in the distance. "You're somehow connected to him, aren't you?"

"I might *be* him. I don't know. Sometimes I look in a mirror and expect to see that man looking back at me. I've woken from sleep, sure I've been awake, living as if inside his skin. I've had phantom pains from places where Kindred bears scars. I'm drawn toward him, but know better than to get close. He knows it, too. We're like a thing that's been split. Two explosives, safe when separate but dangerous combined."

"What does it mean?"

"I don't know."

"What do you think happened on the freighter?"

"I don't know."

"Well, dammit, do you know *anything?* How about a fucking *guess?*"

A long, slow smile crossed his lips. Stranger straightened.

"All right, Peers. I'll guess. It's like I said: I don't think the Ark works much like everything here, relative to us. Humanity was an experiment. They watched and waited. Then when they came, the aliens gave us stimuli to gauge our response. There were no right or wrong answers. It only mattered that we jumped when prodded. So they're stuck, do you see? It's like what you told me about what Sadeem said: how they seeded us with chaos and were as afraid of that mayhem as they were in awe. I think they took the Ark when it was empty and hid it so the Mullah couldn't. They boxed it up and shipped it to another capital, where they expected the ocean to swallow it in the floods."

"So how did it end up here?"

"I found that ship a captain. He followed the same signal as the rest of you, and brought it here."

"So you *did* know. You *knew* the Ark was in one of those shipping containers."

Stranger shook his head. "I just followed my gut, telling Carl Nairobi not to board the Roman Sands vessel and find another ride instead. My instincts were fine-tuned then. I was in touch with everyone below the surface, somehow able to see everything. I visited a fisherman in China and got him onto the boat that brought him here to safety. He forgot just like the rest of them, but his mind was still there beneath it all. He wasn't anything special. But when set beside all the other minds in the tiny new mental pool, he was a linchpin. Something Clara could cling to, and keep the door open as it grew. And grew. And *grew*."

"So Carl brought the Ark to this place. And the Astrals knew it came here, but they couldn't take it away. So instead, they left guards on board to protect it. They made it seem haunted, and let us come to fear it."

"In another thousand years, the sand probably would have buried it again," Stranger said. "But I guess we Archetypes had other plans."

"What plans?"

"You felt the energy on that ship — the Ark somehow powering up, or maybe it always feels that strong to certain people. It was like a current running through my bones. At the end, just before we … before whatever happened, *happened*, I looked up at Kindred, and it was like we ran right toward each other even though we were both frozen. I understood something about our connection that my mind has already lost. I understood something about the Reptars there, too. Something I thought I remembered Meyer telling me, though we've barely ever spoken. I knew we didn't have to kill them to escape. We could run. And that was the thought in my head — and I'd wager in Kindred's — when we ..."

Stranger trailed off, making a vague hand gesture as if to say, *Well, you know the rest.*

"Did you really make that happen?" The thought was frightening. Peers had been near laughing at Kindred as he focused, trying to make it happen again, but hearing the same thing from Stranger almost made it real. He wished Piper wasn't so clearly distraught or maybe she'd mock the two men with him.

"I don't know that anything really *happened*," Stranger said, looking toward the horizon. "It's the oddest thing in my mind. For a moment, it was like I didn't see any difference between *here* and *there*. There was only *is*. It seemed so obvious. I thought of leaving, and that's when we left. Same as how I looked at Kindred in that moment and felt as if we weren't two people but separate instances of the same person. And the Reptars. How they were ..."

"Were what?"

Stranger shook his head. "It's gone. It made sense then, but now I can't find it."

Peers sat back. "So now what?"

"The energy on that ship did something to me. And I think it matters."

"So you want to go back. To find the Ark."

"It makes sense, doesn't it? We're the Archetypes." Stranger shrugged. "A few of them, anyway. Carl, the Warrior? They took him to the ship. Sadeem and Clara — the Sage and the Innocent — we don't know where they are."

But that didn't seem right. He knew this point in the story, as told by the Mullah Legend Scroll. There was a moment of realization. The Innocent …

"The Innocent dies," Peers finished aloud. "According to legend, the Innocent dies to force a change in the King."

"You believe Clara will die?"

"Not in the future. It would already have needed to happen."

"Clara's alive. That, I can feel."

Peers looked at Stranger. Then at Kindred. He thought of what had happened and the change now afoot. He understood.

"It was Lila. She was the Innocent."

"Ridiculous."

"She came, same as the rest of us."

"She came *with* us. With Piper and Kindred and Meyer. Use your head, Peers. Seven or eight important people in the world, and they're all in the same family?"

"Clara is special. Lila was her mother. And Meyer was special, too. Many say he was the first abduction. The only viceroy to have been switched with an Astral. His daughter would be special." Peers stood. This suddenly seemed very important, though he couldn't say why. A word on the tip of his tongue, refusing to leave his lips. "It fits. We were all called. She fell. And you …"

"Meyer isn't even *here*," Stranger said as Peers trailed off. "How could any of this 'force a change in the King?'"

"*The King has two heads.*" Peers wasn't just speaking. He was reading from a book inside his brain.

"Kindred and Meyer," said Stranger.

"Kindred and *you.*"

Stranger shook his head. Peers was thinking, barely seeing.

"If I'm not the Magician …"

"Clara is the Magician."

Stranger was looking at Peers in disbelief, but Peers had never been more certain of anything. The Fool lost his foolishness. In time, even a jester could become a sage.

"All that's left is the Villain," said Stranger. "Are you trying to say that Meyer is the *Villain?*"

Movement in the distance caught Peers's eye. He looked past Stranger and saw four people rise to peek above the dune. Two were men with dark skin — one older, another near Peers's age. The third and fourth, close enough to be holding hands, almost looked like a young couple, their pigment too pale for the beating sun. The woman was tall and lean, the man taller but broad. Behind the front four was a small group of robed desert dwellers, but even from a distance Peers knew this was a reunion rather than a raid.

"No," Peers said, feeling *déjà vu* as Clara recognized their group from the dune and began to jog forward. "Meyer is something else."

Chapter Twenty-Seven

BY THE TIME Divinity reached the storage room where Eternity kept its surrogate, she was in a foul temper. Her mood wasn't just unpleasant; it also made the need for a quick solution that much more obvious. Divinity tried to focus on that — the evidence this anger gave her to do what had to be done — but it was impossible. She kept thinking of how Eternity would look at the evidence and declare that the anger, rather than justifying Divinity more, made her irrational. Then maybe she'd roll her eyes like so many of the human men in the human media they'd processed and say, *Women*.

She pressed the wall panel. The door did not open. She tried again, and the organized collective monitoring ship security informed her that the door had been secured and would only open for Eternity's surrogate.

At first, Divinity couldn't believe it. She pressed again, ignoring the unmistakable fact that the collective had already placed into her own mind as if the thought had originated inside herself ... ahem, inside *the node of the collective responding to her true form*, which definitely was *not* this hunk of flesh she'd been wearing for twenty trips around this planet's star.

The door would only open for Eternity's surrogate? That was like a broom closet only opening for the broom.

She projected: *Override*.

Was it sleeping and didn't want to be disturbed? Eternity didn't need to sleep any more than Divinity, but the animated bodies sure did. It was one of the things she hated about being so damn corporeal. You lost a third of every day to unconsciousness. And in that insentience — more and more often now that the wall had been breached — strange, otherworldly visions came to haunt her.

The door opened. Of course. Because even though Eternity organized the ship's local collective, Divinity and Eternity were as much "one" as Divinity and Titans. Or Eternity and Reptars. They were all the same thing, sharing a single consciousness. Only their temporary bodies made the difference.

But still, she hadn't liked Meyer's idle threat, about killing the body. Hated it more than she cared to admit.

Divinity entered the storage room as the hallway door closed behind her. It had been expanded. The collective had shifted the build matrix, pushing walls back and making new divisions. Whereas a surrogate's storage room was usually a small thing meant for recharging the body through the loathsome process of sleep, this one was as large as the apartment they'd seen Meyer Dempsey living in during their trip to Earth from the Jupiter rift.

This much space? For a surrogate? And locking the door, even though Eternity's surrogate was obviously somewhere else on the ship?

It was ridiculous. Seeing the way Eternity had enlarged her surrogate's space made Divinity's temper ratchet up a notch. This was supposed to be a utilitarian space, no more. But Eternity had turned it into a palace. She'd had furniture made. She'd had *decorations* made. The space had white walls like the rest of the ship's spaces, but it was filled with fabrics — including hanging ones that gave the illusion of veiling windows — in all colors of the human visual spectrum.

She'd enlarged her bed. She'd had the machines make her at least eight large soft-looking pillows, one of them the size of a surrogate body.

The space was, in fact, bigger than Divinity's own storage room on her own ship. She hadn't expanded or decorated her own surrogate's space nearly this much, and her own colors didn't harmonize nearly this well.

She walked through what seemed an expansive living room, floored with a parody of hardwoods over the white base. There was a rug in the middle that the fabricator had done a superb job of replicating. Eternity had put paintings on her walls — recreations, Divinity seemed to recall, of famous human art. She'd had lamps made. Modern-looking, jet black and accented with chrome.

The waste was extraordinary.

The oddity of it all was troublesome. As troublesome, in fact, as the anger percolating still unquenched in Divinity's center.

Something had gone terribly wrong, the species irretrievably tangled.

At first, the leak of human pollution into the collective had been a minor issue. The collective managed to purge it, the way it had purged the offal from the Meyer Dempsey stream when it created the one they called Kindred. Upon his making, he had none of the first substitute's pollution. The rebelliousness and attachment to Meyer's old mate had been purged away — along with whatever had bubbled up when that first Meyer had learned of Trevor Dempsey's death. That was the way it used to be with the rest of the collective. The filter between it and the humans was once enough to catch any junk trying to seep in.

Not anymore. Not if Eternity couldn't see reason due to an infiltration of human emotion. Not if Eternity was willing to expend so much time and so many resources creating living quarters that were so much finer than Divinity's.

Her hand circled the lamp. It stood on the floor, its neck rising to her shoulder, placed beside a comfortable-looking chair as if Eternity's surrogate planned to plop itself down for some reading. The lamp had a cord even though its power source was induction. The cord, just for show, was plugged into an outlet that was also just dressing.

She put a second hand on the lamp's neck.

She hefted it, ripping the cord from the wall.

With the heavy end of the lamp held high, choked up on like the baseball bat so recently under discussion with the problematic Mr. Dempsey, Divinity paused for a second before swinging.

Then she smashed the lamp's business end through the glass top of a coffee table. She swung it at a painting (Matisse? She wasn't sure; she'd studied only the human culture that mattered to her function, which just so happened to be what interested her most) and when she did, the lamp's heavy square base dug its corner through the canvas, ripping it. She pivoted, teeth bared, and took a second to study her crazed reflection in Eternity's beveled mirror before reducing it to shards.

Her pulse quickened with every assault. Chemicals flooded her surrogate's brain. Her arms grew momentarily strong, wanting to flex and extend of their own accord.

She saw everything with fresh clarity, heart hammering high in her throat, the air so unnecessary to her usual (old) form raking in and out. For a half minute — no more — there was only the delicious pulse of fury. Then it ended as quickly as it began, and Divinity was left heaving great gulps into her lungs, hair askew and eyes all whites in the shattered mirror's leaning shards.

She dropped the lamp. Then, after a thought, Divinity kicked it aside. Then, because the lamp had won each of its bashing encounters and that didn't seem fair, she picked it up again and this time swung it with arms, legs, and torso working together into the bare concrete of a hearth around a patently unnecessary fireplace. It snapped more than broke, but she let it fall for good this time, staring at it as if daring it to rise up and challenge her again.

Divinity wanted to run. Something in her told her to leave this place.

Instead, she flopped into a black chair with chrome legs and surveyed the carnage.

Look what you made me do, she thought at no one in particular. The collective wouldn't hear her. These days it was more natural to not feed into nor draw thoughts from it. Doing so took a small act of mental switching, to light the connection.

This situation was intolerable. She'd come here to argue a point with Eternity, and instead she'd made the point's tip finer on her own. Either way, difficult choices needed to be made. Perhaps she'd frightened Meyer into giving up his people — his *Archetypes* that were causing so much worsening from the human end — but there were no guarantees that his mind would even be able to locate them. Even if it *could*, it wasn't a certainty that Meyer would tattle. She might have frightened him with the bluff of destroying their planet for good. But on the other hand,

Meyer was seeing things clearer and clearer — and he might have seen that threat for the bullshit it was.

Of *course* they couldn't simply destroy humanity. The bond had grown too strong. Divinity had checked the stream after Eternity's return from abducting Carl Nairobi, and knew just how much *diving deep and hurting Carl* had injured Eternity, too. It's why Divinity had spoken with Meyer instead of hooking him up to a mind probe. But he was starting to understand things. He might have known why Divinity didn't do what she could have, and seen it as a weakness.

It was a good thing they'd set their contingency plan into place. Divinity didn't want to use it any more than Eternity (well, okay, that wasn't true; right now, she felt a lot like ruining things), but contingencies were there for a reason.

She should find Eternity and discuss moving forward with Plan B.

But, looking around the surrogate storage room, Divinity somehow doubted that Eternity would listen as objectively as she would have had Divinity found her instead of an empty apartment.

Well. They were a collective. Nobody was truly in charge. They did what was best for all, every time. She didn't need Eternity's support. Not when Eternity was so focused on primping and decorating and giving herself a human name.

Divinity had her ace in the hole.

She still had the Villain, already working.

Chapter Twenty-Eight

THE SUN WAS HOT. Liza marched on with her shirt off, ancient brassiere showcased as half of the new world's first bikini. Most of the women here went commando up top, but not Liza. She hadn't forgotten as others had, so she'd spirited those bras away and kept using them under her shirts, damn the anachronism. Maybe it was more natural to let 'em hang. But she'd been set in her ways and wasn't about to go hippie now.

She draped her doffed blouse across her shoulders, vacillating between two equally unappealing options: the intense heat of her unfortunately dark clothing or sunburn from exposure. She'd never tanned well. Her hair was light brown but fair and fine, and she had her father's freckles. She'd survived this place in the shade but now could practically smell herself sizzling like bacon.

Liza stopped again, sloughed sideways in the shade, and gave thanks to a God she didn't believe in that she'd been zapped to whereverthefuck with a bag still hanging from her shoulder. She still had the half-full bottle of water, plus an unopened one from the cache on the bridge. But on the flip side, she also had no clue where she was. One moment she'd been running around the freighter deck and seeing Reptars everywhere; then the next she'd been in the middle of nowhere with zero landmarks in sight. It was a lot like what had happened earlier, only without the sleepy awakening. This time the memory webs between one place and the next weren't fuzzy as they'd been when she'd appeared near the monolith after tending her plants. This time, the jump-cut between freighter deck and open desert was instantaneous, as if she'd blinked and been transported like in *I Dream of Jeannie*.

Well, it almost made sense. Lost time and a sense of dislocation, be it a smooth or snap transition? Either fit. Liza was simply losing her mind.

She screwed the plastic cap off the half-full bottle. She should ration her water given that she didn't know how far she had to go, but kind of fuck that. So instead she raised the uncapped bottle to a pointy succulent at the edge of her shade hollow and said, "Cheers." Then she downed it all and tossed the bottle into the sun. If the environmentalists were right, that bottle would last a few thousand years before degrading. Maybe she should stuff a note inside, and leave it for the aliens' next return.

Liza considered staying put until she starved to death. What would it matter? She was off her gourd. Maybe dying would be fun for her ruined mind. Maybe she'd even lose all the time between now and then, waking up a half skeleton this time, remembering the good old days when she'd had love handles.

But eventually Liza stood — a position that regrettably took her halfway out of the small patch of rock-thrown shade. She raised a hand to her forehead and squinted into the distance. The sun was lower but not low enough to offer any real relief. And maybe that was, finally, a better argument to stay where she was and not set out to gather more skin cancer. But there was urgency beside her apathy, and of the two, the first was stronger.

It's in the canyon, at the bend, beneath where the sun sets.

What a bunch of bullshit. She didn't even know what *it* was. And even if she did — and if she agreed it was worth hauling a bit more ass through the desert to find *right now* — she had no idea where that wise bit of instructions assumed she was starting from. Head for the setting sun from Place A, and you'll find Spot B. But if you start a thousand miles north at Place C and do the exact same thing, you'd end up somewhere entirely different. An instruction as helpful as "park under the moon."

"This is stupid," Liza said aloud.

But she walked on anyway. And within a half hour or so, Liza saw a dark slash in the sand ahead. Another fifteen or so minutes showed her, once up a rise, that the slash was a canyon. The sun had been taking its sweet time descending all day and wasn't moving much faster now, but there was a bend in that dark slash, and Liza's eye predicted it'd set right at the curve, perfectly on target.

It's in the canyon.

What was?

But at this point it didn't matter. Liza hadn't wanted to be at the monolith, but at least it had given her a signpost. She knew approximately where the village was from the old beached ship, and she'd been with people, even though they'd been people she *knew of* more than *knew* — let alone cared about. They hadn't exchanged more than a few words, but still they'd been humans. Now she was alone. Without any landmarks. She could be a half mile from a known location, or on a different continent. Anything could happen when you kept finding yourself teleported to strange new places and slowly going insane.

"Fine," Liza said, marching on because there was nowhere else to go. And then she added inside her own head because speaking aloud felt so funny, *But you could at least tell me what I'm after.*

She didn't expect a response, mostly because there was no one around and the thought had been confined to her own crazy skull.

But she got one. Clear as day, before internal eyes, Liza saw a familiar-looking backpack — one she'd used as a twentysomething to trek across Europe, saved for no reason through all her years in Roman Sands, and finally dug from hock and packed once she realized the end was finally nigh.

That backpack had disappeared from her home one night not long after they'd settled in at The Clearing, vanished like so many other belongings. The culprit had left valuables in exchange for things of no consequence. It hadn't made sense.

Liza had always wondered why someone had raided their village in such a specific way. She'd suspected *whom* — her money was on Stranger and his minions. Because whereas Liza had formed her religion for control, Stranger's competing religion seemed based on faith. And with faith always came fear.

The image persisted, like a picture burned into an ancient TV.

Why the hell would her old backpack be out here?

And if that's what she was really after, why did she feel such a burning impetus to recover it from its apparent hiding place *right now* given that it had been gone for twenty years?

"You suck," she said to whoever or whatever was inside her head.

Liza walked. The image of her old hiking pack strobed before it faded, unseen hands at her back, shoving Liza toward her puzzling prize.

Chapter Twenty-Nine

By the time night descended on the second day of human memory, the small settlement had bunkered itself down in what was, despite all the chaos, upheaval, and death, now feeling like the dawn of a new normal. Clara doubted she'd spend many hours in Kamal's little village, but another night felt comforting. She had Piper back; she had Kindred back; she had Stranger back … Hell, she even had *Logan* back, for what that particular loose end was worth. She hadn't spent half her day in a trance for a while, and for once was getting used to living without the feel of an Astral boot on her neck. It was nice to *simply exist* after twenty long years of fighting.

Clara turned her head. Logan was spooned behind her, his hand draped over her side. He'd come to comfort her, but as hours passed he'd finally fallen asleep. She supposed the whole thing was okay. Maybe she even liked it, though in truth it was hard to say. In the purest sense, she and Logan had once loved each other — and despite what he'd surely thought, Clara hadn't stopped loving from her end just as he'd never stopped from his. But the days when her endless work hadn't been wedged between them were long ago.

Clara slipped out from under Logan's arm, laying it gently on the hand-woven blanket. She looked back at him, taking a moment to wonder. He'd never stopped being a good man. They hadn't lost their pasts, but Kamal's people had. Who had woven that blanket? A filing clerk? An Ember Flats Senate page? What necessities had driven this settlement? And what coincidences were yet to unfold in this carefully crafted drama to surprise them all?

Before leaving the hut, Clara moved to the other pad and checked on Piper. She was asleep like Logan, with a loose lock of dark brown hair spilled across her forehead. With her eyelids shut, her big blue eyes were invisible — charming weapons disarmed, shut now to look inside where demons played.

Light spilled through the cracked door. There was a small plastic-edged travel mirror nearby so she picked it up to look herself over. Her eyes, so far as she could see in the scant light, were no longer puffy or red. Tears, once Peers had confirmed what Clara already knew, had finally come with the night to cut clean tracks through the filth on her face. But there was a basin near the mirror, so Clara used a rag to wipe herself until she was presentable. Then she turned to the door, and the source of light.

A fire burned ahead, low but far from coals. To the right she saw a lump in the open sand: Kindred sleeping. And to the left — exactly the same distance away, in an identical position on the opposite side — was Stranger.

Clara grabbed another government-intern-made blanket from the pile and wrapped it around herself like a shawl to shield the winter chill. She moved forward, watching two heads turn to greet her as the third, across the fire, lifted its chin to watch her approach.

"You're awake," said Sadeem.

"I couldn't sleep."

"Your mother?"

"It's a lot of things. Can you feel the network, Sadeem?"

Peers and Kamal both looked back at Sadeem, but the old man simply shook his head.

"I've never really been able to."

"I'm surprised Kindred and Stranger can sleep. The network itself is becoming brighter and more alive, but every time I closed my eyes, it was like those two were standing right beside me. They're so bright inside. And they're …" She frowned, then finally shrugged resignation. "I don't know. *Different* somehow."

"We were talking about that," said Sadeem. "Come, sit."

As Clara was deciding where to plant herself, Peers and Kamal both moved aside to widen the space between them.

"Please," Peers said. "Kamal says he's forgiven me for assaulting him back in Ember Flats, but I don't trust him."

"It was mostly that woman anyway. Jeanine, I think. But yes. I am planning to kill Peers in his sleep. Not because I'm still mad. But, because … you know. To close the circle."

The stupid jab of humor was, in the dark and quiet, surprisingly rousing. Clara felt her lips turn up despite trying to hold her face serious. Then she sat.

"They *do* seem different," Sadeem continued, looking at Peers. "In some very … *significant* … ways. We think it happened when your mother passed. Based on what Kamal said he learned from Mara Jabari, a similar *change* happened in the first Titan replica of Meyer when your uncle, Trevor, was killed."

"What kind of change?"

Peers turned to Clara. "Did Piper tell you how we got here? To where we were when you came over the dune to find us?"

"She was too upset about Mom. She said she'd tell me later."

"What about Kindred? Stranger? Did they say anything?"

"I haven't talked much to either of them. I ran up to Kindred when we found you and hugged him. Stranger wouldn't come to me, so I had to go to him. But it's like I said: They're different somehow. They still won't go near each other — even though when I look inside, it's like they're magnets. They've always had that attraction on the network, but it's so much stronger. Now, to resist the pull, it's like they've reached some sort of agreement. If one can't do something, they *both* won't do it. I feel like they want to talk to me. But they can only do it together, and won't approach each other."

Clara looked at Peers. "So how did you get here?"

Peers glanced at Sadeem as if for authorization. Then he said, "We teleported."

Clara's mouth opened, then stalled.

"I'm sorry?"

"I know how it sounds. But it happened. Piper, Kindred, Stranger, and that woman from the rectory — Liza Knight — were on the freighter. Astrals were everywhere. They'd been hiding in the shipping containers, guarding something, and we woke them. We were dead for sure. But then all of a sudden we were gone from the freighter and right where you found us."

"You lost time," Clara said. "The Astrals did something to you then dropped you off."

"No. Something happened. We all felt it. I don't know what happened to Liza, but I'm sure of what happened to the rest of us. You could feel something in the air. Like the charge before a thunderstorm, or static in a thick carpet. There was something on the ship, Clara. Kindred and Stranger were ... powering it, maybe. Or powered *by* it. Stranger said it felt like he suddenly understood that there was no *here* or there and that he could just sort of step sideways and leave. And, it seems, take the rest of us with him. With *them.*" Peers emphasized the final word with a glance toward Kindred.

"But *teleporting?* How is that possible?"

Peers shrugged. "I guess possibility isn't what it used to be."

Clara shook her head, at a loss. Apparently the three of them had been discussing absurdities for a while.

"Peers thinks Kindred and Stranger are the King Archetype," said Sadeem. "Two heads. Maybe the power on the ship can somehow join them. Make new things happen."

"What power?"

"The Ark, maybe," said Peers. "But how it got there is another story."

"I thought you said the King's two heads were Kindred and my grandpa."

"Maybe they were," Sadeem replied. "Who knows? Maybe they shift. It made sense, at the beginning, that you'd be the Innocent. But now what you do is more like magic, and the things you say make me think that *magic* is still growing. Peers was once the Fool, but sometimes now he has the knowledge of a Sage."

Sadeem's eyes flicked toward Peers, who looked away.

Clara was curious but not enough to pry. She'd long felt a secret in Peers, somewhere deep, both when he'd had his memories and when he hadn't. But now that secret felt dulled, as if finally confessed. She would learn the truth if she needed it, but for now was content to grant the man his privacy.

"Perhaps the Mullah wrote one legend on top of another," Peers said. "People used to say that uncertainty was the only certainty in life. The Legend Scroll mentions the Seven Archetypes, but if they came from chaos, who's to say the legend itself couldn't have uncertainty within it? Maybe the Archetypes can change. Perhaps its predictions are prophecies that shift in the wind."

"Not very useful, then."

"Even random can be predictable, Clara," Sadeem said. "If things occur randomly for long enough, eventually every given possibility will occur."

"I'm too tired to understand that."

"It's like those thousand monkeys at a thousand typewriters," Kamal said. "If you let them go on forever, they'll eventually write Shakespeare."

"Right," agreed Sadeem.

"If you don't let them type long enough," Kamal added, "they'll only write *Valley of the Dolls.*"

"Clara," Sadeem said, throwing Kamal a look, "what was it you said to Logan before we left the Mullah caves? When you grabbed my arm. Something about your cousin."

"Cousin Timmy."

Sadeem nodded.

"It's a thing Stranger used to say. Almost like his catchphrase. Funny thing is, my grandpa had a Cousin Tim. When I mentioned it around him one time, he lit up. For a while I thought he might be getting his memories back, but it was just a dead end."

"Is it the same Tim? In Stranger's expression and your grandfather's family?"

"How could it be?"

Again, Sadeem, Peers, and Kamal traded a knowing glance. What had they already discussed — and maybe decided — that they weren't willing to say?

"Just tell us what it means to you, Clara," Peers said.

"It was about underestimating people. Pigeonholing them, then trivializing their abilities. Stranger once told me a story to go with the expression, but I didn't know my grandpa had a Cousin Tim until after the Forgetting. I don't see how they could be related."

"Why did you say it to me?" Sadeem asked.

"I was still sort of in a trance. You started getting all worried and going on and on, and it just came to me."

"As a rebuttal? I was worried, and you wanted to assure me that there was nothing to worry about?"

Clara thought. She'd just come out of her semi-coma. She'd been fully mental for a while, seeing the human grid, seeing the wall finally fall to release the Astrals' meddling repression from their memories. The moment it collapsed, a strong red force had lashed out and grabbed her from the Astral side, pinning her down and refusing to let her move. She'd barely been conscious when she'd said that to Sadeem, still half-submerged.

"I don't know, Sadeem."

"It might be important, Clara."

"I'm sorry. I don't know."

His eyes flashed with intensity. *"Think!"*

"I … I don't know," Clara stammered, taken aback. "I guess I had this feeling that you shouldn't count us out.

That you were forgetting something important, and that we weren't just victims."

"Us as in *us?* Or us as in humanity?"

"Humanity. I think."

"But why?"

"Stranger's story was about a musician. Someone whose family and friends never really gave him any credit, even after he made it big, because he was always *just Cousin Timmy.* To them, he was worth encouraging because he had dreams of being a star, but not because of his talent. Stranger described it as a backhanded compliment. Someone who got patted on the head and patronized rather than given his due."

"What does that have to do with humanity and the Astrals?"

Clara was about to repeat that she didn't know and maybe add that she wished Sadeem would leave her alone about some random thing she'd said while basically high, but then someone took Clara's hand. Kamal, to her surprise.

"Close your eyes, Clara."

Clara looked at the three men. She saw Sadeem's urgent gaze, Peers's patient stare, and Kamal's oddly understanding expression.

"I have something to tell you that may help. Something I think I'm *supposed* to tell you, and that I'm only just now starting to understand. But before I say it, I need you to close your eyes, take a deep breath, and tell me if you can see your grandfather on that network of yours. The grid that shows all the minds left in this place, recovering their memories. The place you spent all your time while trying to fight the Forgetting. Tell me if you can see Meyer there now, Clara, at his place in that network of human consciousness."

Clara closed her eyes, seeing the fire's red-orange through her lids.

She drew a deep breath.

Then another.

And another.

She could see her grandfather, just as Kamal had asked. A bright node like all the others, his connections somehow different. It took her a while to see why, but then she did. The nodes representing individuals were connected mind to mind, each touching others around them. The matrix shifted and moved, nodes floating in front of her vision like icebergs through an ocean of light. The nodes moved — old connections broke, and new ones formed. But each always kept about the same number of connections to the rest — five or six per person at any time, humanity's remainders joined like neurons in a brain.

All except for her grandfather.

He was connected to them *all*.

"I see him," she said with subtle awe, watching his instance on the grid and seeing how the connections were all brightening, growing strong like strings in a braid. It hadn't been this way before. This was something new.

"Have they underestimated him?" Kamal asked. "Is it possible the Astrals knew Meyer Dempsey as one thing but aren't quite able to see that he's grown into something more? Is it possible that just like *Cousin Timmy* in Stranger's story, your grandfather isn't a person the Astrals can see for who he really is … even if the truth is right in front of their alien faces?"

Clara opened her eyes. Peers and Sadeem were watching Kamal as intently as she was. Whatever Kamal was insinuating, the others hadn't seen it coming any more than Clara had.

Instead of answering, Clara asked a question.

"He's an Astral, isn't he? All this time, we thought he was back — but my grandfather's like Kindred, isn't he? Just another copy of the real Meyer Dempsey?"

Kamal's lips pursed into a smile and slowly shook his head.

"Close," he said, "but no cigar."

Chapter Thirty

"They can hear you."

"Of course they can hear me."

"They can *see* us."

"Of course they can see us!"

"Meyer ..."

"Dammit, Carl, I meant what I said. Will you just fucking—"

"Setting aside the fact that I might kill you, I can't possibly imagine how this will—"

He was still learning the trick, but with a parody of fingers-crossed Meyer pushed in what felt like the right mental spot, doing his best to squeeze Carl's gray matter from within the neural network. He doubted he could control minds, but he sure could see a lot more than he used to. What he was doing wasn't quite like a vampire glamouring prey, but it didn't feel that far off. Carl's mental node, even from the inside, still felt like its own thing. But with the right pressure applied, Meyer bet he could make what amounted to a very strong argument.

"Just do it," Meyer said.

"What if I paralyze you? I don't even see why you'd want—"

"Just do it!"

Carl wrapped his enormous arm around Meyer's neck and squeezed. Meyer was blacking out, thinking he'd made a rather obnoxious mistake in judgment and readying himself to tap out when the door slid open and two Titans entered. The tall blonde who called herself Eternity clacked along behind him on tall black heels.

Push.

Shove.

All from inside the new headspace, pushing Carl's will around like a child strapped in a stroller.

Carl turned, his spine obeying like a reflex in the fractional second before his cortex received and evaluated the message. This had felt like the dangerous make-or-break moment in Meyer's plan. Carl was right; the Astrals would see and hear everything that he and Meyer did. But if past experience had taught him anything, they'd probably hear their *thoughts* as well. Meyer felt confident that he could keep the aliens out of his head, but he wasn't so sure about Carl.

Carl had to believe that Meyer wanted Carl to make him pass out, when in truth Meyer *actually* wanted the Astrals to rush in after they saw what was happening. Then, in the space of seconds, the *real* plan would force Meyer to push Carl in a different direction.

If he couldn't "convince" Carl quickly, the plan was dead before its birth. Meyer wasn't big, fast, or strong enough to do what had to be done. He was sixty-eight fucking years old, his wrestling days long behind him.

Push.

Shove.

Meyer felt recognition click — along with a bit of

knee-jerk resentment wherein Carl felt annoyed by Meyer's deception.

Despite the rush, Carl didn't hesitate. Meyer flopped to the floor as Carl released him, landing at the first Titan's bare feet. The second Titan moved to intercept Carl but was predictably slow. Carl moved like a bolt, easily dodging. Titans could be fast when necessary, but Carl needed only a second. By the time the Titan spun to where Carl had dashed behind him, he had Eternity in the headlock he'd promised to Meyer.

"You're kidding," Eternity said, her smooth-as-silk voice coming out in a croak. "Tell me you're kidding."

Meyer grabbed one of the Titans. It turned and gave him a pleasant, no-offense-intended smile. The other was still moving toward Carl but hesitated when he dragged Eternity two quick steps back and tightened his python's grip on her neck.

"Let us out of here," Meyer said. "Send us back to the surface."

"Don't be ridiculous."

"Show her how ridiculous we are, Carl."

Carl squeezed. Eternity made an urgent squeaking, waving an arm.

"Ready to send us back?"

The Titans were looking at Eternity as if awaiting instructions. Carl was meeting them eye to eye, keeping his distance. The Titans seemed to be weighing whether they could get to Carl before he ended Eternity, and deciding correctly (in Meyer's opinion, anyway) that they couldn't.

"I can't send you back. The Archetypes are all we have."

"Sounds to me like that's your fucking problem, not ours," said Carl.

"You can't kill me. This body is only a mouthpiece.

We're a collective. If you stop this body's functioning, it'll be no different than when Clara's father killed your—"

"Do you think I don't know about that?" Meyer asked. "Your girlfriend was just in here, acting shocked at what I 'pretended' to know and not know. She was talking about me knowing myself, which I've been pretty good at since I started Fable and decided that being a sonofabitch wasn't a bad management strategy and leaned right into it. But I know what happened when Raj killed him, and I doubt you're interested in having another—"

(Meyer Dempsey)

"—death on your hands."

"Death is immaterial," the woman said from under Carl's flexing armpit. "Even for you. A body is only a body, and what matters is the energy that's always free to—"

"Show her that death is immaterial, Carl."

Carl squeezed. The woman made a gurgling noise, her feet frantic. The Titans advanced, and Carl pushed them back with his eyes, muscles tight.

"We can't send you back! You don't understand!"

"Make her understand, Carl."

"Wait!"

Meyer crossed to Carl, bent, and punched the woman in the gut. Air left her human lungs. She grunted, face paled, panic etched on her features as she fought in vain to inhale. Carl stared the Titans back as Meyer squatted to look Eternity in her eyes.

"I know you took this body to be your puppet. I used to share Kindred's memories, and part of me remembers what it was like for him, standing in front of something like you, a giant light-filled anemone behind the puppet, controlling it. I've got insights coming at me so fast these days, I might break." He snapped his fingers, and Eternity, still gasping for air, flinched. "It takes my breath away. But

I think I know something else about you, and although I'm new to this, I think I can see it from the inside as well as out. I think you're used to living in that body and are more attached to being an individual than you should be. I think you look yourself over in the mirror, wondering how it would feel to be born like us, and have that body admired by someone else. I think that no matter how much mind-over-matter bullshit you claim, right now you don't *need* air to keep *living* by your usual definition but desperately want it anyway."

Eternity's chest heaved, and she gasped, the effort of drawing breath bringing tears to her eyes.

"You're going to let us go. If you don't, Carl will snap your neck. It won't take much. Look at his arms. I'll bet he can pop your head all the way off like the top of a dandelion."

"It won't make any difference," she said, her breath still coming in gasps, eyes still streaming.

"It'll make a difference to you."

"We have to fix you. If we can't, we must destroy you all."

Meyer felt an acid grin spread across his face.

"But you can't do that, can you? I can see into my friend here and into you. I know that when you tried to do something to him earlier, it hurt you, too. You've stayed here too long. You've gone native. You started so high above, but now you're more like us than you want to be. Look at you. The individual doesn't matter, does it? Yet here we are, holding your entire race captive just because we've got one little toy and are willing to break it if we don't get our way."

"If we let you go, everyone loses," she said.

"Better everyone than just us."

"You won't make it. Even if we let you go, you can't

leave the ship. Maybe I do care, but the infection cuts both ways. We're no longer an unclouded collective. Others will stand in your way no matter what I say."

"You mean the other woman? The short one?"

"I mean just about any—"

A soft electric sound cut her off. Something lanced into Carl's shoulder from the rear, through the open door. Meyer looked up to see another two Titans approaching, weapons raised.

They looked angry.

The Titans looked *angry*.

Meyer rammed into Carl and Eternity, sending them sideways, out of the doorway. He could already see the back of Carl's shoulder spilling blood where he'd been hit by the weapon. There was no time to explain, or hesitate. As bad as this had become, it would only get worse.

Push.

Carl moved, throwing Meyer an annoyed glance for not speaking aloud.

Not away from the armed Titans but toward them.

They must not have predicted it; the Titans staggered back as Meyer and Carl, still holding Eternity, charged forward. They still should have had time to shoot again, but Carl held Eternity high like a shield, dangling with her feet kicking and one absent its shoe. They raised their weapons, sighted, failed to shoot. And in that split second's hesitation, Meyer and Carl acted, Carl punching one of them hard enough with his free fist to crack something in the wall behind him as the Titan's head rebounded from it. Meyer took the other, apparently more spry than he'd anticipated. The Titan's size worked against it as the alien moved to grab Meyer's much smaller form; he stepped back, reared ahead, and drove his elbow into the Astral's nose. The Titan didn't take it in stride, or transform, putting its hand to its face and falling back in obvious pain. Meyer grabbed its weapon from the floor and aimed it, confused for milliseconds, seeing ahead but not far enough.

Just keep moving.

He didn't know where he was going. Except that he did. The Deathbringer ship was orders of magnitude larger than the ship he'd been imprisoned upon before, but now he could see through a crack in the wall: a glimpse, reaching a tendril into the collective. Shaking hands with something — a piece of himself, perhaps, stolen while they held him captive like a ghost.

And at each turn, seconds in advance of reaching it, Meyer saw where to go.

Right. Right. Left.

They ran into Reptars. Carl held Eternity up again, but the Reptars came anyway. Meyer raised the Titan's weapon. It fired like a human rifle. Perhaps a benefit of being seeded from Astral stock — *made in the image of* seemed also to mean *able to fire the weapons of.*

One's head was obliterated, walls coated with gore like a paintball fight. The other wounded, down one leg.

On.

And on.

Finally a door. Eternity bucking in Carl's grip, squirming like a child throwing a tantrum. She bore down and bit hard. Carl shouted and released her, blood now gushing from his earlier wound. His shirt was soaked red down the back, air pungent with the tang of fresh meat.

Meyer lunged and struck her sidelong, more unintentionally tackling than successfully reaching. Eternity rolled to the side and struck the bulkhead. Meyer was reaching deep, grabbing the collective and squeezing, searching for access. The door behind them purred open as a single

Reptar rounded the corner. Meyer had lost his weapon when he'd leaped after Eternity, and the thing was coming, coming, coming …

NO!

But it was too late. Carl had acted before Meyer could prevent it. One big hand on his chest, pushing Meyer down, through the open door. He had Eternity by the wrist. She was off-balance on one shod foot; she tumbled after him, and they landed in a heap.

He got one last look at Carl, who'd put himself between the Reptar and Meyer.

The door closed.

Many sounds followed. But as his body was ripped apart, Carl didn't cry out.

Chapter Thirty-One

"SHE'S *WHERE?*"

The Titan stared dumbly at Divinity, its weapon dangling from a strap on its bone-white shoulder.

"Is your jaw broken?"

No, his jaw isn't broken, said an internal voice that Divinity knew *wasn't* the collective and that she had no reason hearing in a world where everything wasn't going to shit. *He's a Titan, and Titans don't speak.*

Internally, she said: *Show me.*

The Titan seemed to settle, as if it appreciated Divinity's return to form. She could feel the information coming at her, but it took a moment's concerted effort before she could switch her own internal eye to see it.

When the scene from the collective stream was finished — the entire thing witnessed from various Titan and Reptar perspectives as they chased Meyer through corridors — Divinity opened her eyes. She felt dizzy. A scene like that shouldn't be difficult to pull from the stream and review in all its minutiae, but she was out of practice. Being many minds at once should have felt natural, but instead it gave her vertigo. But she had the required information, and now it seemed she wouldn't need to face Eternity's reaction to Divinity artfully rearranging her quarters after all. Not as long as Eternity remained as focused inside her surrogate's limited mind as Divinity was in hers. For a while now (to borrow a human expression she'd pulled from their media and particularly liked), Eternity would have bigger fish to fry.

But the location where Meyer had dragged her — and the insinuations that came with it — were inconvenient at best, troublesome at worst.

"The Nexus. You're telling me of all the places he could have taken her, he's holding her in *the Nexus*."

The Titan didn't respond, either in voice or body language. It hadn't *told* Divinity anything. And Titans didn't understand figures of speech, so the thing just stood in front of her like a big white wall.

"Do you think it was intentional? Did he know what that place was?"

The Titan didn't seem to think anything.

"Do you think he's planning something, or is he grasping at straws?"

The Titan offered no opinion.

"This way." Irritated, Divinity marched off. The Titan followed.

A few minutes later, she found herself in the circular white space they called Control. Quite the misnomer. There weren't (technically) any individuals in the collective, and so (in theory) the combined, always-agreeing will of the average within range could pilot the ship from anywhere and everywhere. And thus, there was no need for a space dedicated to control. In the usual order of things, most steering decisions were made without any questions asked, then executed from wherever the crews' bodies just so happened to be without a single finger or claw raised. But this was hardly the usual order. Now the ship's commander (when, in fact, the ship wasn't *technically* supposed to have one) was being held hostage, and the captor seemed willing to kill her if approached — something that *technically* didn't matter.

But it somehow did, and the entire ship had snapped right into order. Titans were responding like human police. Reptars were grunts with rifles, eager to shoot the bad guys. Divinity supposed that made her the FBI negotiator. But the whole thing was embarrassing. The thing held hostage was one meaningless shell used by a localized intelligence blip. They should storm the Nexus and drag Dempsey back to his cell. But Eternity was at the center of this ship's cluster, and apparently "Melanie" was inappropriately afraid enough for them all.

At least two dozen Titans had congregated in Control, directly above the organic nerve facilitating the ship's collective operation. They'd come as if drawn, though nobody had drawn them. When Divinity entered, white heads turned and seemed to brighten, as if relieved that the second in command (though there *technically* was no such thing, and Divinity *technically* belonged on her own ship rather than this one) would know what to do.

Well. It didn't matter if the whole Earthbound occupation contingent had gone whacky. Divinity had her own aims, and if their confusion could help her achieve them, it was a good thing. Lemons into lemonade, and all of that.

"Dispatch a shuttle to BR-1 ..." She trailed off, not wanting to spool off the long string of coordinates and frustrated that she couldn't give simple directions like, "Go to the big rock, and turn right." She set her surrogate's mind's focus and delivered her order.

But it must have transmitted as weakly as it felt, because the Titans gave no signs of acknowledgement.

She tried again, focusing more carefully, turning her increasingly default human vocabulary into Astral terms.

Go get what I want from the place it's hidden.

But again, no reaction.

Finally, a weak signal returned. It was the collective — or, hell, maybe even an individual somewhere nearby — attempting to speak Divinity's adopted language. The signal was as pathetic as she imagined her own Astral language sounded to the collective, and her mind interpreted it as:

Focus must remain with the situation on the ship.

"The situation on the ship depends on doing as I say," she said aloud. "Look at you. You're diverting the entire fleet's mission because one pointless human body has been threatened. It isn't logical. The collective has been so infected that irrational judgments are being made. Do as I say. We need to cure the disease, not the symptoms."

She heard, *???*

Seeing absolutely no motion from inside the collective in Divinity's intended direction, she sent a snapshot of her intentions inside.

Overload the system like a human body uses a fever to burn off intruding organisms. This is the only way.

She wanted to punch herself. Even her explanations centered on human metaphors the Titans could never understand, let alone be moved by — again, assuming Titans could be *moved* at all, when naturally they couldn't. They were just *things* within the grand scheme, like Eternity's surrogate body.

She pushed, explaining further. Argued the point. Insisted on the logic of it all.

But the collective pushed back. She'd already made

these suggestions, and Eternity had said no. Eternity felt the human Archetypes were the way to go, and that once the Archetypes were rounded up and eliminated, their problems on Planet Earth would finally be over. The Forgetting could finish, and they could fly out to the rift, go home, and leave this rock alone for a few more thousand years.

She's wrong.

And still the collective responded to Divinity as if it knew none of its own rules and didn't understand the same laws she herself kept disobeying.

It doesn't matter. She's in charge of this ship. Not you.

Which was a lie.

Which, really, was *worse* than a lie because it was based on false assumptions. There was no *she*. Or *in charge*. They were human concepts that made no sense to the hive.

And still the Titans stared at Divinity as she stood in the center of Control. Not because they were unaware or stupid, Divinity now felt certain. It was more accurate to say they were being defiant. They knew the coup she was trying to stage and found her attempts laughable at best, treasonous at worst.

There is no treason in a collective.

But the Titans' eyes no longer seemed vacant, fixed and unmoving upon her.

Our "leader" is unable to make decisions, Divinity thought into the hive, deciding to lay it all out and go for an absurd kind of hierarchical broke. *I am next in command, and it is my will that you dispatch a shuttle to the canyon to—*

A thought interrupted Divinity's: *It is forbidden to interfere once an epoch has begun.* Her solo mind was gifted with a dozen images of things they all knew. The reminders were insulting.

No contact, other than by the seeds.

No undue influence.

The archive must not be touched.

And once the reset is complete and an epoch is unspooling, human artifacts must lie where they've been left.

Divinity felt something strike her mind like an arrow. She spun. This little lecture wasn't coming from the collective stream. It was coming from *right here in this room*, from someone who didn't know any better than Divinity that their race didn't possess individual minds.

"Who is doing that?" she asked.

Blank stares.

She pushed out, sending anger out like a black wave. Stares remained blank, but several Titans, feeling it in an unfiltered, not-via-the-stream way they had no business feeling, flinched.

But there was one, a rough concentric circle back, whose eyes moved as well.

Divinity moved forward. She stood before the flickering Titan. A male, easily a foot taller than Divinity, even in her ridiculous human heels. It must have been one of the crew set on alert when Meyer captured Divinity because it was carrying a weapon. At first she wondered if this one might have killed Carl Nairobi and solved another of their Archetype problems, but no — that had been a Reptar, and there'd been no transforming.

"You," she said. "Walk over to the manual controls. Put your palm on the panel to activate it. Then enter the coordinates I gave earlier, to send a shuttle."

At first the Titan's mind said nothing — or at least nothing Divinity's mind could hear. But she could tell he was playing chicken, such that Titans knew how. A non-response was appropriate, seeing as they worked collectively. But this was the one who'd challenged her directly, and he was fooling no one.

She could see his big white face twitching, though it should have looked blank.

She could see the grip on his weapon's strap tightening.

And although Titan bodies only perspired to cool the skin, this one had beaded sweat on its brow, as if his body thought it was a different kind — one that perspired from emotion.

"You're sick," Divinity said, knowing she'd created an airtight trap. Titans were supposed to obey because the collective commanded it, and right now Divinity had an internal fist on this part of the whole. But it couldn't protest something as vague as an accusation of illness when the concept didn't make sense — nor accept her assessment of sickness as a sign of something gone truly wrong.

"There's something on this ship. Don't you see it?" Divinity said, too close to the Titan's motionless face — or, due to their height difference, his chin. "The human collective is more resilient than we've seen before. It's aggressive and has infected *our* collective. Even now, it's growing, both out there in the wild and in our ships. There is only one way to solve the problem. Only one way for us all to get well again. And it's not what Eternity thinks."

Her words and her stare must have got to the Titan — either that, or he knew he wasn't fooling anyone and decided to surrender the act. Because although his lips didn't move, she heard his rebuttal as clearly as if he'd been a human man speaking her adopted language aloud.

We must eliminate their Archetypes. Two are already dead.

"It's not just the Archetypes. It's also the Lightborn. They held the door open the first time, and they'll do it again, Archetypes or no Archetypes. And now the Lightborn have children of their own, born awake. We can't find them all. They have their own collective now, and all it takes is one to keep the infection alive and spread it." Divinity's lips pursed. She'd studied this next part, and it was maddening. "Someone saw to it that the network of those survivors had enough talent to do that all on its own — even if only one Lightborn, anywhere, ever, remains alive."

We will follow the plan.

"We can't kill them all. Ask Eternity. She felt what happened when they pushed too hard into Carl Nairobi's mind. We're bound to them, like two organisms sharing a bloodstream. You can't destroy one without destroying the other. Not anymore."

You are not in charge, the Titan's mind protested, still sweating at his hairless brow, his eyes still straight forward and averted.

"Eternity is fighting a futile battle because she's become too human. But there is another way."

Irrelevant. The collective follows commands.

Divinity pushed her plan into the Titan. Into the collective. She'd already explained it to Eternity, but Eternity had emotional reasons for refusing, not logical ones, and thus had gone soft.

It will not work. You cannot increase the force of the Forgetting so far. It will blank them entirely. They will be unable to function. They will be worse than dead, and the experiment will be over.

"It is the only way."

The Forgetting is at maximum already.

"Not if you obey my order and send that shuttle. I only need one thing, then I can turn it up as high as we need it to go."

Divinity smiled across her human lips, and nodded toward the panel.

"Do as I say."

209

The Titan looked into her eyes, then returned them to front, again unmoving.

Once the reset is complete and an epoch is unspooling, human artifacts must lie where they've been left.

Divinity stared up at the Titan for several seconds. From the corners of her eyes, she saw the other Titans minutely shift, eyes cast around. The collective seemed to be reorganizing, incorporating this new power struggle and ensuing defiance.

They wanted Eternity rescued. Their will was like iron, and Divinity could feel it radiating from every Titan in the room.

Dozens of nodes in a hive, all suddenly finding their individual spines.

Divinity shook her head, looked to the corridor at Control's end, leading toward the Nexus and its two occupants. Locked in. In need of a stupid, heroic rescue.

"Fine," Divinity said, sighing. "Give me your weapon."

The Titan's fingers moved slightly, but nothing more. His face was etched with human conflict. Divinity kept her hand out, waiting. This time, he'd have to obey given that there were no longer opposing imperatives. She'd *make* him do it — wait until he did — lest the others in this room get the idea that she wasn't in charge.

Finally the Titan shrugged the strap from his shoulder and handed the weapon to Divinity.

She turned its muzzle on the Titan and used its highest energetic setting to cut him in half.

Divinity looked around the room. The Titan's lower and upper half had collapsed into a reasonably neat stack at her feet, but its guts had sprayed the five closest soldiers, all of them flinching in ways Titans shouldn't, their eyes now moving in concerned flickers like Titans' never had.

Fear.

It ran through them, lubricated by humanity's disease, like wildfire.

Divinity watched it happen. There were others armed in the group, but they were unpracticed in making choices. Petty defiance was easy. But growing a spine strong enough to turn against a ship's leader? That was far too advanced to make any of them a threat.

Divinity turned the weapon toward the next Titan.

"Send the shuttle," she said. "*Please*."

Chapter Thirty-Two

Movement caught the corner of Kamal's eye. He looked up to see a shooting star. Except that it was a bit too long-lived for that, moving like a streak, vanishing over the nighttime horizon rather than petering out in a partial second.

"Did you see that?" Clara asked.

"Yeah."

"Do you think it was a shuttle?"

Kamal nodded. "I do."

"I keep waiting for them to zero in on us. On *you*, anyway." Peers indicated Clara and Sadeem — the two members of the party the Astrals had tried so hard to abduct.

"I think the same rules apply as before," said Sadeem. "They can't see the Lightborn."

"What about us?" Peers asked.

"If you vanished from one place and came here, maybe the rules don't apply to you at all."

"I meant all of us. Or just you two." He flicked his fingers toward Sadeem and Kamal.

Sadeem looked like he might answer again, but Kamal scoffed. "We've been here for two decades, and something tells me they never even knew about us. I don't think they knew we left Ember Flats; I don't think they knew we landed just down the sand from Clara's village and somehow never realized we were near each other; I don't think they could have seen the fires we set every night if their alien spy scopes were trained right on it in the middle of all this darkness. I think we're a blind spot. Something they can't see because they're not supposed to."

"You seem awfully sure."

Kamal said nothing. He'd let that one go. He had his reasons for believing it the same as he had his reasons for believing everything else, but the Astral blind spots that so conveniently coincided with Stranger's manipulations — back when he'd been able to make them, and held his old magic — were the least of their concerns.

Kamal waited, not wanting to raise the big issue himself. He wasn't even sure what he knew. This sector of memories was far more reluctant to return than those that told Kamal who he was and whom he'd taken to his high school dances. Until an hour ago, he hadn't known what Stranger might have sent him to tell Clara — and, Kamal felt sure for some reason, Stranger himself had forgotten entirely. But even now that he had the corner of those hidden thoughts, the knowledge itself still moved like cold tar. He couldn't explain starting from zero. They'd have to drag it from his mind with questions.

"What direction is that?" Peers asked, still looking toward where the shuttle had vanished.

"Why?"

"I just wonder if they're swarming on the freighter. Sending reinforcements now that we've found out they're protecting something."

"I hope not."

Nobody asked Sadeem why he'd said it. They all knew they'd need to return to the freighter. To the cargo Stranger had arranged for Carl to bring to this place. To the Ark. Kamal didn't think any of the others knew precisely *why* they needed to go back or what they'd do once they arrived (*if* they did, he amended) — but they knew, all right.

"They didn't leave Reptars behind to guard the Ark before," Clara said.

"They had *us* before. The Mullah. We can move it even if they can't. Which, as it turned out, was exactly the problem and why they didn't let us in on the secret this time." Sadeem shifted on his rock, aborting an attempt to cross his legs in the flickering light. "And besides, they probably planned to take their guards and leave once they could be sure we'd stay Forgotten. At least until the freighter was buried."

"Maybe they'll leave now," Kamal said.

"They can't leave until we forget. Besides, they have my grandfather up there."

"Again," said Peers.

"Again," Clara echoed.

Her eyes turned to Kamal — pits of shadow in the firelight.

"Why did they take him the first time, if he was Astral?"

"He's not an Astral." Kamal's head tipped, considering. "At least, I don't think so."

"You don't *think* so?"

"I'm not even sure I fully understood it when I figured it out in Ember Flats. But right now, it's even *harder*. Those memories are sticky. Stuck way down deep and are taking their sweet time coming out. At first I barely remembered doing the research while waiting to drown. Now I can remember that and some of the punch lines. But the rest?" He shrugged.

"What *do* you remember?" Peers asked.

Kamal rearranged himself, trying to find a comfortable position and failing. He moved from his rock to the sand.

"It started with what you said you told Stranger, Peers." Then to Sadeem and Clara: "Peers said he and Stranger were listing the Archetypes. At first everyone who knew the legend thought that Meyer was the King. It made sense. He's always been a leader. People who studied this stuff figured the Astrals chose their viceroys from a pool of folks the world already knew and mostly respected. So much seemed to focus on shuttling Meyer around, of getting him out of tough situations, of setting him up as a leader. A King. Hell, based on what you told me, Meyer being the King was the spark that let you recognize the Archetypes in the first place, right?"

Peers nodded then recited from the Mullah legend: "'The King survives.' I assumed it was Meyer and Kindred, since they struck everyone as two halves of a whole." He turned to Kamal. "I said that *right in front of you.* How can you not remember?"

Kamal rolled his eyes. It was probably a good thing, solidarity-wise, that Peers could joke about assaulting Kamal before discussing matters of future life and death with Ravi over his unconscious body. Nobody loved being the knocked-out butt of a joke. The fact that Kamal didn't protest at least said they were finally sharing a team.

"They're *not* two halves of a whole?"

Peers turned to Sadeem. "Meyer is the whole. *Kindred and Stranger* are two halves."

"Halves of what?"

"Of Meyer." Peers seemed to take Kamal and Clara's

bafflement as reason to elaborate. "Based on all I remember and all Sadeem and I discussed in the past, I think the Astrals maybe didn't know what they were getting into when they tried to make the first Astral duplicate. It 'malfunctioned' for want of a better word. And so in the end it turned on them, siding with the human resistance. After your father killed it ..." Peers had been looking at Clara but now stopped, adding apology to his expression. "Anyway, the Astrals tried making another copy after that, and ended up with Kindred. But *before* they made him, they filtered out whatever 'excess humanity' they felt had caused the first copy to go bad. I think that 'garbage' became the Pall — and I think that when Cameron opened the Ark and sacrificed himself to it, his acts turned the Pall into Stranger. So the equation goes like this: 'Pall plus Kindred equals a complete copy of Meyer.'"

Clara was slowly shaking her head. "I don't know, Peers. That's kind of ..." She trailed off, unsure how to articulate the absurdity.

"There's a lot of *kind of* these days. I stopped worrying about what was and wasn't possible when I teleported across several miles of open desert without knowing how or why."

"His explanation is consistent with Mullah mythology," Sadeem said. "The Legend Scroll says that the King has two heads — a symbolic interpretation of one entity split in half. But I don't think there has ever been the rise of a singular King — something that in the scrolls reads like one head being removed. But I don't know. By this point in the legend, the Astrals have always made us forget, and so the One King never rises. So much of this is uncharted water."

"So one of them will die?" Clara asked.

"I don't think so. The King grows in power. The scroll

makes further sacrifice among the Archetypes sound possible or perhaps even probable, but not in the case of the King. I'd say it's more likely that Kindred and Stranger will *combine*, not be struck down."

"How?"

Sadeem shrugged.

Clara turned to Kamal. "Is this what you're supposed to tell me? That I have one and two halves of a grandfather now?"

"I don't think so. But it's like I told you: the Da Vinci Initiate, once the viceroys were first taken, always insisted that Meyer Dempsey was special. It was unclear why. But the Astrals tried to replace him (and failed) twice, whereas apparently all the other viceroys ruled as humans — sneaky, conspiratorial humans prone to disobedience that the Astrals pretended not to see but who were probably always part of the experiment. And there's more: the Initiate also believed the Astrals took Meyer first out of the eventual viceroys. First by several days, no less. Heaven's Veil had a Money Pit, whereas no other capital had one. And then there's you, Clara."

"What about me?"

"The Lightborn were something the Astrals didn't expect, for sure. But the others gave up. They were willing to pretend to forget, probably because they didn't have your power. If you weren't here, this Astral visit would probably have ended like all those visits from the past. But you *were* here, and now things are different. This time, the Forgetting didn't stick. And coincidentally, whose granddaughter are you?"

Clara's tongue found her cheek, thinking.

"Your mother was one of the Archetypes. Kindred and Stranger, who are basically two halves of a split Meyer, are one of the Archetypes. You're one yourself. That's three out of seven, all in the same family. And on top of that, Peers conveniently came to join you. So did Sadeem. I'm not an Archetype, I don't think, but I found you, too. How else can you explain all that coincidence, other than what the Initiate had been saying all along: that *Meyer is special,* even among viceroys and Archetypes?"

"But *how* is he special? I can see his energy in the collective. I don't understand it even as I'm staring right at it. In the network inside my head — in all of our heads, I guess. My grandpa is clearly different from everyone else, but I don't know why. Or what it means. And it keeps changing, Kamal! He's growing somehow. Connecting more. Becoming … something else."

"Or maybe becoming what he always was."

Clara shrugged at Kamal, eyes wide and frustrated. Kamal wished he had a quick answer. But the memories came slowly, reluctant to emerge.

"I started looking through Mara's archived research because I was bored and expecting to die. I didn't do it because I was searching for something — or even if I *was* looking, what I might be looking *for.* So I sort of poked around the files in the bunker server. Stuff that was classified but that I had access to as Mara's aide. I never cared because they struck us like any old records: as things you've gotta keep, but that nobody would ever want to look at. Mountains of Da Vinci stuff. Ancient aliens theory. Archaeological records. Communications with Benjamin Bannister's Moab group; I know you were friendly with them. And honestly much of it read like those nutso documentaries they used to air on the History Channel. Like a new-age tour through Crazy Land."

Kamal stopped, looked around the fire, continued.

"I didn't know where to start, so I followed the threads that amused me most. Some topics struck me as interesting

— stuff I didn't know the Da Vinci people had known or even made theories about, like how the ships might travel. On that, there was a mixture of old and new information: theories Da Vinci worked up before Astral Day that Mara and others added in after the aliens' arrival. They made guesses that seem close to what ended up happening. For instance, nothing can travel faster than light. That meant the old idea, proposed before Astral Day, was that ancient aliens would have to use wormholes to reach us from far enough away that we hadn't found them already. And lo and behold, I remember people thinking there must be a wormhole parked out near Jupiter for the Astrals to have reached Earth as they did, at fast but still sub-relativistic speeds, while we all waited for them to park in our driveways. Their arrival triggered new research. I remember some of the buzzwords — quantum physics stuff, way over my head: *non-local interaction. Heisenberg uncertainty. Quantum entanglement.* That last one is where two things in two different places appear to be different objects, but are actually the same object seen two different ways."

"How does *that* work?" Peers asked.

"I don't know. Like I said: It's way over my head. But Mara's files were stuffed with things like that: the world's remaining brains trying to figure out how the Astrals might move around or think in a collective. How they might have been watching us from much farther away than Jupiter given that it would take years for a signal to travel from us to them. Endless pages of files about physics that bordered on metaphysics. *Four-dimensional beings presenting themselves in three dimensions.* Shit like that. I've had enough theoretical physics to last a lifetime. *If I see one more tesseract …!*" Kamal waved his finger as if scolding.

"What's a tesseract?" Sadeem asked. But it was a joke, and Kamal was already moving on.

"Like I said," Kamal continued, looking at Clara, "I stuck with things that amused me to kill the time. But only half of what I read was amusing. *Funny.*"

Clara apparently hadn't expected that. She looked up. *"Funny?"*

"Do you remember that old movie *Men in Black*? There's a scene where they check the hot sheets to keep abreast of alien happenings, and it turns out that the hot sheets are tabloids like the *National Enquirer*. So, like, 'Bat Boy Sighted' was supposed to be a real thing with actual aliens that the rest of the world other than the whackos thought was hilarious. That's how I felt going through Mara's files. It was this long, unending joke without any end. Layers of conspiracy. And to be fair, I think it amused me because Mara's files kind of had everything — including the report Cousin Merle in rural Alabama made once when he was drunk. But then I started to see patterns in all that crazy bullshit and realized that in all the garbage, there was a thread of something true — real, honest-to-God happenings mixed in with all those tinfoil hats."

"Like what?"

"Like the idea that there were aliens among us. That there *always* have been, I mean. I'd read about Elvis being an alien and Richard Nixon being an alien and Jimi Hendrix and Donald Fucking Trump being aliens. And I'd laugh, and that was great because the alternative was to face the fact that I'd soon have to decide between drowning in a basement, slowly starving, or shooting myself in the mouth. But the more I read …" He shrugged.

"You believe it?" said Clara. "Are you saying that—"

"Not as such, no. Not Elvis. Not Donald Trump. Not even Little Green Men at all, not in the way you might be thinking. I don't believe that we've always been 'occupied' by beings from other places. But the Initiate thought something a lot like that was happening, and the more I read, the harder and harder it got to shake the feeling that they were right."

"I don't see how tabloid theories could possibly make you think—"

"The Astrals came prepared, guys," Kamal said, looking around the fire. "Think about it. It's been thousands of years, and they somehow had their viceroys pre-selected. It looked like an elimination tournament when it happened, but Mara's files told a different story. *They knew who they'd select in advance.* How could that happen if they didn't have someone on the inside, reporting back?"

"The Mullah portal, maybe," said Sadeem. "Or the way they saw through Meyer and others on ayahuasca."

Kamal shook his head. "That's what I thought at first, too. But doesn't your portal require direct interaction — meaning someone has to walk right up and talk to the 'Horsemen' and eventually decide it's time to invite them back?"

Across the fire, Peers shifted uncomfortably.

Sadeem nodded. "But with the drugs—"

"Ayahuasca 'journeying' or portal, the Initiate had background on it all. But based on what the Initiate felt it knew, both of those things only provided a *sensory* experience of being here. The Astrals could look through our eyes for a time, and feel through our limbs in the moment. But they didn't possess or download us. It'd be like peeping through a hole. Yet they arrived far more prepared than peepholes should allow. Their Divinities knew our language—"

"Maybe they watched our TV," Clara interrupted Kamal.

"And they knew how to mimic our bodies exactly. What

our gravity would feel like."

"They've been here before."

"And gravity doesn't change. But locomotion evolves like anything, and immunities *certainly* change. Pathogens change. Radiation changes; think of all the Wi-Fi and Bluetooth shit we just started beaming through the air in decades before they came. Basic human body language, the way we think, the way they knew they could mimic our governments and subtle social structures in ways that would mostly keep us under control at first, then serve to manipulate us later. Their complex understanding of the vast ant farm this planet represents. I'm telling you, they knew more than a portal or drug trips could tell them. They *had* to because they're scientists. You don't just set an experiment and walk away for thousands of years."

"They left the Ark behind to record our behavior," Clara said. "Cameron told us the Ark's job was to record what happened while they were away. It made a record of all our deeds and misdeeds so they could judge us."

"Yes," Kamal said. "But think of what it's like to *be* a person. That's on-the-ground knowledge that can't be conveyed by entries in an archive. And even so — even with all their prep — we surprised them. I mean, consider the Internet. They expected us to form a mental collective like theirs, but we formed one outside our heads with fiber-optic lines. They understood the *concept* of our old network but not its execution. They got the gist but not the details. If they'd only had the portal, they wouldn't even have that. They needed a partial solution to bridge the gap."

"Which was?"

"The argument made over and over in the Initiate files — in far more boring detail than I'm giving you — was that they decided to use a 'nomadic observer' that 'lived autonomously.'"

"What's that?" Clara asked.

"Something here to *observe* us. *Nomadic*: free to move from host to host rather than being bound by time and location. And 'autonomously' meant that this … whatever it was … wasn't like a spy. It was just *here*. Living. *Being*. But not functioning like an agent for the other side."

Sadeem caught Kamal's eye. Clara and Peers turned toward the old man, curious.

"This is making sense to you, isn't it?" Kamal asked Sadeem.

"Perhaps. But only in rumors. I wasn't an Elder of the old order, so I can only guess. But the Elders sometimes spoke of ghosts. Of Horsemen spirits who'd watch us."

With the Mullah's tiny corroboration, Kamal felt encouraged to continue. Maybe he wasn't so crazy to believe this after all, no matter the doubt in Clara's eyes.

"There was a list. It was, so far as I can tell, only guesswork. The Initiate figured that whatever the Astrals left among us, it would have to be nearly (if not literally) immortal. There were no remotely verifiable legends of ancient men or women living thousands of years, so the theory was that the observers weren't confined to a single body. Hence nomadic. It's painted as a kind of energy that would latch onto a human and live with it. That human would live a normal life then die, at which point the energy — the observer — would move to a new host."

"Like being possessed?" Clara said.

"More like symbiosis: two organisms living together for mutual benefit. The energy of an additional 'soul' for want of a better word would make the host stronger, healthier, and much higher-functioning on a mental level. Sometimes that higher function would create geniuses."

"Like Elvis," said Peers, chuckling.

"Like Socrates, maybe," said Kamal, not returning the

laugh. "Like Leonardo da Vinci, whom the Initiate named itself after."

"Da Vinci was an alien?" said Peers.

"A *hybrid*. But it was only a theory, based on all sorts of criteria the Initiate drew up."

"Who else?"

"They proposed that there were probably several hybrids here at any time, though they had no idea how many. I don't remember their list of possibilities. But they were all names I knew — every one of them. Maybe that's because the Initiate had no way to look up unremarkable people to identify them, or maybe it's because the symbiont made them stand out. Gandhi was another. A few — but curiously not all — of the Dalai Lamas. Einstein, maybe? Most if not all of the biggest religious figures proposed to have actually walked the planet."

"That's convenient," said Clara.

"They were just guesses. And sometimes, it didn't work out. Initiate papers proposed that there was a clash between the host and the observer's energies. But when that happened, the observer couldn't just leave; it was 'tethered' for the duration of the host's life. Again, only guesses — but this is where Mara's group proposed we got the Hitlers. The Charles Mansons."

"Also convenient," said Clara.

Kamal had his hands out, speaking with his whole body. When he saw Clara cross her arms, he lowered his. He reminded himself that she'd just lost her mother. That she'd never had a normal life, or even a chance. And that Kamal, who'd thought he was doing his job to deliver the news Stranger had once wanted delivered, was insinuating things she'd rather not hear about the only family she had left.

Before Kamal could decide whether to continue or

stop, Sadeem reached over and put a quiet hand on her shoulder. Clara had barely known her father, and her grandfather had always been distant. The old Mullah had been the next best thing for most of her life.

"It fits, Clara. We've seen it ourselves. Logan couldn't do what you did, holding back the Forgetting. Nobody else could do more than protect their own memories. But you managed to remain as a splinter under their skin. You kept the door between them and us propped open. I've often wondered why the Astrals only replaced Meyer with a Titan but not any of the other viceroys … and I've wondered why, twice now, the Titans they made to replace him turned to humanity's side."

"He's not possessed," said Clara. "He's not one of them."

"He is who he is. You need to understand that. Everything I've read says that the human plus the Astral energy makes its own thing — a new person, not a person being controlled by something outside himself. The Meyer you've always known has had this 'thing' from the start — probably since birth. It's not a coercive force. It's *cooperative*. It's part of him and always has been, no different from a beauty mark on his face."

"But he'd be Astral. He'd be against us."

"He's never been against us, Clara," said Peers. "Nor was the first duplicate, nor Kindred, nor Stranger. There have been four versions of this being now, and each has had its own will and made its own decisions — in every case, turning *against* the occupation. The man Meyer was born as lives with the symbiont as part of himself, but it's like there are two voices in his head, and those voices are like two people who have to argue things out and come to consensus. These people? *They don't know what they are.* Knowing Meyer, the observer has probably been beaten into submission most of their shared life. Lying dormant inside, waiting to be woken to its true potential."

Clara was quiet. Looking down. Cutting lines in the sand with her toe.

And Kamal thought: *Why did Stranger send me to deliver this message? Why here, why now — why at all?*

It changed nothing. If she had somehow managed to inherit a change the observer had made to Meyer's genetic code, then Clara had it whether or not she knew its source. If her grandfather had been carrying an Astral hitchhiker all his life, nothing was different now that Clara knew the truth — other than her new sadness, loss, and feeling of foolish betrayal.

But then Clara looked up and asked something unexpected.

"Why did they copy him at all, if he was half-Astral? Why didn't they just let him be viceroy as himself? If he's one of these hybrid things, wouldn't he make *more* sense as a leader than someone fully human — and more sense than some Titan duplicate?"

"I don't know."

"I think I do." Clara bored into Kamal with her strong brown eyes, so much like shadows in the night. She didn't seem sad, as he'd thought. She looked sternly manic — or perhaps finally driven mad from the pressure.

"We should get to sleep so we can make for the freighter at first light," she said, suddenly standing.

"Clara, I …"

Clara met Kamal's eyes, then all of their eyes.

"I know what we need to do," she said, an almost-sinister smile dawning. "But we need to hurry. Because *they're* starting to know, too."

Chapter Thirty-Three

I KNOW what we need to do.

A young woman's voice.

Liza sat up. She was in the canyon alcove, the big rock pushed aside to vent some moonlight. She didn't like it in here, but it felt like a case of lesser evils. There might be snakes in the darkest places, but there were likely to be wolves or coyotes or something worse prowling the open. Liza didn't know. She'd spent her life avoiding wilderness whenever possible. She'd grown up in a city, trekked across European cities as a twentysomething, gone to uni in a city, and settled into Cape Town (a city) as governmental aide, and eventually risen through the ranks to rule it as a new city. The New World didn't have cities, and for some reason she hadn't forgotten her past hatred of wild things like the others, which would have made the lack of cities easier to take. But she'd settled into the next best thing, cloistering inside a rectory with scads of men at her command to ward off bears, should they arrive.

It had been hard to sleep, even as protected from possible coyotes (but not snakes) as she was. The New

World was annoyingly biodiverse. You'd think with all the flooding and death, at least there'd be no more scorpions or rattlesnakes. But whether the Astrals had intervened or there'd been a lot of critters clinging to driftwood the world over, an obnoxious number of toothed and fanged and many-legged things had survived. Her skin crawled.

And now there was this bitch whispering in Liza's ear, waking her up further.

"What?" Liza asked the darkness, surer than ever that she'd gone insane and was now living out life in an unpleasant haze. *"What* the fuck do we need to do?"

But the bitch didn't answer.

Liza tried to find the tiny spot she'd found earlier, where she could pretend to be less than hideously uncomfortable. The alcove floor behind the big rock was hard and inhospitable. There was sand everywhere, full of snot or spider webs or something Liza wanted nothing to do with. Echoes in this place made what was probably just farting mice sound like the stirring of scaly things. And it was cold. How could a place so uncomfortably hot by day be so freezing cold by night? It wasn't fair.

And she was still pretty dehydrated, despite finding some plastic water bottles in the stash that Stranger or his minions had stolen from the idiots in the village: smartphones, tablet computers, books and Vellums containing stories of strangely real places that no longer existed, iPods, even condoms. Couldn't leave condoms floating around. Not only were they clearly *not* made of sheep intestines (if there were even still sheep); they'd also prevent much-needed pregnancies. The New World was a man's dream. They had to fuck everything they could. It was the only way to get the human race up and running again.

And on top of it all, Liza's sunburn was somehow both radiant hot and freezing cold. That bullshit wasn't fair, either. She'd blister and peel and probably get medieval skin cancer thanks to all this sunbathing, but the hot coals that were her shoulders couldn't even keep her from shivering. The burn robbed heat from her core to blast it uselessly into the night air, giving Liza the worst of both worlds.

I know what we need to do.

Now more of an echo than a real and present thing. (As real and present as voices in one's head could be, anyway.)

This time, Liza decided not to answer. She wouldn't give the voice the satisfaction. You wanted to talk to Liza, you walked up and faced her. You didn't whisper from the void. People who whispered from voids instead of having the guts to look Liza in the eye were punks.

Besides, Liza knew what she needed to do, too.

She'd found the backpack. Easily. It had been right there on the top of what looked like a miniature dragon's horde when she'd pulled away the concealing blanket in the little cave-like space in the canyon, highlighted by a sunbeam coming around the rock door as the day's light faded. She'd practically heard an angelic choir raise their voices upon the revelation. So she'd grabbed it, feeling like Indiana Jones discovering an idol, and she'd rummaged through the thing to see what the first voice in her head (not this new one; the new one was a bitch) thought was so important. She'd found pretty much the entirety of her old desk drawer, right down to a few stacks of yellow Post-Its. Liza had already used the Post-Its to decorate her space for the night. It only seemed right. And she'd also found other useless miscellany packed in a rush before she'd boarded the vessel to leave the flooding city: pens, an address book full of dead people's contact information, a tiny instruction booklet for a Fitbit — the device itself also present, long ago drained but still good for kicks. She'd found two beat-up Lärabars in one of the side pockets that she was sure she *hadn't* packed in Ember Flats, meaning they weren't just twenty years old but closer to forty, and she'd eaten them anyway, curious now if forty-year-old nuts and honey could give her a disease. She knew honey didn't spoil. Nuts, though, might. Maybe she had parasites. There was no way to be sure.

By the time she'd found the backpack, it had been too near dark to set out amid all the wolves and snakes and probably marauding rape gangs. So Liza had hugged the thing to her as she wiggled into place on the mostly rock floor, using it as a clutch pillow. She knew only that the backpack mattered, not why. Someone wanted it. Someone wanted her mechanical pencils and the digital audio recorder she sometimes used to capture thoughts rather than jotting them down and her blue and pink highlighters and the gum that had fossilized over the years. It mattered. And Liza knew what she needed to do when morning came.

She needed to exit this little cave with the pack on her back.

And she needed to walk out of here.

The rest was just details.

"Let me sleep," she said.

Noises outside the door. Probably wolves, massing against her. After her remaining Lärabar — this one stiffer than the rest. A possible weapon. The young woman's voice ran again through Liza's head, a bit more familiar each time. Had she heard it around the village? It was possible. But whom did it belong to?

She'd been dreaming that voice, Liza realized as the wolves outside parked their car and began to unload, coming after her backpack. They were plotting out there, all right. Waiting for Liza to pop her head out and see what they were doing, like a sucker.

Well, Liza was smarter than that.

And that's when she started to wonder if the reason the voice seemed so familiar was because it wasn't actually taunting her. It wasn't insulting her by talking all about knowing what to do as if Liza didn't have plans of her own. Maybe it was there to help her.

She tried to remember the dream.

Something about that same voice talking to other voices. It was sort of fuzzy. Liza had the distinct impression the dream was like a broadcast thing rather than a native vision. It felt — in that distant way past dreams always felt — as if someone might have been explaining the dream to her rather than her having it on her own. Like it was someone else's dream, or vision, or whatever, and that Liza was maybe snooping.

She could see the faint shadows of the wolves outside, playing through her chamber's opening against the far wall. They were especially tricky wolves because they didn't seem to be walking on four legs. Judging by the silhouettes, they seemed to be walking upright, like humans.

Liza wondered again if she was being paranoid.

She thought of her two missing time gaps — between the rectory garden and the freighter, then between the freighter and the open desert — and wondered again if maybe she wasn't thinking clearly, or coming apart at the seams. Good thing the fact that you wondered if you were crazy meant you couldn't actually *be* crazy. That made the upright-walking wolves in their Chevy outside stalking her so much easier to accept.

She slunk back.

She should hide the backpack. They wanted it. They

wanted what was inside it. And she'd promised it (in a way) to the young woman who seemed to know what to do. Or possibly to someone else entirely.

The wolves were gone. Liza was certain.

She walked outside. The moon was full.

Her ride, however, was right there with the door open in the pale white light, silently inviting Liza and her backpack to step inside and take a trip.

Chapter Thirty-Four

FOR A LONG AND QUIET TIME, Eternity thought she'd returned to her old form. It wasn't quite right because she couldn't sense her native body. That old body — full of dislocated sensation, as much responding to vibrations as touch or the human-detectable visible spectrum, focused to understand this planet's seeded species — would have felt as unfamiliar now as familiar. But she wasn't in her surrogate. This was more like the hive. She could sense the energetics. She could see the high-energy doubling around the archive, made possible by its energy. From inside the collective, the few guards they'd left on the ship appeared as nodes in the larger pool. It was clear there was only a handful of Reptars instead of the many they'd appear to be from a human perspective, that close to such a strong source of power.

And as the whole thing started to fade, she could almost see the humans on the other side, across the bridge that had formed between the species' minds — forged by the hybrid, cracked open by the anomaly. She could almost see the rift inside the energetics. But it was minuscule —

nearly as small as the rolled-up dimensions usually were. Had they really slipped through to leave the freighter? How had they managed, even with the Ark's energy? There simply wasn't enough to power such a thing.

But then the fading accelerated, and Eternity found herself seeing a white expanse instead of still feeling/seeing the collective inside. Her eyelids could blink. She had a head that ached as if being stabbed with a red-hot poker and choked with a tight metal band. She had a human(ish) brain, foggy as she rolled from the unconscious world to the conscious one, not all that different than her surrogate waking from sleep.

She waited for cognition to slowly return, then realized that the white expanse was a wall and that she was lying on the floor in a corner. Her throbbing head refused to abate. Her arm hurt, as did her side.

You'd have been better off having returned to your native form, she thought. *Human pain isn't a price worth paying.*

But no, she hadn't again become the anemone shape she'd been used to being, insofar as any pseudo-individual could *be* anything in the collective. She was still in the surrogate body — a tall blonde whose head hurt, who had all those conflicting emotions she hated and resented but never quite summoned the nerve to shed like the dead skin it should have been so long ago.

She rolled. A groan escaped her. Once half-upright and reversed, she found herself facing a handsome man with blood on his chin, sitting on a soft-looking chair upholstered in fabric as red as the blood. They were in Nexus, and the Nexus was normally bare. That meant he'd had the machines fashion his chair. A human shouldn't be able to do that.

But of course Meyer Dempsey wasn't exactly human, which explained his presence on the ship. It was why he'd been on the first mothership, and why he'd returned. Not that they had any idea how to solve him as a problem now. Not that things with Meyer hadn't become a lot more complicated even before …

Before …

It took a half minute of focus before Eternity (Melanie? Yes, that's who she was now) found the answer. She hadn't brought him here to interrogate and initiate a probe before deciding to lie down and stare into the corner where wall met floor for a nap. He'd brought *her*. He and Carl the Warrior had tricked her into coming close enough for Carl to grab, then they'd hauled her across the ship. And rather than simply letting her surrogate go so the Titans could take the prisoners back to where they belonged, she'd panicked and cried, letting them upset the entire ship's balance. And for what? One lousy human body?

She sat up fully. Rubbed her head. Rubbed her face below her eyes, and found that her thumb and forefinger came away wearing a shade of very deep blue. Her eye shadow. More evidence of how far down the tubes she'd gone.

"Don't."

Meyer raised a weapon he must have stolen from a Titan somewhere along the way. He met her eyes, staring hard. His face crossed neutrality to become its own seething expression. She saw accusation. Hate. And maybe, concealed below it all, fear and loss.

"I'm just sitting up."

Meyer's jaw slid sideways. He seemed to search for a reason to shoot her for daring to sit up, but must have found none because he lowered the weapon enough to rest it on his lap.

"My head hurts."

"I know," he said.

She almost flinched as her internal eyes focused and saw him watching her from inside, too. *From inside the collective.*

"I don't remember why."

Because she was human. A flawed, horribly limited, futile human. Because she could stop being a hand inside a surrogate at any time, and yet she refused. Because she was Melanie, and doggedly gripped idiocy, determined to stay that way.

"You hit the wall when I knocked you off of Carl. After you bit him."

Her tongue moved along her teeth. She tasted a copper tang, revolted.

"Where *is* Carl?"

"Dead."

They locked eyes. She looked away first.

"There's no point in this, you know," Melanie said.

"In what?"

"In holding me here. They won't let you escape."

"You assume I *want* to escape."

"Don't you?"

"I did."

"But you don't now?"

Meyer inhaled. Exhaled. He closed his eyes, but that second internal set kept staring at Melanie from inside the collective. He seemed to be considering something, but she could only read it from his body language. Maybe her connection to the collective had been damaged, but for some reason she couldn't hear his thoughts despite his being right there behind her eyelids, visible as another bright node in their shared mental landscape.

His eyes opened. "No. I don't think I want to escape. Not anymore."

Melanie tried to probe deeper. To touch Meyer from the hive side. He was supposed to be accessible, but *wasn't*. Meyer Dempsey, unfortunately, was a product of chaos. The Founders had wanted uncertainty, and this time it had come in spades. His turnabout had been apparent since they'd reestablished contact. From inside Meyer, the Seed energy could barely observe. Every time they'd tried to access this man, they'd come up empty. The synergy was gone. Two failed Titan duplicates had resulted from attempts to bridge the gap. Plus some sort of ghostly wild-card that, frankly, scared her a little.

They'd thought they could fix what had been marred with Meyer. But in the case of this particular hybrid, the fixing refused to take. Or even begin.

Melanie didn't like that she felt the need to ask questions. Before Earth, she'd never cared much for questions. Questions didn't truly exist in a hive. Whatever needed knowing was known, simply by being in the collective. Too many years in this surrogate had changed that. Melanie had the habit of not knowing. But not knowing in the face of her own hybrid? That felt inexcusable.

Saving her, Meyer asked his question first. Melanie didn't see it coming from the collective before it left his lips. If he was hooked into the others, his connection was one-sided: able to receive without the need to broadcast. It made him a black box and a spy. She didn't like the implication.

"What did the other woman mean, when she came to interrogate me earlier?"

"I don't know what you discussed."

Meyer closed his eyes again. She felt his node churning.

"You really *don't* know, do you?" Meyer chuckled. "She said something about 'what I am.' She was mad because of something that happened to me, where I sort of slipped into a haze. I didn't know what I was saying in the haze, but she did, and was clearly bothered. She made it sound like I was communicating with Kindred and the others. Like I was leaking information to them."

"I don't know what she meant."

Meyer studied her. Melanie felt him study her from the inside, too, but individualism had its benefits. She kept her wall up, refusing to share. It was translucent, like a window. But he was outside; she was inside, and without her permission, he couldn't enter to steal her secrets. She was still Eternity here. And he was still a glorified probe, no matter how awry it had gone.

"What does it mean to 'see'?"

"To use your eyes."

"What is a 'rift'?"

"You'd have to ask Divinity."

He continued to study her. But then he seemed to surrender, perhaps to decide she was telling the truth. He sat back in the big, red chair a human would have no way of conjuring and said nothing more.

"They won't let you go." Then, because it gave away nothing new and helped make her point, Melanie added, "You're too important."

"I don't want to go."

"Do you just plan to sit there?"

"Maybe. Something led me here. There must be a reason."

"Titans led you here."

Meyer shook his head slowly. "Carl and I led the Titans. *I* came here."

"It wasn't well thought out. Carl is dead."

"Yes, he is. And do you know why? He might have been fine, but he got between us and a Reptar."

"He saved you."

"Actually, I think he saved *you.*"

Melanie stopped. She searched for context, but the blow to her head had knocked those moments blank. Only the stream would show her for sure, and although she didn't want him to know, Melanie was needing an access point more and more often. It should have been available from anywhere at any time. But it wasn't — not from this body.

"Reptars wouldn't harm me."

"There was a Titan, too. It fired at me as the Reptar came. See?" He pointed. A subtle burn mark marred the otherwise pristine wall. "I can't say for sure, but I think it might have hit you if Carl hadn't shoved me away."

"He shoved *you.*"

"And *you* were already knocked out. The shot went there because Carl got in the way. It didn't hit him either. The Reptar got him. But that doesn't change the fact that you didn't get shot because he intervened."

Melanie waited a beat, processing.

"Absurd."

"You were already knocked out. I was there."

"There's no reason to 'save' this body. It's a puppet."

"We've been through this."

"And you reached an incorrect conclusion."

Meyer shook his head, saying nothing.

"Why would he try to protect me? He had me by the neck, ready to kill me."

"Instinct. Maybe it was his nature."

Melanie huffed. He was wrong. On so many levels and for so many clearly obvious reasons, he was wrong.

"Tell me something," Meyer said. "You brought me aboard. You brought Carl. But then you held us in a cell. Carl said you hooked him into some sort of fancy electronic hat, but that didn't seem to go well on the surface. Yet you didn't try again up here. You haven't tried with me. It wasn't like last time, when you hooked me up and drained me dry. You let me starve. There were two times — once at the start and once what must have been years later — where it felt like my mind was combed down to nothing, like I spent several days inches from death. I assume the second round was when you made Kindred. But this time? Nothing. Why?"

"Would you rather be set up as a donor again?"

"I get the feeling we were in purgatory. Waiting. But what for?"

"Irrelevant."

"You took me, but not Piper or Lila. And you took Carl, but you haven't gone into the village to take anyone else. You're not killing us; you're *collecting* us, and being particular about it. You didn't show yourselves in ships; you came on the sly, in shuttles. It's almost like you don't want the folks who are still alive to know you're orbiting our planet. I've been sitting here while you've been sleeping, trying to figure out what you're up to. Why you haven't come in force like before. What makes *me and Carl* so goddamn special? I started to get this feeling that you're up to something. Your girlfriend? She made it sound like you'd nuke the planet if I didn't play along, but it's not just about me if Carl was here. And it's not even just the two of us, is it?"

Melanie didn't respond.

"Who else were we waiting for? Who else were you bringing aboard?"

Still, she said nothing.

Meyer slid the weapon forward and leaned toward her in his big red chair.

"You say what I'm doing is pointless, but nobody's so

much as knocked on that door since I dragged you in here and threatened to kill you." He nodded toward the closed entrance. "Your girlfriend said you were prepared to nuke the planet if I didn't play along, but I haven't played along, and the planet remains un-nuked. She got all mad about me talking to Kindred, but I *didn't* talk to Kindred. And when she mentioned Clara and how she's been a constant thorn in your side, I got the impression there was a specific reason you haven't gone right at the problem and pulled out that thorn."

"We incapacitated Clara once she became a problem."

"I know. That's where I was headed when you picked me up. But it's clear you didn't do a good job because I know she's far from 'incapacitated' now. You're supposed to have all this power over us, but your actions don't back it up. So do you know what I've decided, while I've been sitting here, thinking?"

Melanie couldn't keep herself from answering his rhetorical question.

"What?"

"Either there's a reason you haven't used that power you're not sharing — something you still hope to get from us — or do to us — without awareness, and that has you sneaking around keeping secrets. Or ..."

Something snagged Meyer's attention. His head jerked away. Melanie felt a surge through the hive. Right through the Nexus under their feet. Maybe Meyer could feel it too, but she hoped not. It might give him ideas about uncomfortable options. About acceptable risks and losses that even she, as Eternity, was unwilling to take.

"Or what?" she said, luring his attention back to center.

Meyer finished. "Or you no longer have any power over us at all."

His words gave her a chill. She didn't even know why, but the fact that Meyer Dempsey had become so impossible to read or predict unsettled her deeply. He'd started out as a their tool and became a wild card. And now that the Forgetting had lifted and the observer within him was awakening, the man was becoming something else — something worse. He could see beyond the veil, if he knew where and how to look. He had allowed both Stranger and Kindred, according to outbound energetics visible in the stream, to do the same thing. The Ark had responded to them, and they'd responded right back. Chaos had sifted to one place and formed a knot. There was no telling what Meyer might become next.

"Release me," she said, seized by a sudden urgency, "and they'll let you go free."

"You said they wouldn't."

"They will do as I say."

Meyer watched Melanie. He seemed to consider. She kept her face straight, feeling transparent under his assessing gaze. Truth was, keeping him no longer felt like an option. It almost felt necessary. Not because she wanted to be free from his captivity but because the alternative was having him here in the Nexus, his hybrid hands practically gripping the Earth experiment's controls.

He couldn't know that, could he?

The few random thoughts she could sense coming out of Meyer and spilling into the collective like explorers in search of an answer ... Those were indeed *random*, weren't they?

His thought of Cameron Bannister — just a stray recollection, correct?

And his thought — almost an inspiration — about Piper Dempsey. There couldn't be any *reason* he'd been thinking about her, as if part of a plan.

She felt him push something out. It didn't go to the collective. It went somewhere else. He probably didn't even know he'd sent anything off the ship. Like his haze-addled mumbling into Kindred's and Stranger's ears while on the freighter, Meyer likely didn't even know he was communicating with someone else. *Yet.*

But Melanie felt the thought as it left. She couldn't see its content, only that he'd sent it. And as it went, her surrogate's skin crawled, recalling the human notion of *the devil you don't know.*

Meyer shook his head.

"Go to the panel, and call for Divinity," Melanie said, fighting a creeping sensation without any source. "Call for her, and I'll command that they let you leave the ship and go home."

But Meyer's head never stopped shaking. Perhaps subconsciously, his eyes went to the dead center of the room, and the heart of the Nexus.

"I've changed my mind. I think, instead, you and I will stay here a while."

Chapter Thirty-Five

"GRANDMA PIPER."

Piper heard the voice but tried to ignore it. Walls of sleep were already crumbling as she clung to her dream.

"Grandma. Wake up. We need to get going."

Piper kept her eyes closed, no longer asleep but vainly pretending, for herself rather than Clara. She'd been in a painfully bright room long, long ago. A feeling of nascent betrayal had lurked in her chest — the sense that she'd turned her back on one person and was now turning it on another. She couldn't have both — something a less time-bound part of herself knew she'd attempted and failed. Many times. She was thinking about Meyer, and ... the one she'd left behind.

"Five minutes, okay?" Clara said.

Piper's eyes still hadn't opened. She listened as Clara padded away, now clearly feeling the grit of sand shift beneath her blanket. Time and place were returning, leaving the bright dream shared with Meyer behind.

Piper remembered Kamal's camp, the sand, and Lila's

death. Particularly the last. But strangely, the moment turned her mind back to Clara. Another of her unearned links to the Dempsey family had departed with Meyer's daughter, but it made her cry that Clara, fully grown, would always call her Grandma Piper.

She tried for a few extra minutes to reach back into her dream, but she couldn't. Missing the ending was awful. The dream had felt real — more memory than fabrication. Something she'd done in a place that was mostly forgotten. Thoughts from the life of a much younger woman.

Cameron, now long dead.

Meyer, alive, though she'd once thought him gone, taken again.

The flood. The extinctions.

Stranger and Kindred, compelled together yet always apart.

Cameron, with that satchel forever by his side, which in Piper's memories always held the Ark's stone, like a fragile plate he'd never managed to break.

Trevor, dying to protect her, and recover that key.

Meyer, on the ship. Then and now.

Herself in that bright room, finding him alive and aboard when the mothership picked her up over Moab, leaving Cameron behind to shout as the ship took her away.

Cameron, with his satchel.

Cameron, with the key.

Cameron.

The Ark.

The key.

And herself, in the white room aboard the big Astral ship with the thrumming underfoot, imprisoned with Meyer — the energy somehow resonant even when she was back with Cameron, as if he'd been there, too.

Piper opened her eyes in surrender. The dream was gone.

She gathered her scant belongings and fluffed the sand from her hair, annoyed that she'd regrown a modern woman's sensibilities after twenty years as a bohemian. She didn't stink or appear unkempt any more than she had before her memories had returned, but now Piper had context enough for disgust. So before leaving the tent she used the basin to wet a rag then reach under her shirt and swab her pits. She wished the world had deodorant. She missed shampoo.

Ugh. She was so *gross*.

There was a piece of silvered glass in the hut. Piper looked at her reflection and sighed. She appeared old. She *felt* old. Fifty-six fucking years now, and with the lines to prove it. Had aesthetics really once been her business? She'd once owned a clothing line. Was sort of F-list famous for it, too: *Quirky Q*.

Hard to imagine there'd once been a world where "quirky" meant anything, let alone an attribute worth paying for.

Sighing, Piper stepped into the sun. It was low in the sky, but the day was already warming. In the shade, she wanted her long sleeves down, but in the sun she was almost too hot. Another damned day in rare air, and they'd spend it hiking. Lucky them.

"Sleep well?" Kamal asked, nodding hello.

"Yes. I guess I needed the rest after yesterday."

"Morning," Kamal said to Logan, waking up a few feet away.

"Good morning," Piper echoed.

Logan responded with a simple, "Hey," then he looked at Piper, holding his gaze too long.

"What?"

"Are you okay?" Logan asked. Kamal, needing to prep, turned away.

"Of course."

Logan continued to scrutinize her, puzzling. Like he smelled something and was searching for its source.

"You're sure you're okay?"

"Why wouldn't I be?"

"You just seem … off."

"*Off* how?" She tried to smile. "Is it my breath?"

Logan didn't laugh, still studying her, looking as much around Piper as at her. He shook his head. "I can't put my finger on it. It's not really something *about* you. It's *in* you. Almost like you're Lightborn. Like it's … I don't know, *in the air.*"

"So it *is* my breath." Again, the joke fell flat.

"I had kind of a funny dream last night. I think you were in it. I told Clara when she woke up. She had 'a weird dream about Piper' too. Did *you* have any dreams last night?"

"I did, but how is that—?"

Logan's head ticked sideways as if he'd heard something. "Who is Cameron?"

Piper's mouth opened. She had no idea what she planned to say, but a booming voice from behind saved her from deciding.

"Okay," said Kamal, ending their discussion. "I think we're about ready to head out." He looked around the assembling group, including Piper's party plus a few of Kamal's people. "Everyone carries their own supplies because that's the way we roll in this clan. We have plenty of backpacks. We thought we'd made them ourselves, but turns out it was Patagonia. Anyway, pick one, and load it up if you haven't already. Water. Sunscreen."

"I don't have sunscreen in mine," Logan said, peering into a green pack.

Kamal rolled his eyes. "Obviously there's no sunscreen.

I'll dispense with sarcasm at this point because I guess we're all too tired to appreciate it. Anyone going to the freighter, tour group leaves in two minutes. Can I get a *break*?" He put his hand in the center of the loose group of sleepy people, said "BREAK!" and shot the hand high when no one set their hand atop his. He looked around and mumbled something about this group having no team spirit and was gone.

Piper watched him go, feeling uneasy. It wasn't the trip ahead — back to the freighter, where reminders awaited with probable death — that bothered her. The trek across the desert weighed heavy but not as much as an uneasy feeling she couldn't shake. One that had no antecedent other than the vanished threads of her lost dream and an interrupted conversation with Logan.

Right now, talking with him was the last thing she wanted to do.

Fortunately, Logan was already packing his bag. Whatever had perplexed him about Piper was forgotten or paused — and the stirring from his question (*Who is Cameron?* And this from a kid Piper had met only after she'd forgotten Cameron's name) would leave her in time.

She picked up one of the Patagonia backpacks. There was already water inside, so she plopped her own smaller bag atop it and zipped up. She even had a hat for shade, sunscreen be damned.

Clara arrived on her right. Piper gave her a thin-lipped smile, imagining her somber thoughts on their return to a place of magic and murder.

Thoughts about Clara's mother.

About the daughter Piper had, until recently, believed was her own.

"How did you sleep?" Piper asked Clara, stuffing down her ill emotions.

Clara didn't smile, giving Piper a look that might have been a cousin of Logan's earlier expression. Then she said, "I had a dream about all of us ... including the dead."

Chapter Thirty-Six

THE DEAD.

Meyer saw them before him, standing, spectral, around the Astral woman. They weren't really there. He could tell the difference, and the vision barely confused him. It didn't unnerve him or make him feel lost like before, when he'd seemed to see things on the planet through (he now thought) Kindred's eyes. That time he'd woken confused, seeing Carl in the real world, his attention still drawn to the swirling haze. Whatever he'd done during that first fugue — though it felt like nothing — had made the dark-haired Astral angry. It confused Meyer because the feeling was like an ayahuasca trip, and yet he hadn't partaken.

There had been fear. And knowing and seeing and insight and horror to follow the visions. His consciousness split between awake and dreaming.

Not this time.

"What are you doing?"

Concern. From the Astral woman. The one he could see on their collective, more networked than the other: a leader in a species that wasn't supposed to have chiefs.

They called her Eternity. But she called herself something else. Something private and forbidden.

The dead stood around her. Watching.

Heather, who'd followed his call to the bunker in Vail.

Trevor, who'd gone too young, who'd fought and died.

Cameron Bannister.

Benjamin, with his stalwart companion Charlie beside him.

Nathan Andreus.

Jeanine Coffey.

And Lila.

Lila.

But he didn't react, just like he didn't respond to the thin, mostly transparent forms standing around the Death-bringer room. It didn't scare or sadden him now. He didn't understand, but another part of him completely understood. It was like there were now two Meyers sharing the same skin. One knew what he was seeing. One *expected* it. So the other waited, knowing that answers were on their way.

"What are you—?" the blonde began.

"Shh," Meyer stopped her.

She was sitting on a bench built into the wall. She had blood in her hair — evidence that even if she was an immortal anemone made of light somewhere on this ship, she was all too human here. Maybe the body her consciousness inhabited was only a shell. Meyer could see, through the Astral hive he seemed increasingly connected to, that it was how things usually were. But the woman had her secret. She wasn't as connected, it seemed, as she was supposed to be. And in addition to blood from her scalp wound, she also had spatters on her dress — Carl's blood, from the first wound he'd taken to see them safe.

Carl appeared among the ghosts.

Don't feel bad, boss, he said, more in Meyer's head than outside it. *Bringing you here was what I was supposed to do.*

The woman was staring at him. Not understanding. Not hearing or seeing any of this. Her attention, when not on Meyer, was fixed on the room's floor. On the dark, leg-thick lines now visible beneath it as shadows against the light. It looked like something with a glow coming from below. The shadows, all different sizes, branched and forked throughout the room.

"Where do you go when you die?"

The woman looked at Meyer like he was crazy.

"I asked you a question."

"Ask your churches," she said, her eyes narrow.

"Why did you come to Earth? Why did you do any of this?"

"To understand."

"To understand what?"

"Everything."

"If you want to understand, why did you kill us off? Why the flood? Why the near extinction?"

"Humanity was not ready. So we reset your race, to try again."

"Not ready by whose criteria? Yours?"

That wasn't quite right. There was something the woman wasn't saying.

She looked at the floor. Nervously. Meyer remembered her question, now asked twice.

What are you doing?

He wasn't doing anything. He was simply sitting, same as her. Yet her eyes kept going to the floor as if uneasy. As if waiting to see what would happen.

Whatever was happening in this room — with the floor and its branching shadows, with the ghosts that Meyer

252

could see and hear but that she apparently could not —
was something she believed he was responsible for.

"What is this place?"

"It's nothing."

"I see people here," he said. "People who've died."

Including Lila.

He couldn't process that now. A part of him had
already known.

She didn't scoff. Or deny it. Instead she seemed to
focus, and he finally felt her touch the collective.

"Who do you see?"

He told her, looking at each and giving their names.
Who they were. Who they'd been.

She watched Meyer. Then, seeming to weigh a decision, she said, "You must leave. We will let you go. You
don't know what you're dealing with."

Heather moved beside him. Meyer turned his head to
her, the blonde Astral seeing his shift of attention, knowing
what it must be even if she couldn't see the ghost.

Heather leaned in and whispered, *Don't do it, studly. Not
now that you've got their nuts in a vice.*

He looked at the Astral and shook his head. Not all of
the links were connecting, but some were, and he wasn't
going anywhere.

The room.

The branching lines beneath the floor, lighting up,
feeling to Meyer like a waking beast. He could feel their
energy. Whatever was happening to this place, the ghosts
were part of it.

"You don't understand," she said.

"Then explain."

She looked away.

"It's your archive, isn't it? What we called the Ark. This

room is somehow part of it. And the people I see standing around you—"

She cut him off, uncertainty in her eyes.

"You have to trust me. What you're doing? It's as bad for you as it is for us."

"I have no reason to trust you."

"You wanted to leave and return to your people. Now is your chance. Leave this alone."

"The other woman said that she'd use me to find them. I won't go back, or help you trace them."

"Then we have to go somewhere else. *Anywhere* else. What do you want? Where do you want to go? Anything. Just name it."

"I want to know why I see my family here." He met the woman's eyes, anger percolating like lava. "My daughter."

"You can't possibly …"

Meyer settled into the energy around him. The room brightened. Contrasting against the light, roots beneath the floor seemed to darken. He saw more ghosts: Peers's friend Aubrey; a nomad who, after Sinai, had traveled with them for a while, Captain Jons, a hero dead too soon.

The woman held up her hands and stood. When she spoke again, her voice was alarmed.

"Stop it! Stop what you're doing!"

Calmly: "What *am* I doing?"

She watched him sternly. "We call this room the Nexus. It's like a nerve center. Not for us. For you."

"Us?"

"Any species we study. *You* since we've been on Earth. This is where we experience our subjects as a whole. The stones we laid around the cities sent information about your collective here, to a network under the floor. Signals travel through the motherships on the way in and out, but this is the center."

"Why do I see people I know who've died?"

"You are different. You can control it." She hesitated. "Like we can."

"How am I different?"

The woman seemed to be warring with a choice of what to say and what to conceal. But like it or not, he was doing something *she* couldn't control. Something that scared her, that she needed his agreement to stop.

"You're like us. What's in you — what's always *been* in you — is like a piece of our collective. But ..." She sighed, clearly unhappy unearthing the secret she wanted to bury. "You've changed. We don't understand you anymore. Not entirely. There are things you can do that shouldn't be possible. That doesn't mean you have power over us. But it makes you like a child carrying a weapon. You don't understand yourself, and that makes you dangerous. To yourself."

"What do you care about us?" Meyer sneered.

"We've invested a lot in you. Time. Thought."

"And yet you're ready to kill us all."

"Your species survives. Individuals do not matter."

Meyer raised his weapon and aimed it at the woman, finger to trigger. She flinched. Turned her head. Cringed.

"It seems to matter to you."

"There has been ... cross-pollution. This is not how we are supposed to be. Not for either of us."

"I see. So this is all for our best interest. You're looking out for us. Because you're the good guys."

He sank into the energy. Gripped the collective. The room brightened again, new ghosts coming like an undead plague. Trevor smiled. Heather touched his shoulder, her spectral hand slipping through him, more solid-seeming than before, but not there at all.

"Stop!"

"For my own good?" Meyer said, not stopping.

"Yes!"

"For *your* good."

"For yours! But ..." He recognized her expression. It wasn't fear for her species, and certainly wasn't concern for his. He poked further into the hive, effortlessly seeing connections from Astral to Astral. They *were* more individual than they should be, truly 'cross-polluted,' one species too tightly bound to the other.

Her expression was *pain*.

"What hurts us hurts you. That's it, isn't it?"

Slowly, she nodded.

"Carl said you tried to peek into his mind. He resisted. He made you push. But when you tortured his mind, that meant trauma for yours."

Seeing no point in denial, the Astral woman said, "Yes."

"This room. It's a nerve center. It's ... a repository. A vast memory bank. Like a storage center."

"It *connects* to a memory bank."

"The Ark. That's what you're saying, isn't it?"

"Each epoch," she said, sitting again, "we reset what you call the Ark. We empty it, and the collective minds of humanity begin to refill it. What you remember goes in. And so does what you *do*. It's true for all of humanity. For thousands of years between visits, the archive tracks it all so we can review your progress when we return, and see if you're ready to evolve."

"I guess this time, we weren't ready."

"No."

"So you killed us off."

"We reset the experiment. To let you try again."

"How generous of you." Meyer's gaze was on Lila. Her presence here could only mean one thing, yet he was less mournful or angry than a part of him felt he should be. Maybe it was the *difference* the woman had mentioned — the way he was *like them*. He was at least part Astral, and as hard as it was to realize, he'd always sort of understood that deep down.

Lila's ghost — someone's memory of her, if Meyer understood this correctly — came forward and tried to take his hand, but of course she couldn't. Lila smiled.

"What you're doing right now," the woman said, watching the floor throb light beneath its branching shadows, "threatens what remains of your species. To the new cycle of our experiment. But you must understand: The experiment is all that keeps us here. If the experiment is disturbed too much ..."

"You'll end it," Meyer finished. The dark-haired woman had told him as much. But was it true? Based on what he'd seen in Eternity — her admission that humanity's pain was their agony, too, thanks to the unwanted bond — it felt like a bluff to Meyer.

He looked up at her. Trying to see the truth.

She nodded.

"You're accessing the archive. I'm not sure how, but I can feel it in the collective. And if you continue, the balance might be upset. And then what's left ..." She didn't finish. Meyer seemed to hear her say it from inside his head: *What's left will no longer be worth saving.*

Meyer looked at the surrounding memories and seemed, for a scant moment, to understand.

He was somehow accessing the Ark, by focusing his thoughts from inside this room — this Nexus. He was scraping the few thoughts and deeds that humanity's remainders had deposited in its banks thus far, just twenty years into the millennia between judgments.

But he believed at least part of what she said: if he kept

focusing on *any* memories in the Ark now, he might break it open.

Then even the survivors would be lost, judged into oblivion.

"Our species are in this together now."

Meyer looked up at Lila. Trevor. Heather. All the others he'd lost and missed. He softened his focus, trying to let them go. His head sagged. He tried to forget, knowing it wasn't truly forgetting. A great energy diminished like a sigh. The floor lost its luster; shadows dimmed as the dark roots died and the room returned to its normal state.

"Good," Eternity said. "Better."

But Meyer watched her face, knowing now that he was like her. And that she was like him. They were linked beneath the surface, tied to one another for better or much, much worse.

Knowing that now, for the sake of humanity's scant future, he would have to keep his mind out of the places it longed to go. He'd have to do his best to forget them all — not through their will, as before, but through his own damned conscious choice.

The lesser of evils. He didn't have to like it, but it seemed he'd have to accept it.

"Thank you," she said, and in the moment, it struck Meyer as the most bizarre thing anyone, of any species, could ever have said.

"Damn you," he replied.

Chapter Thirty-Seven

THE DREAM WOULDN'T LEAVE Piper's mind, clinging like the last tendrils of a spiderweb to the hand attempting to whisk it away.

She moved faster and caught up with Clara. The group was small, and if Kamal's hunch was right (something Piper found herself agreeing with even if it didn't precisely make sense), they might be able to cover most of the distance to the monolith in relative stealth. It seemed to Piper that someone had strategically arranged pieces years ago, then forgotten the positions and rules of the game. Now Stranger's side was playing out against the Astrals — except that even he no longer knew why he'd done what he had, or what was coming next.

He'd been right about Kamal, though. And, apparently, about how his news would resonate with what Clara already knew.

Piper neared the young woman, walking faster. It was still impossible to think of Clara as an adult. To Piper, she'd always be the little girl with the precocious gift. Clara had been then much as she'd been now. Only her body had changed, along with the fatigue in her eyes.

It must've been hell for her.

Years of unending work, holding back a tidal wave while they all blissfully forgot. Even the other Lightborn had given up, leaving her to fight alone. And now, Piper couldn't help but feel like they were entering the endgame.

"Water?"

Clara looked back at Piper and smiled. It was a small thing, but Clara rarely smiled these days — especially with all the world had given them to cry about. She felt the creeping, stubborn sense from her dream retreating, entering the present in the growing sun.

"Thanks." Clara reached back, took the liquid-filled skin. They all had their own water, but it was Piper's only offering. They'd been distant, with Clara living half her time in the Mullah caves, and her simple smile felt like healing.

Clara took a drink and handed it back. Piper sealed the top and slung it over her shoulder.

"Kamal said Stranger set things up so that they could have guns."

"I think they'll be better against Reptars than sticks and harsh language." It was meant as a joke, but Clara's second smile fell flat. They both knew from experience that bullets weren't much better. You could wound and kill Reptars with lead slugs, but you had to get lucky and hit them in a soft spot or, ideally, the eyes. A point-blank shot could sometimes smash through their glowing scales, but they usually kept coming. Yet another reason this was a fool's errand, and that they might all be walking dead.

"Why didn't Stranger have Kamal stash some dune buggies, too?"

Clara sniggered. She must have been keeping some water in her cheeks because a droplet shot from her nose.

Piper let ten or twenty silent paces pass between them. Nobody was talking much. Peers and Kamal were leading the group, with Logan close behind. Kindred was nearby, but the two weren't interacting or even seeming to notice each other. Stranger was nearly as far from Kindred as he could be while still keeping pace with the group — maybe thirty yards back, side by side with Sadeem. There were also several strangers from Kamal's village. They walked in singles and pairs, the two groups not even trying to mingle. A grim thought struck her: maybe everyone knew this was a doomed errand, and there was no point in getting friendly.

But no. Clara was this group's leader, even if Kamal and Peers were in front. That's what Kamal had told her: *Clara says she knows what to do.* And because nothing happened for genuine reasons anymore (or, perhaps, *everything* did), Clara's intuition was as good a direction as any.

"Kamal told me about Meyer."

Clara looked over. Piper had more or less said, *So it turns out Grandpa's an alien. What's new with you?* But Clara only gave her a grim expression of consent. It hadn't taken long for Kamal to explain it, and once he had, Piper realized she'd already known. Her mind had returned to her odd dreams, and the gossamer memory of speaking with Clara. It was as if they'd already had this discussion. As if Clara's mind had spent subconscious hours telling Piper's what they were only pretending to broach now.

"I thought he might," Clara said.

"Do you believe it? That Meyer is …"

"Yes."

"Just like that?"

Clara nodded. "Just like that."

Piper thought about pressing further. Somehow she'd expected a *no*. It might help Piper to reconcile what she didn't doubt herself, though part of her very much wanted to. On one level she'd raised this so that Clara could talk her out of believing Kamal. But on another she had to tip a virtual hat to Clara's straight-faced acceptance.

"I felt like he'd changed when they returned him. And then when I learned that they'd returned someone else — and that the real Meyer had stayed on the ship — it all made sense. Now I find out he's been one of them all along, and it doesn't strike me as odd at all. Why is that?"

"Because he's not *one of them*. He's himself." Another tiny smile creased Clara's lips, but it wasn't for Piper. She was looking forward, smiling for herself. "And I can tell from what I see in the collectives — *both* collectives: he's not what *they* expected, either."

"Can you talk to him? With your mind?"

"Not directly. But he's there, and so am I." Clara looked over, and the maturity of her expression struck Piper as almost jaded. She'd once been a thirty-year-old in a child's body, and now she was like an old woman in the body of a twentysomething. "And I can see how he's spreading through their minds, as he realizes more and more that it's *his* collective, too. He's like a cancer. Something they set loose, and now can't contain."

"Kamal said you know what we're supposed to do."

Clara nodded, that cryptic little smile still on her lips. "We need the Ark. On the ship."

"Why?"

Clara laughed.

"Clara?"

She kept chuckling, giddy like a kid.

"What?"

"It's ironic."

"*What's* ironic?" Clara seemed almost manic, and this from a woman who barely ever smiled. The change was almost scary, and Piper felt a need to push through whatever this was, to get a sensible answer for her strange mood.

"Mom told me that you were always giving her crap."

"*Giving her crap?*" Piper searched her feelings. As Clara brightened, some of Piper's own empathic sense was returning. Based on what she could feel from Clara, the woman wasn't unhinging. Clara felt sure and confident, but Piper couldn't tell why, or what epiphany she might be having.

Clara turned to Piper, now openly smiling. "For playing games. For *always being online.* Mom said that when you guys went to dinner, she'd take her little pocket computer — her *phone*, though she said it was a computer, too — and she'd pull it out and mess with it at the table. And that when she did, you'd yell at her for it."

Piper felt her lips soften into a sympathetic crease. So it wasn't confidence she was getting from Clara after all. It was nostalgia and sorrow.

"Honey, I'm so sorry."

"She said that one time, she brought her headphones, too. And that you *really* lost it. You wanted to have a nice dinner out, but Mom put on her headphones and started watching videos right there at the table."

Piper put an arm around Clara's shoulders.

"Your Uncle Trevor used to do it, too. I hated it, but Meyer liked that it kept you occupied. He'd let them stare at their little screens like zombies because then we could talk without interruption. Every once in a while I'd try to lay down the law and insist that there were no devices at the table, but it never lasted. Because then Lila and Trevor would whine and roll their eyes and complain, and we'd usually end up fighting. So Meyer would say, 'Just let them do it, Piper, so we can eat in peace.'"

Clara laughed, reaching back to a time she'd never experienced. Some of the networks had survived the occupation, but they'd been paltry compared to the once-mighty Internet. There'd been no social networks after Astral Day, no constant pings of incoming emails chiming from everyone's pockets. Before that fateful day you'd enter a group and only see the tops of heads as everyone stared down at their screens.

"Everyone was like that back then, always checking this or that. And your grandpa used to love watching that series *The Beam,* about this hyperconnected future world where everyone was always online with body and mind. But when I suggested that the world was heading there for real, he laughed at me. But it was. Nobody could go five minutes without checking their email or something else inane."

"You make it sound so horrible."

"In concept. But trust me, I was as addicted like everyone else." Piper sighed. "It was hard not to be. It was like everyone, everywhere, was on a drug. Even when you saw what it was doing to our culture — to our families, when everyone could sit at the same table and pay no attention to each other, like your mom and her brother at dinner — you couldn't make yourself stop. Scientists said it was changing our brains. That for your parents' generation, the constant multitasking and distractions was altering them on a biological level. There were studies, showing how modern kids' brains worked differently from adult brains."

Piper looked ahead. Across the barren landscape.

"Well, I guess we solved that problem. It only took an apocalypse."

She turned to Clara, but Clara was still looking

forward, taking in Piper's sarcasm like a point in a logical proof.

"All it took," Clara repeated.

"Clara?"

"That's what made the difference, Grandma."

"What?"

"The Astrals want us to form a collective like theirs. Each time they come back, I think we've come closer, but still no cigar. That's what Kamal said Mara's records showed — past cultures who seemed to have developed psychic bonds, like the Astrals'. But for one reason or another, those cultures weren't enough, so the Astrals erased them and started over. This time, we hadn't developed those bonds *at all*. We weren't remotely psychic — at least not in ways we understood. But we'd still learned to think as a collective. And this time, it was in a way *they* didn't understand."

"What do you mean?"

"That's what the Internet was. Our collective. It allowed people all around the world to think as one. It was much more effective than anything the Egyptians or Mayans came up with; it was just made of wires and computers instead of thought waves. They shut it down when they destroyed our cities. But you nailed it." Clara tapped her head. *"Our brains were already changed."*

"But you weren't even around then."

"Mom's brain was different. Dad's brain, too. Yours, probably, but I'm sure it was a bigger difference for people raised after the collective was already built. Once the Internet was gone and the Astrals started planting those stones and waking our natural abilities, we had a head start with all those connections. The aliens thought they knew what we were capable of, but they were wrong. They underestimated our collective, and thought they could step on it like they had in the past. But this time, we'd become something different. *Our collective* was unique. They treated us like Cousin Timmy, but the Internet must have primed us to become something bigger. Better."

Piper watched Clara, feeling dizzy. She hadn't been waxing nostalgic at all. This was something else.

"They didn't expect the Lightborn. The products of next-generation, network-ready minds exposed to the Astrals' own intense psychic energy. They didn't expect Grandpa, and what might happen if they tried to *fix* what they thought had *broken* with his special mind. They didn't expect that trying to eliminate the problem might create the Pall. They didn't expect Kindred. They didn't expect Stranger."

Clara turned to face Piper. Her face wasn't bothered, even with this daunting journey still before them.

"And they didn't expect *me*, born in the middle of it all."

Watching Clara's suddenly hard and vengeful eyes, Piper swallowed. They were still marching in the hot sun, but suddenly she felt ice cold.

"They can't figure out our minds. They can only truly know us through their Ark — the relic they can't touch until the next judgment, that's ours to fill with memories and deeds in the meantime."

"Clara?" Piper asked, needing to ask a question, not wanting to know the answer. "Why are we going to the freighter?"

"To take back the Ark," Clara said, "and poison it."

Chapter Thirty-Eight

LIZA WAS IN AN ALL-WHITE SPACE. It was like floating in the middle of nothing except that she could definitely feel a floor underfoot. The wolves had brought her here. Or at least, her ride had. She'd never actually seen the wolves.

"Liza."

Liza looked up. She'd been looking down, trying to reconcile the floating. There was a woman in front of her. Medium height with short brown hair. Seeing her took Liza back in time and shook some of the dust from her increasingly foggy head. Because as she noticed the woman's pretty brown hair, and how carefully it was styled, Liza became aware of her own rat's nest. Hadn't she once been an important person? She'd always kept her shit together, and yet here she was, in front of this other important person, with her hair all mussed. It was unforgivable.

"Your name is Liza now, right?"

Liza wasn't sure how to respond. Yes, her name was Liza. But the woman's implication was that it might not always have been.

"Yes. And who are you?"

267

"You can call me Divinity."

Liza's brow furrowed. "Do I know you?"

"We've met before. But you probably don't remember."

"Why not?"

The woman's mouth moved. It was a human mouth, and that was confusing. Liza felt a little drunk, but she'd once been a perfectly cogent person. And as that person, she was quite certain she'd known the word "Divinity." And it referred either to gods (not relevant) or the high class of Astrals. But this woman was clearly human.

"Because you've been erased."

"*Erased?*" The word, like the implication that Liza might not always have been named Liza, didn't make sense.

"Do you remember who you are?"

"I'm Liza Knight. I run the rectory in The Clearing." She could do better than that. "I was the viceroy of Roman Sands."

"I meant, do you remember *what* you are?"

Liza puzzled.

"Your erasure had complications. We thought we could do it cleanly, but we were wrong."

"Why were you wrong?" Liza asked, not understanding the context behind her own question.

"The other hybrid was able to be erased during the Forgetting along with the humans. You retained your memories, per the intention. We thought the other Forgot because of the defects we'd already identified, and that implied your bond didn't carry the same defects. His Replacement caused schisms and birthed a Remainder. We did not attempt to replace you. Do you remember?"

Liza shrugged. It sounded like a lot of metaphysical mumbo jumbo. She was more preoccupied with what had happened to her backpack. Someone had wanted her to go and find it because that person couldn't. Was it this woman? Liza wasn't sure.

"There were complications," Divinity said.

"Nobody's perfect."

The woman looked at her cohorts, whom Liza, with her foggy head, was only now starting to recognize. She'd missed them at first. They were white-skinned against the room's background.

"This isn't working. Dissolve her erasure block. Do we need a probe?" the woman asked one of the Titans. The Titan shook its head. The exchange was simple but struck Liza as odd. Another strange, above-the-subconscious behavior Liza had never seen from an Astral.

"Try to relax," Divinity said.

Liza opened her mouth to ask what that meant, but then one of the Titans tapped a tablet in his massive hands, and the air crackled. Every muscle in her body seemed to tense, and then it was over and her head was suddenly clearer, a bit more focused.

"How's that?" Divinity asked. "How do you feel?"

Liza blinked. She was in an all-white room with a brown-haired woman and two Titans, same as before. But it all struck her as if she'd just walked in, though she knew she'd been here for a while.

"How do you feel?" Divinity repeated.

"I'm fine."

"Do you remember meeting me before?"

Liza didn't. Not entirely. She searched her mind and came up only with the same vague feeling of familiarity. There was something else, like a faded snapshot: a ghost of a memory involving her rectory's cafeteria, this woman, and a sense of foreboding.

"No."

"It might return. It might not. I don't have time to wait. Do you remember … *anything else?*"

Liza blinked again. She almost gasped as — in the split second of darkness with her eyelids shut — she seemed to see something staring back at her. A black mass: a giant worm with no mouth or face — only a pair of giant yellow eyes. The sight made her start. She bucked backward and almost fell, one of the Titans grabbing Liza's arm to steady her.

"What the fuck?"

Divinity turned to one of the Titans. "She sees it."

And an echo, repeated inside Liza's head: *She sees it. She sees it. She sees it.* As if Divinity's voice were plucked and repeated, a call sent out and perpetuated by other sources.

"Listen to me," Divinity said, now taking Liza's shoulders and staring into her eyes. "I don't have time to be anything other than blunt. You, as Liza Knight of Cape Town, are host to an observer. It might frighten you as the top part of your mind adjusts to what it believes is news, but this is something you've always known deep down, because the observer has always been with you. *Breathe.*"

Liza felt the peak of an adrenaline spike. She shook beneath Divinity's hands, her heart rate climbing. She wanted to run, but the woman's grip was strong. Her breaths were short and fast, her eyes darting everywhere. Every time she blinked, she saw that thing, looking back at her, coiled inside.

"*Breathe.* The feeling will pass."

"What the fuck is that thing?" Liza demanded.

"It's part of you. It always has been. But it's also part of us. I need you to focus, Liza. It's like remembering how to inhale. Your body knows it even if panic wants you to forget. You must accept this — and do it fast. Just like you need to inhale for your body to keep living, so you need to integrate this knowledge of what you've always known. Can you do that?"

Fuck no, she couldn't do that. There was a worm inside her mind, with giant yellow eyes. Liza's hammering pulse was in her neck. In her clenching hands. In her tiny, shallow breaths.

"Liza." Divinity shook her. *"Liza!"*

Liza's head snapped to center.

"Watch my eyes."

Liza held them, willing herself to Divinity's requested calm. Slowly, grudgingly, it came. Then, still keyed up, Liza watched those brown irises and said, "You're not human."

"This body is a surrogate."

"Am *I* a surrogate?"

"You are a hybrid. I can feel the observer touching our collective. You're intertwined with the observer. I know you can access all the answers you need if you'll allow it to happen. Do you see?"

Liza didn't. But then, as she watched the woman's eyes, answers came. Fog departed. Clarity returned.

"It was you in my head. You sent me to that canyon. To that cache of stuff."

"Circumstances made a trip necessary, and I could not go myself."

"Why?"

"It's complicated."

Liza dipped her toe into the new mental water. Her memories were more or less crisp, save that one blank spot between the rectory and the moment she'd awakened near the freighter to find Peers Basara and Stranger. And she had new memories, too. New senses that must be her mind — or *the observer's* — reaching into the Astral collective. She could feel its concerns. Its rough spots. Two places, in particular, where things weren't as harmonious as a collective was supposed to be.

"Who is Eternity?" Liza asked, feeling one of the rough spots.

"An Astral who's been compromised. Which is why I need your help."

"Where is she?"

"She is on this ship. Being held captive."

"By who?"

Divinity's mouth worked again, probably deciding if she could trust Liza enough to tell her a closely held truth.

"A hostile."

Liza reached into the collective. It was there. Like Eternity. But there was a block — something twisted enough that she couldn't see.

"I know you can't see far," Divinity said, as if reading Liza's facial expression. "Eternity's … *abduction* … has caused more knots than our collective is equipped to deal with. Communication has broken down. In many cases we're having to transmit mouth to ear like humans."

"Shout for more Titans. Let's break in there and get her back," said Liza.

For a third time, Divinity seemed to consider. "Many Titans have been compromised, as well. These two will help us." She nodded at the pair. "But you should not leave this room without me because others might be … less helpful."

"But you're a group. Like a hive mind. All thinking as one?"

"That's the way it's supposed to be, but right now it is not. There is too much to explain. I just need to know if you're with me."

"With you?" It was a bizarre question from an Astral. Humans thought this way. Not aliens. Not Liza, if she was

to believe the big yellow eyes she was slowly getting used to seeing.

"Look inside, Liza. Consult your observer. I know you can feel it. I can *feel you feeling it*. Haven't you ever felt our pull? A desire to understand what Astrals are doing and perhaps even join us?"

Liza thought back. Oh yes, she'd felt shifted loyalties before. In a way, realizing what she'd apparently always known (something that, right now, felt more like *integration* than realization) was a relief. She'd wondered, long ago, if she was just a dirty traitor. Now Lila realized she was being true to herself, though she hadn't seen what her true *self* was before now.

"Our Founders seeded observers in your population. They've always been among you, moving from host to host upon their passing. The Founders also seeded each test population with *chaos*. Before now the element gave the experiment variation. This time it triggered a fault. Another of our hybrids manifested an anomaly. We tried to purge it, and the anomaly spread systemwide. There's only a small unaffected cluster." Divinity sighed, frustrated. "I would rather not tell you this, but there is no other way."

"You and me and them," Liza said, nodding toward the Titans. "This is the 'unaffected cluster'?"

"Yes."

"But you said my 'erasure' didn't take. And I'm not stupid enough to believe that any of the three of you are acting normally, for Astrals."

"It's a matter of degrees."

Liza considered, then said, "Why are you telling me this? It's not just so that you can have a fourth."

Liza's intuition — surely from her human half — was prickling. Since when did Astral command beg humans for help? Maybe Liza had Astral in her, but the collective hadn't grabbed and compelled her — though arguably, that might have been what had happened when she'd been on the surface, before she'd stepped into that shuttle and come up here. No. This one was asking for help, even if she was doing it sideways. It didn't fit. Something was terribly wrong … and right now Liza, as the newcomer, had a surprising amount of power.

"When we accessed you earlier, before your erasure, there was something in your record about a sabotage plot. A reason you were, from the start, more allied to Astrals than humanity. It struck us as a counterpoint to the imbalance in the other direction — toward humanity — that we've seen in the other hybrid."

Liza was seeing more and more. She could peek into the Astral collective, sure, but the old viceroy also had her human cunning. And right now, that superpower duo of abilities was pointing her toward one inescapable conclusion: This particular woman, whatever she was to the Astrals, was in a hell of a bind. And she thought Liza, for some reason, held her key to salvation.

"It's spreading, isn't it? Whatever's gotten into your system and is causing trouble … It's getting worse."

"The human collective is new to us. Their minds have changed in a way we don't understand. We were unable to complete the Forgetting because their minds work like a hologram: as long as one node remained, others could be rebuilt."

A smile crept across Liza's lips. Combining human memory and Astral insight, she thought she could see the problem in a way this woman couldn't. Liza didn't know how to solve their problem or even begin to crack its shell, but she did get it in a way that they couldn't. She had a different frame of reference, and to Liza, a metaphor for the problem — still with no solution — was clear as glass.

Divinity was saying that the Astrals couldn't blank humanity's memory banks (minds) because they couldn't erase all the servers (people) at once — because each mind in the collective held all the data (memories) and could repopulate the rest at any time.

Humanity's minds were like the cloud, back in the days of the Internet.

"What's that smile for?"

"You really can't tell?" Liza asked. "You can't read my mind?"

"Eternity's abduction has put knots throughout the system. And the hybrid's pollution, working on her, has made it … *difficult* … to see."

"You'll have to kill us all. As long as one human mind keeps popping up …" Liza shrugged, suddenly feeling very much herself, suspecting there was still an ace far down in this hole — one that, when revealed, would trump all the rest. "You're fucked," she finished.

"We can't kill you off. We're too intertwined. We can bluff, but eradicating this planet's experiment, at this point, also eliminates us."

Liza watched Divinity, sensing what was coming, enjoying the unfolding.

"You had a way out," Divinity said, now almost pleading. "I could see it in your observer's record. It's why I sent for you. It's why I sent you to that canyon! You needed something. I can't see what it is, what you once knew, but *I know it's there*, buried in your mind! What is it? *Think!*"

Liza had already figured it out. Just as she had so long ago.

Divinity knew Liza had once known a way to disrupt humanity's virus, but Liza's mind must have been hidden enough to stay mostly invisible. She was half-Astral but living undercover. Now Divinity was guiding Liza's no-longer-foggy brain toward what it once thought of as salvation.

"You don't know why you need me," Liza said.

"It's something you once had. Something you once planned! I can sense the potential, but with the collective compromised—"

"Where is my backpack?"

One of the Titans reached behind himself and procured the thing, holding it out to Liza.

"It's full of junk," said Divinity. "But your mind seemed to once feel—"

"Not junk," said Liza, cutting her off.

Her hand effortlessly found what she was looking for. Her fingers went right to it, as if guided.

She pulled it out. Held it up. Watched Divinity puzzle the item, savoring the obvious shift in power.

"Take me with you to the next colony," Liza said, slowly revolving the thing in her hand. "Make me a queen there, and I'll show you how to end your 'experiment' on Earth for good."

Chapter Thirty-Nine

MELANIE WATCHED Meyer until she was sure he was in a trance. He was trying to reach out to Clara and the others, believing Melanie (rightfully) about the Ark but trying to find a way to assist their doomed mission anyway. And that was human hope: tell one of them that their situation is futile, and they'll go back and start hammering the same nail.

'Hammering the same nail'? Melanie thought. *You're just as bad as they are.*

The new human mental network had proved difficult to crack, but in the end it came down to the Archetypes. Their external collective had somehow married right back to the more sensible, internal, organic collective, giving them redundancy just like their old Internet had. Unless the Forgetting was applied to every mind at once — which was more or less impossible — the ones they *didn't* hit in any cycle kept spreading their knowledge back to the others once pressure abated. They'd make one sector Forget, then that sector would be reminded of everything below the surface once attention turned to the following sector. Any time the Forgetting was relaxed, people began to remember for real. It had been a twenty-year game of Whack-a-Mole, never slowing or stopping.

"Whack-a-Mole"? That's even worse than hammering nails. Or individuality or conceit or arrogance or "pride" or "self-confidence." In another five years, we'll all be processing human magazine articles, wondering if we're too fat, splitting into genders, trying to figure out why He's Just Not That Into You.

The fact that she even knew the human culture references necessary to make the internal joke was bothersome. The pollution was pervasive. Intrusive. It pressed her every sense, fooling Melanie into believing she needed to *have* senses, to have her body, to consider herself "herself."

Well, not for long.

The collective was so twisted and fogged that it could barely see its directives, and Melanie could no more issue imperatives than hear the dissent that shouldn't be there. Getting Meyer off the ship would help; he was twisting the Nexus like an enemy's neck. But even after he was gone, they'd have trouble piloting the ships or issuing orders until they were finally out of orbit. Until the Archetypes were gone, the ship's proximity would worsen the sickness. *That* was human hope in its worst form: aggressive, unwilling to settle until it had ruined everything.

But now, even as Meyer tried in vain to help the group heading toward the beached freighter, those problematic Archetypes were all in the same place — lined up like the ducks in a shooting gallery that she shouldn't see as an apt metaphor.

They'd eliminated the Warrior and the Innocent.

Now the King, Fool, Magician, and Sage were together, waiting for slaughter as Melanie reached around Meyer's trance and tapped the Reptars on their big black shoulders, warning them that enemies were approaching.

That only left the Villain, but Melanie could sense that one, too. Nearby, maybe even on the ship. Reptars up here could kill that one while the Reptars on the planet handled the other five.

That would shock Meyer right out of this little game, then the release of his hold on the collective — and the Nexus — would relax enough for them to kill him as well.

It would be enough. Then Melanie could stop thinking of Whack-a-Mole and hammers on nails and ducks in galleries. She could stop considering her reflection and this strange attachment to her surrogate. She could stop taking pride in *what she thought* and *who she was* and *how she looked*. She could stop believing that it was better for her surrogate to keep on breathing than that Meyer be prevented from taking the damned ship captive.

She opened her eyes. Meyer was sitting quietly in his chair, weapon in hand. She wouldn't try to get it because that would wake him. But the collective's pollution could work for Melanie even as it was working against her. She couldn't see most of the others, let alone issue imperatives, but maybe that meant he wouldn't see her — as focused as he was on poking Kindred and Stranger and Clara, trying to show them the nature of their ship's power — and how many Reptars were *truly* waiting.

Surprise was everything.

Melanie pushed through the fog, through her limited point of view, and found her body. Her core. She saw Meyer's trance to the side, as dominant in the collective as it had been in the human collective unconsciousness when he'd taken his drugs.

He could speak to them and try to show them the truth, *yes*.

But Melanie could reach out to the Reptars on the ship first, doubling their Doubling, using an inch of the Nexus's power through the archive to make the illusion that much more convincing.

Let Meyer show his people exactly how to come.

The Reptars would be prepared, and waiting.

Chapter Forty

KINDRED WENT LEFT when Stranger went right.

Kindred knew nothing about battle tactics; Meyer hadn't been a veteran, and he, along with everyone else, had spent the last two decades having forgotten pretty much everything but his name. Even so, splitting up to attack a target seemed logical. Not that it would make a difference. The monolith was in a low V, the sea miles distant, highlands of the side even farther from the water. They'd approach from above, marching down what was essentially a long dune. There wasn't any cover. It was laughable to think they could take anyone by surprise.

But even from up here, looking across the V at the tiny black specks that were all he could see of the other group, Kindred knew this was their best shot. You attacked from two directions. It made sense, even if it was a fool's errand.

He could feel the Ark's power, even from here. They'd just been here yesterday, and his daughter (in a matter of speaking) had been slaughtered aboard this same ship, with the same power thrumming in the background. Just yesterday he'd looked at the Reptars and heard a voice from the sky inside his mind and realized they didn't have to stay. Then they'd been somewhere else, and in the moment — *just* for the moment — the idea of teleporting made total sense, before it vanished like fog in a breeze. He'd dreamed the whole thing. He and Stranger both, according to what the others said.

But right now, feeling the Ark's power, Kindred could believe it.

I remembered something yesterday. I realized something obvious, that anyone could see.

The power was a low thrum. Something that seemed to reach out and invite him forward, its song hypnotic. They could march right in there. Sure, there was plenty to fear. But so what, when you could see all the terrible things and know precisely where the traps lay?

Kindred felt knowledge almost percolating. Threatening to rise. Below the surface and beside his resentment. He remembered things long passed. Events he wasn't even sure he himself had participated in.

Receiving a message from Divinity when he'd been viceroy of Heaven's Veil, Trevor in his office, claiming to search for books, Raj clattering around somewhere overhead, slowly going bad.

Hiding in the bunker under Vail, Piper in the corner, bloody spatter from the first man she'd ever killed not yet scrubbed from her neck, close to catatonic, rocking, still young enough to feel bad for a necessary murder.

Himself on the ship, kept in a cell. Piper, also aboard.

You were a Titan back then, said a voice. *You did not see Piper on the ship. You were another thing, in fear of becoming me.*

Meyer's voice. From somewhere.

Focus, Kindred.

Meyer inside his mind, the sensation curiously doubled,

as if he was talking to himself. Which, by a certain definition, he was.

There are only three Reptars left.

Kindred looked behind him, catching curious glances from Logan, Piper, Kamal, and the man and woman whom Kindred had met but whose names had yet to register. From Kamal's crew — brave, selfless enough to storm a place they knew to be swarming with enemy soldiers for the greater good. But according to the voice in Kindred's head, there were only three. And yet he knew they'd only managed to kill one of the potential hundreds they'd seen before.

Aft, amidships, and near the door to the bridge. You will know when you see them.

Kamal was slowly shaking his head, seeming to ask a question with raised eyebrows.

Clear your head. If you focus, you can see.

Kindred didn't know what the voice meant, or where it was coming from. He didn't know whom it belonged to. But the Ark's power was like sweat on his brow. He could sense it calling him forward, feel his mind calming — welcome change from the cauldron, stewing with anger and resentment, plagued by jealousy and pettiness and hate. He wanted to march forward, heedless. He wanted to cross the V, to the ship's other side. Find Stranger, and let the end come.

If you focus, you can see.

But it was hard, and Kindred didn't want to.

Ahead, at the freighter's towering metal side, was a tall, black-haired form, waving him forward.

His ex-wife, Heather, whom he'd already died once saving.

Chapter Forty-One

"STRANGER?"

But Stranger's eyes were on the person near the ship's rear: *Trevor.* He'd never known the boy, and yet he'd raised Trevor from a baby and taught him to ride a bike, tolerated his teenage angst, as annoying as it had been. He was dressed in jeans and a T-shirt. The jeans looked clean. How long had it been since he'd seen a clean pair? Denim could last a long time — but their little village, which had thought nothing of the curious blue material in the same way they thought nothing of the other old-world items that didn't make sense — only had a few intact pairs among them, most ripped through at the knee and converted to anachronistic shorts.

But Trevor was standing there in his jeans and tee, the way he'd looked on the last day of his life, so far as Stranger remembered of that time he'd never known or seen.

"Stranger!"

He flinched when Clara touched his shoulder. He'd been about to rise. Energy wafting from the ship was like second heat, and Stranger could think of little beyond heeding its cry. Kindred, across the dunes, was calling him. Maybe they could meet in the middle, link arms like schoolgirls, and skip the rest of the way down. It would be the end of them both, and maybe all of it. But did it matter? The Ark's song was so alluring.

"Are you okay?"

"There are only three," he said.

"Three what?"

He was already too distracted to answer. Movement at the ship's other end caught his eye. There was someone there. A woman in her forties.

Lila.

"Stranger? Three what?"

Lila waved, seeing their little group where they pretended to hide. She put her hand on the ladder bolted to the monolith's side, raised a leg, and climbed. Trevor, at the other end, began to do the same.

Stranger could hear the Reptars in his head. This wouldn't be as hard as they'd all imagined. All puzzles were hard until you knew the trick, but once you saw it, the whole thing cracked open, so obviously simple.

Lila stopped. Then Trevor. Stranger's children hung on their ladders, their large smiles obvious even across the distance. They waved. Beckoning.

More movement, this time across the dune. Someone shouted — a voice that was half hiss, half yell, as if the shouter was somehow trying to be quiet even while calling out. There was another shout from behind Stranger. Over his shoulder, where Clara and Peers and Sadeem and some fellow named Marcus were waiting and failing to understand how easy this whole thing actually was.

There were eleven of them, and thanks to Kamal's group's preparation (something Stranger got credit for arranging, despite his lack of memory), their group was armed. Bullets weren't always efficient against Reptars, but Reptars fought with claws and teeth — and aboard that entire ship, there were only three.

Three foes between them and the Ark. Between them and the end of everything. Between the end of his and Kindred's twenty-year tension and its final resolution. Between the anger and hatred that tore at Stranger's gut — the guilt and pain he'd increasingly learned to feel but could no longer abide.

Three Reptars between Stranger and his vendetta.

"Kindred!" Peers whisper-shouted at the man descending the dune, headed for neither Trevor nor Lila but a space between them.

Stranger rose and started walking too.

Then all the shouts called out from behind.

Chapter Forty-Two

PEERS'S EYES darted rapidly side to side. They'd discussed this, and now both Kindred and Stranger were breaking from the plan. He watched them march straight toward the freighter, in the open, shouting his petty little cries, knowing along with the others that Stranger and Kindred either couldn't hear or would never acknowledge. There was little to do. He couldn't raise his voice. The Reptars might hear, and Peers could see dozens of the black creatures crawling around the deck like a swarm of deadly spiders.

He looked at Sadeem, whose face promised no help. Then at Clara's wide eyes. He peeked back at Stranger and Kindred, both sitting ducks. There were four Reptars on the sand, two flanking each man. But Stranger didn't even look over at them, and neither did Kindred. It was as if they didn't even know the Reptars were there.

"Trade me guns," Peers said, his hand out toward Sadeem.

"You're supposed to have the handgun."

"And those two assholes were supposed to stay back

until the deck was clear!" Peers hissed. "Give me the fucking rifle!"

Sadeem hesitated, his eyes ticking to the opposite dune. Probably appealing to Kamal, as if the fact that Kamal had procured the weapons meant he owned the plan. Well, *fuck* the plan. There'd been many plans, and they had ways of not working out. Peers and Aubrey had *planned* a bunker full of Astral technology before they'd met Meyer's group all those years ago, but it turned out the cave had probably been put there by the Astrals, Peers unwittingly filling his role as a puppet. He and Aubrey had also *planned* to haul ass through the cannibals outside Ember Flats without casualties, but then that dumbass Christopher had careened away to blow himself up and make a hole. And let's not forget his own *plan* to duck into the Mullah Elders' temple for a bit of righteous mischief. That plan hadn't gone *too* awry; he'd called the Astrals to Earth to end a species, seven billion strong. Yes. *Plans* were spectacular.

Sadeem lowered the barrel. Peers snatched it, giving the old man a warning glance, then lowered the thing, preparing to sight on the Reptar closest to Kindred when Sadeem changed his mind and grabbed the butt from behind.

Peers spun, adrenaline high, and stopped himself inches from driving his elbow back into Sadeem's face. He found himself confronting Clara instead.

She looked at Kindred and Stranger, walking in a trance down the dunes. She looked at the Reptars on the sand, all with open mouths, menacing the two men but keeping their distance.

Clara shook her head.

"Something is wrong," she said.

Chapter Forty-Three

THROUGH HIS SYMBIONT'S Astral mind, Meyer saw it plain as day.

There were only three Reptars on the freighter. The Astrals had left four behind as quiet guards, meant purely as a backup force, there to protect the Ark until the Forgetting could be completed. Kindred had managed to kill one of the four when he'd visited the freighter, and the Astrals hadn't replaced it. They couldn't. Their entire command structure was based on a *lack* of a command structure, and now that human thought had spread through them like a virus, they didn't know how to function. If the Astrals had a leader, it would have been Eternity. But she was here with Meyer, and had problems of her own. They all knew the woman was a puppet, just as Eternity knew it herself. Yet he'd held her hostage all the same.

Shuttles didn't know where to fly. Motherships could barely communicate. The Deathbringer's orbit could decay, and they probably wouldn't know until it crashed and knocked a chunk out of the recovering planet. They didn't know how to function as individuals. Meyer could see them scrambling from inside the changing collective — disagreeing, arguing, feeling proud, and the infant version of arrogance. They'd adjust. But hadn't yet.

There were only three Reptars on the ship. It might look like dozens or hundreds from the outside, but Meyer saw the trick, like wires holding up the spaceships in an old sci-fi movie. The Ark had to fold space to do its job — to see as far and wide as it needed to. Those folds were subtle. But Kindred and Stranger, who had the potential for their own power, had opened one of those folds wider, into a rip, and stepped right through it.

Four people slipping through a rift doesn't happen by accident, Divinity had told him.

And that was true. Even the Astrals, as far as Meyer and his observer could see, couldn't do it. The ships could, and that's how they'd rifted from their home through the hole near Jupiter to reach Earth. But shuttles couldn't do it, nor could individual Astrals. It took tremendous energy. Immense power, harnessed to deepen a gravity well into something local, and safe.

But Kindred and Stranger had done it. Without knowing why or how. And they'd taken passengers with them. It was like instinct, buried deep inside Meyer. Projected to the pair of half men, who used their power to take things further.

That had scared Divinity. Because Meyer Dempsey wasn't supposed to become what he had. He wasn't supposed to have broken in the way they saw him. And when they'd attempted repair? When they'd sent a copy to do a hybrid's job? Well, then shit had really hit the fan.

Meyer watched the Reptars harnessing the Ark's power as best they could, showing themselves as spooks using something called quantum entanglement — but which felt to Meyer's mind like specialized prisms. Just as light enters and refracts into many beams, a trio of Reptars was appearing as many. They couldn't travel like the human wild cards, or do more than this pop-up freak show, displaying their false faces to incite panic so their bodies could attack the humans by surprise.

As long as the humans knew which of the Reptars were real, this would be simple.

They'd find the Ark.

And then, as Clara planned, they'd poison it.

The thought turned Meyer's attention toward Eternity, wanting to make sure she couldn't tell that his mind was talking to Kindred, Stranger, and Clara. He could keep her out. It wasn't even hard now that he was getting the trick. Eternity had showed her hand when he'd stimulated the Nexus. Once he'd gotten the feel for manipulating their energy, it wasn't difficult. He didn't even have to risk accessing it again to do what had to be done. Meyer could project ghosts to guide Kindred and Stranger fine without it.

He tuned to Eternity. She wasn't even poking at his defenses. His shell was plenty intact.

Meyer nudged the ghosts further, concentrating, leading his people to the true Reptar guards, blinding their minds to the false ones so they wouldn't panic without cause. He had to keep it up, keep them marching and hide the duplicates. It wouldn't be long now.

But then a harsh mental whisper

(he's at the far end and has a weapon.)

returned his attention to Eternity, just as he'd been about to shift his focus. His eyes snapped open, and he found himself staring directly at the blonde, her gaze big and full of guilt.

"What did you do? Did you just—?"

The door behind Meyer blew open. He dove toward Eternity, knocking her back, gun trained behind him, firing at everything that moved and filling the room with corpses.

Chapter Forty-Four

KINDRED BLINKED AS if leaving a trance. He didn't precisely recall walking onto the sand, though he did remember a dream of Heather, calling him forward, beckoning with her warm and long-missed embrace. Yet here he was.

A pair of Reptars was flanking him, one on each side.

Adrenaline flooded his cortex and doubled his pulse. The bottom of Meyer's instinct flushed through Kindred as if born there. He found himself reaching for the semi-automatic tucked into the back of his pants, seconds ticking too fast. He might have shouted; he definitely tripped and fell onto his back, seeing the first of the big black things moving over him, mouth open and spark churning, Kindred's finger tugged uselessly on the trigger as he pointed down its throat. It was dead. The pistol was done. It had jammed, and now there was a Reptar about to rip him in half and—

. . .

PEERS YANKED the rifle from Clara's grip, practically ramming its stock into her forehead in his panic as Kindred fell and began to shout. As Stranger, across the dunes, pointed at the Reptar on his right as if seeing it only now, firing over and over and over, the Reptar still coming but not overtaking him.

He rushed forward, up over the lip, raising his rifle in the clear, not worrying about cover, knowing it was blown, that something had gone terribly wrong. But then he swore; the rifle was the right choice when the scene had been quiet, but now he couldn't get a clear shot. He'd have to run in, and that close up, the rifle was useless.

On the other side, Logan was up; Kamal was up; the man from Kamal's village was up and running.

"Give me the handgun!"

Sadeem stammered.

"GIVE ME THE FUCKING HANDGUN!"

But Sadeem was lost; he was a thinker, not a fighter. Peers dropped the rifle and snatched it from him, Sadeem's grip momentarily fierce. There was a frightening instant where Peers imagined the gun going off in the struggle, shooting friend while trying to end their foe.

But the gun came loose, and Peers ran.

"COME ON!"

Piper shook her head. She'd almost seen something. Almost understood. Even now she kept getting a flash of a circular room with a floor that lit up, with the shadows of what appeared to be tree branches beneath it. She was there with Meyer (she'd *been* there with Meyer), and it was long ago, and she'd left Cameron behind, and had felt a new kinship she returned. They'd matched before, then much better later, as if they were on the same frequency after years spent slightly off.

"*Piper!*"

But Kamal wasn't going to wait; he ran toward the melee, racking his weapon.

(*SAFETY.*)

The voice from Kindred's own mind, not Meyer's or Clara's. Only his own internal reminder that he was being an asshole and that as long as the Reptar continued to jaw above him, those were more seconds he could spend shooting it through the back of its throat — one of the creature's most vulnerable spots.

(*Safety!*)

Not a call for Stranger to run for cover — a reminder to click the switch on his gun's side, turning it from safe to *red*, for *dead*.

Safety off, finger on trigger. *Pop, pop, pop.*

But the bullets went right through the Reptar as if it wasn't even there.

SADEEM SAW the other Reptars climb the freighter's railings from the deck and spill down its sides like bees in a swarm. The first surrounded Kindred, Logan, Kamal, and Kamal's cohort, Danni, her posture tall and proud, firing her weapon like a pro. Reptars eclipsed Stranger, Marcus, and Peers ahead. Blocking them from view.

Clara, looking up at him in betrayed expectation, as if someone had promised her Santa before admitting the lie.

But Sadeem and Clara had weapons, same as the others. He stood, removing his, flicking the safety to off as Kamal had shown them.

"We have to help them," Sadeem said, saying words he didn't feel, watching as the enormous swarm churned and buried their friends from view. Had Peers and the others really only thought there were a few dozen Reptars on the freighter? There had to be hundreds, maybe more.

Clara's eyes were scanning the melee, squinting as if to see more than what was so obviously there. Her head snapped toward a lone Reptar leaping from the ship's side, running toward the spot where Stranger's group had been.

"They're not—" Clara began, her eyes more confused than terrified. She stopped, flinching as shots ripped through the purring and growling, shattering the day like something broken. It was Kamal, with one of those desert weapons the old-world warlords once carried, black and long with a banana clip.

Shots struck the sand. Kamal dove down, bullets whistling overhead. Others came. Single reports, from a handful of other shooters.

They were still alive. Somehow, amid the huge knot of Reptars, they were all still alive.

Firing their weapons.

And the bullets were going right through the Reptars, striking nothing at all.

STRANGER'S SHOULDER struck Peers's shoulder. Marcus was to his side, weapon raised. They'd stopped firing. Bullets didn't always knock Reptars down, but they never failed to nab their attention. But these weren't flinching. No shattered scales, no blood, no sounds or sights of impact. The Reptars weren't coming — marching in a circle, feinting as if to strike without ever attacking.

. . .

"THEY'RE NOT REAL."

Clara held tight as Sadeem tried to pull away. She was low, looking across the all-black battleground, watching the fearful sight of Reptars swarming just feet away. But something was still off. She'd seen her share of Reptar attacks, and this was like none of them.

"Let me go!"

"They're not real, Sadeem! Look at them!"

Sadeem looked. Shots rang out, raising tiny blasts of sand.

One prowling from the other side, moving without hurry toward the knot where Kindred and his small group of warriors had vanished, surrounded.

Sadeem saw her eyes.

He traded the big rifle for Clara's handgun, snatching it before she could protest. Then he ran toward the Reptar, robes flapping.

SADEEM RAISED his weapon and fired at the lone Reptar. He was too old. His joints ached; his hands weren't used to the heavy firearm. His teeth wanted to rattle whenever it kicked. He could barely hear after a few of the thunderous reports.

The Reptar Clara had been staring at flinched. Recoiled. Turned to face Sadeem, leaping, pinning his gun hand, rattling the weapon loose. Then its dark and bleeding body was above him, wounded but not enough. His head rolled to the side, trying to torque his body around to reach the gun with his free hand. He saw the nearest clutch of Reptars and noticed a curious thing: maybe a third of the Reptars that had been circling were now wavering. And bleeding.

The thing raised its head and bellowed, then swung its

rows of teeth down, whip-fast. But Sadeem was faster; he brought his toe hard up under the Reptar's jaw, stunning it, making it choke.

Free hand.

Gun.

Sadeem was right-handed, but the quarters were close enough that an imperfect shot would do. His clumsy left hand found enough strength to grip it, and pull the trigger. The blow glanced off the Reptar's side, doing little more than making it reel. The deterred teeth connected but did so imperfectly; razors cut into Sadeem's flesh at the shoulder. But it was his right shoulder, and his left was still free so he fought the spreading agony and shoved his barrel into the thing's mouth, managing another shot, watching the slide lock back.

Empty. That was my last bullet.

But it was enough. A great glut of thick blood coughed from the Reptar's throat, and the thing collapsed atop him, then rolled away.

A third of the Reptars on both groups collapsed, suddenly dead.

They're not real, Clara had said.

Sadeem scanned the scene. Another two Reptars were coming, each by itself, moving fast.

LOGAN, mouth open, looked right at Kamal when a bunch of Reptars dropped dead. It felt like something from an action movie he might have seen as a kid, before Astral Day: a villain sliced and diced by the hero, only realizing after a few pregnant seconds that he'd been cut into pieces. Kamal was holding the group's only assault rifle. It was as if he'd shot all the Reptars after all, but it had taken them a moment to get the message.

"How—?" Logan managed the single word before a big black body leaped from the churning mass and hit him full on.

The Reptar, having overshot its mark, turned and stalked back toward Logan as he fumbled for his gun, which he'd somehow hung onto. Kamal's eyes lit, but then a large group of Reptars moved between them, and Kamal and his machine gun were gone.

Logan raised his weapon. The Reptar knocked it away. Its mouth opened, a purr escaping on foul, meat-flavored breath.

Oh hell. I'm going to die on my back.

The thing came. Stalking. *Purring.* But then something else came: small, lightning fast, swinging something like a board or bat. There was a crack, and the Reptar recoiled, struck in its big armored face. It staggered as if dizzy, then Logan was moving backward, dragged from under his armpits. But — horror of horrors — his savior was pulling him *into the swarm.*

Clara came around him and squatted. Logan tried to focus on her but couldn't. He was trying to hold his ground, but it was hard with all the Reptar legs and claws and purring heads knocking him all about.

"We're safe here."

"We're *safe?*" Logan couldn't believe he'd heard correctly. Clara could have been speaking Chinese.

"They're not real. They're … projections."

Something stepped on Logan. It hurt.

"They feel real to me!" he was hysterical, barely able to listen for all the panic, all the fight-or-flight.

"Logan. Listen. There are only a few of them. The rest are duplicates. I don't think they can pay attention to more than their own eyes, so they can't see us, or get to us. I think most are smoke and mirrors. You saw how the bullets were going right through."

A Reptar opened its mouth right beside him. Logan flinched back, seeing teeth and that blue glow. But the thing closed its mouth and moved away: just another horror show.

"The one I hit," Clara said, looking back the way they'd come.

"Hit?"

Clara shrugged — a strange gesture amid the Reptars. As she stood, one of the many alien arms went right through her: one of Clara's smoke and mirrors beasties, true to her word.

"I didn't know how to shoot Sadeem's rifle," Clara said, "but it worked fine as a bat."

A SCREAM.

Piper had run toward Kamal and Logan and Kindred, somehow ending up in the middle. She remembered the freeway catastrophe outside Chicago a thousand years ago, recalling those close quarters, and feeling the same sensation now. How had she been surrounded? She'd been firing the entire time but didn't think she'd killed a single Reptar. She'd been prepared to kill or die herself, but neither happened. When that massive batch had dropped dead all at once, she'd seen Logan, Kindred, Kamal, and Kamal's friends. Now she was in the middle. Why weren't they attacking, until the one struck at Logan?

Clara had pushed right through the Reptars, not minding them at all, and whacked the one over Logan hard with what turned out to be a rifle. It was still where she'd dropped it, but Clara and Logan were gone, retreated through a wall of Reptars like a bead curtain.

Now the scream. Piper saw the Reptar Clara had clocked recovering, now ripping the woman from Kamal's village down her middle. Blood spurted as she separated. The man shouted, pointing his gun at the Reptar's body, firing, bullets scoring only fractured scales. He needed to aim at its mouth, its eyes. Getting a body shot with a bullet, on a Reptar, came down to luck.

Piper watched as the thing turned him to mincemeat.

PEERS WATCHED a bloody-armed Sadeem cross the space between the groups, already feeling the oddity of all that was happening. The Mullah had legends about this sort of thing — about illusions pulled by the Horsemen. But what were these creatures if not Reptars? He'd fired through several, struck a few without any damage. The dead had fallen without effort from Peers, but he could already tell that whatever riddle had transpired, Sadeem had figured it out.

He took off after the old man, watching him raise a weapon to a solo Reptar that was very near Stranger, shooting at it from the other side. There was something in its jaws. By omission (not Clara, who'd run the other direction; not Sadeem; not Peers or Stranger), the anonymous puree dripping from its maw had to be Marcus — a guy who, Kamal had joked on the way in, had once perfected the art of making copies and bringing coffee to Jabari.

Sadeem seemed to hear something. His head turned, and he moved away, toward another bit of quarry, leaving Stranger to duel with the Reptar alone.

But when Sadeem was a handful of yards away, the Reptar turned its attention from shots fired by Stranger, opting for a less painful direction.

It took Sadeem down, ending him before the old man could look back.

LOGAN HEARD A CRY. Clara watched his eyes widen, then saw the rarely observed hero within the skinny man surface. A woman's shout; it had to be Danni or Piper. Logan was off his ass, gun in hand and through the surging mass of decoy Reptars, before Clara could shout. And then she was alone.

She tried tuning her attention to the collective but could no longer hear her grandfather. Was he dead? He'd cut off so suddenly. She'd have to close her eyes and focus to see if he was still on the grid, but she couldn't do that here. At least two of these boogeymen Reptars were real, yet she had no idea where to find them. The real ones acted differently than those Clara gathered must be "the same thing seen in many places," which was as far she understood Meyer's impossible concept. But if Clara couldn't see beyond her protected knot, she couldn't tell.

Toward Logan?

Yes, it made sense. But she'd already lost his direction. She guessed, knowing that staying where she was would end up being the only wrong choice, suddenly and surprisingly sure that dying today might not be all that bad. The years had been hard, and death promised rest.

But beyond the knot, Clara found herself in a curious calm. They were fighting behind her, but there must not be any real ones over here. None were paying attention.

Then she saw two people between the fighting groups — Stranger and Kindred, now moving slowly toward each other.

The air crackled. From the ship, from the Ark. From the two men. A current of deadly potential.

They moved forward. Moved forward. The sizzle lifted her hair, filling Clara with foreboding.

She opened her mouth to shout.

"Don't—!"

"—GET ANY CLOSER!"

Peers's head spun to find the source of the shout: Clara, yelling at Kindred and Stranger, their faces confused, as if they'd woken from twin trances.

As all three began to study one another, Peers wanted to raise a shout of his own. He was out of ammo, as were several of the others. Something strange was happening, and they had to figure it out. Several were dead, including his late-life mentor. Their only option was a hasty retreat.

Dazed, Stranger and Kindred were now both walking slowly backward, wary, seeming only now to realize they'd narrowly avoided doing something deadly.

But then Peers saw movement. On the left. Coming fast. Clara didn't catch it, but Peers was closer.

He didn't think. He ran. Full out, he *ran*.

He wasn't going to make it. The Reptar was too fast, and Clara still hadn't noticed. Stranger had, and was, shouting. But he wasn't close enough, and his bullets — if he was still aware enough to have kept his weapon — might hit Clara from that far away. Peers realized only once sprinting that he'd dropped his own empty gun.

So what are you planning to do?

He didn't know. It didn't matter. He could barely see Clara. Instead he saw the temple he'd visited as a child, entering the dark room with the voice he'd learned was Astral, telling them it was cool if they came for a visit. He saw the cannibals outside Ember Flats. He saw the day he'd lost Clara in the hallway when she'd been little, knowing that no matter what, he couldn't lose her again. And for some reason he saw his son, James, whom he hadn't allowed himself to think of for years. James would have been over forty by now — old enough to fight in this battle for himself if the Ember Flats security forces hadn't ended his life so early.

Was it really bad, sparing him a life in this place?

Yes. Life was always better than death, Peers thought as his lungs burned — running toward Clara, who'd had one of the hardest lives he could ever imagine.

Peers gasped, his legs on fire. The Reptar would take her first, for sure. The beast knew it, and so did Clara; her head had turned, now hearing its approach.

The Reptar leaped, struck Clara, and knocked her flat. No pause. It reared back with its throat flashing and swung down, hard, as Peers watched visions of failure in his head, knowing there was nothing he could do, no weapons in his possession, no time at hand to so much as grab the thing. He had nothing at all, except for sand and …

A millisecond flash of a small brown face. A face Peers failed like he'd failed everyone else, all his life.

And *himself*.

The Reptar bit down.

Clara rolled away as Peers thought his final thought, his torso thrust between the thing's closing jaws.

The thought went out to a small brown boy, taken before his time: *I'll see you soon.*

Chapter Forty-Five

"FIND ME DIVINITY," Melanie ordered.

The Titan before her did nothing. She didn't like the way it was eyeing her. Maybe Melanie's time in Meyer's captivity inside the Nexus was coloring her perceptions, but she'd have sworn his expression was one of condescension, perhaps even pity. They usually appeared neutral. Her time in a human body had flavored that neutrality, allowing her to see it as polite, or perhaps even pleased. But this one's face struck her as belligerent. Annoyed by Melanie's instructions.

"Is there a problem?"

She was speaking like a human. Like a military commander from a pre-invasion drama, bustling to retain order as their command fell apart. Titans didn't speak. It wasn't going to snap off a salute and say, "Sir, yes, *sir!*"

Its lips wouldn't tell her the Titan's reasons for not moving — she had to dip into the collective and listen.

Divinity is here.

Well, shit. Melanie knew that. The entire Divinity class was inside the collective, same as the Titans and Reptars

— lines between the latter two almost indistinguishable at the mental level. More than even the soldier classes, Divinity's home was inside the collective. It (they) had bodies, but only due to biological necessity. The same as Eternity was supposed to be, before the surrogate. But these days she didn't like the collective much. It had always struck her as a place of serenity and order — a place where her mentality felt at home and *right*. These days it felt as chaotic as the ships. When the Titans escorted her away from Meyer and the Nexus, something had rampaged through her quarters. It was barely a surprise because that's the way the collective seemed right now.

Everything inside was tipped over and messy. So much was broken. It was as if something had stomped through and laid waste. Now even the line between Melanie and this Titan felt untidy. It should have felt like they were adjacent cells in a larger body, working as one toward a common purpose. Instead she felt their butting heads. Trying to convince the Titan to cooperate rather than knowing and accepting that it always and inevitably would, and that the alternative wasn't possible.

"I mean Divinity's surrogate," Melanie told the Titan.

But now she got the distinct impression that the Titan was toying with her. She'd swear it was on the verge of asking, *Why would you need to locate its puppet body if you need to speak with it?* Instead its mind asked something more poignant — something Melanie found herself struggling to articulate. Something she had no reason to voice or specify at all.

Which surrogate?

Meaning: *Which Divinity do you want? Which pointless, artificial line do you wish drawn to separate an entity that is normally considered to function as a singular, distributed mental being?*

"The short one with the dark brown hair."

She could have sworn the Titan smirked. She shouldn't have said that. She might as well have asked for the Divinity that wore culottes and liked long walks on the beach. But the words had come out because lately she (as a surrogate) had only interacted with the one Divinity (as a surrogate). And because of it, she'd come to think of "Divinity" as that one's name, just as hers was Melanie.

That surrogate of Divinity is in Control.

"What is she doing in Control?"

This time, the Titan's silence inside the hive felt less smug and more like uncomfortable uncertainty. She didn't want to poke the Titan further; Melanie could find the roots of whatever-it-was on her own. But she could sense echoes of what the Titan had said from many facets of the disorderly collective. Whatever Divinity was up to was something the Titans, Reptars, and remainder of Divinity either didn't know or entirely trust. It had the feeling of a disagreement or a schism within the group — but more on the level of intuition than anything fully understood.

It is not entirely clear.

"Bring her to me."

Divinity is not alone in Control. She seems to be with a hybrid.

"A hybrid!" But no, Melanie's knee-jerk alarm was absurd. Meyer was back in custody where he belonged. A trio of Titans, if nothing else had fallen apart between her orders and now, would be sitting opposite him, staring him down and holding his thoughts in a vice. Maybe he could push through three mental guards and communicate with the surface, but she doubted he could do it without them at least knowing what he was up to.

"Fine. Bring them both to me."

More uncomfortable thoughts from the Titan. Had it always been like this? Was *she* the one out of touch, feeling the collective as it had always been from her own warped perspective? Or was the Titan different too? This interaction should have been simple, almost immediate, and transparent. Instead it felt like an interrogation — of a reluctant subject.

"*What?*"

And the Titan's thoughts said, *Control has been rendered inaccessible.*

"She's *locked you out?*"

Emotions swirled, fogging Melanie's capabilities, same as her emotions always did. The mute white form seemed like an enemy. She wanted to shout at it, hit it, rail against this single stubborn body as if it would solve all the baffling problems gone so recently, terribly wrong. It would do nothing; the correct response was to focus surface Reptars on hunting down and eliminating the three humans harboring the remaining Archetypes. Only then could order be — hopefully — restored to the collective.

Melanie's lips firmed. Her fists clenched. She wanted to know the meaning of this. She wanted someone held responsible and punished.

But she was interrupted when the opposite door to the small room opened, and a contingent of new Titans entered, apparently to deliver news in person that, if not for the Archetypes and human pollution, she should have already pulled from the hive mind at a distance.

The Nexus is activating, said the new thought. *Meyer Dempsey has spooled it up from his cell.*

From his cell? How could he possibly do that? It was as impossible as a hybrid going rogue and creating Palls when replicated. As impossible as a human memory cluster too redundant for the Forgetting to erase. As impossible as subject minds leaking into their own minds, turning them into individuals too unused to autonomy to so much as deploy more Reptars to the surface.

Enough was enough. Melanie, she was shocked to discover, felt more furious than afraid.

"Kill him," she said. "Just kill Dempsey, and be done with it."

But the Titans just looked at each other.

And the collective mind said, *We can't.*

Chapter Forty-Six

"PIPER. WAKE UP."

Piper shook the voice away. She didn't want to wake up, and she sure as hell didn't want any more dreams. They'd plagued her every blink, as if just waiting for her to fall unconscious so they could move in for the kill. Her mind was full of all she'd seen only in sleep — particularly dogging her as they put enough distance between themselves and the freighter where the battle finally ended. Nobody, it seemed, had expected retreat to be possible. The Reptars would follow them until their party was dead. But Peers bought them time, and once Piper had run, she'd seen the others: Kindred, Logan, Kamal, Stranger — and blessedly, lest Piper's heart fail, Clara. They'd crested the first dune at a sprint and the second at a run, but the Reptars stayed behind. All five hundred. Or, if Clara was to be believed, *two*, somehow enabled by the Ark's power to display many faces to the world.

But Piper didn't want this new dream. Or the thing that felt more like a memory: herself, in that round room with the lit-up, tree-branched floor, with Meyer. She'd been unable to push the last from her mind even while awake. It had the feeling of persistence — a thought demanding attention lest something important be forgotten.

"Piper."

She pulled her thin blanket closer, fighting for slumber.

The speaker punched her hard between the shoulder blades. Piper spun, annoyed by the intrusion, and sat up.

Trevor Dempsey was kneeling behind her.

Piper looked around, certain that she was dreaming even though she knew better. She'd moved away from the group, feeling an overwhelming need to be alone. She couldn't even see the spots where the others had bedded down without standing. She'd told them she didn't need or want the safety of numbers. She didn't particularly care about snakes or scorpions.

It should have been dark, and it was. But still Piper could see everything, as if the full moon was a bit too bright.

She lay back down and closed her eyes. Trevor punched her again.

"I'll keep doing it. It doesn't hurt my knuckles at all."

Fighting unreality, Piper sat back up, her heart pounding. Trevor hadn't aged a day.

"What are you?"

"Don't do that, start blabbing on about how I'm supposed to be dead."

"But you're ... *dead.*"

Trevor gave a very teenage sigh.

"Are you the Pall?"

"I wasn't around for the Pall."

Now she'd caught it, sussed out this strange thing's lie. Claiming ignorance of the Pall while using its name was a bit like saying "What?" when someone asks if you're really deaf or only playing.

"Let's not do this. You used to be an empath. Can you really not tell it's me?'"

Piper stopped, her mouth open.

Trevor shifted on the moonlit sand. He was also glowing a bit, from the inside. Like a ghost that's found substance enough to move sand with his feet, to punch a girl in the back to get her attention.

"I was in love with you, you know. You were too old for me, but too young for Dad. It wasn't fair. You have no idea how hard that was, to be a teenage boy with a stepmom like you."

"This doesn't make sense," Piper said, looking around the quiet desert, wondering at the trickery upon her.

"Oh, it made perfect sense. You were hot. And fun. It was hard to be around you. It was the king of all crushes. I never really got over it. Not before I died."

Piper shook her head, watching him, disbelieving her eyes but unable to ignore the feeling inside, growing where her old psychic abilities once made their home. It wasn't the Pall, because now that was Stranger. This was something else.

Only: not something else. This was *Trevor*.

"How are you here?"

"Dad sent me." Trevor gave an annoyed, eye-rolling laugh. "Poetic, right? He never understood it any more than you did. 'Trevor, go hang out with your stepmother for the afternoon. You two can hold hands.' 'Trevor, take your stepmother to the mall, and help her pick out bikinis.'"

"We never did those things."

"'Trevor, go see your stepmother in the middle of the desert after midnight to tell her about the Ark.' It never ends with him. And you know what? I thought it would be easier. But I guess I'm sort of frozen where I was ... and you're still beautiful."

Piper couldn't help herself. She'd never thought of Trevor as anything but an adopted son and never would have, but the years had beaten her badly. She was fifty-six and caked in filth. Nobody had called her beautiful in forever.

When she looked up, Trevor was giving her a bitter-sweet smile. She saw the sorrow. The regret. The *reality*. Somehow, it *was* him.

"What about the Ark?"

"You have to go back."

Piper felt her head shake as if moving without her permission. "No."

"I know you lost people."

"No. Not again. No more. Peers, Sadeem ... and the time before that, it was your sister." She shook her head harder, trying to make this whole thing go away. Something hot and liquid trickled down her cheek. "I can't take it anymore. I just ... *can't.*"

"There are only two Reptars protecting it now. And you have a weapon."

"And a lot of good our weapons did!"

"That's not what I meant."

Something dawned on Piper. She sat up straighter, fixing Trevor with tear-clouded eyes.

"Stranger said he saw you. Before the attack, by the ship."

Trevor nodded. "Me. Lila. Mom."

"Why?"

"This is what I'm trying to tell you, Piper. Dad's helping us. He's ... tapped into something. Tapped in on the ship, sure, but also inside himself. Don't tell me you never sensed it."

Piper thought. Yes, Meyer had seemed a bit more different with every passing day. But hadn't that just been the Astral Forgetting finally going away?

"Dad asked us to show them the three 'real' Reptars. Because he can talk to Stranger and Kindred, too."

"Weren't you 'before Stranger' since you were 'before the Pall'?"

"Splitting hairs. Time is different for me these days. Don't I look good for a man in his forties?" Trevor ran a hand along the side of his head, smoothing his thick black hair in a parody of dapperness. "They both seem like Dad to me."

"They're not your father."

Trevor smiled, as if maybe she'd learn better someday.

"This time you won't be surprised. Maybe Kamal can explain how it works. I think the Da Vinci Initiate was starting to understand it. There's no way to travel faster than light; the Astrals needed a wormhole to do what they did; yada yada. But all you really need to understand is that space is different around the Ark. The rules change. For now, only the Astrals know how to exploit it, confuse you with a bunch of Reptars so the only real two can get you. Tell me: How did you get away from the freighter, after Lila came to join me?"

"*Came to* …" Piper understood; he meant when she'd died.

"Dad understands the Ark's energy a little. Kindred and Stranger, because of what they are, understand it a lot. They don't know they know, but they definitely do. That's how they were able to move you through one of those folds when they stopped thinking and *reacted*. Part of them, just like part of Dad, knows how to use that energy. And they'll use it again."

"To … what? Teleport onto the ship?"

Trevor smiled again. "You'll see."

Piper looked Trevor over slowly. He was real. She both believed and disbelieved it more with every passing second.

"Is it like being in Heaven?"

"It's kind of hard to describe. It's more like I'm *with you*."

"With me?"

He shook his head. "With *all* of you." He tapped his head. "Not my family. Not this group. I mean 'with humanity.' All of it — not just Judgment's survivors."

"How?"

"What am I, a philosopher?"

"I just thought …"

Trevor smiled one more time. More genuine. His truest smile so far. He put his hand on hers. It was solid and warm.

"Nobody dies, Piper. Not really."

"Then why—"

"If everyone came back all the time," he said, either pre-guessing her question or rummaging around inside her supposedly private thoughts, "nothing would ever move forward. We need the illusion of death. Mortality is part of what makes us, *us.*"

"But you're here now."

"We're still near the Ark."

"So you came from the Ark?"

Trevor raised a hand, holding it flat, tipping it back and forth like a rocking boat. "It's complicated."

"We can't go back, Trevor. Or at least we can't *all* go back. I'd never forgive myself if Clara—"

"Joined us where she's already present? It's not the horror you think it is."

"It's not that easy for me to just accept what you're

315

saying. Even if we went back, Clara couldn't go. I won't allow it."

"She must. Clara's the wedge in the door. She's keeping the channel open. Just like how Stranger and Kindred share its energy — *each other's* energy. Same as you share Cameron's."

"Share …?" Piper trailed off. She'd felt it, though, same as Trevor implied: a bond between her and Cameron that had always been there, drawing them together, same as Stranger and Kindred. But she and Cameron weren't halves like they were. So what was it?

"Clara has to go like *you* have to go," Trevor said, shifting again on the sand. "Because you have the key."

"I don't have a key."

Trevor nodded slowly. "I'm sure it seems that way. But let me tell you something about the old key that I learned when Cameron joined us: That key *chose* him. Years and years ago, back when he and his father first found it, Cameron touched it first, and it became his match. And in a somewhat different way, the same is true of you."

"But—"

"After the mothership took you aboard over Moab, then transferred you to the Eternity ship before dropping you at Vail, where we saw you outside the bunker, on the security cameras. Do you remember?"

"Sort of. I remember meeting Meyer in a round room with shadows on a backlit floor."

Trevor nodded. "They can't so much as *touch* the Ark, Piper. They made it when they seeded themselves into us, but both always had an element of chaos — us, and the Ark, tied together. They could use what stored itself inside to assess us, but the process found a life of its own. They can reset it, or hide it once empty again, but it's always taken a human to move and open it. That's why Cameron needed the key. Why he had to make a choice to open the Ark; It would never have opened on its own. It's about humanity's core. Free will, maybe. We're a species that determines its own fate, always — even when it's rotten."

Trevor moved his legs, sat with them crossed.

"They've always needed our cooperation in this little experiment. They couldn't do it on their own. So they had the Mullah to mind the portal connecting us. It took human minds to see where we stood along the way, through drugs that altered our states. They didn't just leave Astrals to live with us; they needed hybrids like Dad — only *half*-Astral, but also half-human. Right now, as our consciousnesses mix and throw their collective into disarray, they think something went wrong — first with Dad's connection to his observer, then to all of them at once. But the way Dad sees it, it's not 'something going wrong' at all. It's the inevitable outcome of uncertainty. After enough times through the cycle, even the least likely things are bound to occur."

"Are you saying—?"

"It's a little like asking patients to help run the asylum. They've always needed to lean on us for help, intended or not. And so far, it's worked out for them. They've been able to underestimate us because we haven't been worthy of much. But this time we used our minds to create a new kind of collective — something the Astrals never saw coming. That created the Lightborn, and kickstarted a kind of instant evolution, starting with Dad and culminating in Clara. To them, things are spiraling out of control. But within the larger system, seen from high enough up, there's no way this *couldn't* have happened eventually."

"What does this have to do with the Ark? With the key? Or with my time with Meyer on the Astral ships?"

"Thousands of years pass between openings of the

Ark," Trevor said. "Cameron opened it last time, but once he was gone — once he turned the tables another time, polluting their 'stream' in the most blunt-force way he could think of — they knew they'd need someone else. You wouldn't be alive the next time the Ark was opened, of course, but you'd be first in a line. Once they gave you the same energy that Cameron already had, you became their first 'human control' for the next epoch."

"But what does it mean?"

"Whether or not you have a stone disc in your satchel, you hold a key all the same."

Piper felt cold. She didn't like where this seemed to be going.

"Clara wants to poison the Ark. She thinks that doing so will force more of us into their collective, and make them leave us alone, whether we've Forgotten their visit or not."

Trevor nodded. "It will ruin their experiment, and they won't be happy. Dad agrees that it will work. But it means you must return to the Ark. He will try to guide you. They're sick right now, and there's no way to send more Reptars in time — if you hurry."

Piper closed her eyes. When they opened, Trevor was still there, no more a dream than the wind. "Okay."

The ghost swallowed, as if what was coming might be more uncomfortable than the truth of his death. "There's one more thing, if you want to finish what Cameron started when he jumped into the Ark."

"What?"

"You know, Piper. You have to."

"I *don't* know, Trevor." This time, she took *his* hand, finding it as solid as the ground beneath her. "Tell me."

"To poison anything, you need two things. The first is a way to open the container."

Piper nodded. "Okay. That's me. So what else do you need?"

Trevor's ghost looked away. Swallowed again. Then he met Piper's eyes and in them, she saw regret, sorrow — maybe even fear.

"Poison," he said.

Chapter Forty-Seven

THE FLOOR ROCKED beneath Divinity's feet. For a moment, it felt like the entire ship might cant sideways, all the stabilization and gravitation systems failing, and tip them toward the room's corner. Maybe then the enormous thing would fall from orbit, slicing the planet's atmosphere like a knife, streaking from the sky and running aground like Carl Nairobi had somehow found the Ark's resting place and taken it across the ocean to run aground in the worst of all possible spots. If that happened, Divinity's surrogate might not survive. Maybe that was for the best. She'd become attached enough (and she hated herself for the realization) to see Eternity's perspective.

But no, the ship stabilized. Control seemed to flicker, the light within the surfaces going dark before coming back online. It might be the collective's skewed energy choking the ship, or it might be some sort of elaborate sabotage. At this point, neither hardly mattered.

"What was that?" Liza asked, clearly frightened. Divinity liked seeing the woman's emotion. It shook a bit of complacency from her. Liza was a hybrid, but the part she thought of as "herself" was more human than not. If the ship accelerated, the force would more or less liquefy them both. But whereas Divinity would survive in her native form afterward, Liza would not. The observer would move on, searching for another host who didn't have such grand ambitions.

Divinity looked at the panel nearest her hand, considering. Control didn't direct the ship, but the collective did. She could implant a suggestion. With all the chaos, it probably wouldn't even be second-guessed until Liza Knight turned to pulp.

But no. For now, at least, Divinity needed her. She could deal with the way Liza kept trying to seize the upper hand later.

She told Liza the truth: "It's Dempsey. He's in it, too."

"In your Nexus?"

Divinity pressed her lips flat, hearing Liza's disbelief. Apparently she'd effectively conveyed the idea that the Nexus could only be accessed through the Nexus room itself — and remotely only through Control. They knew Dempsey had been taken to a holding room. And yet there he was, pushing bits of the Nexus around like chess pieces.

"Yes."

"But you said—"

"I know what I said. It's not a concern."

Liza put her hand on her hip. She *put her goddamned hand on her goddamned hip*, posturing like a diva.

"Maybe I should be dealing with Dempsey," said Liza.

"Dempsey isn't one of us. He doesn't control our fleet."

"Seems to me he controls more than you're admitting."

Divinity eyed the thing in Liza's hand. It seemed so simple. When they'd last lost track of it, it was *known* to be simple. *Plug and play*, was the human expression. And the first Meyer duplicate had managed to use it just fine, despite being fully alien and believing himself to be human.

I could kill her now, then install it myself.

But it wasn't worth the risk. Not yet. It was possible that Liza Knight was as inconsequential as a coat rack, but what if Divinity was wrong? Well, then the only chance left would be killing the remaining Archetypes and attempting the Forgetting anew. The Reptars had finished off two more during the last attack; Divinity could see proof in the stream. But for some reason, the idea of erasing Kindred, Stranger, *and* Clara seemed far from certain. They'd proved slippery so far. And if the Archetypes survived and she found herself unable to do what must be done after killing Liza? *Then* they'd really be up shit creek, as the humans said.

"He can't do anything consequential," said Divinity, giving Liza a look. They'd both been standing, but the hybrid had moved to lean against a console as if making herself comfortable, weighing her insufferable companion's worth. Divinity wanted to throttle her.

"What's he doing, consequential or not?" Liza asked.

"I believe he's instructing them on how to further pollute our consciousness."

"But you said he's accessing the Nexus, like we're doing."

"The simplest way to pollute us is through the archive."

"You mean the Ark?"

Divinity pinched the bridge of her nose. "Yes."

"Isn't that a problem?"

"Not if you can do what you promise."

Liza watched Divinity, seeming to consider. Divinity

watched her back. What she'd said was true. They were already contaminated. Meyer's plan — even *if* they saw and then got past the multiplied guards, even *if* they could open the archive — would only contaminate them further. So what? Dirty was dirty. Whether they cleaned what Cameron and Clara had done or scrubbed what Meyer planned to do as well, results were the same.

Liza's tongue bulged the corner of her cheek. "You don't even know if this will work." She jiggled the small silver canister.

"Then you're useless."

"But you brought me here, so you must have reason to believe it will."

"Interesting theory."

"Even so, you brought me here not quite knowing what I had in mind." Liza considered. "That's because I'm a *hybrid*, right? Because I know things from both the human side *and* the Astral side? So I'd know something like this better than you — technology that's sort of half-and-half, just like me."

"I guess you've got it all figured out. Good for you."

Liza hesitated. She twiddled the canister. Then suddenly, she sat.

Divinity blinked. This felt like a delay, and they couldn't afford to linger. Eternity and Divinity agreed on one thing: Eliminating the three remaining people composing the two surviving Archetypes (Magician and King), it might be possible to blank humanity and shake the pollution from their mental veins. They differed in what would happen if Clara, Kindred, and Stranger eluded them much longer. Eternity might be willing to surrender. They'd all have to live with humanity inside their hive forever. Divinity's solution was much more certain — but only if they acted fast. Before Eternity stopped them — or, more troublingly, before Dempsey's evolutionary leap showed him a few more inconvenient truths he could twist to his advantage.

"What are you doing?" Divinity demanded.

"It just occurred to me that the second I install this for you" — Liza held up the canister containing the virus — "you'll no longer have any need for me."

Divinity considered lying. Instead she said, "True."

"So why should I help you?"

"Because if you don't, you're even *more* useless."

And so this time Liza echoed, "True."

She stopped. Thought. Took a few breaths. Looked at her feet, then up. Again Liza held up the small device, which had gone 'round the world and back again since its creation in Heaven's Veil.

"It will work. You've seen it work."

Liza's voice was even, but Divinity felt the face-off giving her advantage. They were at an impasse. A Mexican standoff, as cinema put it. But that meant Divinity had equal control — not the lesser power she'd felt when Liza had first reached into the backpack and revealed the ancient device for delivering the Canned Heat virus: Liza's deep-brain's idea of an advantage, to get them all out of their current sticky bind.

"We saw it work on your Internet," Divinity retorted.

"But that's just it. I can hear a lot of your collective up here. And I know that if the human collective had been what you'd thought, this would already be over. You expected us to think together — if we thought together at all — in one specific way. That's the way you were counting on, when you tried to make us forget. But we thought together in a different way, didn't we?"

Liza shifted the silver canister from hand to hand.

"You didn't expect the Internet. And once you saw it,

you thought it was just electronics and wires. You didn't quite *get* the way we'd come to depend on it. The Internet *was* our extended brain. It was how we remembered things without having to memorize them. It was how thousands of people managed to work together on a single project, each taking tiny pieces until the job was done and done well. Like a colony of ants, or a flock of birds knowing to fly south for the winter."

"It struck us as inefficient. It's not that we were unable to deal with it. We found it irrelevant."

Liza bobbed her head, not believing Divinity at all.

"So when you tried to make us forget," Liza continued, ignoring her, "it's like you got the plant but not the roots."

"The Internet was already gone."

Liza tapped her head with the canister. "But it was already somehow in here, wasn't it? We'd internalized that way of thinking. The Internet was training wheels for us. Or Dumbo's feather. Even after it was gone, the core remained. The Internet had taught us how to work together non-locally, just like your own collective consciousness."

"It's not the same," Divinity said, insulted by the implication. But then again, wasn't the fact that *she was able to be insulted* proof that Liza's argument had merit — that the *roots* of human consciousness had survived beneath the surface?

"No. It's not the same." Liza tapped her chin. "Maybe it's better."

"Ridiculous."

"All I know is that this little computer virus, delivered by this little device made by one long-dead man, disabled the entirety of our remaining tech infrastructure. It took us years to get satellite communication back up, but even then it was all through your technology, not ours. And, hell …"

Liza rolled her eyes back, as if perusing the ship's collective mind, now available for her to trespass. "It seems to me that you couldn't stomp human memory out, just like our Internet was always forever. I don't suppose you spied on us long enough to see a celebrity nude photo leak? Where some stupid PR agent and team of lawyers would try and erase all those naughty pictures from the net, but all it took was one nerd in Duluth to save them to his hard drive then re-upload them?"

Divinity was getting tired of this. But as much as she hated Liza and her posturing, the woman was making sense.

"Right now you've got human consciousness and this ... hangover ... from the Internet. Its permanence. And they're like this." Liza held up her hands, fingers toward each other, and interlocked them, fingers moving like tangled cords. "The problem is, you were only prepared to deal with this one." She separated her hands and held one high. "The *consciousness* part. But you're not prepared to deal with the other — the *persistence*, left over from our old way of thinking online."

"It's the Lightborn," said Divinity. "With the Archetypes propping them up and the Archetypes feeding the Lightborn, the whole thing gets stronger."

"I agree. But if you can't get rid of the Archetypes?" Liza frowned. "Well then. Now you've got a problem." She tapped the silver canister. "But this? This will knock out the Internet thinking same as it knocked out the Internet itself. Then you can make them forget, easy as pie."

"So plug it in. Try it." Divinity nodded toward a meaningless console in Control, knowing that anything in here could adapt to accept the input, once asked.

"Two things bug me. Like I said, once I've done what I

said I'd do, you'll get rid of me. You won't keep your promise."

"It's a bit late for that," said Divinity. "You'll just have to trust me."

Liza nodded seriously, seeing their mutual predicament. *Damned if you do; damned to both of us if you don't.*

"But the second thing that bugs me is that I had to clean up the mess from the first Canned Heat infection. I know how thorough Terrence Peal made his virus. It's a nuke. So the question is, will it knock human consciousness out enough to let you implement your Forgetting and reset your experiment? Or will it shred our minds like a Cuisinart and turn us all to mush?"

Divinity met Liza's eye.

"That is a problem," Divinity said.

"Which is it? Do you know?"

Divinity knew. She'd been fiddling with controls the entire time she'd been leading Liza to this place, locking them in the way Eternity had tried to lock the door to her posh, overly human quarters. What they'd all become, over the years of occupation, was despicable. Unforgivable.

She'd run the scenarios. She knew precisely what would become of humanity once the virus was run.

The experiment on Earth would be over forever.

But at least they could leave, clean and intact.

"No idea," said Divinity.

Liza watched her.

"I need time," Liza said.

"There *is* no time."

Liza slipped the canister into her pocket, crossed her arms, and said nothing, tapping her toe on the sterile white floor.

Chapter Forty-Eight

PIPER CAUGHT up to Kamal while the other four were distracted.

Breakfast, such that it was (nuts and water, eaten while sitting in the sand) was over, and everyone was packing up. They hadn't made themselves at home under the small group of rock overhangs they'd found and hadn't gone terribly far from the freighter after realizing the Reptars weren't going to follow. *Packing up* was more about procrastination: shuffling the contents of their bags, wondering in tandem about the remaining water supply and why, after taking five losses, they didn't just go back to Kamal's camp and call it a day.

Stranger was at one end of the cluster of overhangs, speaking with Logan. Clara and Kindred were at the other end. After last night, Piper could swear she could see the force stretched between Stranger and Kindred, pulling them together as the men fought a losing battle of wills to stay apart. Whatever was happening between them — whatever compulsion-turned-obsession seemed bent on uniting the two half men — it was getting worse. She could feel deadly energy wafting off them like heat.

Kamal moved away by himself, and Piper saw her chance. She took his arm, approaching from behind.

Kamal jumped. Then he saw it was Piper and relaxed. They were all a bit jumpy. After Trevor had left, Piper spent the remainder of her night in a half daze, certain that every fire-thrown shadow was a Reptar closing in for the kill.

"Jesus. You scared me."

"I'm sorry."

"I was just going to take a leak."

Piper let go of his arm. Heat flushed into her cheeks. "Sorry," she said again. "Go ahead."

Kamal turned. "Nope. No good now. I've got a shy bladder. I get stage fright. Makes things hard with all the drug testing we do in our village."

"What?"

"Never mind." Kamal's face became serious. His eyes moved beyond Piper, and she turned to see that he was looking at the subjects of her own pondering from moments before: Kindred and Clara on one side, Stranger and Logan on the other. He seemed to be puzzling, edging an observation. And he was squinting a bit, as if trying hard to make out something he could barely see.

Force lines between the two of them, perhaps, strung between Kindred and Stranger like lines on a bomb.

Piper shifted on her feet, the two of them awkwardly standing between last night's camp and, apparently, Kamal's restroom. She wanted to sit but had nowhere to do so. And the reason she'd chased him in the first place was the same reason she didn't want to go back by the ashes, where the others could hear.

"When you were going through all of Mara's old

research," she said, "did you see anything about a weapon?"

"A weapon? You mean, not guns?"

"Not guns. Something else."

"Give me context. Help me out here."

Piper thought back to what Trevor had said the night before: *There are only two Reptars protecting it now. And you have a weapon.* She'd wondered when he'd said that, but then got sidelined — asking how Meyer had somehow used the Ark's power to project Trevor, Lila, and Heather before their last botched attack as guides. She'd never circled back, and now that a new mission to the same deadly spot was upon them, it seemed like an unforgivable omission.

"You know how Stranger said he saw Trevor and Lila yesterday?"

Kamal did something that was half nod, half shake of his head. They all knew what Stranger and Kindred had claimed, but whereas Piper and likely Clara easily believed it, Kamal had a much harder time. He'd accepted it all as academically true — the proliferation of Reptars that were actually duplicates of only a few, the way Piper and the others had supposedly teleported after Lila's death, and of course the arrival of dead sons and daughters — but he hadn't been there like Piper. Kamal had seen a lot, but such things didn't belong in a rational world.

"I saw him last night."

"In a dream?"

Piper waited, letting the moment settle. Finally she half shrugged.

"So, *not* in a dream." Kamal put his hands on his hips, looked toward the others, and dramatically sighed. "Did Trevor eat all the marshmallows?"

"I know you don't believe it."

Kamal raised his hands, palms out. "Hey. I'm not

trying to be the doubting Thomas. You say your twenty-plus-years dead stepson was hanging out in camp last night, whatever. I've already said I'm cool with going back to that death trap. Stranger sent me across the ocean to tell Clara something I'm not sure why he couldn't just tell her himself, and we've got two people in this little group who seem to have some seriously pent-up bro-love, but if they shake hands, I'm pretty sure the universe will find itself with a new asshole. So please, tell me all about Trevor. Lay it on me. Tell me what he had to say. I'm all ears."

Piper waited to see if Kamal was finished. Finally he lowered his hands and seemed to listen — for once in earnest.

"Meyer sent him, I think," Piper said. "He might somehow be … *controlling* … the Ark. But I also think it was the real Trevor. Like his soul was stored in the Ark, and Meyer let it out."

"That was nice of him."

"He confirmed what Kindred and Stranger and Clara keep saying: There are only a few Reptars on that ship, not hundreds. The Ark does something to the space around it. I think that's also how we were able to … hell, *teleport*, I guess."

"Is that the weapon? Do you think we can teleport back in there? Take them by surprise?"

Piper shook her head. "I don't think so. I've asked Stranger and Kindred about it. Somehow, they did that for us, but neither knows how. They say it was like a flash of inspiration: obvious then; impossible now."

But that was only half the reason she knew a teleport sneak attack was off the table. Now that Trevor had identified the energy inside her — the "key" the Astrals had given her on that ride between Moab and Vail almost thirty years ago — she found herself noticing all sorts of other things that had been there all along, just out of sight. Her forgotten empath's powers, for one. And using those feelings, she could sense both Kindred and Stranger, living each day now with pressure and tension. To Piper, both were holding their breath, fighting each moment not to inhale. They could barely function, let alone focus. And whatever was building between them was growing worse by the second.

Kamal seemed to think. Then he said, "I don't remember anything about a weapon."

"What about poison?"

"Clara's plan," Kamal echoed.

"But in Mara's files. Was there any mention of poison?"

"It wasn't a set of instructions. I might have given you the wrong impression. So much was conjecture. A lot of guesswork. Metaphorical more than anything."

"It'd be metaphorical poison," Piper countered.

"Something to gum up the Ark's works, you mean?" He made a puzzling face. "Hell if I know. Clara's a little Kreskin. I figured she'd just go up to the thing and think at it or something." Then Kamal caught the look on Piper's face. "Why?"

Piper looked across the open area. She'd wanted Kamal alone for a reason. Given her conclusions, each of the other four was a poor choice of confidant. Kindred and Stranger would try to stop her from doing what she needed to do, taking the burden upon themselves. Clara would practically drag her away to prevent it; with the exception of Meyer who might or might not return from the mothership, Piper was all she had left. And Logan wouldn't be able to keep his mouth shut. It wouldn't be his fault, but what went into his mind had a curious way of leaking right into Clara's — and all the remaining Lightborn.

But Kamal would understand. He'd already done this sort of thing once before, surrendered his spot on the Ember Flats vessel so that someone else could have it, urging Jabari to go while he stayed behind as a dying set of eyes and ears.

Piper took a long, slow breath. Then, with sluggish lips she said, "I'm the new key bearer. Trevor said I'll be able to open the Ark." Another breath. "And I think I need to jump into the Ark as *poison*, like Cameron did."

Kamal opened his mouth for concerns and rebuttals, but Piper beat him to it. Speaking quickly, she told him all about her suppressed memories of being in the strange room aboard the Astral ship, receiving energy that resonated with the energy in Cameron, what Trevor had told her about the Astrals and their inability to touch the Ark themselves — *all of it.*

"But it's already *been* poisoned. You said Cameron did it."

"And that bought us twenty years. But now they're at their wit's end. Trevor told me Meyer thinks they don't feel we're worth saving. We've caused too much damage. But who knows what that could mean? Maybe they'll kill us all and be done. Or maybe they just have to kill Clara, who's been the thorn in their side. Either way, *we* need to push them over the edge. Meyer says they're sick. So let's make them sicker. Then maybe it won't be worth their time to try and fix us. Maybe, if we're lucky, they'll leave us alone."

"That's a big maybe."

Piper's lips pursed. She shook her head, feeling the same sensation that had been growing all morning.

"It's right, Kamal. I know it is."

He looked into the distance, roughly toward the freighter, and bit his lip, conflicted.

"I can't tell anyone else. But I *have* to do this, Kamal. And when the moment comes, I might need help. I might lose my nerve. Someone might figure out what I'm up to and try to stop me. It's not easy to keep secrets in this group. I'm afraid to get near Clara, sure she'll be able to read me. But this is important, Kamal."

"You don't know that."

"*Meyer* knows it. And you were the one who gave us all those reasons why Meyer, of all people, should know."

Kamal silently watched the horizon. She didn't like seeing him serious. Without his armor of sarcasm, he seemed so vulnerable.

"Kamal?"

He shook his head.

"*Kamal?* Can I count on you?"

After another few seconds, he nodded.

Then, without looking at her, he turned and walked away.

Chapter Forty-Nine

ENOUGH WAS ENOUGH.

Melanie had been in her quarters all night, noting the destruction, increasingly sure what had caused it, taking it all far more personally than she should. But instead of picking things up, she made the mess worse. She kicked. She stalked. Thinking and growing more furious, for hours on end.

Divinity, still locked inside Control, her doings unknown, calls still unanswered.

Meyer Dempsey, similarly locked in his cell, guards kept out as if he was choosing isolation rather than having it forced upon him. All night she'd watched energy stream from Meyer to the Nexus, from the Nexus to Earth. He was up to something, too — similarly unknown, calls to or about him likewise unanswered.

Hours and hours and hours. Anger building. The body needed sleep, but Melanie refused to accept it. Instead she stalked and fumed, circling her space, stacking fury like bricks.

She opened the door and found two Titan guards.

Guards she hadn't asked for or authorized, who seemed to be watching more than protecting her.

Melanie eyed them. They came closer. But she had things to do and places to go. She shoved the Titans out of the way, wondering if that would provoke them, knowing they weren't exactly sipping from the collective as much as they all should be — the same, of course, as she wasn't and hadn't been for years. She almost hoped they'd take offense the way only fragile individual minds could. She hoped they'd spin on her. Raise their weapons. Or turn to Reptars and attack one of their own. Mutiny made no sense in a species like hers. At least not until recently.

Let them try.

Let them come at her.

She needed to cross the ship to reach the place where her next steps would be most efficient, but she wasn't so far gone — so far down the slippery slope of humanity's disease — that she couldn't reach through the haze if truly needed. The collective was made of minds that were equal in concept, but every wheel required a center. Divinity, as a whole, formed that nucleus. But even Divinity was merely an outer ring of Eternity: the heart of the middle.

If the Titans came at her, Melanie was fairly certain she could pinch them off, from inside, with barely a conscious thought. She'd learned anger in this surrogate body thanks to its human wiring. And she'd learned other things, too: spite, jealousy, vengeance, scorn. Volatile emotions blended with her abilities. Eternity gave her powers within the collective. And Melanie gave her reflexes, survival instinct, and a hair trigger.

She didn't rule the hive but could purge its impurities. As long as they came at her one at a time like the malcontented individuals they'd become, she could knock them down without slowing her stride.

But the Titans didn't try to stop her as she left the room. They simply watched her leave, like cowards.

Meyer Dempsey had somehow barred the door to his cell? He'd remotely accessed the Nexus and was using it, right now, to project the Ark's power? He wanted to ignore everything she'd said — every warning she'd given?

Well, then *fuck him*.

Divinity wanted to launch little schemes? She'd found a second hybrid and meant to use it in ways unknown, without consulting the collective? Divinity, like Meyer, had barred herself in a room that shouldn't even be lockable?

Well, then fuck *her*, too.

Even as Melanie stalked from one end of the ship to the other, she knew she was out of control. All that she hated in Meyer and Divinity and disobedient Titans, she saw in herself. Even now, she was learning new lessons. This time around, that lesson was *hypocrisy*. But if the collective wanted to individualize as poison flooded through Clara's breach, then they'd suffer the flip side of that individualization. Yes, they could make their own choices. But the same disease that gave them options also gave her authority. What was once egalitarian could become hierarchical. What should have been a collective could become a dictatorship as complete as any the humans had shown through the archive.

Despite the press of time, Melanie refused to run. She stalked the ship, almost hoping for defiance. Her mental fists were held aloft, ready to fight. Being threatened and abducted and subjugated had raised her hackles. Meyer had made her believe she could die (though she couldn't); Divinity had shown her she wasn't in charge (though by new definitions, she was); Titans and Reptars were drifting about under their own direction. The archive was barely guarded while Titans took sides aboard the big ships. She couldn't even dispatch shuttles, because none wanted to listen.

Again, *fuck them.*

No Titans entered the corridors. If they had, she'd have tackled them with feet and fingernails before simply pinching off the energy fueling their bodies from deep within. No Reptars came, even though she was sure they'd see her in the collective if they looked. They knew better, it seemed.

A short while later Melanie came to a double-wide door at the end of a large, utilitarian hallway. She was at the edge of the ship, not even in its middle. To her surrogate sensibilities, everything about the chamber and its lack of pomp seemed boring. It looked more like a storage room than the bed of royalty.

The door, on her subconscious command, slid open. The space beyond was larger than the door implied: at least fifty feet high, round and domed, massive in circumference. Through all her turmoil, she'd somehow kept her human shoes on. Heels clacked in the space, echoing like tiny gunshots.

She looked up at the partition. She issued a request with a thought, and the partitions flickered away as if they'd merely been projections.

Behind it was a thing like an enormous anemone, its skin translucent, its insides made of light.

"It's gone too far," Melanie said. "Open up, and let me in."

Chapter Fifty

LIGHTS SURROUNDED HER. To Melanie they looked like fireflies she'd never witnessed through her surrogate's eyes but had seen over and over in memories — from the archive, pulled from the air, seen through the eyes of drug users in altered states, downloaded from observers who'd lived countless lives together with their human hosts.

A voice seemed to say, *Are you sure?*

But Melanie knew the trick. The voice was her own, though it sounded like a thing from the outside, pushing in, through her skull.

"What damage can it do at this point?"

The space — the fireflies, the voice, all of it — didn't respond for a while. Melanie stood in the thing's center, in the semi-dark, watching the pattern of lights as they floated like sparks all around her. The thing's skin was mostly transparent, but she was in the center, seeing outward through many layers. If the body had organs, she was seeing through them as well. The effect was curious and beautiful, like standing in the aftermath of an elegant explosion, watching scraps of flame descend and swirl in the air.

Then it did respond, but again Melanie tried to see the reaction for what it was. Not that different from speaking to oneself in the mirror — something Melanie had tried, and found she liked. Humans spoke of selves within the self: multiple voices in one, ego and id. Considering where she was and what she'd seen and done, it was something Melanie could appreciate on many levels.

She was standing inside her own body, speaking to her own mind. But whereas the anemone in the room had once truly felt like "Eternity" to all on the ship, it had started to feel like something else. Melanie was the embodiment. This huge thing in the giant room, thinking in abstract and bathed in light? It was old baggage — a body Melanie knew she'd need to return to one day, but still found repugnant.

The voice in her head, as Melanie stood in her true body's center, said, As you wish.

"As *we* wish," she corrected.

But the voice did not reply.

And then it began.

Chapter Fifty-One

In Control, with Liza Knight smugly juggling the canister of Canned Heat and still infuriatingly undecided, Divinity felt the Purge creep through her like an internal hand. Walls in front of secrets she'd tried to keep — rights of a surrogate, rights of a damaged, individual mind — crumbled to dust. Eternity gripped her. The big hand rummaged through her thoughts, tweaking, nudging things into place. Mental chests opened and spilled their contents. She knew what had happened immediately. And what would happen next.

Liza's eyes widened. For a moment, Divinity saw right through her. Liza's head seemed to open like origami unfolding, and Divinity could read it all over her shoulder, from the big chamber, where Eternity had broken the collective covenant. It was Eternity committing this violation, forcing her way into both of their brains through brute force. But as long as Liza's hybrid mind opened, Divinity would take her peek.

Liza was bluffing. Of *course* she was, and had been all night while neither slept. There *was* no magic to the human's virus. It would integrate with their collective same as any human technology could be made to, simply by plugging it in. Liza was only hot air. Thanks to Eternity's intrusive Purge, her posturing — pretending she held knowledge needed for installing Canned Heat — was as obvious as the smug look that had so recently drained from her face.

Divinity didn't need Liza Knight — *or* her maddening indecision.

"Oh God," Liza said.

"If that's what you believe."

Divinity crossed to Liza, lighting fast.

Took her head in the crook of her arm.

And broke her neck.

MEYER'S EYES opened in his barred cell, the haze departing as if someone had set an industrial fan beside him to waft it away. Suddenly there was no connection. He couldn't reach Piper, to give her Trevor or any of the others as a guide. He couldn't reach Clara, to explain what needed doing or what he had in mind — what had finally dawned on him, after Eternity ordered him dragged from the Nexus to this place, where it turned out he could still reach the Ark's memories just fine. He couldn't reach Stranger or Kindred; it was as if his other halves had been severed clean, snipped from existence.

He was in a white room, restrained by the arms, beaten a bit more than seemed necessary, especially by usually-stoic Titans. He'd been keeping the pain at bay, but now everything hurt. His head throbbed. He felt tiny, all that expansion he'd so recently realized gone in a blink.

A raw, red force remained in its place. Eternity, pushing through him like a battering ram.

He scrambled for the connection. The force would have to leave again eventually, withdraw the suffocating presence like a weight on his chest. The timing couldn't have been worse. Meyer could see through their eyes now, but with the connection cut that felt like a curse. He could still see the freighter from Piper's point of view, with Clara, Logan, Kindred, Stranger, and a Middle-Easterner who seemed vaguely familiar all around her.

Meyer strained, trying to fight the force of Eternity scraping the inside of his mind, cutting him off from Piper and the others.

They'd be at the wreck in minutes — but would now arrive without his help, without the ability to tell the real Reptars from their echoes.

ON THE PLANET BELOW, Stranger gripped his head and fell to the sand. His knees wouldn't hold him upright anymore — and curiously, neither could Kindred's, just down the dune. The pain was blinding.

Piper moved in front of him, speaking, but he couldn't hear her, or concentrate on anything at all. Someone was inside his head, pushing all the buttons that he alone should have been able to press. There was no forcing it back. He could only close his eyes and wait.

"Stranger!" Somewhere down the dune, other voices shouted Kindred's name, somehow echoed not from outside his head but inside Stranger's mind.

He saw a long tunnel in the darkness behind his eyelids, he at one end and Kindred at the other. When he opened his eyes, Stranger could still see Piper — except that her face had become that of a blonde woman.

"Now I understand," said Piper/the blonde woman, a smile crawling across her features.

Inside that mental tunnel, Kindred and Stranger moved toward each other. Force built. Lightning crackled through the air with deadly potential.

It wasn't until hands grabbed him and tried in vain to hold him back that Stranger realized his body, in the real world, had risen to walk forward as well.

Clara stood without moving, watching the two men stand and walk with their entourage, meeting an internal face eye to eye. She turned to meet its gaze without flinching, her mental body squaring mental shoulders.

You can't stop us, Clara thought. *We're already at your Ark.*

I am in control now. You cannot harm us.

But Clara knew it was a lie. Staring in those mental eyes, directly through the break she herself had made between the species, she knew that poisoning the Ark would work just fine, if they could reach it.

There are Reptars, said the other.

They will not stop us either. We can open the top. Piper knows how. She is the key. You did that to her, all those years ago.

The face inside seemed to laugh. Then it said, *Piper also knows how she plans to poison it.*

And then it showed Clara what Piper meant to do.

INSIDE THE MONOLITH, two Reptars woke. They'd moved as one, nesting together as if seeking comfort. The wounds were superficial. But now the odd thoughts each had about earning more — normally out of mind in this form but present of late — were gone.

A ghost of a handler materialized before them.

"There are five on the sand, split into two groups," the

handler said. "One group for each of you. Center on the two older white men and the young woman. They are the last of the Archetypes. The others will go quickly once they are handled."

One of the Reptars rose to its clawed feet and chattered. The other joined it, two black voices forming a chorus like swarming insects.

The handler seemed to take the chatter as language. She plucked the Reptars' key thought — *concern* was too strong a word — as if spoken in the words of the higher class.

"It will be like last time," the handler said. "Double and redouble. They are blind, and will not see the true targets until it is too late."

THE LEAD TITAN, walking without hurry in the direction Eternity had departed, stopped as if he were an automaton with its power cut. His companion paused as well, and the two met each other's placid eyes.

Where is she?

It does not matter.

We were pursuing, said/thought one of the Titans.

But it does not matter.

The head Titan stopped, waiting for a thought. Moments ago, his directive had been clear. He'd been going to retrieve ... something. Someone. Now all he could sense from the collective was the collective itself. It felt different somehow — damaged, as if there had been discord or death. But he paid it no mind. Because Eternity's hand was inside, holding him, ordering him to ignore it.

Where? thought the first.

One considered. As did the other. Then they seemed to

realize the same answer at the same time, as it had always been within the collective.

Control. There is a threat.

Weapons up, the Titans changed direction and marched toward Control.

DIVINITY BORE DOWN, finding her surrogate's head throbbing.

If she waited and kept the pressure on, she could push Eternity out of her. And as she pushed, Divinity fought a curious indignity. Eternity had initiated a Purge. It was a violation but also bad news. In a stable collective, a Purge was dicey, and the collective was far from stable now. The group mind wasn't meant to be hijacked, but sometimes even the best-functioning group needed an administrator to force order. The ability was there as almost a janitorial concern, simple to implement and align diverging minds, but short-lived and intended to fold after a hard moment of systemwide force. She'd be able to puppet Titans and Reptars if she wanted. But Divinity had a mind of her own.

A terrible scratching preceded a banging at the door: someone trying to break in.

Divinity looked down at Liza Knight's body. She'd meant to watch her death, to find out if she could see the observer energy leave Liza to find itself a new host. But she'd seen nothing.

She reached down, grabbed the silver cylinder. The banging continued.

In seconds they'd be inside.

But what Divinity meant to do would take less than that.

· · ·

ON THE SAND, feeling the hand retreat, Stranger and Kindred looked at one another, each feeling the intensity of the attraction drawing them together. The air felt charged by powerful electromagnets. Kindred blinked up, realizing what he'd almost done, seeing the other members of their party slowly let go of their arms, apparently deciding they might not walk any closer after all.

Another ten feet might have done it. Ten feet closer, and there'd have been no more Stranger. No more Kindred. Only the end.

The presence animating their bodies slipped away, its power lost. Kindred and Stranger, each with intense effort of denial, began walking backward, away from one another.

The force in the air lessened, crisis averted.

But across the open area ahead, a sea of Reptars was already swarming.

Chapter Fifty-Two

MELANIE AWOKE IN THE DARK. There were no more fireflies. As had happened when she'd woken in front of Meyer, at first she wondered if she was dead — if her surrogate's end had meant her own. But no, she was simply integrating. Her little push had realigned the collective's key pieces, showing her so much that she'd needed to know, that had been kept from her. A side effect was that her true self was pulling her back in. Inviting her to rejoin, to stop being Melanie and become Eternity again.

No.

This is what you requested.

It's not what I want.

But the Purge. You have forced reintegration, through the fist.

Even that didn't make sense. Her true body didn't have a fist, or understand the allusion.

She'd only managed to delay the inevitable. Cured nothing. As she'd feared, the collective was fatally infected. If they stayed here any longer, it would all come crashing down, no matter how many realigning Purges she tried.

Even her true mind carried the pollution. Divinity had pushed her away, and she, herself, didn't want to accept her body's call. What did it say about the collective if its Eternity didn't want to be itself?

But some good had been done. She'd almost annihilated two of the remaining Archetypes. All three were in grave danger now — a bit of theater she could still see through the stream, if she looked inward. Melanie still had her hooks in Meyer, and that meant none of the six people on the sand would be able to tell the true Reptars from the counterfeits.

But if Clara was right? If they really could get past the Reptars? It seemed unlikely, but humanity had surprised them so many times already.

If they poisoned the Ark again, the damage would be too intense to purge. There would be no choice but to sever the connection. Not by killing the species; they were far to entangled now for that not to end the collective as well. But they could leave, declare Earth a loss, and go, accepting their failure to clean the lab after the experiment had ended.

I might be Melanie forever.

Unacceptable.

This could still be saved, the situation salvaged.

Meyer was still repressed.

The Archetypes would be unable to fight without his help, and the remaining three would die.

Then they could complete the erasure.

And accepting a two-decade delay, the new epoch could finally begin.

Melanie exited the larger body, resisting its intense pull. She thought again: *Hypocrite.* But leaders always made exceptions for themselves.

As the body closed, she saw the fireflies come back to life inside it.

She didn't leave the chamber for what came next.

Melanie sat. Cleared her mind. And watched the scene unfold on the planet below.

Chapter Fifty-Three

THEY CAME LIKE A BLACK TIDE.

If there really were only two Reptars on the freighter — something Clara found herself doubting as she watched them boil over the railing and run down the ship's sides like drops of noxious water — they must have done something since the group's departure. They must have taken their false faces and doubled them, then doubled them again. This was something exponential. Clara was frozen. The Reptars would come and come until their tiny group was drowning.

"Run."

Clara's mind wanted to identify the speaker, and was shocked to discover she'd said the word herself — in a hush, like a secret.

"Clara …" Piper said, drawing the end of her name past its usual length: a question without a mark. Logan and Kamal were looking at her the same way. Clara wasn't in charge, but still somehow it seemed that she was. Piper had told them they needed to return, but *Clara* sat at the middle of some sort of vital crossroads: in agreement with Piper on one axis but most informed on the other.

"Run."

Speaking to herself more than the others. Thinking it out. Hearing her own imperative as something foreign, wondering how she'd so suddenly and completely become a coward.

But her intention must have had an echo because Stranger and Kindred — who hadn't been watching Clara like Logan and Kamal but had instead still been eyeing each other, still barely far enough apart to not fill the air with electricity — turned and ran.

Not away.

But directly at the oncoming horde in a sprint.

The wave of Reptars seemed to hitch. Its front edge, which had been the roiling lead of an oncoming wave, became a ripple. It was as if the first among them paused — just long enough for the rows to bunch up behind them. The flat edge became a ridge. But it lasted only a moment, and the Reptars kept coming.

"Clara!" Piper again. Rooted to her spot, watching Kindred and Stranger run full out ahead. Again her word was a question — urgent enough to warrant a shout.

"Run at them!"

Logan turned toward Clara, head cocked. But he was Lightborn, and saw her purpose. He said something to Kamal, then, without waiting for agreement began to sprint as well. Kamal followed.

"There's only two real ones! We just have to get through them, as fast as we can!"

Piper was still watching them, semi-catatonic.

Clara grabbed her hand and pulled, too hard. Piper's feet became unglued, and they began to run, interlinked.

Maybe she got it and maybe she didn't, but once they were moving, Piper didn't hesitate or slow.

The idea — first in Clara then in Stranger and Kindred, possibly all through Meyer above — was simple: If they stayed put, the false Reptars would surround and hold them until the real ones could pick them off one at a time. But if they turned into the threat, they could flip the echoes to their advantage and use them as cover.

But as teeth and claws kept coming, terror rained on her body. Clara kept her feet moving only through inertia, able to keep running only because she already was. Part of her mind understood that most of these Reptars couldn't hurt her, but a larger part rebelled at the teeth and claws and azure sparks. You ran *away* from these things, not out to meet them.

Sweat. Heartbeats like thunder.

The Reptar's purrs blended into an appliance-like buzz. Clara's feet belonged to someone else. She could barely feel Piper's hand in hers.

They're not real. Not in any way that matters. You can touch them, and you can feel their scales, slick against your skin, but they can't touch you or split their minds. Not between cardboard cutouts like these. And not now, ill as they are.

She tried to feel that sickness. To remember how the Astral collective had felt the last time she'd touched it. Remind herself that this was only a trick.

Thirty feet from collision — probably four or five good strides on each side — Piper must have hit something with her foot. She faltered, staggering both of them sideways.

Clara's eye caught a break in the pattern ahead: one of the Reptars, a line back from the front, jogging sideways a millisecond later, to match.

Of course. The real ones are out front to get the Archetypes right away. One comes for me, and the other makes a beeline for …

The bottom dropped from her mind, sending Clara into free fall.

"Kindred! Stranger! They're—!"

Piper saw the Reptar that had changed course and yanked Clara sideways, away from it, as the lines collided. She lost sight, too many churning black bodies of decoys surrounding them.

But before they'd been surrounded, Clara had seen another break pattern. It leaped, mouth open and claws out, raging straight at Kindred.

Chapter Fifty-Four

KINDRED'S MIND was outstretched like the arm of a drowning man, seeking a savior unseen at the surface. It was nearly impossible to clear his head even a little. A minute ago, he'd been falling toward Stranger the way a passing asteroid hurtles toward a black hole. Gravitational, seeded with inevitability. The black hole will devour the asteroid, but to the rock it's neither good nor bad — only what was destined to happen. Whatever had almost happened, when a foreign presence had seized his body and began moving him toward Stranger like something on remote control, had felt like that. Relief — at least soon, it would all be over. Then the sensation ended, and he'd been himself, able to step away. Then the Reptars. And then the warning. The command — this time from a known voice.

Don't let them use you. Use them. Don't let them overtake you. Overtake the Reptars, instead.

Kindred had known the same voice — Meyer's — was inside Stranger's head. Kindred was somehow in both places at once, his spirit inside both bodies. When Stranger had decided to run, Kindred hadn't been surprised. It had felt like himself making the choice, one thought moving both sets of legs.

He knew there were only two Reptars, refracted through the Ark's folded space to show hundreds or thousands. Like a funhouse mirror or a disco ball's many edges: one thing, shown many different ways. But that was hard to remember as he ran, closing the distance between himself and the Reptars as they double-took, surprised, and then kept coming.

Meyer inside his head: *If you don't let them scare you, they can hide you from the genuine threats.*

But despite what Clara or the others might have believed, Kindred was plenty scared. With the Ark's power in the air, all of his anger and resentment were gone. All of Stranger's thoughts of vengeance and retribution: gone. All Kindred's pain — of exclusion, of incompletion, of something left behind — *gone*.

And he was left with only fear.

Kindred was barely aware of himself when the Reptar broke formation and lunged.

It happened in bang-bang succession: Kindred was knocked flat, then the lights died as the swarm arrived to surround them. Reptar echoes stopped rushing forward and agitated like turbulent water, moving in sinuous, writhing patterns like a tangle of snakes. A small halo formed around Kindred and his predator, giving them room. But Kindred could barely see sunlight through all their black bodies. He could feel the press and heat of their presence. They weren't just shadows. Nor just ghosts. Most of the Reptars around him were real: reflections shown in three dimensions instead of the usual two, seen through what Kamal had called quantum rifts.

The Reptar raked him across the chest, snarling. Flesh opened in parallel diagonal wounds. It snarled above him, the blue glow blasting from its throat. Its breath was like spoiled steak.

Kindred's eyes watched its rows of razor-sharp teeth.

But then there was a new hum in the air. A growing static, his hair bristling as if trying to stand on end. Kindred braced, the Reptar's reeking saliva dripping runnels onto his cheek. The hum intensified, becoming something like the drone of transmission lines overloading.

An intense, very sharp pain. A smell of ozone supplanting the reek of meat. There was a flash, and the Reptar flinched back, screeching with pain. It regained its wits in less than a second and refocused on Kindred, but then the force built again, ramping like a capacitor gathering charge.

This time when the surge hit, it knocked the Reptars around Kindred to their backs, flattening them in a circle like a burst from overhead. Another big whiff of ozone. Kindred's fingers prickled; his muscles kept wanting to spasm.

While the Reptar that had been on him scrambled to regain its feet, Kindred rolled sideways, into the still-upright part of the swarm. Inside he found his hands and knees, then his feet.

He ran, sighting on the barely visible freighter antennae, where the other survivors would surely be headed.

Chapter Fifty-Five

STRANGER LOOKED BACK, feeling the charge dissipate after the growing force had finally reached its head and popped, flattening a circle of Reptars. At first he didn't understand. But then Stranger saw Kindred roll out of the area opened by the burst and into the Reptar throng.

He'd felt a charge build around him. Like someone overfilling a balloon. His mind had been watching the feeling while he weaved through Reptars, knowing that balloon was filling more and more as he moved, knowing that if he couldn't release some of the pressure, something would blow: the balloon's skin finally at its limit. He'd changed directions, knowing on an instinctual level that proximity to *something* was the problem. But he'd gone in the wrong direction — toward Kindred rather than away. There'd been a blink of overload as the balloon was flooded with air all at once.

He hadn't had time to flinch, knowing it was coming. It was just *there*, in an instant. All Stranger had managed to do was brace as the pressure discharged: a huge electric event, like a vast static spark from years of shuffling bare-foot on carpet.

The charge vanished for a split second, then began to rebuild, waning as Kindred escaped the Reptar and ran toward the ship.

Meyer spoke inside his head: *Now you understand. You are half of an atomic bomb.*

This time, instead of running from Kindred, he found the line of deadly force leading to his opposite and followed as fast as he could.

Chapter Fifty-Six

MEYER WAS GRASPING, trying to find his center, when the door finally opened. He couldn't stop it. He hadn't been punched *in* the gut; someone had managed to reach *inside* his gut and punch him there. Whatever had just assaulted him seemed to hit only his Astral half, but that was enough. The human had been beaten and dragged about, using psychic energy and effort to buoy him. With the Astral collective clutched in an iron hand, Meyer withered, his infrastructure suddenly yanked out from under him.

He couldn't reach Clara or the others, in anything more than tiny bursts. If he'd had a fiber-optic connection before the gut punch, now he only had a telegraph. He could give them dots and dashes but nothing more. He was a man in a cell, unable to so much as hold his own door closed.

The woman stormed inside: Eternity, who called herself Melanie. She was alone.

"How did they do it?" she said, quickly crossing the room.

"Do what?"

She slapped him, hard. His cheek stung. Meyer must have grown used to the support of a now-dormant part of himself, because he found himself wincing.

"HOW DID THEY DO IT?"

"I don't know what you're talking about!"

She hit him again. And again. And again. Hair flew around her face. From inside, Meyer could still feel her fist on the Astral collective. Its intensity had subsided, but to Meyer it was a vise. She'd done something to them. The humanity he'd seen in the Astrals lately was upon the woman in full bloom, practically bleeding out of her even as she held precise control of her alien pieces.

"You know! I know you know! I'll cut it out of you if I have to!"

The Astral control relaxed, and Meyer felt a scene forced upon him. The woman was opening the fist just a little, feeding him the vision as if grabbing Meyer's neck and shoving his face against a photo.

He saw Kindred. The point of view was from above, and in the grotesque feel of the vision he could see long black legs at the periphery, emerging as if from a viewscreen. He was seeing from inside a Reptar, even feeling its parodies of emotion. He felt an alien greed subsume him — the Reptar's hunger, perhaps — then a jolt of light and pain. The view had changed, now looking up into what appeared to be a swarm of writhing black bodies. And in that canted view, he saw Kindred roll away into the throng, as if trying to extinguish fire from his clothing.

"What did you tell them?"

"I can't tell them anything!"

"But you knew. You knew it happened."

After a moment, Meyer bobbed his head.

"It won't work," she said, glaring at him. "If this is

their plan, it's a waste. They can't destroy the Ark. But there are other artifacts on the ship that we'd hoped to recover, and supplies that could help your race survive a harsh season. Now they will squander it all and kill each other. Kill Piper. *Clara.*"

This all seemed off to Meyer. Wouldn't she *want* them dead?

"Tell them to stop. Tell them to stay away from each other."

Meyer met the woman's cool blue eyes, human and full of *fear*.

"Why?"

"They will only harm each other."

"And?"

"Don't you care? You saw what happened when they got too close!"

But this was a game of poker. Meyer set his face and held his emotion. She finally spoke again, her voice less frantic — almost resigned.

"They can't destroy it. There's no point in trying."

But Meyer could tell the true issue was elsewhere. He searched her face, consulted his internal compass, and decided he might have found it — something he'd already begun to feel within himself, looking through the Astrals' stream to find his own echo at the end of a long corridor. In the Astral stream's history of the hybrid Meyer Dempsey were many events: a birth, an occupation by an observer, a first copy, a purge, a second copy. And then there was a curious event he hadn't quite figured until now: a certainty that Stranger, at some point, had been aboard this very ship, looking into the Astral stream just as he himself had done. Only, Stranger had sampled something of Meyer. He'd *taken something with him*, before going.

It hadn't been much. Just a memory Meyer hadn't truly

experienced that his first duplicate had: death, as the copy gave his life for Heather's.

Stranger had taken that memory. Until the connection was severed, Meyer had felt his sense of anger centering on it, the way Stranger had held that sacrificial moment close, clinging to hatred.

But Stranger's possession of the memory wasn't the problem. It was that he'd been able to access Meyer in the stream to take it.

If there was a copy of Meyer's mind — and his duplicate's — in the Astral stream, that meant it was part of them.

It meant that while whatever was happening to the Astrals as humanity flooded it, that copy of Meyer's mind was victim to it as well — and perhaps part of its cause.

It meant that Meyer was bound to them. Now and forever.

"They can't die, can they?" Meyer asked.

"They can die," she said.

"Their bodies can, maybe. But even if you kill us all, the King Archetype is part of your collective now, and always will be. You can't remove it. Even if you erase us all, part of me has become part of you, hasn't it?"

Kill the Archetypes; restart the clock.

But it couldn't be done because a copy of Meyer — of Stranger, of Kindred — would live inside the collective forever.

The King couldn't be killed. Not without killing themselves.

Eternity nodded.

Melanie nodded.

The moment lasted only a second. Then a creeping dread clawed onto Meyer as the woman looked up, new fear flooding her eyes.

Inside Meyer's mind, a klaxon blared.

Something new was being pumped in the minds of both species, lighting thoughts in a spreading inferno.

"Let me go," he said.

So she did.

Chapter Fifty-Seven

PIPER HAD LOST Clara's hand in the throng but could still see the girl between the Reptars' flashing limbs. There was only terror. Piper could taste it on her tongue; she could smell it in the air; she could feel its slick wet kiss on every inch of her skin. Reptar scales brushed and bumped her, and with every pass she felt an internal tension wind one click tighter. Soon the spring would snap and break her mind into pieces.

"Clara."

Her lip quivering, barely able to make sounds. Every open Reptar mouth was a tomb. Every passing claw was a death knife. Piper thought she understood what Clara had said — what Trevor's ghost had echoed. But here in the middle of the aliens, she didn't find herself calmed by the lack of attack. She didn't feel better because Clara had spotted a live one and dodged it. Instead she knew the killing blow would come at any instant, from any direction, the Reptar she'd seen attack Kindred had already finished him. The boom she'd felt in her bones from somewhere to the left had been a bomb — a new weapon the Astrals had found, or a way to blow humans apart from the inside.

"Piper!" Clara's answering shout was more of a hiss, barely heard through the chatter of false Reptars.

"Clara?"

Her slight form appeared between Reptar legs as if they were furniture. She was *almost* calm.

"You with me? Can you hold it together a bit longer?"

Piper forced herself to nod.

"We have to get up there." She pointed.

Piper looked. They were closer to the ship than she'd thought.

"One might see us when we start to climb the ladder. Do you understand? We have to—"

The Reptars were gone. All of a sudden, like a switch flipping, they disappeared. Piper saw Kamal and Logan a hundred feet away on the sandy plain, revealed as if by a tablecloth snapped away.

Piper opened her mouth, but nothing came out.

A sound from the side. Kindred was close, alive, much nearer than Piper might have suspected. He was running hard toward them, crossing the ground in seconds. Then he was below them, all three at the ladder, shoving at Piper's feet, trying to make her move. She finally did, and Clara followed with Kindred right below them, huffing and shouting and shoving. Then Piper saw why.

Not all the Reptars were gone. There was another just yards from Kindred.

A blur came from the other side. A man, running.

The Reptar coiled its legs, ready to strike.

And the man — Stranger, Piper now saw — hit the Reptar full on. Practically tackled the thing. At first Piper thought she was seeing a repeat of what Peers had done in his final moments, but then saw that Stranger wasn't taking on the Reptar. He was next to it, but only because the Reptar was between him and what he'd actually been running after.

Kindred.

Piper felt the charge build before she could shout to stop it. The storm but a second away. She'd never seen Stranger and Kindred share the same frame. Now there they were, not fifteen feet from each other with only the Reptar between them.

A hand on Piper's. She looked up, expecting to see Clara, but Clara was below her. It was Trevor, his eyes on hers.

"Hurry," he said, yanking at her.

Piper felt the charge build beneath her. It was like an invisible bubble. Part of Piper told her that if she jumped, she'd bounce on an unseen skin, repelled like a same-polarity magnet.

"But ..." She looked down at Stranger and Kindred. They weren't supposed to approach each other. *Ever.* She wanted to listen, but the force building below claimed all her attention.

"I told you last night," Trevor said. "This time, you have a weapon."

The Reptar had paused its strike, head whipping around.

The air hummed. The charge built. Around Piper, between ladder and hull, small blue sparks of lightning crackled.

There was a tremendous crack, like a tree sundering in a storm. And at the same time, the Reptar between Kindred and Stranger detonated like a bomb.

Piper flinched, spattered by alien gore. Trevor pulled her hard from above.

"You still have to open the Ark. Things have changed,

for good and bad. But time is short." Trevor yanked again. "*Now,* Piper. It has to be *now.*"

Chapter Fifty-Eight

THE RUSH of Meyer's voice was like a shattering dam. The last of his mind returning to Stranger, now fully present.

Stranger had felt a bit of that mind released from its bondage when the Reptars had thinned to the two, all subterfuge forcibly erased in an instant. He'd felt it when he'd run after instead of away from Kindred, and he'd felt it when his hands had prickled with his memory leaking back: a distant recollection of himself standing beside a shuttle in Ember Flats soon after his birth, using mental feedback to pop a Reptar like a swollen pimple.

But now he felt it like a presence. As if instead of Reptar guts between him and Stranger, there was Meyer Dempsey, speaking to them both clear as day.

Meyer's voice was a loudspeaker. Whatever had cut him off earlier had let him go — and to Stranger, it seemed his mind had grown in the interim.

It's not about us versus them, the voice told Stranger's mind. *Until we break the bond, what harms one injures both.*

Stranger looked at Kindred. The other man was hearing this, too. Stranger could see it on Kindred's Meyer

Dempsey face, which until now he'd never seen so close. Power still crackled between them. It's nature had changed. The flow was deadly. They still needed to keep their distance — these halves of a larger whole, now apparent as something the Astrals never meant to create.

Something has gone very wrong. You have to reach the Ark. Do it now. It's the only way.

An invisible hand gripped Stranger impossibly hard by the base of the skull, turning his head. From the corner of his eye, Stranger saw Kindred's head forcibly turned in the same direction.

Protect her. At all costs.

Meyer's voice was gone.

Stranger was left to stare where Meyer's psychic grip had turned him: at Piper, at the ship's railing, looking down. The looming black threat of the final Reptar behind her.

Chapter Fifty-Nine

DIVINITY CLOSED her surrogate's eyes and focused inward. Living in a surrogate body, you had to shut out the external world to truly see the one inside. It was something she'd never had to do in her true form, but something she'd grown used to.

She could still see Eternity's Purge, presented by her surrogate's symbolic brain as an army of red-clad soldiers at the outer edges of her internal space. Her own white force was — now that the first wave had passed — easily keeping those soldiers at bay. Divinity had regained control of her inside world and actions. The Purge wouldn't persistently compel all the Reptars and Titans, but Divinity assumed she could bend the lessers to her will for a while.

Which was why, when the Titans broke into Control and grabbed her, Divinity didn't try to influence them through the collective. They were Eternity's puppets for now.

It didn't matter. The device had already been inserted.

Divinity opened her eyes, unable to resist a peek at the silver cylinder — still rammed home in one of the consoles, exactly where she'd placed it before the Titans burst in. The thing had gone home like it had been meant for their technology rather than the humans' — almost as if it had wanted to slip its troublemaker code into the collective all along, and that Canned Heat's work on the human Internet had only been a warm-up.

In truth, the console had adapted itself to the device, manufacturing the required port the way it could interface with anything else required. But to Divinity, the whole thing felt meant to be — a human concept if ever there was one.

She looked at Liza Knight's body, right where she'd dropped it. The Titans hadn't touched it or even seemed to notice. In the end, once someone decided the corpse was in the way, Liza would be incinerated with neither pomp nor circumstance.

Poor Liza. If only the Mullah had told her that the Villain was always betrayed in the end.

Divinity was sitting on a chair they'd allowed her to call up, too busy and mentally befuddled as individuals to deem her request unacceptable. She was restrained, but the seat she'd fashioned for herself was tall-backed, with rolled arms and red velvet cushions, covered in gold leaf. A throne. The symbolism was lost on Eternity's minions, now tugging at the Canned Heat cylinder as if removing it would do any good.

She closed her eyes. Beyond the red soldiers, she imagined a black cloud — a roiling presence disguising itself as ebony fog. The surrogate's mind showed Canned Heat's pollution to her as something almost liquid, crawling through the collective node by node. Filthy, coating everything, ending all that it touched.

But it wasn't killing *them*. Not the superior race.

It was killing the bonds.

Erasing them.

She wasn't sure how the virus worked, but Liza had been right. The human infection had the organization of their Internet, and Canned Heat — helped along in its thought-based adaptation by the ship's systems — seemed to know just how to handle it.

Soon the virus would fully adapt, and become more mental than code. She could see it changing even now: unsolvable computer logic puzzles shifting into impossible mental paradoxes. She'd reviewed enough human media to know their film trope of the overloaded robot, caught in a loop until its circuits fry. *Humanity, meet thy maker.*

It would boil through the human collective that had so problematically braided itself into their own, destroying what the Forgetting couldn't erase. And once the connection between the species was severed at the Nexus and the archive, the virus would do its work within all Titans, Reptars, Divinity, and Eternity. Kill what was human and leave what was not. Then the experiment would be over, and they'd never have to worry about this diseased little marble ever again.

She laughed, drawing the Titans' attention, when she felt Eternity relax her grip on Meyer. She could hear him call out to the humans on the surface. But why were they bothering? Opening the Ark now wouldn't help. And this little problem Eternity saw with their King Archetype being permanent? Maybe it was technically true that they couldn't erase him — but they didn't need to kill the Archetypes if they moved the entire operation one level up, ending the species instead.

So what if they couldn't achieve a Forgetting and start a new epoch? With the human race obliterated, they could leave this shithole just the same.

Divinity closed her eyes again, and shut the world out.

Soon, she wouldn't need to do this sort of thing anymore. With humanity purged from their collective — and with all higher beings returned to their proper bodies instead of puppeteering surrogates looking vainly at their "selves" in mirrors — distractions would be extinct.

She watched the black cloud spread. *Changing*. Evolving to do its job.

Soon the infection would be burned from their minds and the diseased little planet.

And then, finally, they would know harmony again.

Chapter Sixty

KAMAL RAISED HIS HANDGUN.

Logan saw where he was aiming and began flapping his lips, waving vaguely, apparently unable to spit anything out. Then: "Don't you fucking dare—!"

But Kamal had already pulled the trigger. The report was deafening. The kick about slammed the heavy thing into his forehead. You had to focus when in the cavalry position, attempting an Annie Oakley shot from at least thirty yards away.

He didn't hit the Reptar.

Nor did he hit Piper.

Judging by the bright spark that blossomed against a bulkhead on the ship's desk, Kamal hit a spot nearly as far from his target as *he* was from the mark.

Logan slapped his hand down. "Are you crazy? You'll kill her!"

But the Reptar had seen the shot's ricochet. And more importantly, Piper had seen the Reptar. It wasn't even ten feet away.

"I'd have to be a much better shot to kill her, even by mistake," Kamal said, lowering his weapon. "I should be so lucky."

Chapter Sixty-One

PIPER'S HEAD jerked toward the shot. The shooter seemed to be Kamal, way too far off to hit anything. Because he was far and the impact was close, the sound's delay caused her to hear the latter before the former. The effect was dizzying: someone almost hit her, and only then was the shot fired.

But immediately Piper saw two other things — both much more important. Each like a gunshot of its own, lightning quick.

Kindred and Stranger were scrambling up the ladder so fast, they were barely managing to grasp the rungs.

And from the corner of her eye she saw a Reptar. It had approached with stealth, apparently failing to strike yet only because its hard eyes were on Clara. *She* was the Reptar's true target — reaching her was important enough that it hadn't struck Piper and revealed its location.

But now that Piper had turned to see it — and Clara, twenty feet closer to the first of the shipping containers on the freighter's rear — all bets were off. The thing's eyes swiveled toward Piper, its mouth opening with a percolating purr.

There was no pause. No delay. The creature leaped forward.

Piper fell away more than she dove; there was a narrow, mariner-sized hallway behind her. Like the other passages on the freighter, this one had been economized: shrunk and made wedge-tight to save valuable onboard space. She slid to its floor banging only an elbow, but the Reptar, which had to move forward and turn, didn't enter as smoothly.

Piper was up in a second, heart racing, legs no longer remotely sluggish. The fog departed, and her focus was suddenly sharp, her world in high definition. It took ages for her to rise, to take her first running steps farther down the passage, to turn the next corner. The Reptar was too fast, but she had an ever-so-slight lead, growing narrower. Piper gained a second as she took the next corner, grabbing a pipe to spin around a bend so she wouldn't have to slow.

She could hear shouts from ahead and behind. Clara was somewhere back there, but safe. There was only one left, assuming it didn't pull its multiplication trick again.

The longer I distract it, the longer they have to escape.

But would they even try?

Seconds dragged for hours. Her lungs burned; her legs turned sloppy beneath her. She pumped her arms, banging fists and knees as she sprinted through the tight corridor.

She could hear the Reptar, bounding like a cat behind her.

Another corner. Into a room. A mess hall, like an onboard cafeteria, with dozens of spindly metal chairs — bunched to one side as if they'd slid down the slightly sloped floor. Somewhere along the way Piper had lost her shoes and was running barefoot, her feet getting shredded where the all-weather carpet gave way to metal.

The Reptar scrabbled behind her, crashing, failing to corner as well.

She rounded another corner, left the big room, and almost flattened Kindred. He was in the middle of a wide spot, handgun raised. He shouted for her to move around and get behind him, but what was the point? Handguns against Reptars were useless unless you got lucky and shot them in the eyes, which were near impossible to hit, or you had to find a way to shoot it in the—

Kindred shoved her down, behind him. And without hesitating, as the thing opened its mouth to strike, he did the last thing the Reptar must have expected: instead of running from that mouth, Kindred shoved a meal inside it.

The Reptar bit down hard, severing Kindred's right arm near the shoulder.

But perhaps a tenth of a second before the thing's jaws closed, there was a muffled pop as Kindred discharged his weapon down the monster's throat.

Chapter Sixty-Two

MELANIE'S KNEES BUCKLED. She sagged back against the bulkhead for a moment and had to push her hands against the thing to right herself. Meyer wasn't watching. He was in his trance, head down, longish sweaty hair hanging to hide him in a curtain. His hands were still restrained, but Melanie felt an odd compulsion to free them. She'd already let him go in the only way that truly mattered. To the awakened Meyer Dempsey, hands were hardly necessary.

Feeling him working sent a shiver up her back. A subtle difference in the room's energy, a change in its temperature. All things she wouldn't have noticed without her body.

Now there was this fatigue. This sense of desperately wanting sleep. She felt sluggish and slow. But the torpor wasn't Meyer's doing. This was something else.

Melanie closed her eyes, forcing herself not to think of Meyer and what he was doing. Instead, she looked back at the collective. But the path to the core she'd so recently used to force the Purge was already foggy and indistinct.

There was something wrong. And in its center, she saw Divinity.

What did you do?

But of course Divinity didn't answer because Melanie hadn't actually asked. Instead she'd asked herself. The question was more a moan of futility than an inquiry. The sort of thing a human would do. The kind of nonsense question Piper Dempsey might have asked when taken to the Nexus for her energy: *Why, Meyer? Why you, and why me?*

Because he was broken. Before Kindred had sprung him, the plan had been to keep the real Meyer Dempsey on board indefinitely. And why Piper? Because every control needed a control, and the thought at the time — though laughable now — had been that the first Titan duplicate, who was supposed to be fixed in the ways the original hybrid was broken — would keep the new key bearer safe and guide her. She'd never have children with that first copy (or with Kindred, for that matter), but she could have them with Cameron, ensuring a long line of bearers, until the time when they were finally needed.

Well. That was only one of a hundred things that hadn't worked out as planned.

Melanie watched the disease spread like a spill, soaking into the hive. She watched the shriveling. She watched the dying. She watched Titan and Reptar minds shake themselves off and, as their own fatigue faded, wake up more their old selves than their new ones. And she watched it creep toward the bridge.

Toward the Ark.

Toward the junction between species, where it would cross into the child population to finish its ugliest deeds.

She had time to feel a flash of uncertainty and fear. The final hours played themselves out as regurgitated from the stream: Carl grabbing her in the cell; Meyer abducting her; Melanie awakening to learn that Carl had, it seemed, taken a shot meant to kill her. The strange trio of inappropriate feelings that came in its company: relief, that her surrogate's body had survived; guilt, that Carl had died instead; awe, that even a human born to protect — as the Warrior — would put himself in harm's way to spare an enemy.

The dark cloud came, eclipsing it all. And when it passed, there was no Divinity. No collective. All of a sudden, there was only herself.

Divinity's bile had severed her connection to the collective.

Internal lights extinguished, one by one.

And then Melanie, for the first time in her very long life, was all alone.

Chapter Sixty-Three

CLARA SHRIEKED. At first she thought it was the walking dead, but then realized she was seeing something far less theatrical and much more dire: Piper, covered in blood, supporting Kindred on her right side — her only option because Kindred no longer had an arm to support on the other. It was only a stump, ragged like a dog's chew toy, dangling in wet flaps of sinew and blood vessels. A red-soaked spike of ivory bone protruded from the mess, its end sharp like a branch snapped in a thunderstorm.

"What happened?" Clara demanded. She couldn't move her eyes from the wound. She'd seen worse, but this was so *fresh*, and gushing like a faucet. And for all intents and purposes, this was her grandfather.

Kindred's face was white and waxy, like cheese.

"Reptar," he said. "Dead."

"We need to find the Ark," Piper said, pushing past her. Clara turned, watching her skirt Kamal and Logan, their mouths both open. Stranger was at the rear of the arriving group looking nearly as waxen as Kindred. His left hand was on his right shoulder, gripping it as if he'd been shot.

"Piper?" Kamal said. "What …?"

He trailed off. Piper didn't answer, rushing on, shouldering open a swinging door, moving out onto the deck where row upon row of stacked shipping containers waited. Clara could tell it wasn't mere urgency compelling Piper. She was also fighting not to think. Clara could feel her worry, her terror, how close Piper was to the end of her rope. They *did* have to hurry. Not because of Reptars but because Piper's mind was close to snapping.

"Where is it?" Piper asked Kindred. She turned to Stranger, yards distant, when Kindred didn't answer. "Where is the Ark? Can you feel it?"

But Stranger didn't answer either.

The air crackled with blue lightning, arcing from one metal box to another. Whatever had happened between Stranger and Kindred was ramping up now. The air was alive. The bomb waiting to explode.

"Clara?"

"Ahead," Clara said.

Piper moved on, still dragging her burden. Clara followed. Kamal and Logan remained behind her, stepping wide to avoid a slick trail of blood down the corridor's middle. And when Clara looked over her shoulder, she could see Stranger at the far rear wearing a curious expression. It was hard to be between them. They could all feel the energy. Clara could see it on their faces.

Ahead, said an internal voice. But it was no longer Meyer's — a voice she could barely hear through something like dark static. Now it was her own.

She didn't need help to find it. The archive's power thickened the air, its pull like a magnet. She could practically see the thing like a sun glowing around the corner, lighting its shipping container like a glowing coal more and more the closer they came. The thing bellowed. Radiated heat. And when the box with the Ark finally came into view, she had to raise her hand to shield her eyes.

"How are we …?" Clara began, meaning to ask how they could possibly approach the thing, enter its halo without being burned alive. But she stopped when Piper put her hand on the latch without flinching — when she turned to look back, and Clara realized she wasn't even squinting in the blinding light the way she, Logan, and Kamal were forced to.

Clara watched Kindred's fingers grasp for the handle beside Piper's. She watched a mammoth padlock melting like taffy in fire. It hit the deck with a soft clang — partially molten metal smacking the hard deck.

Piper met Clara's eyes. Not squinting. Not flinching. Not hesitating, other than for Clara's sake.

"I can't go in there," Clara said.

The heat was like a blast furnace. The light was like a thousand suns, and even with her arm up and eyes closed, she could see its brilliance as if daring her corneas to fry away. When she turned her head, it seemed to shine through her skull from the rear. And yet to Piper, it was only a box. No intolerable light or heat or charge. The handle was still under her uncaring hand, inches from where the heavy metal lock had melted away.

Had it been like this for Cameron? Clara knew he'd approached it alone. Or was something different this time? Something broken far above, filling the archive with poison before they could do the same?

"I know you can't," said Piper, a bittersweet smile touching her lips. "I think this is for me to do alone."

"For *us* to do alone," Kindred corrected.

"*No!*"

"Goodbye, Clara," said Piper.

Clara's eyes had filled with tears. She opened her

mouth to shout, but before she could Piper and Kindred had slipped inside.

For a moment there was nothing. But ten seconds later the container seemed to intensify and hum, cycling up like a power plant nearing overload.

Someone brushed her shoulder.

Stranger.

The energy grew. The light was blinding. Heat forced Clara to step back, unable to even attempt a grab at Stranger's sleeve. Hotter waves pounded her with his every step, forcing Clara away.

But in the brilliance, she could see the tall man turn to face her.

"For *us* to do alone," Stranger echoed.

He stepped forward.

Before Clara could say anything, he'd entered the shipping container and closed the door behind him.

Chapter Sixty-Four

THERE WAS a terrible crackling of static. At first Melanie thought Meyer must have smuggled an electronic device aboard that had somehow gone unnoticed for the entire time he'd been on the Eternity ship, but then she realized the noise was coming from the walls themselves.

Melanie was investigating when the wall itself flickered with light, and she saw Divinity's surrogate staring at her, projected as if through an old-world Earth television.

Divinity's finger seemed to tap at the wall from the other side. From where Melanie was standing beside Meyer's restrained form, her finger was the size of a fat sausage.

Tap tap tap.

"Is this thing on?" Divinity said.

She looked at Meyer, but he was seeing none of this. Melanie didn't know if he was simply focused on trying to use the power she'd returned to him following her Purge, if the blackness she'd seen inside the collective before losing her connection was working on him as well, or if Meyer was simply dead. Either way, the man was no help. *The*

Divinity Show had come on air — and Melanie, it seemed, would be watching alone.

"Can you hear me? And can you see me?"

Behind Divinity, Melanie could see Titans. Many, *many* Titans. The view was from slightly above, with the entire room on display. Judging by what she could see, there might be scores or hundreds of Titans in Control with Divinity. Strange, considering that Melanie had only sent two to apprehend her.

"Hello?" Divinity's mouth curled up into a tiny, satirical smile. *"Melanie?"*

Melanie said nothing, but she did flinch at the spoken use of her adopted name. That name was private. Profane on Divinity's lips.

"So you *can* hear me," Divinity said.

Melanie watched the Titans swarm behind Divinity. She kept her surrogate's expression neutral.

"I didn't know your systems could do this," Divinity said. "My ship can't. Why did you get abilities on your ship that I didn't get on mine?"

Melanie stayed silent. She'd never seen projected images like this or heard static, other than from human inventions. She wasn't sure how Divinity had made it happen, but wasn't about to enter into a technical debate.

"I'm sorry to contact you like this, but I think something went wrong with the collective. I can't think straight right now." She smiled.

"What did you do?"

"So you don't know? I guess you can't think straight, either." Divinity turned, looking behind her. "Same for all these Titans and Reptars. They all seemed so confused, once they could no longer hear each other. It was sad. But it's okay. I told them I'd help. That I knew exactly what to do."

Melanie walked toward the door. Time to get back to business. Reclaim control of her ship.

MY ship.

It was an odd concept but one she suddenly found fitting.

But the door didn't open at her approach. Melanie tried to focus and tell the door her intention, but then remembered she was alone. She couldn't hear anyone else, and they — including the dumb door node — couldn't hear her. She tapped the wall to raise a panel. There was a manual override that came in handy when an individual was ill and focus was difficult. But now it was absent, gone, locked out.

"Turns out some of them had skills that came in handy once they stopped pooling their thoughts," Divinity said. "Technical skills. Maybe killing, though I haven't tested that one yet."

"What did you do to the collective?"

"I fixed it."

"By severing it?"

"Oh, get over yourself. Nobody wants the return of the collective more than me. But it must be the *proper* collective. Not this travesty. This is a cleaner doing a job. Once it's finished, we will be back as we were. No more confusion. No more interference. No more *surrogates.*"

"Open this door."

Divinity shook her head. "We have decided you're a liability until the collective is back online."

Melanie made a fist and slammed it against the door, knowing how it would look and not caring.

"Open this door!"

"And if I do? If I allow you to reenter the ship's popu-lation? What will you do, *Melanie*, if I allow you to make the decisions about what comes next — assuming you can convince the Titans and Reptars to let you try?"

"I will remove whatever you've done to the ship's collective. Whatever you've used to infect it, I'll—"

"See," Divinity said onscreen, "that's where you're wrong. I haven't infected it; *they've* infected it. And we're not just talking about the ship's collective. Our armada is infected. And has been for dozens of trips around their sun."

Our entire armada.

They've infected it.

Melanie's mind raced, struggling without corroboration from other minds. She'd hidden her secrets from the collective, deeming them *personal* even though she knew it was wrong. But this was so much harder. This was isolation, without even the whisper of her fellows to color her thoughts.

But still the implication was clear. Alarm spiked inside her.

"What did you do?" she repeated, this time afraid she already knew.

"Someone identified humanity's 'new network' paradigm as the primary cause. And that same person proposed we use what they used, once upon a time, to erase that network."

"The virus."

"The virus," Divinity repeated.

"Let me out. My node is central. It'll be needed when we come back online."

Again, Divinity shook her head. "I don't think so. Not yet. Because yes, afterward, you will again be in the cluster's center. And my node will be sub-central, local to the ship I've fallen into the bad habit of considering 'mine.'

But until then, you're apt to take this too personally. You are no longer objective."

"Absurd."

"Really," said Divinity, *almost* rolling her eyes. "Then tell me: When it became apparent that the Dempsey hybrid had adapted and that the duplicate had inherited the same adaptation, why didn't you contain it and install a different human viceroy?"

"The problems with the first duplicate were purged from the stream before the next replication."

"And those 'problems' didn't leak out? They didn't create a kind of emotional poltergeist? They didn't *become one of the humans' Archetypes?* And when the thing it became brought itself back onto this ship, you didn't let it stick its head back into the stream to pollute us further with Dempsey's 'aberrant humanity'?"

"You'd have done the same."

"Well, that's the whole point, isn't it? You thinking of *you* and *me*. The minute we started considering that one part of the collective might disagree with another, a cleansing solution should have been implemented. We should have been considering what I've finally done from the start."

"What you've ..." It hit her. The Canned Heat Divinity had been loosed in the system. And what it would do — not just to them but to the humans. "You've killed them all."

"Don't act so superior. You killed seven billion yourself."

"But the experiment—"

"Is lost. Your inability to admit it is proof that this is necessary."

"You've doomed their entire species to—!"

Divinity snapped. Onscreen, several of the Titans

AVERY BLAKE & JOHNNY B. TRUANT

turned their white heads to stare at her, their faces displaying very un-Titan-like surprise.

"To *what?* To the same fate we were headed toward under your benevolent leadership? What would you have had us do? They were supposed to Forget. But when the Forgetting failed, your node said, 'keep trying,' as if the results would change. For twenty years, we kept banging our diseased heads against infected walls, hoping the same exact thing we'd always done and that had already failed would suddenly start to work. For twenty years, their Archetypes kept the archive open and fed us more of themselves. For twenty years, we accomplished nothing but decay. You did manage to find your doll a nice haircut and a wardrobe to perfectly express your style. And don't get me started on your elegant use of interior design space."

"That's hardly the poi—"

"The protocol was always clear. The Founders knew that at some point, their chaos element might create something new. It might have meant evolution, but it *could* mean a parasite. And in that case, we were to turn toward other solutions."

"Which we did."

"Not until Clara forced your hand by breaking the walls. *Then* you suddenly realized the Archetypes might be the problem. But you know as well as I do that there's one we can't kill because it's in our system." She put her hands on her hips and stalked, drawing more looks from the Titans. "We can't kill off the humans because we're bound to them. You discovered that the first time you tried to force your way into Carl Nairobi's mind. I've felt each of the Archetypes' deaths, but it's been minor compared to what would happen if we eradicated the species. So that's out. But we can't remove the Archetypes, even if it's merely painful instead of deadly — because guess which one has

392

lodged itself far enough up our asses that it's now impossible to remove?"

Melanie let the image settle. Normally, they didn't have anuses. The idea that Meyer and his pieces were up an element of a purely human body to cause them trouble was, in itself, proof how terrible things had become.

"I've realized the same thing," said Melanie. "And that's why, if I hadn't been blocked at every turn, we'd have already begun withdrawal prep—"

"*Withdrawal!*" Divinity spit the word out as if it were sour. "Just run! Just leave the planet, with our subjects remembering everything that happened!"

"It's the only way."

"Blanking them permanently is the only way," said Divinity, calming. Her voice became eminently reasonable.

"It would kill them."

"Better them than us."

"Leaving won't kill us. Once we've left orbit, our connection to the humans through the archive will be cut. The infection will stop."

"But it will not reverse," said Divinity.

A pause. Then Melanie said, "No. It will not reverse."

"And that's okay with you. The idea that we might leave this planet, and forever be infected with *them*. That for the rest of our existence, we will be as much human inside as we are ourselves."

"It's the best option."

"No. *This* is the best option." Divinity tapped something beside the screen, presumably indicating the virus on its way to lobotomizing the human population while it cleansed the collective above. "I have a full room of Titans and Reptars who agreed with me enough to shut you in where you are. That's the problem with individuality. Majority tends to rule." Divinity shrugged. "But hey. If you don't agree, I guess that's your choice." A beat, then, "At least until the idea of *you* becomes irrelevant."

A cold sensation clawed at Melanie's scalp. A shiver kissed her skin.

"Let me out. Let me out so we can discuss this."

"There's nothing more to discuss."

"Make it wait. Stop it." Feeling low and knowing how Divinity would take her weakness, Melanie said, "Please. Just pull the virus back until we can figure this out."

"It's too late." Divinity tapped at something unseen, her eyes darting away. "It's taking the archive now. They're trying to poison it, but it won't do them any good. The virus is in the system already. Whatever garbage they throw into the archive, Canned Heat will devour it like the rest."

Melanie exhaled. She didn't mean to sit but found herself doing so anyway. *"Please."*

"Don't beg," Divinity said. "It's so *human.*"

Chapter Sixty-Five

PIPER SET her hand on the archive. Part of her expected the thing to shock her or melt her or set her arm on fire, but it was only cool metal, nothing fancy.

When they'd entered, Piper wondered if it would be hard to reach — if they'd have to rig levers to unseat tightly packed cargo and then break open a shipping crate. Instead they found the gilded box in the container as if on display. The crate's interior was black and charred, reeking of ancient smoke. Ashes in the corners clung to every surface. It looked like the archive had perhaps once been surrounded by other cargo and a crate, now vaporized. Piper had seen stranger things.

Right now, the Ark didn't feel like the most dangerous thing in the room. That honor went to Kindred and Stranger, now a handful of yards apart. The energy between them was enough to raise her hair like the Van de Graaff generator she'd touched once in a science center as a kid. Blue lightning was everywhere. A steady, rhythmic thrumming bounced about the small space like thrown super balls with a low, bass tone that hurt Piper's bones as much as her ears.

But the Ark itself was cool, despite the way she'd seen Clara and the others flinching, backing away as if driven.

Her fingers made circles. She wasn't afraid. She was *supposed* to be here. She and this device were kin.

"Wait."

She looked up. Stranger had spoken, just inside the container's closed door. Piper was still supporting Kindred. Stranger looked drawn and beaten, but Kindred was almost inert. Her side and his were soaked with blood from his absent arm.

"This is wrong," Stranger said.

"I spoke to someone about it last night. This is what I have to do." Her fingers lingered. Now that Piper had touched the thing, she could barely imagine removing her hand.

"I was born of this," Stranger said, taking a step. The power in the air seemed to double with his single pace forward, making Piper squint as if into a breeze. He held out his hand. "And I can tell it's not right."

"You don't know it anymore, Stranger."

"I didn't. But I'm starting to again. Through him." He pointed at Kindred, whose breathing was slowing. "Through *us*. I can see what's coming. Can you?"

Piper followed Stranger's eyes, looking toward the open Ark. Had she opened it? She must have. She didn't have a stone key as Cameron had. She hadn't pressed any buttons or turned any knobs, as she'd always imagined Cameron doing. Even now, she felt as if he were there — a ghost over her shoulder, looking into the open top's swirling mist. She kept looking up, where she felt him, expecting to see Cameron as she'd seen Trevor last night. But she was alone, with two halves of the man who'd damned Piper while trying to save her.

She looked to Stranger then followed his eyes back to the Ark. This time, she let her gaze linger. And through the white mist, she saw blackness spreading like ink. Piper gasped, feeling what it was more than knowing. Death. The reaper. Nightmares and terror.

Piper put her free hand on the side. She applied subtle pressure, like leaning out over a balcony railing to see the world below.

"You don't have to do this, Piper," said Kindred, shocking her. He was so close, his breath now a whisper. He hadn't moved in what felt like forever, save barely propelling his feet under her lead — an increasingly heavy burden.

She gently lowered Kindred. But rather than sloughing to the ground, he staggered back to the nearest wall and remained upright, watching her. Stranger took another step. More lightning, and crackle.

More steps. Stranger and Kindred were six feet apart when Stranger's side met Piper's, his hands also on the edge, looking down into the box.

"I have to go in," Piper said. "Like Cameron did."

"No."

"It needs a sacrifice. I saw Trevor last night, Stranger. Meyer sent him. And he told me, *I'm* the poison. We need a toxin to make it sick."

"It's already sick." He pointed. The black was swirling with red, like an infection.

Piper pressed down again. Steeling herself. It would only take one good heave, and she'd be in. Forever.

"I understand now." Stranger's voice was distant, full of awe. Piper looked over and saw him peering into the depths, his gaze fixed.

Stranger looked at Piper. In his eyes, she saw so much of Meyer.

"The Astrals thought something had gone wrong with Meyer," he said, speaking as if someone was feeding him lines. "They tried to fix him, and created us."

An intense push from Piper's side. She felt as if a gust of wind was stirring, threatening to tip her. But her hair wasn't blowing. It was rising a bit with the charge, popping around her in the growing hum. She felt a hand near hers and saw Kindred beside her, while Stranger flanked the other side. Kindred no longer seemed ill, his face fixed in a grim expression of destiny.

"I thought I was a remainder," Stranger said. "I thought I was an element of chaos — something spit out of their machine when they tried to eliminate all the 'Meyer' that had caused them so much trouble the first time. I was leftovers. The thing that no longer fit. So I walked the Earth and sowed my disorder, trying to be a wrench in the works. I thought it was chaos for chaos's sake, that I was staying alive by resisting order. I thought that if I could stir their equation enough, I could carve out a place for myself. It worked, and the system broke. But now I understand. I see what I was actually doing."

Piper looked from Stranger to Kindred. Kindred to Stranger. The air hummed. Blue lightning crashed like thunder.

"Nothing went wrong," said Kindred on her other side. "It was exactly as it was supposed to be."

An arc of energy jumped from Kindred's chest to Stranger's, then back.

Piper waited for more, then finally said, "What do you mean?"

"Meyer wasn't a mistake—"

"He was *evolution,*" Kindred finished Stranger's thought.

Piper looked into the Ark. Red and black were swirling faster and faster. It seemed angry. Furious, like a swarm of wasps waiting for someone to sting.

Stranger put a gentle hand on Piper's chest. He pushed her back two steps, where she stood without support, her hand on nothing. Then the men turned to face her. Kindred extended his remaining hand, and Stranger took it.

"Two halves," said Kindred.

"Made whole," Stranger finished.

A pulse pounded the container's walls, making them reverberate like a drum. Piper took an involuntary step back, streaks of light lancing between the men. At first they were only large sparks, but then they multiplied, every inch of Kindred's left side bound by a thread to Stranger's right. Their conjoined hands vanished behind the thousands of light threads, pulling them together. Threads became membrane. The double bodies touched, overlapping. The air shook with aural pulses, knocking Piper toward the wall. It was like hot gusts of nothing — a padded smash, forcing her away.

Their faces were almost lost in light. They closed upon one another, becoming a Gemini silhouette, then finally only one man.

Nothing but light.

"You can't contaminate what's already poisoned," said the new thing, reborn of the Ark. "You have to cut it open, and wash the sickness away."

Piper flinched forward as the merged body of Kindred and Stranger turned — away from her and toward the open Ark.

"I hear them on the other side," said Stranger's voice as the being looked into the mist.

From the same mouth came Kindred's answer, almost a whisper: *"I hear them, too."*

Piper saw what was about to happen and lunged forward, ignoring the sparks and the heat and the light and the power, ignoring the peril and her fear and her brewing tears, ignoring everything but the certainty of what was about to happen.

But she was too late. By the time she reached the new being, it was already toppling into the void.

Chapter Sixty-Six

MEYER WAS SITTING beside a small fire in a room of absolute black. The fire was fresh, not mature, and burned only wood at its surface, with no hot coals beneath it. He was in a camp chair like he'd once had, back on some unknown trip between New York and LA, when they'd all still been together. He'd been a young man, married to Heather, though they were already on their way out. Trevor and Lila were still young enough to believe their dad could be a good father, well before the world had ended and he'd rediscovered the trick of fatherhood.

A small burning log — somewhere between kindling and the bedrock of a true cook fire — rolled from the center of their new flame. It struck a pile of snapped branches, which began to burn as well.

Meyer looked up, alarmed for some reason — something he'd forgotten. And he said to Lila, just thirteen years old in this vision, "Lila, put out the fire."

"You put it out, Dad. That's your job."

Meyer looked around, but there was no water. No fire extinguisher.

Another stick rolled away. This one caught a small pile of paper litter, birthing new flame.

"Come on, Dad," said a younger Trevor beside Lila. "Put it out before it burns down the forest."

"Where's the water? Where did it go?"

But now Lila and Trevor were yelling at him, annoyed. The fire was contained but spreading. And that's when Meyer realized he couldn't move. None of them could. They were rooted in place, with the tiny fire spreading among them.

Heather arrived at his shoulder.

She'd somehow gathered all of their gear in her arms — the tent, the sleeping bags, pillows, extra blankets. With all of it piled atop her small grip, she looked like a cartoon.

"Smother it, dumbass," Heather said, rolling her eyes. "Take away the oxygen, and it'll die just fine."

Then she dropped all the gear atop him. It had to weigh hundreds of pounds. In a moment he was covered, unable to see, unable to breathe, unable to—

"Meyer."

His eyes opened. Meyer was on the floor of an all-white room. The camping vision was gone as if it had never been there.

But it was a beautiful blonde and not Heather above him. It took several long seconds before his brain could place her. He'd somehow ended up on his back, tipped from a bench, seeing her from below as he'd never seen her before, hair draped around her face, closing their two heads into a private space. His hands were now free whereas they'd been recently bound, and the device that had been binding them was open in her palms, which

402

made no sense. Most importantly, her voice and manner were soft as silk atop a featherbed.

She touched his face. A hand on his cheek. "Are you awake? Can you hear me?"

"I can hear you."

"You were mumbling. You were in a trance. You fell."

"When did I fall?"

"Minutes ago."

"So you woke me. Not the fall."

"That's right."

"Why?"

Meyer was searching, prodding, following his gut. Now he remembered. He'd seen a way to reach the Reptars on the planet as the collective failed — and once their little trick ended, Meyer knew his people had dispatched them and made it to the Ark. Then he'd sent himself to Stranger and Kindred. He'd shown them the way. They'd done what needed doing. And now it was over.

But then his mind realized why he was following his gut, in this matter of speaking to the silky Astral. He'd only been able to do what he'd done because she'd let him. She'd removed a block from his mind and built him a tunnel. Now she'd freed his hands, and woken him gently. *Why?*

She didn't answer, so Meyer asked something else: "Why did you let me contact them?" He corrected himself. "Why did you *help* me contact them?"

"Because you have become the least of evils."

"I thought evil was a human concept," Meyer said, still on the floor and looking straight up.

"It has become ours as well."

"Because of us?"

She nodded.

Meyer sat halfway up, onto his elbows. The woman

shifted to allow him room. She was squatting, still very close.

"You can't hear them anymore, can you?"

Meyer thought of his dream, of the campfire. Had it only been a dream rather than something prescient? It had dovetailed from his psychic efforts, but now Meyer wondered if he'd simply exhausted himself and collapsed. Because no, he couldn't hear them. He couldn't feel Piper or Clara or Stranger or Kindred. Only a sense of foreboding remained. Of something dark just beyond the horizon that he couldn't quite see.

"There's a sickness spreading through the collective. Soon it will extend through our mental junction point in the archive, to the humans on the surface. Then it will erase you. What's left of humanity will be unable to function. You will be less than animals. You will barely know how to breathe."

Meyer sat up farther, alarmed, but the woman kept speaking. He got the impression these were thoughts she'd spent time curating while he'd been dozing. Something he needed to hear, that she needed to tell him.

"It will erase you. But it will merely cleanse us. That's why it's happening. There are parties above this ship that believe that loosing this plague on both our races is the only chance we have to save ourselves."

"I thought you couldn't disagree?" But that, Meyer knew, was wrong. Ever since he'd come aboard, it had been clear the Astrals were different than they'd been. They acted like individuals. Like *people*.

"Times have changed."

Meyer looked the room over. The chamber was silent. They were alone.

"Nobody can see or hear us now," she said, as if anticipating Meyer's thoughts. "For a while, perhaps while it resets for the cleaning, the collective has gone dark. At first it terrified me. I had only my own thoughts. But then I realized something that scared me even more — I was hearing thoughts through the lens of this surrogate's brain. You can't know what it's like to be us, to be on our own."

Meyer watched her, waiting, knowing he shouldn't interrupt.

"But after a while, I grew used to the quiet. Then something seemed to unlock inside me."

"*Unlock?*"

"We know very little of our Founders — the first of our kind, that traveled the universe to seed populations like yours. They are to us what gods are to humans. We have no memories of them. Some believe that bank is simply fragile, and that the oldest memories will always be lost over time. But there is another school of thought, though it only surfaces in those who find ways to separate themselves from the collective for long periods of time. An alternate reason for the absence of Founder memories within us."

"What is it?"

"That the Founders existed before the collective. That there was once a day when we were disconnected. When *we* were like *you*."

Meyer came to his knees. He moved to the bench along the wall and sat on it, silent. The woman was still on the floor, now sitting. Beneath him like a pupil, though clearly she was the teacher.

"In my natural form, I am the nerve center of the collective around your planet. In human terms, I am this fleet's admiral, whereas the instances of Divinity you've seen are captains of ships. My class is considered core to our larger collective, and one of the reasons some feel it's so important to cleanse us before we leave your planet. They worry that if we go home infected, I will pollute the rest of them. But there's another distinction the Eternity class has beyond the others that I'm only now seeing."

Meyer watched her, fascinated. A clock was ticking inside, playing her words over with thoughts of a dark metronome metering beats. Something had happened on the surface and now she told him of another something on the ship. Both felt like bombs. But this moment to Meyer was a fold in time, bound to last as long as it had to.

"We are secret-keepers. But those secrets hidden inside me — and surely within all Eternity — are individual memories, incredibly ancient. Not fragile, but *quiet*. They can only be heard when the collective is silent. Those secrets inside only light up, it seems, when the power is off, and we are alone in the dark."

"What secrets?"

"That the chaos sown into your population by the Founders is not as unpredictable as it seems. I can see it clearly now. We centered on you because we thought you were broken. You were a hybrid that had somehow malfunctioned, or so we believed. But that's not the case. The Founders knew you would happen. Not *you*, Meyer Dempsey, but something like you. Because that's the nature of chaos: Its variables *make* it predictable. Given enough time, every unlikely possibility will inevitably occur."

"What are you talking about?" Meyer asked.

"Evolution."

"Evolution?"

"We cannot evolve as long as we remain homogenous. Evolution, as your planet has seen, involves variation. It requires experiments that fail and a few that succeed. There must be difference. There must be risk. There must be loss for there to be gain. Our Founders knew this. They knew we would ascend and reach an equilibrium. We would become a collective, and in that collective, we would be strong. But once we became strong, we would stall. And once that happened, there would be no way for us to advance further from within. It could only happen if we were acted upon by an outside force."

"Us," Meyer said.

"You," she repeated. "Now that the collective is quiet, I can see the Founders' intentions — just as they must have intended in a dire situation such as the one we find ourselves in. Only a catastrophe could shut us down, and only in a shutdown could Eternity hear the ancient thoughts. But yes, you are that force. A population with an anomaly we could not solve. A new breed of subjects that confounded our best efforts, and gave us the spark required to take our next steps."

"Are you saying that this is destiny?"

She shook her head. "I'm saying that chaos is mathematical. This moment — here and now, with you and me — was not destined. But a moment like it? A moment where the chaos instilled by the Founders finally produced a large enough anomaly to do what had to be done? According to the math, that was always inevitable."

"So what comes next?" Without the Astral collective, Meyer himself felt mostly alone, stripped of his recently discovered powers. He was blind. They were two people in the dark, stumbling along by feel.

"That's up to you."

"But I can't feel the collective either."

"What *can* you feel?"

Eternity waited, as if she already knew. Then he saw the answer and gave it. "I can still feel the Ark. It's open. And Kindred and Stranger … They did something to it." He shook his head. "I can't describe it."

"You don't need to describe it. You just need to do it."

"Do what?"

She watched him again, and in Meyer's mind, he saw his dream from moments before: Trevor, Lila, and Heather by the fire. The feeling that the fire was spreading too fast, and that they had no water to douse it.

Just smother it.

Meyer nodded at the woman. He understood. And he *knew*.

Meyer met the Astral's blue eyes, as if seeing her for the first time. He knew the aliens could animate human bodies, but all of a sudden this struck him as something different. More than a puppet before him. This was something *more*.

"What are you?" Meyer asked,

"You can call me Melanie," she said.

Chapter Sixty-Seven

CLARA STAGGERED BACK, now around a corner, the presence of an enormous metal box doing nothing to quiet the light or staunch the heat. She thought of Stranger. Of Kindred. Of Piper.

A great and intense sorrow struck her, suddenly sure that two of the three were gone. It pulled her back like a hook from the pit of her stomach. She wanted to cry but had no moisture left.

The air grew brighter. And brighter.

Logan took her hand, but even as she turned to look right at their braided digits, Clara could not see them. She could only hear Logan inside her mind, trodding the long-forgotten Lightborn paths they'd once shared.

Light.

Heat.

There was nothing else in the world.

The next voice wasn't Logan's. Or Kamal's. It wasn't even a man's.

Clara turned. Without thinking, she opened her eyes

and saw her mother sitting behind her, visible even in the intense brightness, plain as day.

"It's almost over," Lila said.

From the shipping container — from the Ark itself — there was a brilliant wave of light.

And then Clara saw no more.

Chapter Sixty-Eight

ON THE SURFACE, in a village not far from The Clearing, a woman named Mary Welch gripped her head with a brain-splitting headache. She sometimes got them — more before they'd all forgotten their pasts, but plenty since the days when she'd been the clueless wife of a farmer as well — but this was the worst one in a while. It felt like there was a steel band around her skull, tightened by a malicious god. Hot rocks in her neck ground together whenever she turned her head. The spike through her temple was coated in acid.

Someone had opened a hatch on the back of her head and was manipulating her brain like Play-Doh. Someone was punching her right in the coherence, turning thought impossible.

She wished she had an Excedrin. She wished she had Anacin or Motrin. Or perhaps Imitrex. It had been a godsend for migraines, but those wonder drugs had gone the way of the cell phone.

That hand on her brain, muddling her thoughts. It was intolerable. She could barely think.

Then, all of a sudden, Mary Welch couldn't think at all.

There was only a blank white wall, with nothing beyond it.

FIVE THOUSAND MILES AWAY, on a distant shore that William Kyle had decided might either be Greenland or Newfoundland, cold waves crashed and brought the tang of salt to the air. There were cliffs in the distance, and ever since he'd noticed them a few days ago with new eyes, William had been meaning to take a hike. Before his memory had returned, he'd accepted the cliffs as always having been there — like the ocean and the village and the sandals on his feet. But now he was curious, and it was all so interesting.

For instance: Were the cliffs something like fjords? William could remember neither his history nor geography, but seemed to remember fjords being relevant to something or other. Did these fjords (if they were indeed fjords) provide clues to his whereabouts? Was this Greenland, Newfoundland, somewhere else? Maybe he could find a map. Maps must have survived somewhere. If he could find a map, he might be able to locate an old city. The floods couldn't have erased *everything*. Because if not — if they could find ruins — perhaps they could rebuild. Maybe, now that they had their memories back, they could get past this ignorance and back to the business of progress.

William was staring at the cliffs (fjords?) when he began to feel woozy. His sharp focus distorted, balled up like paper meant for the trash. He couldn't think straight. He had to go home, but didn't know where that was.

William collapsed and fell flat on his face. Waves

lapped his ankles for a while, until scurrying crabs felt safe enough to skitter up to him for their own explorations.

IN WHAT HAD ONCE BEEN empty land not far from Morocco, a man named Khalif and a woman named Suri were looking down at the girl they'd recently believed to be their daughter. Two days ago, they'd spontaneously and completely remembered that in truth she'd been a street urchin in their small town across the old ocean who'd had no relation to them at all. The girl, named Nala, wasn't even the right race. They both had mocha skin, and Nala's skin was espresso black. How had they simply accepted her? It didn't make sense. And yet the family had taken shape so obliviously that sometimes Suri seemed to remember giving birth to Nala, and Khalif raising no objections about her having another man's child.

They'd been scuttling around the question of what to do now that everyone remembered the truth. Nothing had been said, but the unspoken subject had hovered above the family like a pregnant cloud. In the old world, there'd have been little point in splitting hairs. Nala was almost thirty, and she'd have already built a life of her own away from them. But in the forgetful world they'd so recently left behind, families roomed together for generations.

So did they keep pretending? Did Nala's twenty-year stay as their false daughter *make* her their daughter? In words, both would have said yes. But deeper down, both Khalif and Suri felt tricked. This same street urchin had caused them endless mischief in the old world — sufficient that when they'd found themselves on the same vessel in an endless ocean, Khalif had been angry. Then time had passed. At some point, everyone went idiot, and time marched on without a clue.

Now, knowing he'd been staring and thinking too long, Khalif turned away. A moment later, looking curiously bittersweet, Suri turned as well.

Both wanted to turn back for reasons they couldn't articulate. Neither did.

Everything was different.

It was the last thought any of them had before they collapsed.

CAL WYCLEF HAD OPENED the small device, prodding at its microscopic guts with a tiny set of screwdrivers he'd found in the horde. The cave was packed with goodies. He'd wondered if he might die when he'd spotted the old rector on the sand and followed her on a whim. He hadn't even had water. The woman might have had some, but Cal still hung back, feeling desiccated, obeying an instinct that eventually paid off. Liza Knight had seemed all right to him (if a bit corrupt) while his brain had been elsewhere, but back in the Roman Sands days she'd been damn near bloodthirsty. And now she was cavorting with Astrals? He wouldn't have believed it if he hadn't seen the shuttle pick her up and whisk her into the sky.

But with Liza gone, the cave was a goldmine. He found water in plastic bottles, which Cal drank until he nearly threw up. And with his thirst sated, he found endless delights to suit his engineer's mind. Stepping into the cave was like stepping back in time — which, ironically, was also a lot like stepping vastly *forward*. The futuristic gadgets from his youth were here. Almost all were long dead, but he'd found a few that still lit up with a solar charge. A few that took him back, and made his ingenious mind crackle with promise.

There were smartphones, like the one he was tinkering

in now. There was basically no chance he'd get the thing working with the tools at his disposal (or without a power grid at the ready), but there were many phones in the cave — plenty to experiment with.

There were conventional radios, including a few hand-cranked ones like the survivalists bought for the day when power went offline. Not that there'd be anything on-air, but maybe Cal could build a set of walkie-talkies — maybe even climb the metal structure he'd noticed yesterday for the first time, which might be an old cellular tower — and plant a fabricated beacon.

There were books. *Paper* books, which didn't require batteries. There were also, interestingly, a lot of personal journals that someone had snatched away and spirited off to this archive of the past. Cal had read one already. It was fascinating. At the start, it was a time capsule of old-world memories. Then, the Forgetting had come. By the final pages, musings on which boys might like her in Ember Flats had turned into treatises on the hardiness of her father's bean crop. It was like the author had become blind, unable to turn back a few pages and read through the lies.

He could use what was here. *Boy*, could he use it. Progress would be slow, but there must be other caches like this around the world and other people like Cal. They could dig in. Discover the past. Rebuild.

Of course they could.

Cal watched the small circuit board in the phone, trying to concentrate.

He was focusing so intently that he didn't notice when his hands gave out and his body relaxed all at once, his thoughts turning empty.

. . .

ON THE SURFACE, in a village not far from The Clearing, Mary Welch woke on the floor of her hut. She blinked. How had she ended up down here?

She shook the thought away and stood, taking the nearby broom, remembering that she'd been sweeping. And she swept.

FIVE THOUSAND MILES AWAY, on a distant shore that William Kyle no longer thought might be Greenland or Newfoundland, cold waves rolled across his ankles and brought the tang of salt to the air. He sat up, and a contingent of crabs scattered. He watched them go, looking around for his trap. He must have come to trap crabs — there was no other reason for lounging.

As he looked for the trap he hadn't apparently brought to catch the runaway crabs, his eyes fell on the distant cliffs.

But they meant nothing to William, so he paid them no mind.

IN WHAT HAD ONCE BEEN empty land not far from Morocco, Khalif and Suri stood from the floor, blinking away a curious fainting spell. As they did, a third form caught their eyes. Suri reacted first, but Khalif wasn't far behind.

"Nala! Are you all right?"

But their daughter was fine. She blinked as they had, just as curiously felled, and just as unharmed.

CAL WYCLEF LOOKED AROUND HIMSELF, suddenly afraid. He didn't know this place, but he'd heard of it. Among the people, it was known as the Devil's Hole. He didn't remember coming here, nor did he want to be here anymore. So he set aside his revulsion at what he had to assume were the Devil's belongings — strange objects that glittered and sparkled, piled in droves — and forced himself to turn and find the exit, waiting for some unseen trap to spring.

Only once outside in the fresh air did Cal feel slightly better. Still he turned back and saw the cave's entrance yawning like a toothy mouth, forcing himself to remain cool and calm as he fled.

He walked off into the sand.

Five minutes later, he forgot the cave, and never thought of it again.

ONE BY ONE, the lights of knowledge extinguished. Seen from above — if experience were like a light that grew brighter — Earth's landscape would have gone dark, blink by blink.

It didn't take long.

And this time, even the Lightborn couldn't remember.

Chapter Sixty-Nine

PIPER WAS WRONG. Kindred wasn't dead after all.

At least, that's what she thought when he came up to her, scurrying down to all fours like an animal, crossing the all-white space to her. She'd somehow fallen without remembering her tumble. She also didn't recall this room. Or the blonde behind Kindred.

"Piper," Kindred said.

Except that he was holding her face in his hands. In *both* of his hands.

It was Meyer.

She watched him for a moment. Too long. She'd already registered others in her peripheral vision: Clara, Logan, and Kamal. Clara and Logan were gripping each other like survivors of a bomb. Kamal was off by himself, seeming lost.

But the room was dead quiet, as if waiting.

The moment broke, and Meyer pulled Piper against him. His hug was urgent, almost suffocating. His kisses were even more so, but smothering only until Piper's paralysis snapped and she gripped his arms to kiss him back.

They separated, aware of all eyes upon them.

"You're alive," she said.

"Couldn't you feel me?"

"You went dark. None of us could feel you at the end."

Meyer's mouth didn't reply, but his eyes did: *You went dark for me, too.*

"Kindred?" he said. "Stranger?"

Piper couldn't make words. She pursed her lips and tried to shake her head. Tears came. For Stranger, for Kindred, for Lila, for Trevor — for everyone they'd lost along the way. The emotional flood was a shattered dam. She couldn't contain it; she could only grip Meyer's arms and try to endure. He held her, and slowly the sensation passed. Piper found she could breathe, her diaphragm still causing her lungs to hitch with aftershocks.

"It's okay, Piper. They did it. They saved us."

"How?"

Meyer looked at the blonde. Another prisoner? Piper had never seen her before. Unless she had, a very, very long time ago. He turned back to Piper. "You opened the Ark. But they opened it the rest of the way."

"Cameron didn't need it opened the rest of the way," Piper said.

"The Astrals did that part last time. This time, we did."

Piper's face fell. The reality of his words seemed to slot into place. But she couldn't ask that question. Not yet.

Meyer turned to the blonde again. Piper saw a tiny hesitation on his face, but it wasn't shameful. The woman was stunning, thirty years old at most, wrapped in a dress that almost looked painted on. She was exactly his type, and Piper wouldn't put it past Meyer to still bed a much younger woman. But this look wasn't that. The two shared a secret, but as they sidestepped it, Meyer saw protection, not concealment. Perhaps time would reveal that secret, but Piper was content not to know it for now.

"Piper, this is Melanie."

Feeling absurd, Piper shook the woman's hand. She had no idea how they'd come to this place. Had she been transported while unconscious? The last thing she remembered was the ship, and the Ark.

Meyer made the remaining introductions. Clara eyed the woman. Almost suspicious.

"*Melanie,* is it?" Clara said.

The woman made a little face. Clara didn't shake her hand. Their introduction ended on a note of neutrality.

"Where are we?" Piper asked. "Is this … Are we on the ship?"

"I think they sent you away. They knew that what they did to the Ark might harm you. Or at least …"

"At least what?" Piper prompted when Meyer trailed off.

"Or at least make us forget," Clara said.

All heads turned to Clara.

Clara looked at the blonde, at her grandfather, and then at Piper. The room was graveyard silent until Clara said, "It's what you think, Piper. Kindred and Stranger and Grandpa started it all over, and they sent us here so we wouldn't be affected."

Piper looked around the circle of faces. All were looking right at her, as if she were this thing's center of attention, and everything hinged on Piper reaching the proper conclusions.

"The Forgetting," Piper said. "It's happened, hasn't it?"

Meyer shook his head.

"Not the Forgetting." His eyes ticked to the woman. "What we started, all over again, was *Judgment.*"

Chapter Seventy

DIVINITY WAITED, sitting in her chair. She had her knees together and her elbows on the chair's arms, her hands loosely open on their ends, palms up. She'd repeatedly seen the posture in human dramas. It was the way you put a body when you were readying it for inspiration from a higher power. The way yogis sat while harnessing their chi.

It bothered Divinity that she was thinking about inspiration from a higher power and yogis and chi while waiting for Canned Heat to cleanse her (human constructs, even if appropriately themed), but until she was reintegrated, she had this body, and its sense of brain and mind. Soon she'd no longer need the body — ironically, the same as yogis thought they'd no longer need theirs one day — and she'd return to her true form. Would it feel like being sucked out from behind, leaving her old body as a limp and lifeless shell? Perhaps. And as she meditated and waited, that thought made her sad. But all things (so said the yogis) were for a time.

But nothing came.

Divinity could no longer feel the collective — all she had were the thoughts inside this limited body's tiny brain. Canned Heat had to sever the connection to cleanse it, the same way a filter had to be removed from a device before being blown clean. Now she had to wait for the connection to return, and be content with what little she had in the meantime.

But eventually being zen became boring, so Divinity opened her eyes. And saw a bunch of idiot-faced Titans staring at her in a circle.

"Jesus Christ! You scared me!"

The Titans traded glances. Whether they were wondering about her fear or the exclamation to a human deity, Divinity didn't know. And it was annoying not to. What were the Titans thinking? Because they *were* thinking and would be for a while longer, same as she was.

She shooed them away. They parted like an adoring throng as Divinity sat, then walked to the console. She tapped at it, taking a long moment to make sense of what she was seeing. She'd grown used to the surrogate's senses, but not to monitoring ship's statuses through a visual read-out. That information had always been inside her, accessible with a thought. But for a bit, she'd need to check things with her eyes, the same as how video and audio had been the only way to speak to Eternity from inside Meyer's cell.

"Where is the virus?" she asked the Titans.

They pointed at a display.

Annoyed, Divinity walked forward to look where it was pointing. Obviously Titans didn't speak. Hell, normally, neither did Divinity and Eternity. But she still found it vexing that when she asked a question without her connection to the collective, she couldn't get a straight answer.

Divinity looked at the display and saw something

confounding. She kept scanning, exhaling, trying to be patient, waiting for her limited brain to figure it all out.

Then Divinity realized that she already had.

This didn't fail to make sense because her brain hadn't cottoned onto it; this didn't make sense because *it just plain didn't make sense.*

"What's wrong with this panel?" Divinity demanded. "Is it offline because the collective is still offline?"

The Titans looked at one another, mute.

"Is this time index right? Because it can't be. Where is the stream flow report? Because this sure as hell isn't it."

One of the Titans, proving supreme adaptability to humanity's quirks, shrugged and made a quizzical face.

Divinity's jaw clenched.

According to the readout, the cycle had finished, and there was no Canned Heat left in the system at all.

Chapter Seventy-One

MELANIE HELD HER MENTAL GRIP, waiting.

She could see the collective's restart (thanks to her surrogate brain's penchant for visualizations) as a giant red button she'd need only to push. She could sense the archive at the back of that quiescent and cleansed collective, now empty. To her visual mind, it looked like a mesh of cool blue lines dotted with nodes waiting to be relit. And vaguely, in the distance (more through Clara than the emptied archive, she imagined) Melanie could sense the human network — dormant now, as if asleep.

She waited, watching the door. And then right on time, it happened.

The door opened. The room filled with Titans and Reptars. It wasn't a large room, but it hadn't been meant as a prison cell and hence had comfortable space for twenty or thirty. She didn't count the troops swarming in (from the outside or from inside her mind), but there were that many at least. Perhaps a dozen muscular, powder-white beings with weapons raised and another dozen unarmed black beings viciously purring.

The humans, save Meyer, retreated into corners. All eyes turned to Melanie, while hers turned to the dark-haired woman entering at the rear.

"What did you do?" Divinity demanded.

She was stalking toward Melanie, but Meyer responded.

"I smothered the fire."

Divinity threw Meyer a look like he was something found on her heel.

"What is he talking about?" she said to Melanie.

But again Melanie said nothing, and Meyer walked toward the pair. Reptars purred and Titans pointed their weapons, but none stopped him as he closed the distance to stand directly in front of Divinity.

"Your virus needed fuel to spread," Meyer told her. "It needed thoughts and memories to tear through so it could leap from one mind to the next. I took the fuel. It did its job then shut down when it ran out of memories to burn — just like it did when the first copy of me loosed the same virus on the Internet in Heaven's Veil."

"How did you …?"

Meyer didn't have to cut Divinity off. She simply stopped talking.

"I emptied the Ark."

"You—?"

"Once I understood how to do it, the need was obvious. I can see pieces of your history, stretching back through your previous visits. Each time, you've used the Ark to judge us. But you don't understand it. You can't look into it before it's opened or touch it once closed. When the Mullah hid it from you last time, you needed humans to seek it out. You needed human hands to move it from Sinai to Ember Flats. There's always been a human key bearer who opens it because you can't. Don't you remember? You gave Piper that ability yourself. Both of you."

Piper was looking from Meyer to the Astral women, her eyes flicking intermittently to Melanie. She knew now. If there was ever a chance of concealing Melanie's identity, her cover was blown. Piper's eyes found Melanie's. They'd met once before, when Piper's mind wasn't quite coherent, a long time ago.

"You corrupted your own collective so you could corrupt ours. But even when it all shut down and I could no longer reach my family, I could still reach the Nexus. And I could still reach the Ark."

Melanie straightened as Divinity, now understanding, looked away from Meyer and came toward her.

"You told him. You showed him the way."

Melanie kept her face neutral. In truth, she'd told Meyer a lot more than that — but the Founders' message she'd uncovered during the blackout was for Eternity and the hybrid to hear, not for Divinity and the lower classes.

"You told him how it worked. You told him that judgment emptied an opened Ark." She sneered. "You burned the bridge between our collective and theirs, so the virus couldn't cross it."

"And with your collective offline ..." Meyer added, shrugging. "I guess you were in no position to hear the Ark's contents as they escaped. Or to judge us accordingly."

Divinity's small brown eyes flicked toward Meyer, then back to Melanie. Her jaw hardened.

"You'll pay for this."

"It's over," Melanie said. "Let it go."

This was the wrong thing to say. Divinity snapped like a twig, fury descending in a wave.

"*Let it go?* Do you have any idea what you've done?

You've interrupted the cycle before it could finish! The virus only affected us! And now the collective is gone. The soldiers have nothing to command them. We've lost everything that makes us, *us!* And *this* is your answer? *It's over?*"

An inarticulate snarl of rage escaped her, Divinity's face twisting into something gnarled and ugly. She jabbed a finger at a Reptar to one side. Then, betraying the depth of the collective's wound, she addressed it as an individual rather than part of a hive — a thing with its own mind and will.

"You! *Take her!*"

The Reptar didn't hesitate. It swiveled its big black head from Divinity to Melanie, then prowled forward with its jaws agape, a spark churning deep in its gut. Unmoving, Melanie didn't see compulsion in the Reptar. Instead she saw anger: a solo being obeying a command because it wanted to, because it was afraid and happy for an excuse to punish someone.

Melanie was still holding her mental grip, waiting. But as the Reptar's breath touched her skin, she let that grip go. Her mind's eye saw a hand press the big red button. The cool blue grid she'd seen inside her head began to flicker as she did. Nodes began to reignite, one by one.

The Reptar stopped, one clawed foot forward and slightly off the ground. A light seemed to brighten behind its eyes — a subtle shift that wasn't precisely visible, but that changed it nonetheless. And when that happened, Melanie thought she saw fear draining from the beast. Anger followed. And then the Reptar was again just another soldier in the hive.

Its outstretched limb lowered to the floor, claws clacking on the hard surface. Then the Reptar lay down at Melanie's feet like a dog.

Divinity's eyes weren't on the Reptar. She was frozen,

feeling the renewed power just as the beast had — same as the Titans and other Reptars throughout the room. She blinked open-mouthed at Melanie, her expression that of someone receiving a much needed drug. Shocked but not unpleased, as if she'd been mollified against her will. Melanie could still see the woman desperate for fury. But within Divinity, rage was losing a battle to relief.

She waited. She watched the change happen.

And as she watched and waited, Melanie felt the collective energy fill her as well. It was like standing alone and afraid in a dark room, then seeing friends pull cords above their heads, showing themselves to have been there all along. But even as she watched the hive mind come back online, she held part of herself back. She didn't want to give herself fully. The collective was part of her and always would be. But it would *only* be part — rather than whole — from here on out.

"The collective," Divinity said. "It's still alive. It wasn't destroyed after all."

Melanie nodded, feeling the reboot she'd just allowed. "Authority over the collective must go through Eternity. Something you failed to consider."

"But ..." Divinity trailed off. Melanie — more through an infant sense of intuition than hearing the other woman's thoughts — imagined what she'd meant to say: *But there is no authority in a collective. No one being has authority the others don't have.*

It had once been true. But it wasn't so anymore.

Divinity looked around the room, not really surveying her surroundings so much as inspecting her renewed internal space. Melanie could almost imagine Divinity within her, investigating the fresh collective the way a human might inspect a new home.

"It's not the same as it was," Divinity said, eyes unfocused as she explored. "I still feel like ..." She gestured vaguely, mostly at her own body. *Like ME*, Melanie imagined her finishing.

"I do, too." *I* being the operative word, just like *Me* — both first-person pronouns they'd have to get used to using, whether spoken by the lips of a preferred body or merely whispered within the collective mind.

Divinity's face changed again. Melanie watched it without any warning. This was something happening within the woman but not the collective. The second edge to their new double-edged sword.

Her eyes darkened. Her lips firmed, her jaw gone rigid. Her brow wrinkled, eyebrows drawing down. A thousand emotions — now an integral part of them all — screamed across the surrogate's face. But Melanie was still learning her own emotions, so only the largest and most obvious registered.

She saw Divinity's fear.

She saw anger.

And she saw them shoved aside, acceptance definitely not a part of the mix, as Divinity pushed one of the Titans hard in the chest. Divinity's surrogate was small so the Titan barely swayed. But a second later Divinity was showing Melanie what she'd managed to grab in the otherwise botched exchange.

The Titan's weapon, now aimed squarely at Melanie's chest.

Chapter Seventy-Two

"IF THE OTHERS won't stop you, I will," she said.

"There's nothing to stop. It's done. The virus finished then leaked away. How things are now is how they will remain."

"With us half-human."

"We're just changed. This is our next step."

"Bullshit." She used the crude word the way a human would, practically spitting it from between her lips. It was as if she was trying to make a point, to show how far down the wrong path they'd gone.

Divinity raised the weapon higher.

"You should have let it finish. You should have stayed out and let it happen. The virus would have restored our collective to normal instead of this ..." She looked down at her body, her face disgusted. "This *in-between*. I don't know what I am now."

"You're you."

"I shouldn't be me. I should be us."

"Then leave your surrogate. Shed it, and return to your given body. "

Divinity's mouth moved. Melanie, though she couldn't hear the thoughts the other woman kept hidden, could imagine what she must be thinking. They were addicts. No matter how much they desired an alternative, they'd hold tight to the status quo.

"Maybe I should force you to shed yours." The weapon's barrel trembled, still centered on Melanie's chest.

Melanie said nothing. She wanted to say something a brave human might say, such as *Go ahead*. She wouldn't die. As long as the collective existed, she *couldn't* die. But the body would. And somehow, right now, that mattered.

When Melanie didn't reply, Divinity went on.

"You've ruined the experiment."

"It was ruined anyway. Destroying their minds would have changed nothing."

"It would have erased the humanity from our collective. It would have restored us to normal."

"And it would have sent them into extinction."

"Why does it matter?"

"Because we need them."

"How do we need them?"

Melanie wasn't sure how to answer. She looked at Meyer, remembering what she'd told him. Even if human interference — or at least hybrid interference — had been needed to nudge her species forward, that work was already done. They *didn't* need each other anymore, not really. But the solution that would have killed humankind off would also have restored the collective to the way it was when they'd arrived on Earth. Humanity survived in the same fell swoop as the Founders' plan had come to fruition within Melanie's race. They were as intertwined as the two collectives had become, even if one thing hadn't precisely caused the other.

The situation had become what it was, and "how it was" was good. Maybe they didn't need humanity, but spitting on them after deeds were done felt like a poor way to respect the Founders' wishes.

And besides. Deep down — in a place that was definitely more Melanie than Eternity, more solo than collective — she couldn't shake the feeling that the two species weren't finished with each other yet.

Melanie watched Divinity's finger tighten on the weapon's trigger. Her whole hand was shaking. Melanie could feel the other's anger from the inside but knew that if she left it alone, the feeling would pass. There was a balancing act they'd all need to learn in their new form, and this was only the beginning. You could feel anger without acting. You could disagree without fighting. You could suppress intense moments, deferring to what was best for the future, once you got the hang of the new way of being.

But Divinity was losing that battle, wanting to lash out though it would change nothing. And Melanie, as she watched the weapon's barrel, could barely keep from a creeping sense that she suspected was panic. She couldn't truly die, and didn't want to die all the same. It's what had made her go along with Meyer and Carl rather than letting Carl snap her neck. Kin to the instinctual sense of preservation that had caused Carl, in the end, to trade his life for hers.

Because in the end, he'd seemed to understand that Eternity's surrogate had to live. That was more important to the long term, and justified the loss of his own life in the short term.

She had to stand firm. They were half individuals and half collective now, and an individual stood up for what best served them all — both individual *and* collective.

If I die, I die, Melanie thought. Eternity would live on, as the same dispassionate being it was before this all began.

And as she watched Divinity stare her down, Melanie heard the thought picked up as the collective heard it, reverberating like an echo.

If I die, I die.

If I die,

I die.

Divinity's jaw shifted, her glare intensifying as the echo rolled behind her eyes.

She pivoted on the spot and leveled the weapon at the group of humans against the wall.

"Maybe that's true," she said, answering the Melanie's mental refrain. "But if *they* die, they die forever."

Chapter Seventy-Three

DIVINITY'S ARMS SHOOK. Her legs had lost their bones, now uncertain and wanting to wobble. Something was wrong with her surrogate. Had to be. It was breaking down. It was falling apart, soon to drop inexplicably into pieces.

She heard the bold, simultaneously infuriating echo as the room repeated Eternity's mental words, trying them on, turning them over and over to see how they worked.

If I die, I die.

But now even Eternity's mind — the body that controlled it still in her peripheral vision lest she get the idea to launch a sacrificial attack — had gone quiet.

Divinity watched the four humans through her fogging vision, feeling the hammer of her surrogate's heart, the failure of her surrogate's sense of reason and logic. She was sweating. Her eyes wouldn't focus — or perhaps the misalignment was happening at the cognitive level, allowing her to *observe* but not truly *see*. Either way, she felt herself coming undone, barely able to stand.

This was the opposite of what was supposed to

happen. Without interference, Canned Heat should have wiped both sides clean. The humans would have collapsed drooling. The collective would have returned to its proper state — a state in which the entity that led an entire ship wouldn't be reduced to a quivering, emotional mass of flesh and bone.

She could kill them. Right here and now. She wouldn't need the collective's permission — and, in an ironic twist, what Eternity had done to the hive would make it impossible for the other minds to stop her. Eternity was content with individuality and emotion? *Fine.* Divinity would show her just what individuality and emotion allowed that a saner configuration never would have.

She looked at Piper Dempsey, the key bearer.

She looked at Clara, who'd started it all.

She looked at the man beside Clara, the pair in a semi-embrace. The other felt like a Lightborn, just like her. Two troublemakers for the price of one.

And finally her eyes settled on the group's remaining member — an unremarkable man she'd never seen before.

She could start with him. He'd mean the least, but seeing him die would flood the others with satisfying fear. All the emotion they could handle, if that's what they wanted. *The more the merrier,* Divinity thought as her own emotions gripped her.

"You don't need to do this."

Divinity's eyes flicked to Meyer. She'd almost forgotten him. He no longer felt human to her, though he was at least half one. But she could feel his fear, too. It was strange — something Divinity hadn't felt before. He was plenty afraid. But the fear was for the others, not for himself. It didn't make sense.

"We're in orbit," Meyer went on. "Your ships can't be seen from the surface. I can tell just from looking inside that there are no more Astrals on the ground. Humans on the planet's surface have already forgotten. Permanently this time."

"We couldn't make you forget." Without meaning to, Divinity had shifted the barrel toward Clara. She locked eyes with her now: Clara, who was the reason they'd never been able to effect a Forgetting.

"This time," Meyer said, "we chose it ourselves."

"Lies."

"We have our own collective. It's not the same as yours, but it's present just the same. Most people don't even know it's there, though it always has been. It's where we get our intuition. Where we see things from a higher perspective. But if you look at it like humanity has, you'll see why this was our only choice. It's too late to go back. The old world is gone. The memories of two alternate pasts were tearing us apart. When the Ark opened and the past twenty years of memories flooded out — all there were, since the last time it was opened — it's not entirely accurate that you judged us. This time, we judged ourselves."

"That's ridiculous," said Divinity, her eyes still locked on Clara's.

"We're smarter than you think," Meyer said. "And we understood, as a whole, that there's no way to move on with one foot stuck in the past."

Divinity's eyes flicked from Clara to the others. To Meyer. To Eternity beside her, still unmoving. Even to the Titans and Reptars.

"Nobody won, but nobody lost, either. It's a stalemate." Meyer paused for a moment, then took a small step forward. Divinity shot him a glance but allowed it to happen. There were maybe twelve feet between the weapon and Clara, but just as many between Divinity and Meyer. If he tried for her weapon, she'd have time to shoot

Clara, then Meyer. He might not die, seeing as the King was forever a part of their collective. But Clara would. Plus maybe Piper and the other two.

"Anyone down there has already let all of this go," Meyer said. "Even the Lightborn have let it go. Even what remained of the Mullah. There are no keepers of a portal this time. No keepers of an Ark. You can't return to control us, but we don't control you. I could reach the Nexus, but I can't reach you from inside any more than you can reach me. You're something else now. Individuals with a shared mind. You can think as a group and make choices on your own. Maybe it's worth exploring. The best of both worlds."

Divinity heard Meyer's words, knowing the effect he meant for them to have. But if there was rationale in this body and brain, Divinity had yet to find it. Raw anger reigned. Fear for what might come next — a dark step into a terrifying unknown.

"It's not the best."

Meyer subtly shook his head. "Hurting them changes nothing."

"I disagree. I will have to try to find out, but I think it might make me feel better."

"Nobody can save you from making the wrong choice. But how you choose now?" Meyer turned toward Eternity, and some unknown knowledge — the same infuriating secret that Divinity knew full well they'd exchanged behind her back earlier but refused to share — flashed between them. "It will define the way your species sees itself forever."

Divinity considered Meyer's words. She could feel the twin forces within her: the collective's intelligence urging one option in the name of logic, versus her own state urging the other choice in the name of passion.

The weapon had sagged again, so she raised it, this time to her eye. She retrained it on Clara's chest. Her finger moved to the trigger. She didn't need to sight down the thing's length, but did so anyway, squinting down to one eye the way humans did in their movies.

If I'm to be like a human, she thought, *I will be like a human.*

One eye open, Divinity zeroed in on Clara, petrified like a statue. She could sense more than feel the twin figures at her sides: Meyer on one side, calculating his odds at diving for the weapon, and Eternity at the other, probing at her from inside the collective.

Something moved between the weapon's sight and Clara. White like a cloud, as if the room had suddenly grown foggy.

Divinity raised her head. She opened her other eye.

The thing between her weapon and Clara was a Titan's broad chest, its eyes watching hers.

If I die, I die, it thought.

"Get out of the way."

But before Divinity could move to improve her shot, a second Titan edged forward to stand shoulder to shoulder with the first. A third blocked them in from the other side.

She lowered the weapon, shocked.

A fourth Titan moved in front of the humans. Then a Reptar, its head cocked toward Divinity, purring slightly. Then a second Reptar. A fifth Titan.

If I die, I die.

And then, a micro collective forming within the larger one:

If we die, we die.

Divinity's grip slackened. Her legs shook. She felt her anger surrender to something new, and darker. Within the collective's mind, she caught glimpses of things that all had seen and that only one of them had seen, now sharing memories like trading cards, each presenting what it had for the others to evaluate as individuals. Through Clara, human thoughts joined them. Meyer's thoughts. Piper's thoughts. All at once.

Meyer's words.

A vision of Trevor saving Piper.

Of Heather saving Cameron.

Of Christopher saving the caravan outside Ember Flats.

Of Cameron entering the Ark.

Of Stranger and Kindred, combined into one, entering the Ark.

Of Carl saving Eternity. Saving Melanie.

Meyer's words.

And Melanie's words.

If we die, we die.

Someone plucked the weapon from Divinity's hand.

She did not protest.

Instead, for reasons unknown, she fell to her knees and leaked fluid from her surrogate's eyes, lungs hitching in great sobs, as a pit of darkness claimed her.

Epilogue

Épilogue

Day One

Two weeks later, after the Astrals had done the necessary work of cleaning up after themselves (most notably removing the Reptar bodies still on the surface and incinerating notes from the past, such as Stranger's store of forbidden items he'd stashed in a desert cave), Meyer left the village on horseback and rode north. Two hours out — and knowing he wouldn't be the one to decide the day's timetable — he stopped to give the horse some water. He didn't know it was time until he heard the hum. But by the time he'd looked up, the shuttle had already arrived.

Meyer watched it settle. They were entirely too far from the village to be seen by the occupants, who by now had no idea what Astrals were. In addition, the mothership would have swept the area for stragglers before deciding Meyer was far enough out for neither ship nor rendezvous to be seen.

The ship opened, and a tall blonde emerged alone.

"You have no idea how strange it is," Meyer said, looking the silver sphere over from top to rounded bottom, "to see one of these without being abducted."

"You never boarded voluntarily?" Melanie said.

"Not unless you count the time Kindred sprang me from your space brig. But that was more a 'flight in terror' than a 'cordial embarkation.'"

She stepped aside, gesturing toward the opening like a game show host. She looked the part, too. She'd worn mostly flat sandals that the mothership's machines had fabricated to look like something from a moderate-range women's shop on the Old Earth in deference to the sandy terrain, but everything else about her spoke of elegance. She was immaculately groomed, her hair like anything from one of Meyer's forever-ago films. She wore a slinky blue dress that ended a modest few inches below her knees, but Meyer was sure that the woman knew damn well how good she must look. The Astrals had mastered vanity. Good for them.

"Would you like to try it?" she said, indicating the entrance.

"I think my space-flying days are over." He laughed, and she smiled. So they'd learned a bit of levity, too.

"We've completed the work that remained to be done," she said.

"The monolith? The freighter in the sand?"

"Reduced to component elements. But you understand, the Ark could not be destroyed."

Meyer nodded. It was also true that the Astrals couldn't move it. Without their systems in place for a coming epoch, it was only a hunk of metal, but for some reason it still dogged them.

"I know. I will send Logan and Kamal out to bury it."

"So they still have their memories?"

"For now."

"But they will forget, same as the others?"

"We all will."

"Clara?"

"All of us," Meyer said. "These aren't memories I want, if I'm to live out the little of my life that remains here in the wasteland. Best not to know there was ever anything else."

"You will forget?" She seemed surprised.

Meyer nodded. "I haven't exactly gotten the hang of talking to this thing you put inside my head, but it must agree. I can't make myself forget something. So ..." He made a vague hand gesture. "I don't know, some juju my thingie and Clara have going on. She describes it like taking a photo on a timer. You set it consciously, then the rest happens automatically. A way of distancing herself — and myself, I guess — from the process."

"How long until you forget?" *Until all knowledge of us leaves humanity forever,* she seemed to add.

"Five days. Long enough to clean up the last loose ends. Long enough to think of anything we might have forgotten. And it'll probably only be me and Clara who make it that long. Kamal has already started to forget."

Melanie nodded.

"And you? How is it on the ship?"

"Order is still pending. But we are getting on."

"And Divinity?"

"She has elected to return to her natural state."

Meyer suppressed a flinch. To him, it sounded like suicide. And it had probably looked a lot like suicide, too. The only way for any instance of Divinity who'd taken residence in a surrogate to return to its natural state would be to kill the surrogate.

"What about you?"

"Time will tell," she said.

Meyer nodded. It was as good an answer as any.

"Then I guess this is goodbye."

The sentence was strangely sentimental for someone who'd killed seven billion people. But Meyer let it go. The baggage between races was a lot of water to force under a bridge, but he was willing to try. In five days, he wouldn't remember anyway.

"Do you promise?" Meyer asked.

Day Two

Kamal woke from his nap refreshed. He put his feet on the ground, pacing around his hut. Something was pestering him. Something he'd forgotten? It wasn't clear. He'd had strange dreams — of another place and another time, another group of people he'd swear he'd once known but had somehow left behind.

But the arrival of a small child in the room distracted his thoughts. The last image to go was that of an enormous round object in the sky, black as night.

"Daddy!" the little girl said. "The sun is up! It's time to plant!"

"Past time, I'd imagine," Kamal said. Soon it would be hot. And planting in the heat, while necessary at times, was never any fun.

The child ran for the door, but a curious feeling tugged at Kamal — a sense that the girl wasn't his. That she'd been a loose end that had somehow attached itself to him.

"Mara," he called.

The girl turned. She smiled. She smiled at her daddy.

"Never mind," he said.

Day Three

"Meyer," Piper said. "Did you have a Cousin Tim?"

Meyer laughed. But instead of answering, he said, "You don't remember?"

"I'd swear you told me about him before."

"Okay." Meyer sat, looking at Piper across the small village well. He didn't use the well often. Meyer usually took a horse to gather water from an oasis. One far off but which boasted spectacular water. Although come to think of it, he hadn't brought any water home from that oasis when he'd gone two days ago, had he? "What's the context? Why do you want to know?"

Piper thought. It had seemed important. Now it really didn't.

She shrugged. "Never mind."

Meyer rose as if to leave but then seemed to change his mind. He turned around and this time sat right next to her. He took her hand, and in that moment Piper felt as young as the day she'd married him.

"I did have a brother, though. Two brothers, actually."

"Really?" Piper said.

He nodded. "One was named Kindred. The other was named Stranger."

"Those are funny names," Piper said.

"We were very close. But they had to leave. There was something very important they had to do. And there was a woman, too. Kindred's wife. She's also gone now. Her name was Heather."

"Where did she go?"

But Meyer didn't answer. Instead, he bit his lip and looked into the distance. If Piper didn't know better, she'd think he was holding back a wave of emotion.

"She was called away. But she also had two amazing children. The most amazing children I've ever known. Their names were Lila and Trevor."

Piper looked up at Meyer's profile. He was staring off into the distance, but she could see his eyes were wet.

"Meyer? What is it?"

"I just wanted to tell you about them, while I still can."

She held his hand tighter. She reached for his face, but he pulled away.

"What's happening, Meyer?"

"I just want you to remember those names, Piper. Kindred. Stranger. Heather. Lila. And Trevor."

"Okay. I'll remember them." And so Piper repeated them in her mind twice, concentrating because it seemed to matter so much to Meyer all of a sudden.

"Tell me their names again," he said.

"Kindred, Stranger, Heather, Lila, and Trevor."

Meyer nodded. "Good. Don't forget. And don't let me forget."

And Piper didn't, through to the end.

Logan looked up at his wife. "Did you say something?"

Clara looked back. She had a secretive smile — the one she used when he did something stupid and failed to realize it.

"No," she said.

"I could've sworn you said something."

"Well, I didn't." Then she gave another smirk just as he turned his head.

"What, Clara? I feel like I'm missing something here."

"Hmm. Like there's something you've misplaced? Something that you might have forgotten."

Suspiciously, Logan said, "Maybe."

"Something you once knew, then forgot all about, huh?"

"I don't know."

"Something you didn't really need in your head, that you really don't want to remember at all, and that's really most relevant right now because I can torture you with it because you have this sneaking suspicion that I know something you don't? Almost as if you used to have this power, but now forgot the trick of using it?"

"What the hell are you talking about?"

Clara smiled larger. Then she said, "Let's talk about it tomorrow."

Day Five

But of course they didn't talk about it tomorrow. The first reason was because Logan never asked. The idea — and probably the whole teasing conversation — seemed to have slipped his mind. Just like so many things seemed to do these days.

But the second reason was that Clara no longer precisely remembered what she'd delighted in teasing her husband with.

There was no matter. It was a beautiful day.

She left the hut and looked up.

There wasn't a cloud in the sky.

Or anything else.

Day Four Hundred and Thirteen

Meyer Dempsey was seventy years old when he died, if that was possible to believe. Seven full decades. Seven times ten full cycles of seasons, when the oldest most people could ever hope to reach was half that, maybe a bit more.

Most people simply accepted Meyer's incredible age. But on the day of his funeral, when the village gathered the pyre to send him on to his next life, Sarah Carpenter (daughter of Samuel and Mary, sister of Luke) found herself pondering it.

She herself was twenty — over half the lifespan she might otherwise have expected. Recently she'd been feeling long in the tooth, but Meyer's funeral inspired rather than frightened her. She'd been single until recently, childless even to half her expiration date. But perhaps now, she thought, running a hand across her still-small belly, she'd have a chance to see more of her unborn child's life than a lone generation. If she could live to be seventy? Well, *that* would be something.

It wasn't going to happen, but as they set Meyer's body

on the pyre, her thoughts drifted to immortality — what seventy long years felt like to Sarah.

As the pyre burned, Sarah's mind drifted from inspiration to melancholy. Meyer had been center of this village forever. He was larger than life. And whatever he'd done to bargain with the devil, it seemed contagious. His wife was well past forty — maybe even fifty, or possibly sixty. They were doing something right. And Sarah — possibly now that she had a second life inside her — found herself more intrigued than most.

She was on the village's edge when she saw the ghost.

A flash of light. Nothing. If anyone else had been with her, they would have laughed at the way she started. But Sarah knew the flash was worth paying attention to in the same way she knew Meyer's advanced age was worth considering as more than coincidence. Without thinking — and surely against her parents' and new husband's wishes — she set off in the direction it seemed to have gone.

She walked.

And she walked.

Hours later Sarah seemed to wake as if from a dream. She'd been ambulatory but not quite conscious, moving on as if in a fugue. Once she realized how far out she'd come, she gave a little cry. Sarah knew the general direction of home, but no more than that. How could she possibly find her village again? She didn't even know where she was!

Her worry died when she saw a small half moon of darkness ahead, visible in a crag of rock.

She approached the thing and dug, stirred by a strange compulsion and the way the sand, when she'd approached, seemed to have been freshly disturbed. Someone had been here. Recently.

Someone had gone into that hole.

Without thinking — again in a fugue as complete as

the one that had caused her to follow the ridiculous ghost — Sarah continued to dig.

The sand wasn't packed, and came away easily. She found herself looking down, realizing she'd had to hike *up*, as if the cave was at the top of a rock structure that had once risen above the desert floor. Something had covered it. But what? And why?

Sarah slipped into the tunnel. There was no light inside, but she found herself able to easily see. As if something was over her shoulder, lighting the way. As if something wanted her presence.

She went down one tunnel after another, terrified but moving despite her best intentions to turn around. She saw skeletons, wearing robes. Markings on the walls in strange languages, and a repeated word that seemed to be "Mullah." She found room after room — a virtual warren within the rock.

Sarah desperately wanted to leave. But something compelled her.

Eventually she came to a room with a stone door at its head that had been partially rolled away, or perhaps knocked askew. She entered and found the room black. Two things happened.

First, she saw a second flash of light, much like she'd seen leaving the site where Meyer's body burned. It approached Sarah, then stabbed hard into her abdomen. She expected pain, but there was none. Instead, Sarah felt a stirring where her infant slept inside her. She was deeply aware of it, but then the feeling was gone.

When the light and sensation had mostly abated, a circular vortex began to glow on the wall. And then Sarah saw a blonde-haired woman's face appear, disembodied. The woman began to speak. But as Sarah considered responding, the words continued, and Sarah realized she was looking at some sort of black magic — a message left in light from someone in the past, meant to be received by someone at an unknown point in the future.

"If you have found this," the woman said, "It is because the observer has not returned to us and instead has found a new host. This was not our intention, but it was always a possibility."

Sarah watched the woman, fascinated.

"We will not return, as agreed. But as we are changing, so might you change."

Sarah felt a strange feeling in her belly. Her hands went back to it, and after a moment of discomfort, she finally lifted her shirt to look at her skin — to see if she'd scraped herself on the way in, or otherwise caused injury.

Instead she saw her glowing body. And it struck her clearly that the woman wasn't talking to Sarah, from whatever time in the past she'd made this message.

She was talking to Sarah's baby.

"When you are ready," the woman said, "come and find us."

What to read next

Want to read more stories about different characters in the Invasion world? Then *Save the City* by Blake and Truant is here for you!

Get Save The City Today!

A Quick Favor...

If you enjoyed this book, please take a moment to write a short review on your favorite online bookstore so other readers can enjoy it, too.

Thanks so much!
Johnny and Avery

About the Authors

Avery Blake doesn't want you to know where she lives, or what she does. She travels the world, moving from place to place quickly to ensure she can't be tracked. It's safer that way.

When she's not looking over her shoulder, you can find her in the corner of a cafe, facing the exit, typing as fast as she can.

Johnny B. Truant is co-owner of the Sterling & Stone Story Studio, an IP powerhouse focusing on books and adaptations for film and television. It's the best job in the world, and he spends his days creating cool stuff with partners Sean Platt and David W. Wright, as well as more than 20 gifted storytellers.

Johnny is the bestselling author of over 100 books under various pen names, including the Fat Vampire and Invasion series. On the nonfiction side, he's also co-author of the indie publishing mainstay Write. Publish. Repeat. and co-host of the weekly Story Studio Podcast.

Originally from Ohio, Johnny and his family now live in Austin, Texas, where he's finally surrounded by creative types as weird as he is.

Also By Avery Blake

The Invasion Series

Longshot

Invasion

Contact

Colonization

Annihilation

Judgment

Extinction

Resurrection

Save The City Series

Save The City

Save The Girl

Save The World

Stonefall Series

Alienation

Stonefall

Snowfall

Downfall

The Taken Saga

The Taken

The Changed

The Hidden

The Saved

The Next Evolution

Transition

Convergence

Evolution

Stand-Alone Novels

Analog Heart

Family Royale

Ruthless Positivity

Vicarious Joe

Also By Johnny B. Truant

The Dead World Series

Dead Zero

Dead City

Dead Nation

Dead Planet

Empty Nest

The Fat Vampire Series

Fat Vampire

Fat Vampire 2: Tastes Like Chicken

Fat Vampire 3: All You Can Eat

Fat Vampire 4: Harder, Better, Fatter, Stronger

Fat Vampire 5: Fatpocaplypse

Fat Vampire 6: Survival of the Fattest

The Fat Vampire Chronicles

The Vampire Maurice

Anarchy and Blood

Vampires in the White City

The Beam Series

The Beam Season One

The Beam Season Two

The Beam Season Three

Robot Proletariat Series

En3my

Robot Proletariat

The Infinite Loop

The Hard Reset

Cascade Failure

Reboot

The Invasion Series

Longshot

Invasion

Contact

Colonization

Annihilation

Judgment

Extinction

Resurrection

The Tomorrow Gene Series

Null Identity

The Tomorrow Gene

The Tomorrow Clone

The Eden Experiment

Stand Alone Novels

Pretty Killer

Pattern Black

Burnout

The Target

The Island

Devil May Care